Praise for *New York Times* bestselling author Linda Howard

"Howard's writing is compelling."
—*Publishers Weekly*

"Linda Howard writes with power, stunning sensuality and a storytelling ability unmatched in the romance genre. Every book is a treasure for the reader to savor again and again."
—#1 *New York Times* bestselling author Iris Johansen

"You can't read just one Linda Howard!"
—*New York Times* bestselling author Catherine Coulter

"[A]...master storyteller."
—*RT Book Reviews*

"Ms. Howard can wring so much emotion and tension out of her characters that no matter how satisfied you are when you finish a book, you still want more."
—*Rendezvous* on *Mackenzie's Pleasure*

"Linda Howard is an extraordinary talent whose unforgettable novels are richly flavored with scintillating sensuality and high-voltage suspense."
—*...k Reviews*

"Linda Howard k... ...es to be different."
—*...e Coeur*

"Linda Howard ex... ...best of the romance genre."
—*RT Book Reviews*

LINDA HOWARD

RECKLESS

HQN™

HQN™

Recycling programs for this product may not exist in your area.

ISBN-13: 978-0-373-79997-8

Reckless
Copyright © 2016 by Harlequin Books S.A.

The publisher acknowledges the copyright holder of the individual works as follows:

Midnight Rainbow
Copyright © 1986 by Linda Howington

Tears of the Renegade
Copyright © 1985 by Linda Howington

This edition published by arrangement with Harlequin Books S.A.

For questions and comments about the quality of this book, please contact us at CustomerService@Harlequin.com.

® and TM are trademarks of Harlequin Enterprises Limited or its corporate affiliates. Trademarks indicated with ® are registered in the United States Patent and Trademark Office, the Canadian Intellectual Property Office and in other countries.

www.HQNBooks.com

Printed in U.S.A.

CONTENTS

MIDNIGHT RAINBOW

CHAPTER ONE

HE WAS GETTING too old for this kind of crap, Grant Sullivan thought irritably. What the hell was he doing crouched here, when he'd promised himself he'd never set foot in a jungle again? He was supposed to rescue a bubble-brained society deb, but from what he'd seen in the two days he'd had this jungle fortress under surveillance, he thought she might not *want* to be rescued. She looked as if she was having the time of her life: laughing, flirting, lying by the pool in the heat of the day. She slept late; she drank champagne on the flagstone patio. Her father was almost out of his mind with worry about her, thinking that she was suffering unspeakable torture at the hands of her captors. Instead, she was lolling around as if she were vacationing on the Riviera. She certainly wasn't being tortured. If anyone was being tortured, Grant thought with growing ire, it was he himself. Mosquitoes were biting him, flies were stinging him, sweat was running off him in rivers, and his legs were aching from sitting still for so long. He'd been eating field rations again, and he'd forgotten how much he hated field rations. The humidity made all of his old wounds ache, and he had plenty of old wounds to ache. No doubt about it: he was definitely too old.

He was thirty-eight, and he'd spent over half his life involved in some war, somewhere. He was tired, tired enough that he'd opted out the year before, wanting nothing more than to wake up in the same bed every morning. He hadn't wanted company or advice or anything, except to be left the hell alone. When he had burned out, he'd burned to the core.

He hadn't quite retreated to the mountains to live in a cave, where he wouldn't have to see or speak to another human being, but he had definitely considered it. Instead, he'd bought a run-down farm in Tennessee, just in the shadow of the mountains, and let the green mists heal him. He'd dropped out, but apparently he hadn't dropped far enough: they had still known how to find him. He supposed wearily that his reputation made it necessary for certain people to know his whereabouts at all times. Whenever a job called for jungle experience and expertise, they called for Grant Sullivan.

A movement on the patio caught his attention, and he cautiously moved a broad leaf a fraction of an inch to clear his line of vision. There she was, dressed to the nines in a frothy sundress and heels, with an enormous pair of sunglasses shading her eyes. She carried a book and a tall glass of something that looked deliciously cool; she arranged herself artfully on one of the poolside deck chairs, and prepared to while away the muggy afternoon. She waved to the guards who patrolled the plantation grounds and flashed them her dimpled smile.

Damn her pretty, useless little hide! Why couldn't she have stayed under Daddy's wing, instead of sashaying around the world to prove how "independent" she was? All she'd proved was that she had a remarkable talent for landing herself in hot water.

Poor dumb little twit, he thought. She probably didn't even realize that she was one of the central characters in a nasty little espionage caper that had at least three government and several other factions, all hostile, scrambling to find a missing microfilm. The only thing that had saved her life so far was that no one was sure how much she knew, or whether she knew anything at all. Had she been involved in George Persall's espionage activities, he wondered, or had she only been his mistress, his high class "secretary"? Did she know where the microfilm was, or did Luis Marcel, who had disappeared, have it? The only thing anyone knew for certain was that George Persall had had the microfilm in his possession. But he'd died of a heart attack—in *her* bedroom—and the microfilm hadn't been found. Had Persall already passed it to Luis Marcel? Marcel had dropped out of sight two days before Persall died—if he had the microfilm, he certainly wasn't talking about it. The Americans wanted it, the Russians wanted it, the Sandinistas wanted it, and every rebel group in Central and South America wanted it. Hell, Sullivan thought, as far as he knew, even the Eskimos wanted it.

So where was the microfilm? What had George Persall done with it? If he had indeed passed it to Luis Marcel, who was his normal contact, then where was Luis? Had Luis decided to sell the microfilm to the highest bidder? That seemed unlikely. Grant knew Luis personally; they had been in some tight spots together and he trusted Luis at his back, which said a lot.

Government agents had been chasing this particular microfilm for about a month now. A high-level executive of a research firm in California had made a deal to sell the government-classified laser technology his firm had developed, technology that could place laser weaponry in space in the near future. The firm's own security people had become suspicious of the man and alerted the proper government authorities; together they had apprehended the executive in the middle of the sale. But the two buyers had escaped, taking the microfilm with them. Then one of the buyers double-crossed his partner and took himself and the microfilm to South America to strike his own deal. Agents all over Central and South America had been alerted, and an American agent in Costa Rica had made contact with the man, setting up a "sting" to buy the microfilm. Things became completely confused at that point. The deal had gone sour, and the agent had been wounded, but he had gotten away with the microfilm. The film should have been destroyed at that point, but it hadn't been. Somehow the agent had gotten it to George Persall, who could come and go freely in Costa Rica because of his business connections. Who would have suspected George Persall of being involved in espionage? He'd always seemed just a tame businessman, albeit with a passion for gorgeous "secretaries"—a weakness any Latin man would understand. Persall had been known to only a few agents, Luis Marcel among them, and that had made him extraordinarily effective. But in this case, George had been left in the dark; the agent had been feverish from his wound and hadn't told George to destroy the film.

Luis Marcel had been supposed to contact George, but instead Luis had disappeared. Then George, who had always seemed to be disgustingly healthy, had died of a heart attack...and no one knew where the microfilm was. The Americans wanted to be certain that the technology didn't fall into anyone else's hands; the Russians wanted the technology just as badly, and every revolutionary in the hemisphere wanted the microfilm in order to sell it to the highest bidder. An arsenal of weapons could be purchased, revolutions could be staged, with the amount of money that small piece of film would bring on the open market.

Manuel Turego, head of national security in Costa Rica, was a very smart man; he was a bastard, Grant thought, but a smart one. He'd promptly snatched up Ms. Priscilla Jane Hamilton Greer and carried her off to this heavily guarded inland "plantation." He'd probably told her that she was under protective custody, and she was probably stupid enough that she was very grateful to him for "protecting" her. Turego had played it cool; so far he hadn't harmed her. Evidently he knew that her father was a very wealthy, very influential man, and that it wasn't wise to enrage wealthy, influential men unless it was absolutely necessary. Turego was playing a waiting game; he was waiting for Luis Marcel to surface, waiting for the microfilm to surface, as it eventually had to. In the meantime, he had Priscilla; he could afford to wait. Whether she knew anything or not, she was valuable to him as a negotiating tool, if nothing else.

From the moment Priscilla had disappeared, her father had been frantic. He'd been calling in political favors with a heavy hand, but he'd found that none of the favors owed to him could get Priscilla away from Turego. Until Luis was found, the American government wasn't going to lift a hand to free the young woman. The confusion about whether or not she actually knew anything, the tantalizing possibility that she *could* know the location of the microfilm, seemed to have blunted the intensity of the search for Luis. Her captivity could give him the edge he needed by attracting attention away from him.

Finally, desperate with worry and enraged by the lack of response he'd been getting from the government, James Hamilton had decided to take matters into his own hands. He'd spent a small fortune ferreting out his daughter's location, and then had been stymied by the inaccessibility of the well-guarded plantation. If he sent in enough men to take over the plantation, he realized, there was a strong possibility that his daughter would be killed in the fight. Then someone had mentioned Grant Sullivan's name.

A man as wealthy as James Hamilton could find someone who didn't want to be found, even a wary, burnt-out ex-government agent who had buried himself in the Tennessee mountains. Within twenty-four hours, Grant had been sitting across from Hamilton, in the library of a huge estate house that shouted of old money. Hamilton had made an offer that would pay off the mortgage on Grant's farm completely. All the man wanted was to have his daughter back, safe and sound. His face had been lined and taut with worry, and there had been a desperation about him that, even more than the money, made Grant reluctantly accept the job.

The difficulty of rescuing her had seemed enormous, perhaps even insurmountable; if he were able to penetrate the security of the plantation—something he didn't really doubt—getting her out would be something else entirely. Not only that, but Grant had his own personal experiences to remind him that, even if he found her, the odds were greatly against her being alive or recognizably human. He hadn't let himself think about what could have happened to her since the day she'd been kidnapped.

But getting to her had been made ridiculously easy;

as soon as he left Hamilton's house, a new wrinkle had developed. Not a mile down the highway from Hamilton's estate, he'd glanced in the rearview mirror and found a plain blue sedan on his tail. He'd lifted one eyebrow sardonically and pulled over to the shoulder of the road.

He lit a cigarette and inhaled leisurely as he waited for the two men to approach his car. "Hiya, Curtis."

Ted Curtis leaned down and peered in the open window, grinning. "Guess who wants to see you?"

"Hell," Grant swore irritably. "All right, lead the way. I don't have to drive all the way to Virginia, do I?"

"Naw, just to the next town. He's waiting in a motel."

The fact that Sabin had felt it necessary to leave headquarters at all told Grant a lot. He knew Kell Sabin from the old days; the man didn't have a nerve in his body, and ice water ran in his veins. He wasn't a comfortable man to be around, but Grant knew that the same had been said about himself. They were both men to whom no rules applied, men who had intimate knowledge of hell, who had lived and hunted in that gray jungle where no laws existed. The difference between them was that Sabin was comfortable in that cold grayness; it was his life—but Grant wanted no more of it. Things had gone too far; he had felt himself becoming less than human. He had begun to lose his sense of who he was and why he was there. Nothing seemed to matter any longer. The only time he'd felt alive was during the chase, when adrenaline pumped through his veins and fired all his senses into acute awareness. The bullet that had almost killed him had instead saved him, because it had stopped him long enough to let him begin thinking again. That was when he'd decided to get out.

Twenty-five minutes later, with his hand curled around a mug of strong, hot coffee, his booted feet propped comfortably on the genuine, wood-grained plastic coffee table that was standard issue for motels, Grant had murmured, "Well, I'm here. Talk."

Kell Sabin was an even six feet tall, an inch shorter than Grant, and the hard musculature of his frame revealed that he made it a point to stay in shape, even though he was no longer in the field. He was dark—black-haired, black-eyed, with an olive complexion—and the cold fire of his energy generated a force field around him. He was impossible to read, and was as canny as a stalking panther, but Grant trusted him. He couldn't say that he liked Sabin; Sabin wasn't a man to be friendly. Yet for twenty years their lives had been intertwined until they were virtually a part of each other. In his mind, Grant saw a red-orange flash of gunfire, and abruptly he felt the thick, moist heat of the jungle, smelled the rotting vegetation, saw the flash of weapons being discharged…and felt, at his back, so close that each had braced his shoulders against the other, the same man who sat across from him now. Things like that stayed in a man's memory.

A dangerous man, Kell Sabin. Hostile governments would gladly have paid a fortune to get to him, but Sabin was nothing more than a shadow slipping away from the sunshine, as he directed his troops from the gray mists.

Without a flicker of expression in his black eyes, Sabin studied the man who sat across from him in a lazy sprawl—a deceptively lazy sprawl, he knew. Grant was, if anything, even leaner and harder than he had been in the field. Hibernating for a year hadn't made him go soft. There was still something wild about Grant Sullivan, something dangerous and untamed. It was in the wary, restless glitter of his amber eyes, eyes that glowed as fierce and golden as an eagle's under the dark, level brows. His dark blond hair was shaggy, curling down over his collar in back, emphasizing that he wasn't quite civilized. He was darkly tanned; the small scar on his chin wasn't very noticeable, but the thin line that slashed across his left cheekbone was silver against his bronzed skin. They weren't disfiguring scars, but reminders of battles.

If Sabin had had to pick anyone to go after Hamilton's daughter, he'd have picked this man. In the jungle Sullivan was as stealthy as a cat; he could become part of the jungle, blending into it, using it. He'd been useful in the concrete jungles, too, but it was in the green hells of the world that no one could equal him.

"Are you going after her?" Sabin finally asked in a quiet tone.

"Yeah."

"Then let me fill you in." Totally disregarding the fact that Grant no longer had security clearance, Sabin told him about the missing microfilm. He told him about George Persall, Luis Marcel, the whole deadly cat-and-mouse game, and dumb little Priscilla sitting in the middle of it. She was being used as a smoke screen for Luis, but Kell was more than a little worried about Luis. It wasn't like the man to disappear, and Costa Rica wasn't the most tranquil place on earth. Anything could have happened to him. Yet, wherever he was, he wasn't in the hands of any government or political faction, because everyone was still searching for him, and everyone except Manuel Turego and the American gov-

ernment was searching for Priscilla. Not even the Costa
Rican government knew that Turego had the woman;
he was operating on his own.

"Persall was a dark horse," Kell admitted irritably.
"He wasn't a professional. I don't even have a file on
him."

If Sabin didn't have a file on him, Persall had been
more than a dark horse; he'd been totally invisible.
"How did this thing blow open?" Grant drawled, closing his eyes until they were little more than slits. He
looked as if he were going to fall asleep, but Sabin
knew differently.

"Our man was being followed. They were closing in
on him. He was out of his mind with fever. He couldn't
find Luis, but he remembered how to contact Persall. No
one knew Persall's name, until then, or how to find him
if they needed him. Our man just barely got the film
to Persall before all hell broke loose. Persall got away."

"What about our man?"

"He's alive. We got him out, but not before Turego
got his hands on him."

Grant grunted. "So Turego knows our guy didn't tell
Persall to destroy the film."

Kell looked completely disgusted. "*Everyone* knows.
There's no security down there. Too many people will
sell any scrap of information they can find. Turego has
a leak in his organization, so by morning it was common knowledge. Also by morning, Persall had died of a
heart attack, in Priscilla's room. Before we could move
in, Turego took the girl."

Dark brown lashes veiled the golden glitter of Grant's
eyes almost completely. He looked as if he would begin

snoring at any minute. "Well? Does she know anything about the microfilm or not?"

"We don't know. My guess is that she doesn't. Persall had several hours to hide the microfilm before he went to her room."

"Why the hell couldn't she have stayed with Daddy, where she belongs?" Grant murmured.

"Hamilton has been raising hell for us to get her out of there, but they aren't really close. She's a party girl. Divorced, more interested in having a good time than in doing anything constructive. In fact, Hamilton cut her out of his will several years ago, and she's been wandering all around the globe since. She'd been with Persall for a couple of years. They weren't shy about their relationship. Persall liked to have a flashy woman on his arm, and he could afford her. He always seemed like an easygoing good-time guy, well-suited to her type. I sure as hell never figured him for a courier, especially one sharp enough to fool me."

"Why don't you go in and get the girl out?" Grant asked suddenly, and he opened his eyes, staring at Kell, his gaze cold and yellow.

"Two reasons. One, I don't think she knows anything about the film. I have to concentrate on finding the film, and I think that means finding Luis Marcel. Two, you're the best man for the job. I thought so when I...ah...arranged for you to be brought to Hamilton's attention."

So Kell was working to get the girl out, after all, but going about it in his own circuitous way. Well, staying behind the scenes was the only way he could be effective. "You won't have any trouble getting into Costa Rica," Kell said. "I've already arranged it. But if you can't get the girl out..."

Grant got to his feet, a tawny, graceful savage, silent and lethal. "I know," he said quietly. Neither of them had to say it, but both knew that a bullet in her head would be a great deal kinder than what would happen to her if Turego decided that she did know the location of the microfilm. She was being held only as a safety measure now, but if that microfilm didn't surface, she would eventually be the only remaining link to it. Then her life wouldn't be worth a plugged nickel.

So now he was in Costa Rica, deep in the rain forest and too damned near the Nicaraguan border for comfort. Roaming bands of rebels, soldiers, revolutionaries and just plain terrorists made life miserable for people who just wanted to live their simple lives in peace, but none of it touched Priscilla. She might have been a tropical princess, sipping daintily at her iced drink, ignoring the jungle that ate continuously at the boundaries of the plantation and had to be cut back regularly.

Well, he'd seen enough. Tonight was the night. He knew her schedule now, knew the routine of the guards, and had already found all the trip lines. He didn't like traveling through the jungle at night, but there wasn't any choice. He had to have several hours to get her away from here before anyone realized she was missing; luckily, she always slept late, until at least ten every morning. No one would really think anything of it if she didn't appear by eleven. By then, they'd be long gone. Pablo would pick them up by helicopter at the designated clearing tomorrow morning, not long after dawn.

Grant backed slowly away from the edge of the jungle, worming himself into the thick greenery until it formed a solid curtain separating him from the house. Only then did he rise to his feet, walking silently and with assurance, because he'd taken care of the trip lines and sensors as he'd found them. He'd been in the jungle for three days, moving cautiously around the perimeter of the plantation, carefully getting the layout of the house. He knew where the girl slept, and he knew how he was going to get in. It couldn't have been better; Turego wasn't in the house. He'd left the day before, and since he wasn't back by now, Grant knew that he wasn't coming. It was already twilight, and it wasn't safe to travel the river in the darkness.

Grant knew exactly how treacherous the river was; that was why he would take the girl through the jungle. Even given its dangers, the river would be the logical route for them to take. If by some chance her departure were discovered before Pablo picked them up, the search would be concentrated along the river, at least for a while. Long enough, he hoped, for them to reach the helicopter.

He'd have to wait several more hours before he could go into the house and get the girl out. That would give everyone time to get tired, bored and sleepy. He made his way to the small clearing where he'd stashed his supplies, and carefully checked it for snakes, especially the velvety brown fer-de-lance, which liked to lie in clearings and wait for its next meal. After satisfying himself that the clearing was safe, he sat down on a fallen tree to smoke a cigarette. He took a drink of water, but he wasn't hungry. He knew that he wouldn't be until sometime tomorrow. Once the action was going down he couldn't eat; he was too keyed up, all his senses enhanced so that even the smallest sound of the jungle crashed against his eardrums like thunder. Adrenaline was already pumping through his veins, making him so high that he could understand why the Vikings had gone berserk during battle. Waiting was almost unbearable, but that was what he had to do. He checked his watch again, the illuminated dial a strange bit of civilization in a jungle that swallowed men alive, and frowned when he saw that only a little over half an hour had passed.

To give himself something to do, to calm his tightly wound nerves, he began packing methodically, arranging everything so he would know exactly where it was. He checked his weapons and his ammunition, hoping he wouldn't have to use them. What he needed more than anything, if he was to get the girl out alive, was a totally silent operation. If he had to use his carbine or the automatic pistol, he'd give away their position. He preferred a knife, which was silent and deadly.

He felt sweat trickle down his spine. God, if only the girl would have sense enough to keep her mouth shut and not start squawking when he hauled her out of there. If he had to, he'd knock her out, but that would make her dead weight to carry through vegetation that reached out to wrap around his legs like living fingers.

He realized that he was fondling his knife, his long, lean fingers sliding over the deadly blade with a lover's touch, and he shoved it into its sheath. Damn her, he thought bitterly. Because of her, he was back in the thick of things, and he could feel it taking hold of him again. The rush of danger was as addictive as any drug, and it was in his veins again, burning him, eating at him like an acid—killing him and intensifying the feeling of life all at once. Damn her, damn her to hell. All this for a spoiled, silly society brat who liked to amuse herself in various beds. Still, her round heels might have kept her alive, because Turego fancied himself quite a lover.

The night sounds of the jungle began to build around him: the screams of the howler monkeys, the rustles and chirps and coughs of the night denizens as they went about their business. Somewhere down close to the river he heard a jaguar cough, but he never minded the normal jungle sounds. He was at home here. The peculiar combination of his genes and the skills he'd learned as a boy in the swamps of south Georgia made him as much a part of the jungle as the jaguar that prowled the river's edge. Though the thick canopy blocked out all light, he didn't light a lamp or switch on a flashlight; he wanted his eyes to be perfectly adjusted to the dark when he began moving. He relied on his ears and his instincts, knowing that there was no danger close to him. The danger would come from men, not from the shy jungle animals. As long as those reassuring noises surrounded him, he knew that no men were near.

At midnight he rose and began easing along the route he'd marked in his mind, and the animals and insects were so unalarmed by his presence that the din continued without pause. The only caution he felt was that a fer-de-lance or a bushmaster might be hunting along the path he'd chosen, but that was a chance he'd have to take. He carried a long stick that he swept silently across the ground before him. When he reached the edge of the plantation he put the stick aside and crouched down to survey the grounds, making certain everything was as expected, before he moved in.

From where he crouched, he could see that the guards were at their normal posts, probably asleep, except for the one who patrolled the perimeter, and he'd soon settle down for a nap, too. They were sloppy, he thought contemptuously. They obviously didn't expect any visitors in as remote a place as this upriver plantation. During the three days he'd spent observing them, he'd noted that they stood around talking a great deal of the time, smoking cigarettes, not keeping a close watch on anything. But they were still there, and those rifles were loaded with real bullets. One of the reasons Grant had reached the age of thirty-eight was that he had a healthy respect for weapons and what they could do to human flesh. He didn't believe in recklessness, because it cost lives. He waited. At least now he could see, for the night was clear, and the stars hung low and brilliant in the sky. He didn't mind the starlight; there were plenty of shadows that would cover his movements.

The guard at the left corner of the house hadn't moved an inch since Grant had been watching him; he was asleep. The guard walking the grounds had settled down against one of the pillars at the front of the house. The faint red glow near the guard's hand told Grant that he was smoking and if he followed his usual pattern, he'd pull his cap over his eyes after he'd finished the cigarette, and sleep through the night.

As silently as a wraith, Grant left the concealing jungle and moved onto the grounds, slipping from tree to bush, invisible in the black shadows. Soundlessly, he mounted the veranda that ran alongside the house, flattening himself against the wall and checking the scene again. It was silent and peaceful. The guards relied far too heavily on those trip lines, not realizing they could be dismantled.

Priscilla's room was toward the back. It had double sliding glass doors, which might be locked, but that didn't worry him; he had a way with locks. He eased up to the doors, put out his hand and pulled silently.

The door moved easily, and his brows rose. Not locked. Thoughtful of her.

Gently, gently, a fraction of an inch at a time, he slid the door open until there was enough room for him to slip through. As soon as he was in the room he paused, waiting for his eyes to adjust again. After the starlight, the room seemed as dark as the jungle. He didn't move a muscle, but waited, poised and listening.

Soon he could see again. The room was big and airy, with cool wooden floors covered with straw mats. The bed was against the wall to his right, ghostly with the folds of mosquito netting draped around it. Through the netting he could see the rumpled covers, the small mound on the far side of the bed. A chair, a small round table and a tall floor lamp were on this side of the bed. The shadows were deeper to his left, but he could see a door that probably opened to the bathroom. An enormous wardrobe stood against the wall. Slowly, as silently as a tiger stalking its prey, he moved around the wall, blending into the darkness near the wardrobe. Now he could see a chair on the far side of the bed, next to where she slept. A long white garment, perhaps her robe or nightgown, lay across the chair. The thought that she might be sleeping naked made his mouth quirk in a sudden grin that held no real amusement. If she did sleep naked, she'd fight like a wildcat when he woke her. Just what he needed. For both their sakes, he hoped she was clothed.

He moved closer to the bed, his eyes on the small figure. She was so still.... The hair prickled on the back of his neck in warning, and without thinking he flung himself to the side, taking the blow on his shoulder instead of his neck. He rolled, and came to his feet expecting to face his assailant, but the room was still and dark again. Nothing moved, not even the woman on the bed. Grant faded back into the shadows, trying to hear the soft whisper of breathing, the rustle of clothing, anything. The silence in the room was deafening. Where was his attacker? Like Grant, he'd moved into the shadows, which were deep enough to shield several men.

Who was his assailant? What was he doing here in the woman's bedroom? Had he been sent to kill her or was he, too, trying to steal her from Turego?

His opponent was probably in the black corner beside the wardrobe. Grant eased the knife out of its sheath, then pushed it in again; his hands would be as silent as the knife.

There…just for a moment, the slightest of movements, but enough to pinpoint the man's position. Grant crouched then moved forward in a blurred rush, catching the man low and flipping him. The stranger rolled as he landed and came to his feet with a lithe twist, a slim dark figure outlined against the white mosquito netting. He kicked out, and Grant dodged the blow, but he felt the breeze of the kick pass his chin. Moving in, he caught the man's arm with a numbing chop. He saw the arm fall uselessly to the man's side. Coldly, without emotion, not even breathing hard, Grant threw the slim figure to the floor and knelt with one knee on the good arm and his other knee pressed to the man's chest. Just as he raised his hand to strike the blow that would end their silent struggle, Grant became aware of something odd, something soft swelling beneath his knee. Then he understood. The too-still form on the bed was so still because it was a mound of covers, not a human being. The girl hadn't been in bed; she'd seen him come through the sliding doors and had hidden herself in the shadows. But why hadn't she screamed? Why had she attacked, knowing that she had no chance of overpowering him? He moved his knee off her breasts and quickly slid his hand to the soft mounds to make certain his weight hadn't cut off her breath. He felt the reassuring rise of her chest, heard the soft, startled gasp as she felt his touch, and he eased a little away from her.

"It's all right," he started to whisper, but she suddenly twisted on the floor, wrenching away from him. Her knee slashed upward; he was unguarded, totally vulnerable, and her knee crashed into his groin with a force that sent agony through his whole body. Red lights danced before his eyes, and he sagged to one side, gagging at the bitter bile that rose in his throat, his hands automatically cupping his agonized flesh as he ground his teeth to contain the groan that fought for release.

She scrambled away from him, and he heard a low sob, perhaps of terror. Through pain-blurred eyes he saw her pick up something dark and bulky; then she slipped through the open glass door and was gone.

Pure fury propelled him to his feet. Damn it, she was escaping on her own. She was going to ruin the whole setup! Ignoring the pain in his loins, he started after her. He had a score to settle.

CHAPTER TWO

Jane had just reached for her bundle of supplies when some instinct leftover from her cave-dwelling ancestors told her that someone was near. There hadn't been any sound to alert her, but suddenly she was aware of another presence. The fine hairs on the back of her neck and her forearms stood up, and she had frozen, turning terrified eyes toward the double glass doors. The doors had slid open noiselessly, and she had seen the darker shadow of a man briefly outlined against the night. He was a big man, but one who moved with total silence. It was the eerie soundlessness of his movements that had frightened her more than anything, sending chills of pure terror chasing over her skin. For days now she had lived by her nerves, holding the terror at bay while she walked a tightrope, trying to lull Turego's suspicions, yet always poised for an escape attempt. But nothing had frightened her as much as that dark shadow slipping into her room.

Any faint hope that she would be rescued had died when Turego had installed her here. She had assessed the situation realistically. The only person who would try to get her out would be her father, but it would be beyond his power. She could depend on only herself and her wits. To that end, she had flirted and flattered and downright lied, doing everything she could to convince Turego that she was both brainless and harmless. In that, she thought, she'd succeeded, but time was fast running out. When an aide had brought an urgent message to Turego the day before, Jane had eavesdropped; Luis Marcel's location had been discovered, and Turego wanted Luis, badly.

But by now Turego surely would have discovered that Luis had no knowledge of the missing microfilm, and that would leave her as the sole suspect. She had to escape, tonight, before Turego returned.

She hadn't been idle since she'd been here; she'd carefully memorized the routine of the guards, especially at night, when the terror brought on by the darkness made it impossible for her to sleep. She'd spent the nights standing at the double doors, watching the guards, clocking them, studying their habits. By keeping her mind busy, she'd been able to control the fear. When dawn would begin to lighten the sky, she had slept. She had been preparing since the first day she'd been here for the possibility that she might have to bolt into the jungle. She'd been sneaking food and supplies, hoarding them, and steeling herself for what lay ahead. Even now, only the raw fear of what awaited her at Turego's hands gave her the courage to brave the black jungle, where the night demons were waiting for her.

But none of that had been as sinister, as lethal, as the dark shape moving through her bedroom. She shrank back into the thick shadows, not even breathing in her acute terror. Oh, God, she prayed, what do I do now? Why was he there? To murder her in her bed? Was it one of the guards, tonight of all nights, come to rape her?

As he passed in front of her, moving in a slight crouch toward her bed, an odd rage suddenly filled

Jane. After all she had endured, she was damned if she'd allow him to spoil her escape attempt! She'd talked herself into it, despite her horrible fear of the dark, and now he was ruining it!

Her jaw set, she clenched her fists as she'd been taught to do in her self-defense classes. She struck at the back of his neck, but suddenly he was gone, a shadow twisting away from the blow, and her fist struck his shoulder instead. Instantly terrified again, she shrank back into the shelter of the wardrobe, straining her eyes to see him, but he'd disappeared. Had he been a wraith, a figment of her imagination? No, her fist had struck a very solid shoulder, and the faint rippling of the white curtains over the glass doors testified that the doors were indeed open. He was in the room, somewhere, but *where*? How could a man that big disappear so completely?

Then, abruptly, his weight struck her in the side, bowling her over, and she barely bit off the instinctive scream that surged up from her throat. She didn't have a chance. She tried automatically to kick him in the throat, but he moved like lightning, blocking her attack. Then a hard blow to her arm numbed it all the way to her elbow, and a split second later she was thrown to the floor, a knee pressing into her chest and making it impossible to breathe.

The man raised his arm and Jane tensed, willing now to scream, but unable to make a sound. Then, suddenly, the man paused, and for some reason lifted his weight from her chest. Air rushed into her lungs, along with a dizzying sense of relief, then she felt his hand moving boldly over her breasts and realized why he'd shifted position. Both terrified and angry that this should be happening to her, she moved instinctively the split second she realized his vulnerability, and slashed upward with her knee. He sagged to the side, holding himself, and she felt an absurd sense of pity. Then she realized that he hadn't even groaned aloud. The man wasn't human! Choking back a sob of terror, she struggled to her feet and grabbed her supplies, then darted through the open door. At that point she wasn't escaping from Turego so much as from that dark, silent demon in her room.

Heedlessly, she flung herself across the plantation grounds; her heart was pounding so violently that the sound of her blood pumping through her veins made a roar in her ears. Her lungs hurt, and she realized that she was holding her breath. She tried to remind herself to be quiet, but the urge to flee was too strong for caution; she stumbled over a rough section of ground and sprawled on her hands and knees. As she began scrambling to her feet, she was suddenly overwhelmed by something big and warm, smashing her back to the ground. Cold, pure terror froze her blood in her veins, but before even an instinctive scream could find voice, his hand was on the back of her neck and everything went black.

Jane regained consciousness by degrees, confused by her upside down position, the jouncing she was suffering, the discomfort of her arms. Strange noises assailed her ears, noises that she tried and failed to identify. Even when she opened her eyes she saw only blackness. It was one of the worst nightmares she'd ever had. She began kicking and struggling to wake up, to end the dream, and abruptly a sharp slap stung her bottom. "Settle down," an ill-tempered voice said from somewhere above and behind her. The voice was that of a stranger, but there was something in that laconic drawl that made her obey instantly.

Slowly things began to shift into a recognizable pattern, and her senses righted themselves. She was being carried over a man's shoulder through the jungle. Her wrists had been taped behind her, and her ankles were also secured. Another wide band of tape covered her mouth, preventing her from doing anything more than grunting or humming. She didn't feel like humming, so she used her limited voice to grunt out exactly what she thought of him, in language that would have left her elegant mother white with shock. A hard hand again made contact with the seat of her pants. "Would you shut the hell up?" he growled. "You sound like a pig grunting at the trough."

American! she thought, stunned. He was an American! He'd come to rescue her, even though he was being unnecessarily rough about it…or was he a rescuer? Chilled, she thought of all the different factions who would like to get their hands on her. Some of those factions were fully capable of hiring an American mercenary to get her, or of training one of their own to imitate an American accent and win her trust.

She didn't dare trust anyone, she realized. Not anyone. She was alone in this.

The man stopped and lifted her from his shoulder, standing her on her feet. Jane blinked her eyes, then widened them in an effort to see, but the darkness under the thick canopy was total, she couldn't see anything. The night pressed in on her, suffocating her with its thick darkness. Where was he? Had he simply dropped her here in the jungle and left her to be breakfast for a jaguar? She could sense movement around her, but no sounds that she could identify as him; the howls and chittering and squawks and rustles of the jungle filled her ears. A whimper rose in her throat, and she tried to move, to seek a tree or something to protect her back, but she'd forgotten her bound feet and she stumbled to the ground, scratching her face on a bush.

A low obscenity came to her ears, then she was roughly grasped and hauled to her feet. "Damn it, stay put!"

So he was still there. How could he see? What was he doing? No matter who he was or what he was doing, at that moment Jane was grateful for his presence. She could not conquer her fear of darkness but the fact that she wasn't alone held the terror at bay. She gasped as he abruptly lifted her and tossed her over his shoulder again, as effortlessly as if she were a rag doll. She felt the bulk of a backpack, which hadn't been there before, but he showed no sign of strain. He moved through the stygian darkness with a peculiar sure-footedness, a lithe, powerful grace that never faltered.

Her own pack of pilfered supplies was still slung around her shoulders, the straps holding it even though it had slid down and was bumping against the back of her head. A can of something was banging against her skull; she'd probably have concussion if this macho fool didn't ease up. What did he think this was, some sort of jungle marathon? Her ribs were being bruised against his hard shoulder, and she felt various aches all over her body, probably as a result of his roughness in throwing her to the floor. Her arm ached to the bone from his blow. Even if this was a real rescue, she thought, she'd be lucky if she lived through it.

She bounced on his shoulder for what seemed like

days, the pain in her cramped limbs increasing with every step he took. Nausea began to rise in her, and she took deep breaths in an effort to stave off throwing up. If she began to vomit, with her mouth taped the way it was, she could suffocate. Desperately she began to struggle, knowing only that she needed to get into an upright position.

"Easy there, Pris." Somehow he seemed to know how she was feeling. He stopped and lifted her off his shoulder, easing her onto her back on the ground. When her weight came down on her bound arms she couldn't suppress a whimper of pain. "All right," the man said. "I'm going to cut you loose now, but if you start acting up, I'll truss you up like a Christmas turkey again and leave you that way. Understand?"

She nodded wildly, wondering if he could see her in the dark. Evidently he could, because he turned her on her side and she felt a knife slicing through the tape that bound her wrists. Tears stung her eyes from the pain as he pulled her arms around and began massaging them roughly to ease her cramped muscles.

"Your daddy sent me to get you out of here," the man drawled calmly as he began easing the tape off of her mouth. Instead of ripping the adhesive away and taking skin with it, he was careful, and Jane was torn between gratitude and indignation, since he'd taped her mouth in the first place.

Jane moved her mouth back and forth, restoring it to working condition. "My daddy?" she asked hoarsely.

"Yeah. Okay, now, Pris, I'm going to free your legs, but if you look like you're even thinking about kicking me again, I won't be as easy with you as I was the last time." Despite his drawl, there was something menacing in his tone, and Jane didn't doubt his word.

"I wouldn't have kicked you the first time if you hadn't started pawing at me like a high school sophomore!" she hissed.

"I was checking to see if you were breathing."

"Sure you were, and taking your time about it, too."

"Gagging you was a damned good idea," he said reflectively, and Jane shut up. She had yet to see him as anything more than a shadow. She couldn't even put a name to him, but she knew enough about him to know that he would bind and gag her again without a moment's compunction.

He cut the tape from around her ankles, and again she was subjected to his rough but effective massage. In only a moment she was being pulled to her feet; she staggered momentarily before regaining her sense of balance.

"We don't have much farther to go; stay right behind me, and don't say a word."

"Wait!" Jane whispered frantically. "How can I follow you when I can't see you?"

He took her hand and carried it to his waist. "Hang on to my belt."

She did better than that. Acutely aware of the vast jungle around her, and with only his presence shielding her from the night terrors, she hooked her fingers inside the waistband of his pants in a death grip. She knotted the material so tightly that he muttered a protest, but she wasn't about to let go of him.

Maybe it didn't seem very far to him, but to Jane, being towed in his wake, stumbling over roots and vines that she couldn't see, it seemed like miles before he halted. "We'll wait here," he whispered. "I don't want to go any closer until I hear the helicopter come in."

"When will that be?" Jane whispered back, figuring that if he could talk, so could she.

"A little after dawn."

"When is dawn?"

"Half an hour."

Still clutching the waistband of his pants, she stood behind him and waited for dawn. The seconds and minutes crawled by, but they gave her the chance to realize for the first time that she'd truly escaped from Turego. She was safe and free...well almost. She was out of his clutches, she was the only one who knew what a close call she'd had. Turego would almost certainly return to the plantation this morning to find that his prisoner had escaped. For a moment she was surprised at her own lack of elation, then she realized that she wasn't out of danger yet. This man said that her father had sent him, but he hadn't given her a name or any proof. All she had was his word, and Jane was more than a little wary. Until she was actually on American soil, until she knew beyond any doubt that she was safe, she was going to follow poor George Persall's ironclad rule: when in doubt, lie.

The man shifted uncomfortably, drawing her attention. "Look, honey, do you think you could loosen up on my pants? Or are you trying to finish the job you started on me with your knee?"

Jane felt the blood rush to her cheeks, and she hastily released her hold. "I'm sorry, I didn't realize," she whispered. She stood stiffly for a moment, her arms at her sides; then panic began to rise in her. She couldn't see him in the darkness, she couldn't hear him breathing, and now that she was no longer touching him, she couldn't be certain that he hadn't left her. Was he still there? What if she was alone? The air became thick and oppressive, and she struggled to breathe, to fight down the fear that she knew was unreasonable but that no amount of reason could conquer. Even knowing its source didn't help. She simply couldn't stand the darkness. She couldn't sleep without a light; she never went into a room without first reaching in and turning on the light switch, and she always left her lights on if she knew she would be late returning home. She, who always took extraordinary precautions against being left in the dark, was standing in the middle of a jungle in darkness so complete that it was like being blind.

Her fragile control broke and she reached out wildly, clawing for him, for reassurance that he was still there. Her outstretched fingers touched fabric, and she threw herself against him, gasping in mingled panic and relief. The next second steely fingers grasped her shirt and she was hurled through the air to land flat on her back in the smelly, rotting vegetation. Before she could move, before she could suck air back into her lungs, her hair was pulled back and she felt the suffocating pressure of his knee on her chest again. His breath was a low rasp above her, his voice little more than a snarl. "Don't ever—*ever*—come at me from behind again."

Jane writhed, pushing at his knee. After a moment he lifted it, and eased the grip on her hair. Even being thrown over his shoulder had been better than being left alone in the darkness, and she grabbed for him again, catching him around the knees. Automatically he tried to step away from her entangling arms but she lunged for him. He uttered a startled curse, tried to regain his balance, then crashed to the ground.

He lay so still that Jane's heart plummeted. What would she do if he were hurt? She couldn't possibly carry him, but neither could she leave him lying there, injured and unable to protect himself. Feeling her way up his body, she scrambled to crouch by his shoulders. "Mister, are you all right?" she whispered, running her hands up his shoulders to his face, then searching his head for any cuts or lumps. There was an elasticized band around his head, and she followed it, her nervous fingers finding an odd type of glasses over his eyes. "Are you hurt?" she demanded again, her voice tight with fear. "Damn it, answer me!"

"Lady," the man said in a low, furious voice, "you're crazier than hell. If I was your daddy, I'd *pay* Turego to keep you!"

She didn't know him, but his words caused an odd little pain in her chest. She sat silently, shocked that he could hurt her feelings. She didn't know him, and he didn't know her—how could his opinion matter? But it did, somehow, and she felt strangely vulnerable.

He eased himself to a sitting position, and when she didn't say anything, he sighed. "Why did you jump me like that?" he asked in resignation.

"I'm afraid of the dark," she said with quiet dignity. "I couldn't hear you breathing, and I can't see a thing. I panicked. I'm sorry."

After a moment he said, "All right," and got to his feet. Bending down, he grasped her wrists and pulled her up to stand beside him. Jane inched a little closer to him.

"You can see because of those glasses you're wearing, can't you?" she asked.

"Yeah. There's not a lot of light, but enough that I can make out where I'm going. Infrared lenses."

A howler monkey suddenly screamed somewhere above their heads, and Jane jumped, bumping into him. "Got another pair?" she asked shakily.

She could feel him hesitate, then his arm went around her shoulders. "Nope, just these. Don't worry, Pris, I'm not going to lose you. In another five minutes or so, it'll start getting light."

"I'm all right now," she said, and she was, as long as she could touch him and know that she wasn't alone. That was the real terror: being alone in the darkness. For years she had fought a battle against the nightmare that had begun when she was nine years old, but at last she had come to accept it, and in the acceptance she'd won peace. She knew it was there, knew when to expect it and what to do to ward it off, and that knowledge gave her the ability to enjoy life again. She hadn't let the nightmare cripple her. Maybe her methods of combating it were a little unorthodox, but she had found the balance within herself and she was happy with it.

Feeling remarkably safe with that steely arm looped over her shoulders, Jane waited beside him, and in a very short time she found that she could indeed see a little better. Deep in the rain forest there was no brilliant sunrise to announce the day—the sunrise could not be seen from beneath the canopy of vegetation. Even during the hottest noon, the light that reached the jungle floor was dim, filtered through layers of greenery. She waited as the faint gray light slowly became stronger, until she could pick out more of the details of the lush foliage that surrounded her. She felt almost swamped by the plant life. She'd never been in the jungle before; her only knowledge of it came from movies and what little she'd been able to see during the trip upriver to the plantation. During her days at the plantation she'd begun to think of the jungle as a living entity, huge and green, surrounding her, waiting. She had known from the first that to escape she would have to plunge into that seemingly impenetrable green barrier, and she had spent hours staring at it.

Now she was deep within it, and it wasn't quite what she'd expected. It wasn't a thick tangle, where paths had to be cut with a machete. The jungle floor was littered with rotting vegetation, and laced with networks of vines and roots, but for all that it was surprisingly clear. Plant life that lingered near the jungle floor was doomed. To compete for the precious light it had to rise and spread out its broad leaves, to gather as much light as it could. She stared at a fern that wasn't quite a fern; it was a tree with a buttressed root system, rising to a height of at least eight feet, only at the top it feathered into a fern.

"You can see now," he muttered suddenly, lifting his arm from her shoulders and stripping off the night vision goggles. He placed them carefully in a zippered section of his field pack.

Jane stared at him in open curiosity, wishing that the light were better so she could really see him. What she *could* see gave wing to hundreds of tiny butterflies in her stomach. It would take one brave hombre to meet this man in a dark alley, she thought with a frightened shiver. She couldn't tell the color of his eyes, but they glittered at her from beneath fierce, level dark brows.

His face was blackened, which made those eyes all the brighter. His light colored hair was far too long, and he'd tied a strip of cloth around his head to keep the hair out of his eyes. He was clad in tiger-striped camouflage fatigues, and he wore the trappings of war. A wicked knife was stuck casually in his belt, and a pistol rode his left hip while he carried a carbine slung over his right shoulder. Her startled eyes darted back up to his face, a strong-boned face that revealed no emotion, though he had been aware of her survey.

"Loaded for bear, aren't you?" she quipped, eyeing the knife again. For some reason it looked more deadly than either of the guns.

"I don't walk into anything unprepared," he said flatly.

Well, he certainly looked prepared for anything. She eyed him again, more warily this time; he was about six feet tall, and looked like…looked like… Her mind groped for and found the phrase. It had been bandied about and almost turned into a joke, but with this man, it was deadly serious. He looked like a lean, mean, fighting machine, every hard, muscled inch of him. His shoulders looked to be a yard wide, and he'd carried her dead weight through the jungle without even a hint of strain. He'd knocked her down twice, and she realized the only reason she wasn't badly hurt was that, both times, he'd tempered his strength.

Abruptly his attention left her, and his head lifted with a quick, alert motion, like that of an eagle. His eyes narrowed as he listened. "The helicopter is coming," he told her. "Let's go."

Jane listened, but she couldn't hear anything. "Are you sure?" she asked doubtfully.

"I said let's go," he repeated impatiently, and walked away from her. It took Jane only a few seconds to realize that he was heading out, and in the jungle he would be completely hidden from view before he'd gone ten yards. She hurried to catch up to him.

"Hey, slow down!" she whispered frantically, catching at his belt.

"Move it," he said with a total lack of sympathy. "The helicopter won't wait forever; Pablo's on the quick side anyway."

"Who's Pablo?"

"The pilot."

Just then a faint vibration reached her ears. In only a moment it had intensified to the recognizable beat of a helicopter. How could he have heard it before? She knew that she had good hearing, but his senses must be almost painfully acute.

He moved swiftly, surely, as if he knew exactly where he was going. Jane concentrated on keeping up with him and avoiding the roots that tried to catch her toes, she paid little attention to their surroundings. When he climbed, she climbed; it was simple. She was mildly surprised when he stopped abruptly and she lifted her head to look around. The jungle of Costa Rica was mountainous, and they had climbed to the edge of a small cliff, looking down on a narrow, hidden valley with a natural clearing. The helicopter sat in that clearing, the blades lazily whirling.

"Better than a taxicab," Jane murmured in relief, and started past him.

His hand closed over her shoulder and jerked her back. "Be quiet," he ordered, his narrowed gaze moving restlessly, surveying the area.

"Is something wrong?"

"Shut up!"

Jane glared at him, incensed by his unnecessary rudeness, but his hand was still clamped on her shoulder in a grip that bordered on being painful. It was a warning that if she tried to leave the protective cover of the jungle before he was satisfied that everything was safe, he would stop her with real pain. She stood quietly, staring at the clearing herself, but she couldn't see anything wrong. Everything was quiet. The pilot was leaning against the outside of the helicopter, occupied with cleaning his nails; he certainly wasn't concerned with anything.

Long minutes dragged past. The pilot began to fidget, craning his neck and staring into the jungle, though anyone standing just a few feet behind the trees would be completely hidden from view. He looked at his watch, then scanned the jungle again, his gaze moving nervously from left to right.

Jane felt the tension in the man standing beside her, tension that was echoed in the hand that held her shoulder. What was wrong? What was he looking for, and why was he waiting? He was as motionless as a jaguar lying in wait for its prey to pass beneath its tree limb.

"This sucks," he muttered abruptly, easing deeper into the jungle and dragging her with him.

Jane sputtered at the inelegant expression. "It does? Why? What's wrong?"

"Stay here." He pushed her to the ground, deep in the green-black shadow of the buttressed roots of an enormous tree.

Startled, she took a moment to realize that she'd been abandoned. He had simply melted into the jungle, so silently and swiftly that she wasn't certain which way he'd gone. She twisted around but could see nothing that indicated his direction; no swaying vines or limbs.

She wrapped her arms around her drawn-up legs and propped her chin on her knees, staring thought-fully at the ground. A green stick with legs was drag-ging a large spider off to be devoured. What if he didn't come back…whoever he was. Why hadn't she asked him his name? If something happened to him, she'd like to know his name, so she could tell someone—as-suming that she could manage to get out of the jungle herself. Well, she wasn't any worse off now than she had been before. She was away from Turego, and that was what counted.

Wait here, he'd said. For how long? Until lunch? Sundown? Her next birthday? Men gave such inexact instructions! Of course, this particular man seemed a little limited in the conversation department. Shut up, Stay here and Stay put seemed to be the highlights of his repertoire.

This was quite a tree he'd parked her by. The bottom of the trunk flared into buttressed roots, forming enor-mous wings that wrapped around her almost like arms. If she sat back against the tree, the wings would shield her completely from the view of someone approaching at any angle except head-on.

The straps of her backpack were irritating her shoul-ders, so she slid it off and stretched, feeling remarkably lighter. She hauled the pack around and opened it, then began digging for her hairbrush. Finding this backpack had been a stroke of luck, she thought, though Turego's soldiers really should be a little more careful with their belongings. Without it, she'd have had to wrap things up in a blanket, which would have been awkward.

Finally locating the hairbrush, she diligently worked through the mass of tangles that had accumulated in her long hair during the night. A small monkey with an indignant expression hung from a branch overhead. It scolded her throughout the operation, evidently angry that she had intruded on its territory. She waved at it.

Congratulating herself for her foresight, she pinned her hair up and pulled a black baseball cap out of the pack. She jammed the cap on and tugged the bill down low over her eyes, then shoved it back up. There wasn't any sun down here. Staring upward, she could see bright pinpoints of sun high in the trees, but only a muted green light filtered down to the floor. She'd have been better off with some of those fancy goggles that What's-his-name had.

How long had she been sitting there? Was he in trouble?

Her legs were going to sleep, so she stood and stomped around to get her blood flowing again. The longer she waited, the more uneasy she became, and she had the feeling that a time would come when she'd better be able to move fast. Jane was an instinctive creature, as sensitive to atmosphere as any finely tuned barometer. That trait had enabled her to hold Turego at bay for what seemed like an endless succession of days and nights, reading him, sidestepping him, keeping him constantly disarmed, and even charmed. Now the same instinct warned her of danger. There was some slight change in the very air that stroked her bare arms. Warily, she leaned down to pick up her backpack, slipping her arms through the straps and anchoring it this time by fastening the third strap around her middle.

The sudden thunderous burst of automatic weapon fire made her whirl, her heart jumping into her throat. Listening to the staccato blasts, she knew that several weapons were being fired, but at whom? Had her friend been detected or was this something else entirely? Was this the trouble he'd sensed that had made him shy away from the clearing? She wanted to think that he was safe, observing everything from an invisible vantage point in the jungle, but with a chill she realized that she couldn't take that for granted.

Her hands felt cold, and with a distant surprise she realized that she was trembling. What should she do? Wait, or run? What if he needed help? She realized that there was very little she could do, since she was unarmed, but she couldn't just run away if he needed help. He wasn't the most amiable man she'd ever met, and she still didn't exactly trust him, but he was the closest thing to a friend she had here.

Ignoring the unwillingness of her feet and the icy lump of fear in her stomach, Jane left the shelter of the giant tree and began cautiously inching through the forest, back toward the clearing. There were only sporadic bursts of gunfire now, still coming from the same general direction.

Suddenly she froze as the faint sound of voices filtered through the forest. In a cold panic she dove for the shelter of another large tree. What would she do if they were coming in this direction? The rough bark scratched her hands as she cautiously moved her head just enough to peer around the trunk.

A steely hand clamped over her mouth. As a scream rose in her throat, a deep, furious voice growled in her ear, "Damn it, I told you to stay put!"

CHAPTER THREE

JANE GLARED AT him over the hand that still covered her mouth, her fright turning into relieved anger. She didn't like this man. She didn't like him at all, and as soon as they were out of this mess, she was going to tell him about it!

He removed his hand and shoved her to the ground on her hands and knees. "Crawl!" he ordered in a harsh whisper, and pointed to their left.

Jane crawled, ignoring the scratches she incurred as she squirmed through the undergrowth, ignoring even the disgusting squishiness when she accidentally smashed something with her hand. Odd, but now that he was with her again, her panic had faded; it hadn't gone completely, but it wasn't the heart-pounding, nauseating variety, either. Whatever his faults, he knew his way around.

He was on her tail, literally, his hard shoulder against the back of her thighs, pushing her onward whenever he thought she wasn't moving fast enough. Once he halted her by the simple method of grabbing her ankle and jerking her flat, his urgent grip warning her to be quiet. She held her breath, listening to the faint rustle that betrayed the presence of someone, or something, nearby. She didn't dare turn her head, but she could detect movement with her peripheral vision. In a moment the man was close enough that she could see him plainly. He was obviously of Latin ancestry, and he was dressed in camouflage fatigues with a cap covering his head. He held an automatic rifle at the ready before him.

In only a moment she could no longer see or hear him, but they stayed motionless in the thick tangle of ferns for long, agonizing minutes. Then her ankle was released and a hand on her hip urged her forward.

They were moving away from the soldier at a right angle. Perhaps they were going to try to get behind their pursuers, then take off in the helicopter while the soldiers were still deep in the jungle. She wanted to know where they were going, what they would do, who the soldiers were and what they wanted—but the questions had to remain bottled up inside her. Now was definitely not the time for talking, not with this man—what *was* his name?—practically shoving her through the undergrowth.

Abruptly the forest cleared somewhat, allowing small patches of sunlight to filter through. Grasping her arm, he hauled her to her feet. "Run, but be as quiet as you can," he hissed in her ear.

Great. Run, but do it quietly. She threw him a dirty look, then ran, taking off like a startled deer. The most disgusting thing was that he was right behind her, and she couldn't hear him making a sound, while her own feet seemed to pound the earth like a drum. But her body seemed cheered by the small amount of sunlight, because she felt her energy level surge despite her sleepless night. The pack on her shoulders seemed lighter, and her steps became quick and effortless as adrenaline began pumping through her veins.

The brush became thicker, and they had to slow their

pace. After about fifteen minutes he stopped her with a hand on her shoulder and pulled her behind the trunk of a tree. "Rest a minute," he whispered. "The humidity will wipe you out if you aren't used to it."

Until that moment Jane hadn't noticed that she was wringing wet with sweat. She'd been too intent on saving her skin to worry about its dampness. Now, she became aware of the intense humidity of the rain forest pressing down on her, making every breath she drew lie heavily in her lungs. She wiped the moisture from her face, the salt of her perspiration stinging the small scratches on her cheeks.

He took a canteen from his pack. "Take a drink; you look like you need it."

She had a very good idea what she looked like, and she smiled wryly. She accepted the canteen and drank a little of the water, then capped it and returned it to him. "Thanks."

He looked at her quizzically. "You can have more if you want."

"I'm okay." She looked at him, seeing now that his eyes were a peculiar golden-brown color, like amber. His pupils seemed piercingly black against that tawny background. He was streaked with sweat, too, but he wasn't even breathing hard. Whoever he was, whatever he was, he was damned good at this. "What's your name?" she asked him, desperately needing to call him something, as if that would give him more substance, make him more familiar.

He looked a little wary, and she sensed that he disliked giving even that much of himself away. A name was only a small thing, but it was a chink in his armor, a link to another person that he didn't want. "Sullivan," he finally said reluctantly.

"First or last?"

"Last."

"What's your first name?"

"Grant."

Grant Sullivan. She liked the name. It wasn't fancy; he wasn't fancy. He was a far cry from the sleekly sophisticated men she usually met, but the difference was exciting. He was hard and dangerous, mean when he had to be, but he wasn't vicious. The contrast between him and Turego, who was a truly vicious man, couldn't have been more clear-cut.

"Let's go," he said. "We need to put a lot more space between the hounds and the foxes."

Obediently she followed his direction, but found that her burst of adrenaline was already dissipating. She felt more exhausted now than she had before the short rest. She stumbled once, catching her booted foot in a liana vine, but he rescued her with a quick grab. She gave him a tired smile of thanks, but when she tried to step away from him he held her. He stood rigid and it frightened her. She jerked around to look at him, but his face was a cold, blank mask, and he was staring behind her. She whirled again, and looked down the barrel of a rifle.

The sweat congealed on her body. For one moment of frozen terror she expected to be shot; then the moment passed and she was still alive. She was able then to look past the barrel to the hard, dark face of the soldier who held the rifle. His black eyes were narrowed, fastened on Sullivan. He said something, but Jane was too upset to translate the Spanish.

Slowly, deliberately, Sullivan released Jane and

raised his arms, clasping his hands on top of his head. "Step away from me," he said quietly.

The soldier barked an order at him. Jane's eyes widened. If she moved an inch this maniac would probably shoot her down. But Sullivan had told her to move, so she moved, her face so white that the small freckles across her nose stood out as bright dots of color. The rifle barrel jerked in her direction, and the soldier said something else. He was nervous, Jane suddenly realized. The tension was obvious in his voice, in his jerky movements. God, if his finger twitched on the trigger…! Then, just as abruptly, he aimed the rifle at Sullivan again.

Sullivan was going to do something. She could sense it. The fool! He'd get himself killed if he tried to jump this guy! She stared at the soldier's shaking hands on the rifle, and suddenly something jumped into her consciousness. He didn't have the rifle on automatic. It took her another moment to realize the implications; then she reacted without thought. Her body, trained to dance, trained in the graceful moves of self-defense, went into fluid motion. He began moving a split second later, swinging the weapon around, but by then she was close enough that her left foot sliced upward under the barrel of the gun, and the shot that he fired went into the canopy over their heads. He never got a chance at another shot.

Grant was on him then, grabbing the gun with one hand and slashing at the man's unprotected neck with the side of the other. The soldier's eyes glazed over, and he sank limply to the ground, his breathing raspy but steady.

Grant grabbed Jane's arm. "Run! That shot will bring every one of them swarming down on us!"

The urgency of his tone made it possible for her to obey, though she was rapidly depleting her reserves of energy. Her legs were leaden, and her boots weighed fifty pounds each. Burning agony slashed her thighs, but she forced herself to ignore it; sore muscles weren't nearly as permanent as being dead. Urged on by his hand at her back, she stumbled over roots and through bushes, adding to her collection of scratches. It was purely a natural defense mechanism, but her mind shut down and her body operated automatically, her feet moving, her lungs sucking desperately at the heavy, moist air. She was so tired now that she no longer felt the pain in her body.

The ground abruptly sloped out from under her feet. Her senses dulled by both terror and fatigue, she was unable to regain her balance. Grant grabbed for her, but the momentum of her body carried them both over the edge of the hill. His arms wrapped around her, and they rolled down the steep slope. The earth and trees spun crazily, but she saw a rocky, shallow stream at the bottom of the slope and a small, hoarse cry tore from her throat. Some of those rocks were big enough to kill them and the smaller ones could cut them to pieces.

Grant swore, and tightened his grip on her until she thought her ribs would splinter under the pressure. She felt his muscles tighten, felt the desperate twist he made, and somehow he managed to get his feet and legs in front of him. Then they were sliding down in a fairly upright position, rather than rolling. He dug his heels in and their descent slowed, then stopped. "Pris?" he asked roughly, cupping her chin in his hand and turning her face so he could see it. "Are you hurt?"

"No, no," she quickly assured him, ignoring the new

aches in her body. Her right arm wasn't broken, but it was badly bruised; she winced as she tried to move it. One of the straps on the backpack had broken, and the pack was hanging lopsidedly off her left shoulder. Her cap was missing.

He adjusted the rifle on his shoulder, and Jane wondered how he had managed to hold on to it. Didn't he ever drop anything, or get lost, or tired, or hungry? She hadn't even seen him take a drink of water!

"My cap came off," she said, turning to stare up the slope. The top was almost thirty yards above them and the slope steep enough that it was a miracle they hadn't crashed into the rocks at the streambed.

"I see it." He swarmed up the slope, lithe and surefooted. He snatched the cap from a broken branch and in only a moment was back beside her. Jamming the cap on her head, he said, "Can you make it up the other side?"

There was no way, she thought. Her body refused to function any longer. She looked at him and lifted her chin. "Of course."

He didn't smile, but there was a faint softening of his expression, as if he knew how desperately tired she was. "We have to keep moving," he said, taking her arm and urging her across the stream. She didn't care that her boots were getting wet; she just sloshed through the water, moving downstream while he scanned the bank for an easy place to climb up. On this side of the stream, the bank wasn't sloped; it was almost vertical and covered with what looked like an impenetrable tangle of vines and bushes. The stream created a break in the foliage that allowed more sunlight to pour down, letting the plants grow much more thickly.

"Okay, let's go up this way," he finally said, point-

ing. Jane lifted her head and stared at the bank, but she
didn't see any break in the wild tangle.

"Let's talk about this," she hedged.

He gave an exasperated sigh. "Look, Pris, I know
you're tired, but—"

Something snapped inside Jane, and she whirled on
him, catching him by the shirtfront and drawing back
her fist. "If you call me 'Pris' just one more time, I'm
going to feed you a knuckle sandwich!" she roared,
unreasonably angry at his continued use of that hated
name. No one, but no one, had ever been allowed to
call her Priscilla, Pris, or even Cilla, more than once.
This damned commando had been rubbing her face in
it from the beginning. She'd kept quiet about it, figuring
she owed him for kicking him in the groin, but she was
tired and hungry and scared and enough was enough!

He moved so quickly that she didn't even have time
to blink. His hand snaked out and caught her drawn back
fist, while the fingers of his other hand laced around
her wrist, removing her grip from his shirt. "Damn it,
can't you keep quiet? *I* didn't name you Priscilla, your
parents did, so if you don't like it take it up with them.
But until then, climb!"

Jane climbed, even though she was certain at every
moment that she was going to collapse on her face.
Grabbing vines for handholds, using roots and rocks
and bushes and small trees, she squirmed and wiggled
her way through the foliage. It was so thick that it could
have been swarming with jaguars and she wouldn't have
been able to see one until she stuck her hand in its
mouth. She remembered that jaguars liked water, spending most of their time resting comfortably near a river

or stream, and she swore vengeance on Grant Sullivan for making her do this.

Finally she scrambled over the top, and after pushing forward several yards found that the foliage had once again thinned, and walking was much easier. She adjusted the pack on her back, wincing as she found new bruises. "Are we heading for the helicopter?"

"No," he said curtly. "The helicopter is being watched."

"Who are those men?"

He shrugged. "Who knows? Sandinistas, maybe; we're only a few klicks from the Nicaraguan border. They could be any guerrilla faction. That damned Pablo sold us out."

Jane didn't waste time worrying about Pablo's duplicity; she was too tired to really care. "Where are we going?"

"South."

She ground her teeth. Getting information out of this man was like pulling teeth. "South *where*?"

"Limon, eventually. Right now, we're going due east."

Jane knew enough about Costa Rica to know what lay due east, and she didn't like what she'd just been told. Due east lay the Caribbean coast, where the rain forest became swampland. If they were only a few kilometers from the Nicaraguan border, then Limon was roughly a hundred miles away. In her weariness, she felt it might as well have been five hundred miles. How long would it take them to walk a hundred miles? Four or five days? She didn't know if she could stand four or five days with Mr. Sunshine. She'd known him less than twelve hours, and she was already close to death.

"Why can't we just go south and forget about east?"

He jerked his head in the direction from which they'd come. "Because of them. They weren't Turego's men, but Turego will soon know that you came in this direction, and he'll be after us. He can't afford to have the government find out about his little clandestine operations. So...we go where he can't easily follow."

It made sense. She didn't like it, but it made sense. She'd never been in the Caribbean coastal region of Costa Rica, so she didn't know what to expect, but it had to be better than being Turego's prisoner. Poisonous snakes, alligators, quicksand, whatever...it was better than Turego. She'd worry about the swamp when they were actually in it. With that settled in her mind, she returned to her most pressing problem.

"When do we get to rest? And eat? And, frankly, Attila, you may have a bladder the size of New Jersey, but I've got to *go*!"

Again she caught that unwilling twitch of his lips, as if he'd almost grinned. "We can't stop yet, but you can eat while we walk. As for the other, go behind that tree there." He pointed, and she turned to see another of those huge, funny trees with the enormous buttressed roots. In the absence of indoor plumbing it would have to do. She plunged for its shelter.

When they started out again he gave her something hard and dark to chew on; it tasted faintly like meat, but after examining it suspiciously she decided not to question him too closely about it. It eased the empty pains in her stomach, and after washing a few bites down with cautious sips of water, she began to feel better and the rubbery feeling left her legs. He chewed a stick of it, too, which reassured her in regard to his humanity.

Still, after walking steadily for a few hours, Jane

began to lose the strength that had come with her second wind. Her legs were moving clumsily, and she felt as if she were wading in knee-deep water. The temperature had risen steadily; it was well over ninety now, even in the thick shelter of the canopy. The humidity was draining her as she continued to sweat, losing water that she wasn't replacing. Just when she was about to tell him that she couldn't take another step, he turned and surveyed her with an impersonal professionalism.

"Stay here while I find some sort of shelter for us. It's going to start raining in a little while, so we might as well sit it out. You look pretty well beat anyway."

Jane pulled her cap off and wiped her streaming face with her forearm, too tired to comment as he melted from sight. How did he know it was going to start raining? It rained almost every day, of course, so it didn't take a fortune-teller to predict rain, but she hadn't heard the thunder that usually preceded it.

He was back in only a short while, taking her arm and leading her to a small rise, where a scattering of boulders testified to Costa Rica's volcanic origin. After taking his knife from his belt, he cut small limbs and lashed them together with vines, then propped one end of his contraption up by wedging sturdier limbs under the corners. Producing a rolled up tarp from his backpack like a magician, he tied the tarp over the crude lean-to, making it waterproof. "Well, crawl in and get comfortable," he growled when Jane simply stood there, staring in astonishment at the shelter he'd constructed in just a few minutes.

Obediently she crawled in, groaning with relief as she shrugged out of her backpack and relaxed her aching muscles. Her ears caught the first distant rumble of thunder; whatever he did for a living, the man certainly knew his way around the jungle.

Grant ducked under the shelter, too, relieving his shoulders of the weight of his own backpack. He had apparently decided that while they were waiting out the rain they might as well eat, because he dug out a couple of cans of field rations.

Jane sat up straight and leaned closer, staring at the cans. "What's that?"

"Food."

"What kind of food?"

He shrugged. "I've never looked at it long enough to identify it. Take my advice: don't think about it. Just eat it."

She put her hand on his as he started to open the cans. "Wait. Why don't we save those for have-to situations?"

"This *is* a have-to situation," he grunted. "We *have* to eat."

"Yes, but we don't have to eat *that*!"

Exasperation tightened his hard features. "Honey, we either eat this, or two more cans exactly like them!"

"Oh, ye of little faith," she scoffed, dragging her own backpack closer. She began delving around in it, and in a moment produced a small packet wrapped in a purloined towel. With an air of triumph she unwrapped it to expose two badly smashed but still edible sandwiches, then returned to the backpack to dig around again. Her face flushed with success, she pulled out two cans of orange juice. "Here!" she said cheerfully, handing him one of the cans. "A peanut butter and jelly sandwich, and a can of orange juice. Protein, carbohydrates and vitamin C. What more could we ask for?"

Grant took the sandwich and the pop-top can she offered him, staring at them in disbelief. He blinked once, then an amazing thing happened: he laughed. It wasn't much of a laugh. It was rather rusty sounding, but it revealed his straight white teeth and made his amber eyes crinkle at the corners. The rough texture of that laugh gave her a funny little feeling in her chest. It was obvious that he rarely laughed, that life didn't hold much humor for him, and she felt both happy that she'd made him laugh and sad that he'd had so little to laugh about. Without laughter she would never have kept her sanity, so she knew how precious it was.

Chewing on his sandwich, Grant relished the gooiness of the peanut butter and the sweetness of the jelly. So what if the bread was a little stale? The unexpected treat made such a detail unimportant. He leaned back and propped himself against his backpack, stretching his long legs out before him. The first drops of rain began to patter against the upper canopy. It would be impossible for anyone to track them through the downpour that was coming, even if those guerrillas had an Indian tracker with them, which he doubted. For the first time since he'd seen the helicopter that morning, he relaxed, his highly developed sense of danger no longer nagging him.

He finished the sandwich and poured the rest of the orange juice down his throat, then glanced over at Jane to see her daintily licking the last bit of jelly from her fingers. She looked up, caught his gaze, and gave him a cheerful smile that made her dimples flash, then returned to the task of cleaning her fingers.

Against his will, Grant felt his body tighten with a surge of lust that surprised him with its strength.

She was a charmer, all right, but not at all what he'd expected. He'd expected a spoiled, helpless, petulant debutante, and instead she had had the spirit, the pure guts, to hurl herself into the jungle with two peanut butter sandwiches and some orange juice as provisions. She'd also dressed in commonsense clothing, with good sturdy boots and green khaki pants, and a short-sleeved black blouse. Not right out of the fashion pages, but he'd had a few distracting moments crawling behind her, seeing those pants molded to her shapely bottom. He hadn't been able to prevent a deep masculine appreciation for the soft roundness of her buttocks.

She was a mass of contradictions. She was a jet-setter, so wild that her father had disinherited her, and she'd been George Persall's mistress, yet he couldn't detect any signs of hard living in her face. If anything, her face was as open and innocent as a child's, with a child's enthusiasm for life shining out of her dark brown eyes. She had a look of perpetual mischievousness on her face, yet it was a face of honest sensuality. Her long hair was so dark a brown that it was almost black, and it hung around her shoulders in snarls and tangles. She had pushed it away from her face with total unconcern. Her dark brown eyes were long and a little narrow, slanting in her high-cheekboned face in a way that made him think she might have a little Indian blood. A smattering of small freckles danced across those elegant cheekbones and the dainty bridge of her nose. Her mouth was soft and full, with the upper lip fuller than the lower one, which gave her an astonishingly sensual look. All in all, she was far from beautiful, but there was a freshness and zest about her that made all the other women he'd known suddenly seem bland.

Certainly he'd never been as intimate with any other woman's knee.

Even now, the thought of it made him angry. Part of it was chagrin that he'd left himself open to the blow; he'd been bested by a lightweight! But another part of it was an instinctive, purely male anger, sexually based. He'd watch her knee now whenever she was within striking distance. Still, the fact that she'd defended herself, and the moves she'd made, told him that she'd had professional training, and that was another contradiction. She wasn't an expert, but she knew what to do. Why would a wild, spoiled playgirl know anything about self-defense? Some of the pieces didn't fit, and Grant was always uneasy when he sensed details that didn't jibe.

He felt pretty grim about the entire operation. Their situation right now was little short of desperate, regardless of the fact that they were, for the moment, rather secure. They had probably managed to shake the soldiers, whoever they worked for, but Turego was a different story. The microfilm wasn't the only issue now. Turego had been operating without the sanction of the government, and if Jane made it back and filed a complaint against him, the repercussions would cost him his position, and possibly his freedom.

It was Grant's responsibility to get her out, but it was no longer the simple in-and-out situation he'd planned. From the moment he'd seen Pablo leaning so negligently against the helicopter, waiting for them, he'd known that the deal had gone sour. Pablo wasn't the type to be waiting for them so casually; in all the time Grant had know him, Pablo had been tense, ready to move, always staying in the helicopter with the rotors turning. The elaborate pose of relaxation had tipped Grant off as clearly as if Pablo had hung a sign around his neck. Perhaps Pablo had been trying to warn him. There was no way he'd ever know for certain.

Now he had to get her through the jungle, out of the mountains, and south through a swamp, with Turego in hot pursuit. With luck, in a day or so, they'd find a village and be able to hitch a ride, but even that depended on how close behind Turego was.

And on top of that, he couldn't trust her. She'd disarmed that soldier far too casually, and hadn't turned a hair at anything that had happened. She was far too matter-of-fact about the whole situation. She wasn't what she seemed, and that made her dangerous.

He was wary of her, but at the same time he found that he was unable to stop watching her. She was too damned sexy, as lush and exotic as a jungle orchid. What would it be like to lie with her? Did she use the rich curves of her body to make a man forget who he was? How many men had been taken in by that fresh, open expression? Had Turego found himself off balance with her, wanting her, knowing that he could force her at any time—but being eaten alive by the challenge of trying to win her, of making her give herself freely? How else had she managed to control him? None of it added up to what she should have been, unless she played with men as some sort of ego trip, where the more dangerous the man, the greater the thrill at controlling him.

Grant didn't want her to have that much influence over him; she wasn't worth it. No matter how beguiling the expression in her dark, slanted eyes, she simply wasn't worth it. He didn't need the sort of complication she offered; he just wanted to get her out, collect his money from her father, and get back to the solitude of the farm. Already he'd felt the jungle pulling at him, the heated, almost sexual excitement of danger. The rifle felt like an extension of his body, and the knife fit his palm as if he'd never put it down. All the old moves, the old instincts, were still there, and blackness rose in him as he wondered bitterly if he'd ever really be able to put this life behind him. The blood lust had been there in him, and perhaps he'd have killed that soldier if she hadn't kicked the rifle up when she had.

Was it part of the intoxication of battle that made him want to pull her beneath him and drive himself into her body, until he was mindless with intolerable pleasure? Part of it was, and yet part of it had been born hours ago, on the floor of her bedroom, when he'd felt the soft, velvety roundness of her breasts in his hands. Remembering that, he wanted to know what her breasts looked like, if they thrust out conically or had a full lower slope, if her nipples were small or large, pink or brown. Desire made him harden, and he reminded himself caustically that it had been a while since he'd had a woman, so it was only natural that he would be turned on. If nothing else, he should be glad of the evidence that he could still function!

She yawned, and blinked her dark eyes at him like a sleepy cat. "I'm going to take a nap," she announced, and curled up on the ground. She rested her head on her arm, closed her eyes and yawned again. He watched her, his eyes narrowed. This utter adaptability she displayed was another piece of the puzzle that didn't fit. She should have been moaning and bitching about how uncomfortable she was, rather than calmly curling up on the ground for a nap. But a nap sounded pretty damned good right now, he thought.

Grant looked around. The rain had become a full-fledged downpour, pounding through the canopy and turning the jungle floor into a river. The constant, torrential rains leeched the nutrients out of the soil, making the jungle into a contradiction, where the world's greatest variety of animal and plant life existed on some of the poorest soil. Right now the rain also made it almost impossible for them to be found. They were safe for the time being, and for the first time he allowed himself to feel the weariness in his muscles. He might as well take a nap, too; he'd wake when the rain stopped, alerted by the total cessation of noise.

Reaching out, he shook her shoulder, and she roused to stare at him sleepily. "Get against the back of the lean-to," he ordered. "Give me a little room to stretch out, too."

She crawled around as he'd instructed and stretched out full length, sighing in ecstasy. He pushed their backpacks to one side, then lay down beside her, his big body between her and the rain. He lay on his back, one brawny arm thrown behind his head. There was no twitching around, no yawning or sighing, for him. He simply lay down, closed his eyes and went to sleep. Jane watched him sleepily, her gaze lingering on the hawklike line of his profile, noting the scar that ran along his left cheekbone. How had he gotten it? His jaw was blurred with several days' growth of beard, and she noticed that his beard was much darker than his hair. His eyebrows and lashes were dark, too, and that made his amber eyes seem even brighter, almost as yellow as an eagle's.

The rain made her feel a little chilled after the intense heat of the day; instinctively she inched closer to the heat she could feel emanating from his body. He was so warm...and she felt so safe...safer than she'd felt since she was nine years old. With one more little sigh, she slept.

Sometime later the rain ceased abruptly, and Grant woke immediately, like a light switch being flipped on. His senses were instantly alert, wary. He started to surge to his feet, only to realize that she was lying curled against his side, with her head pillowed on his arm and her hand lying on his chest. Disbelief made him rigid. How could she have gotten that close to him without waking him? He'd always slept like a cat, alert to the smallest noise or movement—but this damned woman had practically crawled all over him and he hadn't even stirred. She must've been disappointed, he thought furiously. The fury was directed as much at himself as at her, because the incident told him how slack he had become in the past year. That slackness might cost them their lives.

He lay still, aware of the fullness of her breasts against his side. She was soft and lush, and one of her legs was thrown up over his thigh. All he had to do was roll over and he'd be between her legs. The mental image made moisture break out on his forehead. God! She'd be hot and tight, and he clenched his teeth at the heavy surge in his loins. She was no lady, but she was all woman, and he wanted her naked and writhing beneath him with an intensity that tied his guts into knots.

He had to move, or he'd be taking her right there on the rocky ground. Disgusted at himself for letting her get to him the way she had, he eased his arm from beneath her head, then shook her shoulder. "Let's get moving," he said curtly.

She muttered something, her forehead puckering, but she didn't open her eyes, and in a moment her forehead smoothed as she lapsed back into deep sleep. Impatiently, Grant shook her again. "Hey, wake up."

She rolled over on her stomach and sighed deeply, burrowing her head against her folded arm as she sought a more comfortable position. "Come on, we've got to get going," he said, shaking her more vigorously. "Wake up!"

She aimed a drowsy swat at him, as if he were a pesky fly, brushing his hand aside. Exasperated, Grant caught her shoulders and pulled her to a sitting position, shaking her once again. "Damn it, would you get up? On your feet, honey; we've got some walking to do." Her eyes finally opened, and she blinked at him groggily, but she made no move to get up.

Swearing under his breath, Grant hauled her to her feet. "Just stand over there, out of the way," he said, turning her around and starting her on her way with a swat on her bottom before he turned his attention to taking down their shelter.

CHAPTER FOUR

JANE STOPPED, HER hand going to her bottom. Awakened now, and irritated by his light, casual slap, she turned. "You didn't have to do that!"

"Do what?" he asked with total disinterest, already busy removing the tarp from the top of the lean-to and rolling it up to replace it in his backpack.

"Hit me! A simple 'wake-up' would have sufficed!"

Grant looked at her in disbelief. "Well, pardon me all to hell," he drawled in a sarcastic tone that made her want to strangle him. "Let me start over. Excuse me, Priscilla, but nappy time is over, and we really do have to—hey! Damn it!" He ducked in time, throwing his arm up to catch the force of her fist. Swiftly he twisted his arm to lock his fingers around her wrist, then caught her other arm before she could swing at him with it. She'd exploded into fury, hurling herself at him like a cat pouncing. Her fist had hit his arm with enough strength that she might have broken his nose if the blow had landed on target. "Woman, what in *hell* is wrong with you?"

"I told you not to call me that!" Jane raged at him, spitting the words out in her fury. She struggled wildly, trying to free her arm so she could hit him again.

Panting, Grant wrestled her to the ground and sat astride her, holding her hands above her head, and this time making damned certain that her knee wouldn't come anywhere near him. She kept wriggling and heaving, and he felt as if he were trying to hold an octopus, but finally he had her subdued.

Glaring at her, he said, "You told me not to call you Pris."

"Well, don't call me Priscilla, either!" she fumed, glaring right back.

"Look, I'm not a mind reader! What am I supposed to call you?"

"Jane!" she shouted at him. "My name is Jane! *Nobody* has *ever* called me Priscilla!"

"All right! All you had to do was tell me! I'm getting damned tired of you snapping at my ankles, understand? I may hurt you before I can stop myself, so you'd better think twice before you attack again. Now, if I let you up, are you going to behave?"

Jane still glared at him, but the weight of his knees on her bruised arms was excruciating. "All right," she said sullenly, and he slowly got up, then surprised her by offering his hand to help her up. She surprised herself by taking it.

A sudden twinkle lit the dark gold of his eyes. "Jane, huh?" he asked reflectively, looking at the surrounding jungle.

She gave him a threatening look. "No 'Me Tarzan, you Jane' stuff," she warned. "I've heard it since grade school." She paused, then said grudgingly, "But it's still better than Priscilla."

He grunted in agreement and turned away to finish dismantling their shelter, and after a moment Jane began helping. He glanced at her, but said nothing. He wasn't much of a talker, she'd noticed, and he didn't improve any on closer acquaintance. But he'd risked his own life to help her, and he hadn't left her behind, even though Jane knew he could have moved a lot faster, and with a lot less risk to himself, on his own. And there was something in his eyes, an expression that was weary and cynical and a little empty, as if he'd seen far too much to have any faith or trust left. That made Jane want to put her arms around him and shield him. Lowering her head so he wouldn't be able to read her expression, she chided herself for feeling protective of a man who was so obviously capable of handling himself. There had been a time in her own life when she had been afraid to trust anyone except her parents, and it had been a horrible, lonely time. She knew what fear was, and loneliness, and she ached for him.

All signs of their shelter obliterated, he swung his backpack up and buckled it on, then slung the rifle over his shoulder while Jane stuffed her hair up under her cap. He leaned down to pick up her pack for her, and a look of astonishment crossed his face; then his dark brows snapped together. "What the—" he muttered. "What all do you have in this damned thing? It weighs a good twenty pounds more than my pack!"

"Whatever I thought I'd need," Jane replied, taking the pack from him and hooking her arm through the one good shoulder strap, then buckling the waist strap to secure it as well as she could.

"Like what?"

"Things," she said stubbornly. Maybe her provisions weren't exactly proper by military standards, but she'd take her peanut butter sandwiches over his canned whatever anytime. She thought he would order her to dump the pack on the ground for him to sort through and decide what to keep, and she was determined not to allow it. She set her jaw and looked at him.

He put his hands on his hips and surveyed her funny, exotic face, her lower lip pouting out in a mutinous expression, her delicate jaw set. She looked ready to light into him again, and he sighed in resignation. Damned if she wasn't the stubbornest, scrappiest woman he'd ever met. "Take it off," he growled, unbuckling his own pack. "I'll carry yours, and you can carry mine."

If anything, the jaw went higher. "I'm doing okay with my own."

"Stop wasting time arguing. That extra weight will slow you down, and you're already tired. Hand it over, and I'll fix that strap before we start out."

Reluctantly she slipped the straps off and gave him the pack, ready to jump him if he showed any sign of dumping it. But he took a small folder from his own pack, opened it to extract a needle and thread, and deftly began to sew the two ends of the broken strap together.

Astounded, Jane watched his lean, calloused hands wielding the small needle with a dexterity that she had to envy. Reattaching a button was the limit of her sewing skill, and she usually managed to prick her finger doing that. "Do they teach sewing in the military now?" she asked, crowding in to get a better look.

He gave her another one of his glances of dismissal. "I'm not in the military."

"Maybe not now," she conceded. "But you were, weren't you?"

"A long time ago."

"Where did you learn how to sew?"

"I just picked it up. It comes in handy." He bit the

thread off, then replaced the needle in its package. "Let's get moving; we've wasted too much time as it is."

Jane took his backpack and fell into step behind him; all she had to do was follow him. Her gaze drifted over the width of his shoulders, then eased downward. Had she ever known anyone as physically strong as this man? She didn't think so. He seemed to be immune to weariness, and he ignored the steamy humidity that drained her strength and drenched her clothes in perspiration. His long, powerful legs moved in an effortless stride, the flexing of his thigh muscles pulling the fabric of his pants tight across them. Jane found herself watching his legs and matching her own stride to his. He took a step, and she took a step automatically. It was easier that way; she could separate her mind from her body, and in doing so ignore her protesting muscles.

He stopped once and took a long drink from the canteen, then passed it to Jane without comment. Also without comment, and without wiping the mouth of the canteen, she tipped it up and drank thirstily. Why worry about drinking after him? Catching cold was the least of her concerns. After capping the canteen, she handed it back to him, and they began walking again.

There was madness to his method, or so it seemed to her. If there was a choice between two paths, he invariably chose the more difficult one. The route he took was through the roughest terrain, the thickest vegetation, up the highest, most rugged slope. Jane tore her pants sliding down a bluff, that looked like pure suicide from the top, and not much better than that from the bottom, but she followed without complaining. It wasn't that she didn't think of plenty of complaints, but that she was too tired to voice them. The benefits of her short nap had long since been dissipated. Her legs ached, her back ached, her bruised arms were so painful she could barely move them, and her eyes felt as if they were burning out of their sockets. But she didn't ask him to stop. Even if the pace killed her, she wasn't going to slow him down any more than she already had, because she had no doubt that he could travel much faster without her. The easy movements of his long legs told her that his stamina was far greater than hers; he could probably walk all night long again without a noticeable slowing of his stride. She felt a quiet awe of that sort of strength and conditioning, something that had been completely outside her experience before she'd met him. He wasn't like other men; it was evident in his superb body, in the awesome competence with which he handled everything, in the piercing gold of his eyes.

As if alerted by her thoughts, he stopped and looked back at her, assessing her condition with that sharp gaze that missed nothing. "Can you make it for another mile or so?"

On her own, she couldn't have, but when she met his eyes she knew there was no way she'd admit to that. Her chin lifted, and she ignored the increasingly heavy ache in her legs as she said, "Yes."

A flicker of expression crossed his face so swiftly that she couldn't read it. "Let me have that pack," he growled, coming back to her and jerking the straps free of the buckles, then slipping the pack from her shoulders.

"I'm handling it okay," she protested fiercely, grabbing for the pack and wrapping both arms around it. "I haven't complained, have I?"

His level dark brows drawing together in a frown,

he forcefully removed the pack from her grasp. "Use your head," he snapped. "If you collapse from exhaustion, then I'll have to carry you, too."

The logic of that silenced her. Without another word he turned and started walking again. She was better able to keep up with him without the weight of the pack, but she felt frustrated with herself for not being in better shape, for being a burden to him. Jane had fought fiercely for her independence, knowing that her very life depended on it. She'd never been one to sit and wait for someone else to do things for her. She'd charged at life head-on, relishing the challenges that came her way because they reaffirmed her acute sense of the wonder of life. She'd shared the joys, but handled the problems on her own, and it unsettled her now to have to rely on someone else.

They came to another stream, no wider than the first one they had crossed, but deeper. It might rise to her knees in places. The water rushing over the rocks sounded cool, and she thought of how heavenly it would be to refresh her sweaty body in the stream. Looking longingly at it, she stumbled over a root and reached out to catch her balance. Her palm came down hard against a tree trunk, and something squished beneath her fingers.

"Oh, yuck!" she moaned, trying to wipe the dead insect off with a leaf.

Grant stopped. "What is it?"

"I smashed a bug with my hand." The leaf didn't clean too well; a smear still stained her hand, and she looked at Grant with disgust showing plainly on her face. "Is it all right if I wash my hand in the stream?"

He looked around, his amber eyes examining both sides of the stream. "Okay. Come over here."

"I can get down here," she said. The bank was only a few feet high, and the underbrush wasn't that thick. She carefully picked her way over the roots of an enormous tree, bracing her hand against its trunk to steady herself as she started to descend to the stream.

"Watch out!" Grant said sharply, and Jane froze in her tracks, turning her head to look askance at him.

Suddenly something incredibly heavy dropped onto her shoulders, something long and thick and alive, and she gave a stifled scream as it began to coil around her body. She was more startled than frightened, thinking a big vine had fallen; then she saw the movement of a large triangular head and she gave another gasping cry. "Grant! Grant, *help me!*"

Terror clutched at her throat, choking her, and she began to claw at the snake, trying to get it off. It was a calm monster, working its body around her, slowly tightening the lethal muscles that would crush her bones. It twined around her legs and she fell, rolling on the ground. Dimly she could hear Grant cursing, and she could hear her own cries of terror, but they sounded curiously distant. Everything was tumbling in a mad kaleidoscope of brown earth and green trees, of Grant's taut, furious face. He was shouting something at her, but she couldn't understand him; all she could do was struggle against the living bonds that coiled around her. She had one shoulder and arm free, but the boa was tightening itself around her rib cage, and the big head was coming toward her face, its mouth open. Jane screamed, trying to catch its head with her free hand, but the snake was crushing the breath out of her and the scream was almost soundless. A big hand, not hers, caught the snake's head, and she dimly saw a flash of silver.

The snake's coils loosened about her as it turned to meet this new prey, seeking to draw Grant into its deadly embrace, too. She saw the flash of silver again, and something wet splashed into her face. Vaguely she realized that it was his knife she'd seen. He was swearing viciously as he wrestled with the snake, mostly astride her as she writhed on the ground, struggling to free herself. "Damn it, hold still!" he roared. "You'll make me cut you!"

It was impossible to be still; she was wrapped in the snake, and it was writhing with her in its coils. She was too crazed by fear to realize that the snake was in its death throes, not even when she saw Grant throw something aside and begin forcibly removing the thick coils from around her body. It wasn't until she actually felt herself coming free of the constrictor's horrible grasp that she understood it was over, that Grant had killed the snake. She stopped fighting and lay limply on the ground. Her face was utterly white except for the few freckles across her nose and cheekbones; her eyes were fixed on Grant's face.

"It's over," he said roughly, running his hands over her arms and rib cage. "How do you feel? Anything broken?"

Jane couldn't say anything; her throat was frozen, her voice totally gone. All she could do was lie there and stare at him with the remnants of terror in her dark eyes. Her lips trembled like a child's, and there was something pleading in her gaze. He automatically started to gather her into his arms, the way one would a frightened child, but before he could do more than lift his hand, she dragged her gaze away from his with a visible effort. He could see what it cost her in willpower, but somehow she found the inner strength to still the trembling of her lips, and then her chin lifted in that characteristic gesture.

"I'm all right," she managed to say. Her voice was jerky, but she said the words, and in saying them, believed it. She slowly sat up and pushed her hair away from her face. "I feel a little bruised, but there's nothing bro—"

She stopped abruptly, staring at her bloody hand and arm. "I'm all bloody," she said in a bewildered tone, and her voice shook. She looked back at Grant, as if for confirmation. "I'm all bloody," she said again, extending her wildly trembling hand for him to see. "Grant, there's blood all over me!"

"It's the snake's blood," he said, thinking to reassure her, but she stared at him with uncontrolled revulsion.

"Oh, *God*!" she said in a thin, high voice, scrambling to her feet and staring down at herself. Her black blouse was wet and sticky, and big reddish splotches stained her khaki pants. Both her arms had blood smeared down them. Bile rose in her throat as she remembered the wetness that had splashed her face. She raised exploring fingers and found the horrible stickiness on her cheeks, as well as smeared in her hair.

She began to shake even harder, and tears dripped down her cheeks. "Get it off," she said, still in that high, wavering voice of utter hysteria. "I have to get it off. There's blood all over me, and it isn't mine. It's all over me; it's even in my hair... It's in my *hair*!" she sobbed, plunging for the stream.

Cursing, Grant grabbed for her, but in her mad urgency to wash the blood away she jerked free of him, stumbling over the body of the snake and crashing to the ground. Before she could scramble away again, Grant pounced on her, holding her in an almost painful grip while she fought and sobbed, pleading and swearing at him all at once.

"Jane, stop it!" he said sharply. "I'll get the blood off you. Just hold still and let me get our boots off, okay?"

He had to hold her still with one arm and pull her boots off with his free hand, but by the time he started to remove his own boots she was crying so hard that she lay limply on the ground. His face was grim as he looked at her. She'd stood up to so much without turning a hair that he hadn't expected her to fall apart like this. She'd been pulling herself together until she'd seen the blood on herself, and that had evidently been more than she could bear. He jerked his boots off, then turned to her and roughly undid her pants and pulled them off. Lifting her into his arms as easily as he would have lifted a child, he climbed down the bank and waded out into the stream, disregarding the fact that his own pants were being soaked.

When the water reached the middle of his calves, he stood her in the stream and bent to begin splashing water on her legs, rubbing the blood stains from her flesh. Next, cupping water in his palms, he washed her arms and hands clean, dripping the cooling water over her and soaking her blouse. All the while he tended to her, she stood docile, with silent tears still running down her face and making tracks in the blood smeared across her cheeks.

"Everything's all right, honey," he crooned soothingly to her, coaxing her to sit down in the stream so he could wash the blood from her hair. She let him splash water on her head and face, blinking her eyes to protect them from the stinging water, but otherwise keeping her gaze fixed on his hard, intent features. He took a handkerchief from his back pocket and wet it, then gently cleaned her face. She was calmer now, no longer crying in that silent, gut-wrenching way, and he helped her to her feet.

"There, you're all cleaned up," he started to say, then noticed the pink rivulets of water running down her legs. Her blouse was so bloody that he'd have to take it off to get her clean. Without hesitation, he began to unbutton it. "Let's get this off so we can wash it," he said, keeping his voice calm and soothing. She didn't even glance down as he unbuttoned her blouse and pulled it off her shoulders, then tossed it to the bank. She kept her eyes on his face, as if he were her lifeline to sanity and to look away meant a return to madness.

Grant looked down, and his mouth went dry as he stared at her naked breasts. He'd wondered how she looked and now he knew, and it was like being punched in the stomach. Her breasts were round and a little heavier than he'd expected, tipped by small brown nipples, and he wanted to bend down and put his mouth to them, taste them. She might as well have been naked; all she had on was a pair of gossamer panties that had turned transparent in the water. He could see the dark curls of hair beneath the wisp of fabric, and he felt his loins tighten and swell. She was beautifully made, long-legged and slim-hipped, with the sleek muscles of a dancer. Her shoulders were straight, her arms slim but strong, her breasts rich; he wanted to spread her

legs and take her right there, driving deeply into her
body until he went out of his mind with pleasure. He
couldn't remember ever wanting a woman so badly.
He'd wanted sex, but that had been simply a physical
pleasure, and any willing female body had been acceptable. Now he wanted Jane, the essence of her; it was her
legs he wanted wrapped around him, her breasts in his
hands, her mouth under his, her body sheathing him.

He jerked his gaze away from her, bending to dip the
handkerchief in the water again. That was even worse;
his eyes were level with the top of her thighs, and he
straightened abruptly. He washed her breasts with a
gentle touch, but every moment of it was torture to
him, feeling her silky flesh under his fingers, watching her nipples tighten into reddened little nubs as he
touched them.

"You're clean," he said hoarsely, tossing the handkerchief to the bank to join her blouse.

"Thank you," she whispered, then fresh tears glittered in her eyes, and with a little whimper she flung
herself against him. Her arms went around him and
clung to his back. She buried her face against his chest,
feeling reassured by the steady beat of his heart and the
warmth of his body. His very presence drove the fear
away; with him, she was safe. She wanted to rest in his
arms and forget everything.

His hands moved slowly over her bare back, his calloused palms stroking her skin as if he relished the texture of it. Her eyes slid shut, and she nestled closer to
him, inhaling the distinctly male scent of his strong
body. She felt oddly drunk, disoriented; she wanted to
cling to him as the only steady presence in the world.
Her body was awash in strange sensations, from the

rushing water swirling about her feet to the faint breeze that fanned her wet, naked skin, while he was so hard and warm. An unfamiliar heat swept along her flesh in the path of his hands as they moved from her back to her shoulders. Then one hand stroked up her throat to cup her jaw, his thumb under her chin and his fingers in her hair, and he turned her face up to him.

Taking his time about it, he bent and fitted his mouth to hers, slanting his head to make the contact deep and firm. His tongue moved leisurely into her mouth, touching hers and demanding a response, and Jane found herself helplessly giving him what he wanted. She'd never been kissed like that before, with such complete confidence and expertise, as if she were his for the taking, as if they had reverted to more primitive times when the dominant male had his pick of the women. Vaguely alarmed, she made a small effort to free herself from his grasp. He subdued her with gentle force and kissed her again, holding her head still for the pressure of his mouth. Once again Jane found herself opening her mouth for him, forgetting why she'd struggled to begin with. Since her divorce a lot of men had kissed her and tried to make her respond. They'd left her cold. Why should this rough...mercenary, or whatever he was, make shivers of pleasure chase over her body, when some of the most sophisticated men in the world had only bored her with their passion? His lips were warm and hard, the taste of his mouth heady, his tongue bold in its exploration, and his kisses caused an unfamiliar ache to tighten within her body.

A mindless little whimper of delight escaped her throat, the soft female sound making his arms tighten around her. Her hands slid up to his shoulders, then locked around his neck, hanging on to him for support. She couldn't get close enough to him, though he was crushing her against him. The buttons of his shirt dug into her bare breasts, but she wasn't aware of any pain. His mouth was wild, hungry with a basic need that had flared out of control, bruising her lips with the force of his kisses, and she didn't care. Instead she gloried in it, clinging to him. Her body was suddenly alive with sensations and needs that she didn't recognize, never having felt them before. Her skin actually ached for his touch, yet every stroke of his hard fingers made the ache intensify.

Boldly cupping her breast in his palm, he rubbed the rough pad of his thumb across her tightly puckered nipple, and Jane almost cried aloud at the surge of heat that washed through her. It had never been like this for her before; the urgency of the pure, brazen sensuality of her own body took her by surprise. She'd long ago decided that she simply wasn't a very physical person, then forgotten about it. Sex hadn't been something that interested her very much. The way Grant was making her feel completely shattered her concept of herself. She was a female animal in his arms, grinding against him, feeling and glorying in the swollen response of his body, and hurting with the emptiness deep inside her.

Time disappeared as they stood in the water, the late afternoon sun dappling them with the shifting patterns of light created by the sheltering trees. His hands freely roamed her body. She never even thought of resisting him. It was as if he had every right to her flesh, as if she were his to touch and taste. He bent her back over his arm, making her breasts jut enticingly, and his lips traveled hotly down her throat to the warm, quivering mounds. He took her nipple into his mouth and sucked strongly, and she surged against him like a wild creature, on fire and dying and wanting more.

His hand swept downward, his fingers curving between her legs to caress her through the silk of her panties. The boldness of his touch shocked her out of her sensual frenzy; automatically she stiffened in his grasp and brought her arms down from around his neck to wedge them between their bodies and push against him. A low, gutteral sound rattled in his throat, and for a brief, terrified moment she thought there wouldn't be any stopping him. Then, with a curse, he thrust her away from him.

Jane staggered a little, and his hand shot out to catch her, hauling her back to face him. "Damn you, is this how you get your kicks?" he asked, infuriated. "Do you like seeing how far you can push a man?"

Her chin came up, and she swallowed. "No, that's not it at all. I'm sorry. I know I shouldn't have thrown myself at you like that—"

"Damned right, you shouldn't," he interrupted savagely. He *looked* savage; his eyes were narrowed and bright with rage, his nostrils flared, and his mouth a thin, grim line. "Next time, you'd better make sure you want what you're asking for, because I'm damned sure going to give it to you. Is that clear?"

He turned and began wading to the bank, leaving her standing in the middle of the stream. Jane crossed her arms over her bare breasts, suddenly and acutely aware of her nakedness. She hadn't meant to tease him, but she'd been so frightened, and he'd been so strong and calm that it had seemed the most natural thing in the world to cling to him. Those frenzied kisses and caresses had taken her by surprise, shaken her off balance. Still, she wasn't about to have sex with a man she barely knew, especially when she didn't quite know if she liked what little she did know about him.

He reached the bank and turned to look at her. "Are you coming or not?" he snapped, so Jane waded toward him, still keeping her arms over her breasts.

"Don't bother," he advised in a curt voice. "I've already seen, and touched. Why pretend to be modest?" He gestured to her blouse lying on the ground. "You might want to wash the blood out of that, since you're so squeamish about it."

Jane looked at the blood-stained blouse, and she went a little pale again, but she was under control now. "Yes, I will," she said in a low voice. "Will you...will you get my pants and boots for me, please?"

He snorted, but climbed up the bank and tossed her pants and boots down to her. Keeping her back turned to him, Jane pulled on her pants, shuddering at the blood that stained them, too, but at least they weren't soaked the way her blouse was. Her panties were wet, but there wasn't anything she could do about that now, so she ignored the clammy discomfort. When she was partially clad again, she squatted on the gravel at the edge of the stream and began trying to wash her blouse. Red clouds drifted out of the fabric, staining the water before being swept downstream. She scrubbed and scrubbed before she was satisfied, then wrung out as much water as possible and shook the blouse. As she started to put the blouse on, he said irritably, "Here," and held his shirt in front of her. "Wear this until yours gets dry."

She wanted to refuse, but she knew false pride wouldn't gain her anything. She accepted the shirt silently and put it on. It was far too big, but it was dry and warm and not too dirty, and it smelled of sweat, and the musky odor of his skin. The scent was vaguely comforting. There were rust-colored stains on it, too, reminding her that he'd saved her life. She tied the tails in a knot at her waist and sat down on the gravel to put on her boots.

When she turned, she found him standing right behind her, his face still grim and angry. He helped her up the bank, then lifted their packs to his shoulders. "We're not going much farther. Follow me, and for God's sake don't touch anything that I don't touch, or step anywhere except in my footprints. If another boa wants you, I just may let him have you, so don't push your luck."

Jane pushed her wet hair behind her ears and followed obediently, walking where he walked. For a while, she stared nervously at every tree limb they passed under, then made herself stop thinking about the snake. It was over; there was no use dwelling on it.

Instead she stared at his broad back, wondering how her father had found a man like Grant Sullivan. They obviously lived in two different worlds, so how had they met?

Then something clicked in her mind, and a chill went down her spine. *Had* they met? She couldn't imagine her father knowing anyone like Sullivan. She also knew what her own position was. Everyone wanted to get their hands on her, and she had no way of knowing whose side Grant Sullivan was on. He'd called her Priscilla, which was her first name. If her father had sent him, wouldn't he have known that she was never called Priscilla, that she'd been called Jane from birth? *He hadn't known her name!*

Before he died, George had warned her not to trust anyone. She didn't want to think that she was alone in the middle of the jungle with a man who would casually cut her throat when he had no further use for her. Still, the fact remained that she had no proof that her father had sent him. He'd simply knocked her out, put her over his shoulder and hauled her off into the jungle.

Then she realized that she had to trust this man; she had no alternative. He was all she had. It was dangerous, trusting him, but not as dangerous as trying to make it out of the jungle on her own. He had shown flashes of kindness. She felt a funny constriction in her chest as she remembered the way he'd cared for her after he'd killed the snake. Not just cared for her, kissed her—she was still shaken by the way he'd kissed her. Mercenary or not, enemy or not, he made her want him. Her mind wasn't certain about him, but her body was.

She would have found it funny, if she hadn't been so frightened.

CHAPTER FIVE

THEY MOVED DIRECTLY away from the stream at a forty-five-degree angle, and it wasn't long before he stopped, looked around and unslung the packs from his shoulders. "We'll camp here."

Jane stood in silence, feeling awkward and useless, watching as he opened his pack and took out a small, rolled bundle. Under his skilled hands, the bundle was rapidly transformed into a small tent, complete with a polyethylene floor and a flap that could be zipped shut. When the tent was up he began stripping vines and limbs from the nearby trees to cover it, making it virtually invisible. He hadn't so much as glanced in her direction, but after a moment she moved to help him. He did look at her then, and allowed her to gather more limbs while he positioned them over the tent.

When the job was completed, he said, "We can't risk a fire, so we'll just eat and turn in. After today, I'm ready for some sleep."

Jane was, too, but she dreaded the thought of the night to come. The light was rapidly fading, and she knew that it would soon be completely dark. She remembered the total blackness of the night before and felt a cold finger of fear trace up her backbone. Well, there was nothing she could do about it; she'd have to tough it out.

She crouched beside her pack and dug out two more cans of orange juice, tossing one to him; he caught it deftly, and eyed her pack with growing irritation. "How many more cans of this do you have in that traveling supermarket?" he asked sarcastically.

"That's it. We'll have to drink water from now on. How about a granola bar?" She handed it to him, refusing to let herself respond to the irritation in his voice. She was tired, she ached, and she was faced with a long night in total darkness. Given that, his irritation didn't seem very important. He'd get over it.

She ate her own granola bar, but was still hungry, so she rummaged for something else to eat. "Want some cheese and crackers?" she offered, dragging the items out of the depths of the pack.

She looked up to find him watching her with an expression of raw disbelief on his face. He held out his hand, and she divided the cheese and crackers between them. He looked at her again, shook his head and silently ate his share.

Jane saved a little of her orange juice, and when she finished eating she took a small bottle from the pack. Opening it, she shook a pill into the palm of her hand, glanced at Grant, then shook out another one. "Here," she said.

He looked at it, but made no move to take it. "What the hell's that?"

"It's a yeast pill."

"Why should I want to take a yeast pill?"

"So the mosquitoes and things won't bite you."

"Sure they won't."

"They won't! Look at me. I don't have any insect bites, and it's because I take yeast pills. It does something to your skin chemistry. Come on, take it. It won't hurt you."

He took the pill from her hand and held it with a pained expression on his face while she took her own, washing it down with a sip of the orange juice she'd saved. She passed the can to him, and he muttered something obscene before he tossed the pill into his mouth and slugged down the rest of the juice.

"Okay, bedtime," he said, rising to his feet. He jerked his head toward a tree. "There's your bathroom, if you want to go before we turn in."

Jane stepped behind the tree. He was crude, he was rude, he was a little cruel—and he had saved her life. She didn't know what to expect from him. No matter how rough he was, he would eventually disarm her with an unexpected act of kindness. On the other hand, when things were going smoothly between them, he would say things that stung, as if deliberately trying to start a quarrel.

He was waiting for her by the opening of the tent. "I've already put the blanket down. Crawl in."

She knelt down and crawled into the small tent. He had spread the blanket over the floor, and she sat on it. He shoved their packs inside. "Put these out of the way," he instructed. "I'm going to take a quick look around."

She shoved the packs into the far corners of the tent, then lay down on her back and stared tensely at the thin walls. The light was almost gone; only a glimmer entered through the translucent fabric. It wasn't quite as dark outside yet, but the limbs he'd used as camouflage made it darker inside. The flap parted, and he crawled in, then zipped the opening shut.

"Take your boots off and put them in the corner next to your feet."

Sitting up, she did as he said, then lay down again. Her eyes strained open so widely that they burned. Her body stiff with dread, she listened to him stretch and yawn and make himself comfortable.

Moments later the silence became nearly as unbearable as the darkness. "A collapsible tent comes in handy, doesn't it?" she blurted nervously. "What is it made out of?"

"Nylon," he replied, yawning again. "It's nearly indestructible."

"How much does it weigh?"

"Three pounds and eight ounces."

"Is it waterproof?"

"Yes, it's waterproof."

"And bug proof?"

"Bug proof, too," he muttered.

"Do you think a jaguar could—"

"Look, it's jaguar proof, mildew proof, fireproof and snake proof. I personally guarantee you that it's proof against everything except elephants, and I don't think we're going to be stomped on by an elephant in Costa Rica! Is there any other damned thing you're worried about?" he exploded. "If not, why don't you be quiet and let me get some sleep?"

Jane lay tensely, and silence fell again. She clenched her fists in an effort to control her nervousness, listening to the growing cacophony of the jungle night. Monkeys howled and chattered; insects squeaked their calls; underbrush rustled. She was exhausted but she had no real hope of sleeping, at least not until dawn, and at dawn this devil beside her would want to start another day of marathon travel.

He was totally silent in that unnerving way of his. She couldn't even hear him breathe. The old fear began to rise in her chest, making her own breathing difficult. She might as well be alone, and that was the one thing she absolutely couldn't bear.

"Where are you from?"

He heaved a sigh. "Georgia."

That explained his drawl. She swallowed, trying to ease the constriction of her dry throat. If she could just keep him talking, then she wouldn't feel so alone. She'd know he was there.

"What part of Georgia?"

"South. Ever hear of the Okefenokee?"

"Yes. It's a swamp."

"I grew up in it. My folks own a farm just on the edge of it." It had been a normal boyhood, except for the skills he'd learned automatically in the swamp, those skills, which had eventually changed his life by shaping him into something not quite human. He willed the memories away, pulling a mental shade down over them, isolating himself. There was no use in thinking about what had been.

"Are you an only child?"

"Why all the questions?" he snapped, edgy at revealing any information about himself.

"I'm just interested, that's all."

He paused, suddenly alert. There was something in her voice, a tone that he couldn't quite place. It was dark, so he couldn't see her face; he had to go entirely by what his ears told him. If he kept her talking, he might be able to figure it out.

"I've got a sister," he finally said reluctantly.

"I'll bet she's younger. You're so bossy, you must be an older brother."

He let the dig pass and said only, "She's four years younger."

"I'm an only child," she volunteered.

"I know."

She searched frantically for something else to say, but the darkness was making her panic. She felt herself move to grab for him, then remembered what he'd said about startling him, and about not making offers she didn't mean. She ground her teeth together and stilled her reaching hands, the effort so intense that tears actually welled in her eyes. She blinked them away. "Grant," she said in a shaking voice.

"What?" he growled.

"I don't want you to think I'm throwing myself at you again because I'm really not, but would you mind very much if I…just held your hand?" she whispered. "I'm sorry, but I'm afraid of the dark, and it helps if I know I'm not alone."

He was still for a moment; then she heard his clothing rustle as he rolled onto his side. "You're really that afraid of the dark?"

Jane tried for a laugh, but the sound was so shaky that it was close to a sob. "The word *terrified* only begins to describe how afraid I am. I can't sleep in the dark. All the time I was at that wretched plantation I was awake all night long, never sleeping until dawn. But at least I could use that time to watch the guards and figure out their routine. Besides, it wasn't as totally dark there as it is here."

"If you're so all-fired scared of the dark, why were you getting ready to hit the jungle on your own?"

A dark, handsome, incredibly cruel face swam before her mind's eye. "Because even dying in the jungle would be better than Turego," she said quietly.

Grant grunted. He could understand that choice, but the fact that she had so correctly summed up the situation illustrated once again that she was more than what she seemed. Then again, perhaps she already had reason to know just how vile Turego could be. Had Turego raped her, or would it have been rape? With this woman, who knew? "Did you have sex with him?"

The blunt question made her shudder. "No. I'd been holding him off, but when he left yesterday…it was just yesterday, wasn't it? It seems like a year ago. Anyway, I knew that, when he came back, I wouldn't be able to stop him any longer. My time had run out."

"What makes you so certain of that?"

Jane paused, wondering just how much to tell him, wondering how much he already knew. If he was involved, he would be familiar with Luis's name; if he wasn't, the name would mean nothing to him. She wanted to tell him; she didn't want to be alone in this nightmare any longer. But she remembered George telling her once that secrecy was synonymous with security, and she quelled the need to turn into Grant's arms and tell him how afraid and alone she had been. If he wasn't involved already, he was safer not knowing anything about it. On the other hand, if he was involved, she might be safer if he didn't realize how deeply she was a part of things. Finally, to answer his question, she said, "I wasn't certain. I was just afraid to stay, afraid of Turego."

He grunted, and that seemed to be the end of the conversation. Jane clenched her jaw against the sudden chattering of her teeth. It was hot and steamy inside the dark tent, but chills were running up and down her body. Why didn't he say something else, anything, rather than lying there so quietly? She might as well have been alone. It was unnatural for anyone to be that soundless, that utterly controlled.

"How was Dad?"

"Why?"

"I just wondered." Was he being deliberately evasive? Why didn't he want to talk about her father? Perhaps he hadn't been hired by her father at all and didn't want to be drawn into a conversation about someone he was supposed to have met, but hadn't.

After a measured silence, as if he had carefully considered his answer, he said, "He was worried sick about you. Surprised?"

"No, of course not," she said, startled. "I'd be surprised if he weren't."

"It doesn't surprise you that he'd pay a small fortune to get you out of Turego's hands, even though you don't get along with him?"

He was confusing her; she felt left out of the conversation, as if he were talking about someone else entirely. "What are you talking about? We get along perfectly, always have."

She couldn't see him, couldn't hear him, but suddenly there was something different about him, as if the very air had become electrically charged. A powerful sense of danger made the fine hairs on her body stand up. The danger was coming from him. Without knowing why, she shrank back from him as far as she could in the confines of the small tent, but there was no escape. With the suddenness of a snake striking, he rolled and pinned her down, forcing her hands over her head and holding them shackled there in a grip that hurt her wrists. "All right, Jane, or Priscilla, or whoever you are, we're going to talk. I'm going to ask the questions and you're going to answer them, and you'd better have the right answers or you're in trouble, sugar. Who are you?"

Had he gone mad? Jane struggled briefly against the grip on her wrists, but there was no breaking it. His weight bore down heavily on her, controlling her completely. His muscled legs clasped hers, preventing her from even kicking. "Wh-what…?" she stammered. "Grant, you're hurting me!"

"Answer me, damn you! Who are you?"

"Jane Greer!" Desperately, she tried to put some humor in her voice, but it wasn't a very successful effort.

"I don't like being lied to, sugar." His voice was velvety soft, and the sound of it chilled her to her marrow. Not even Turego had affected her like this; Turego was a dangerous, vicious man, but the man who held her now was the most lethal person she'd ever seen. He didn't have to reach for a weapon to kill her; he could kill her with his bare hands. She was totally helpless against him.

"I'm not lying!" she protested desperately. "I'm Priscilla Jane Hamilton Greer."

"If you were, you'd know that James Hamilton cut you out of his will several years ago. So you get along with him just perfectly, do you?"

"Yes, I do!" She strained against him, and he deliberately let her feel more of his weight, making it difficult for her to breathe. "He did it to protect me!"

For a long, silent moment in which she could hear the roaring of her blood in her ears, she waited for his reaction. His silence scraped along her nerves. Why didn't he say something? His warm breath was on her cheek, telling her how close he was to her, but she couldn't see him at all in that suffocating darkness. "That's a good one," he finally responded, and she flinched at the icy sarcasm of his tone. "Too bad I don't buy it. Try again."

"I'm telling you the truth! He did it to make me a less attractive kidnap target. It was my idea, damn it!"

"Sure it was," he crooned, and that low, silky sound made her shudder convulsively. "Come on, you can do better than that."

Jane closed her eyes, searching desperately for some way of convincing him of her identity. None came to mind, and she had no identification with her. Turego had taken her passport, so she didn't have even that. "Well, what about you?" she blurted in sudden fury. She'd taken a lot from him, endured without complaining, and now he'd frightened her half out of her mind. She'd had her back to the wall before, and had learned to strike back. "Who are you? How do I know that Dad hired you? If he did why didn't you know that no one ever calls me Priscilla? You were sloppy with your homework!"

"In case you haven't noticed, honey, I'm the one on top. You answer my questions."

"I did, and you didn't believe me," she snapped. "Sorry, but I don't have my American Express card with me. For God's sake, do I look like a terrorist? You nearly broke my arm; then you knocked me out. You've bounced me on the ground like a rubber ball, and you've got the utter gall to act like I'm dangerous? My goodness, you'd better search me, too, so you'll be able to sleep tonight. Who knows? I might have a bazooka strapped to my leg, since I'm such a dangerous character!" Her voice had risen furiously, and he cut her off by resting all his weight on her rib cage. When she gasped, he eased up again.

"No, you're unarmed. I've already had your clothes off, remember?" Even in the darkness, Jane blushed at the memory, thinking of the way he'd kissed her and touched her, and how his hands on her body had made her feel. He moved slowly against her, stopping her breath this time with the suggestive intimacy of his movements. His warm breath stirred her hair as he dipped his head closer to her. "But I wouldn't want to disappoint a lady. If you want to be searched, I'll oblige you. I wouldn't mind giving you a body search."

Fuming, Jane tried again to free her hands, but finally fell back in disgust at the futile action. Raw frustration finally cleared her mind, giving her an idea, and she said harshly, "Did you go in the house when Dad hired you?"

He was still, and she sensed his sudden increase of interest. "Yes."

"Did you go in the study?"

"Yes."

"Then a hotshot like you would have noticed the portrait over the mantle. You're trained to notice things, aren't you? The portrait is of my grandmother, Dad's mother. She was painted sitting down, with a single rose on her lap. Now, you tell me what color her gown was," she challenged.

"Black," he said slowly. "And the rose was blood-red."

Thick silence fell between them; then he released her hands and eased his weight from her. "All right," he said finally. "I'll give you the benefit of the doubt—"

"Well, gee, thanks!" Huffily she rubbed her wrists, trying to keep her anger alive in the face of the enormous relief that filled her. Evidently her father had hired him, for otherwise how could he have seen the portrait in the study? She wanted to remain mad at him, but she knew she would forgive him because it was still dark. In spite of everything she was terribly glad he was there. Besides, she told herself cautiously, it was definitely better to stay on this man's good side.

"Don't thank me," he said tiredly. "Just be quiet and go to sleep."

Sleep! If only she could! Consciously, she knew she wasn't alone, but her subconscious mind required additional affirmation from her senses. She needed to see him, hear him, or touch him. Seeing him was out of the question; she doubted he'd leave a flashlight burning all night, even assuming he had one. Nor would he stay awake all night talking to her. Perhaps, if she just barely touched him, he'd think it was an accident and not make a big deal out of it. Stealthily she moved her right hand until the backs of her fingers just barely brushed his hairy forearm—and immediately her wrist was seized in that bruising grip again.

"Ouch!" she yelped, and his fingers loosened.

"Okay, what is it this time?" His tone showed plainly that he was at the end of his patience.

"I just wanted to touch you," Jane admitted, too tired

now to care what he thought, "so I'll know I'm not alone."

He grunted. "All right. It looks like that's the only way I'm going to get any sleep." He moved his hand, sliding his rough palm against hers, and twined their fingers together. "Now will you go to sleep?"

"Yes," she whispered. "Thank you."

She lay there, enormously and inexplicably comforted by the touch of that hard hand, so warm and strong. Her eyes slowly closed, and she gradually relaxed. The night terrors didn't come. He kept them firmly at bay with the strong, steady clasp of his hand around hers. Everything was going to be all right. Another wave of exhaustion swept over her, and she was asleep with the suddenness of a light turning off.

GRANT WOKE BEFORE DAWN, his senses instantly alert. He knew where he was, and he knew what time it was; his uncanny sixth sense could pinpoint the time within a few minutes. The normal night sounds of the jungle told him that they were safe, that there was no other human nearby. He knew immediately the identity of the other person in the tent with him. He knew that he couldn't move, and he even knew why: Jane was asleep on top of him.

He really didn't mind being used as a bed. She was soft and warm, and there was a female smell to her that made his nostrils flare in appreciation. The softness of her breasts against him felt good. That special, unmistakable softness never left a man's mind, hovering forever in his memory once he'd felt the fullness of a woman against him. It had been a long time since he'd slept with a woman, and he'd forgotten how good it could feel. He'd had sex—finding an available woman was no problem—but those encounters had been casual, just for the sake of the physical act. Once it was finished, he hadn't been inclined to linger. This past year, especially, he'd been disinclined to tolerate anyone else's presence. He'd spent a lot of time alone, like an injured animal licking its wounds; his mind and his soul had been filled with death. He'd spent so much time in the shadows that he didn't know if he'd ever find the sunlight again, but he'd been trying. The sweet, hot Tennessee sun had healed his body, but there was still an icy darkness in his mind.

Given that, given his acute awareness of his surroundings, even in sleep, how had Jane gotten on top of him without waking him? This was the second time she'd gotten close to him without disturbing him, and he didn't like it. A year ago, she couldn't have twitched without alerting him.

She moved then, sighing a little in her sleep. One of her arms was around his neck, her face pressed into his chest, her warm breath stirring the curls of hair in the low neckline of his undershirt. She lay on him as bonelessly as a cat, her soft body conforming to the hard contours of his. Her legs were tangled with his, her hair draped across his bare shoulder and arm. His body hardened despite his almost savage irritation with himself, and slowly his arms came up to hold her, his hands sliding over her supple back. He could have her if he wanted her. The highly specialized training he'd received had taught him how to deal excruciating pain to another human being, but a side benefit to that knowledge was that he also knew how to give pleasure. He knew all the tender, sensitive places of her body, knew how to excite nerves that she probably didn't even know she had. Beyond that, he knew how to control his own responses, how to prolong a sensual encounter until his partner had been completely satisfied.

The sure knowledge that he could have her ate at him, filling his mind with images and sensations. Within ten minutes he could have her begging him for it, and he'd be inside her, clasped by those long, sleek, dancer's legs. The only thing that stopped him was the almost childlike trust with which she slept curled on top of him. She slept as if she felt utterly safe, as if he could protect her from anything. Trust. His life had been short on trust for so many years that it startled him to find someone who could trust so easily and completely. He was uncomfortable with it, but at the same time it felt good, almost as good as her body in his arms. So he lay there staring into the darkness, holding her as she slept, the bitter blackness of his thoughts contrasting with the warm, elusive sweetness of two bodies pressed together in quiet rest.

When the first faint light began to filter through the trees, he shifted his hand to her shoulder and shook her lightly. "Jane, wake up."

She muttered something unintelligible and burrowed against him, hiding her face against his neck. He shifted gently to his side, easing her onto the blanket. Her arms still hung around his neck, and she tightened her grip as if afraid of falling. "Wait! Don't go," she said urgently, and the sound of her own voice woke her. She opened her eyes, blinking owlishly at him. "Oh. Is it morning?"

"Yes, it's morning. Do you think you could let me up?"

Confused, she stared at him, then seemed to realize

that she was still clinging around his neck. She dropped
her arms as if scalded, and though the light was too dim
for him to be certain, he thought that her cheeks darkened with a blush. "I'm sorry," she apologized.

He was free, yet oddly reluctant to leave the small
enclosure of the tent. His left arm was still under her
neck, pillowing her head. The need to touch her was
overwhelming, guiding his hand under the fabric of
her shirt, which was actually his. He flattened his hand
against her bare stomach. His fingers and palm luxuriated in the warm silkiness of her skin, tantalized by the
knowledge that even richer tactile pleasures waited both
above and below where his hand now rested.

Jane felt her breathing hasten in rhythm, and her
heartbeat lurched from the slow, even tempo of sleep to
an almost frantic pace. "Grant?" she asked hesitantly.
His hand simply rested on her stomach, but she could
feel her breasts tightening in anticipation, her nipples
puckering. A restless ache stirred to life inside her. It
was the same empty need that she'd felt when she'd
stood almost naked in his arms, in the middle of the
stream, and let him touch her with a raw sensuality that
she'd never before experienced. She was a little afraid
of that need, and a little afraid of the man who created
it with his touch, who leaned over her so intently.

Her only sexual experience had been with her husband. The lack of success in that area of their marriage
had severely limited what she knew, leaving her almost
completely unawakened, even disinterested. Chris had
given her no useful standard, for there was no comparison at all between her ex-husband—a kind, cheerful man, slender and only a few inches taller than she
was—and this big, rough, muscular warrior. Chris was

totally civilized; Grant wasn't civilized at all. If he took her, would he control his fearsome strength, or would he dominate her completely? Perhaps that was what frightened her most of all, because the greatest struggle of her life had been for independence: for freedom from fear, and from the overprotectiveness of her parents. She'd fought so hard and so long for control of her life that it was scary now to realize that she was totally at Grant's mercy. None of the training she'd had in self-defense was of any use against him; she had no defense at all. All she could do was trust him.

"Don't be afraid," he said evenly. "I'm not a rapist."

"I know." A killer, perhaps, but not a rapist. "I trust you," she whispered, and laid her hand against his stubbled jaw.

He gave a small, cynical laugh. "Don't trust me too much, honey. I want you pretty badly, and waking up with you in my arms is straining my good intentions to the limit." But he turned his head and pressed a quick kiss into the tender palm of the hand that caressed his cheek. "Come on, let's get moving. I feel like a sitting duck in this tent, now that it's daylight."

He heaved himself into a sitting position and reached for his boots, tugging them on and lacing them up with quick, expert movements. Jane was slower to sit up, her entire body protesting. She yawned and shoved her tangled hair back from her face, then put on her own boots. Grant had already left the tent by the time she finished, and she crawled after him. Once on her feet, she stretched her aching muscles, then touched her toes several times to limber up. While she was doing that, Grant swiftly dismantled the tent. He accomplished that in so short a time that she could only blink at him in amazement. In only a moment the tent was once more folded into an impossibly small bundle and stored in his backpack, with the thin blanket rolled up beside it.

"Any more goodies in that bottomless pack of yours?" he asked. "If not, we eat field rations."

"That yucky stuff you have?"

"That's right."

"Well, let's see. I know I don't have any more orange juice...." She opened the pack and peered into it, then thrust her hand into its depths. "Ah! Two more granola bars. Do you mind if I have the one with coconut? I'm not that crazy about raisins."

"Sure," he agreed lazily. "After all, they're yours."

She gave him an irritated glance. "They're ours. Wait—here's a can of..." She pulled the can out and read the label, then grinned triumphantly. "Smoked salmon! And some crackers. Please take a seat, sir, and we'll have breakfast."

He obediently sat, then took his knife from his belt and reached for the can of salmon. Jane drew it back, her brows lifted haughtily. "I'll have you know that this is a high class eating establishment. We do not open our cans with knives!"

"We don't? What do we use, our teeth?"

She lifted her chin at him and searched in the backpack again, finally extracting a can opener. "Listen," she said, giving the opener to him, "when I escape, I do it in style."

Taking the opener, he began to open the can of salmon. "So I see. How did you manage to get all of this stuff? I can just see you putting in an order with Turego, collecting what you wanted for an escape."

Jane chuckled, a rich, husky sound that made him

lift his dark gold head from his task. Those piercing yellow eyes lit on her face, watching her as if examining a treasure. She was busy fishing crackers out of the backpack, so she missed the fleeting expression. "It was almost like that. I kept getting these 'cravings,' though I seldom mentioned them to Turego. I'd just have a word with the cook, and he generally came up with what I wanted. I raided the kitchen or the soldiers' quarters for a little something almost every night."

"Like that pack?" he queried, eyeing the object in question.

She patted it fondly. "Nice one, isn't it?"

He didn't reply, but there was a faint crinkling at the corners of his eyes, as if he were thinking of smiling. They ate the salmon and crackers in companionable silence, with the food washed down by water from Grant's canteen. He ate his granola bar, but Jane decided to save hers for later.

Squatting beside the pack, she took her brush and restored order to her tangled mane of hair, then cleaned her face and hands with a premoistened towelette. "Would you like one?" she asked Grant politely, offering him one of the small packets.

He had been watching her with a stunned sort of amazement, but he took the packet from her hand and tore it open. The small, wet paper had a crisp smell to it, and he felt fresher, cooler, after cleaning his face with it. To his surprise, some of the face black he'd put on before going in after Jane had remained on his skin; he'd probably looked like a devil out of hell, with those streaks on his face.

A familiar sound caught his attention and he turned to look at Jane. A tube of toothpaste lay on the ground beside her, and she was industriously brushing her teeth. As he watched, she spat out the toothpaste, then took a small bottle and tilted it to her mouth, swishing the liquid around, then spitting it out, too. His stunned gaze identified the bottle. For five whole seconds he could only gape at her; then he sat back and began to laugh helplessly. Jane was rinsing her mouth with Perrier water.

CHAPTER SIX

JANE POUTED FOR a moment, but it was so good to hear him laugh that after a few seconds she sat back on her heels and simply watched him, smiling a little herself. When he laughed that harsh, scarred face became younger, even beautiful, as the shadows left his eyes. Something caught in her chest, something that hurt and made a curious melting feeling. She wanted to go over and hold him, to make sure that the shadows never touched him again. She scoffed at herself for her absurd sense of protectiveness. If anyone could take care of himself, it was Grant Sullivan. Nor would he welcome any gesture of caring; he'd probably take it as a sexual invitation.

To hide the way she felt, she put her things back into her pack, then turned to eye him questioningly. "Unless you want to use the toothpaste?" she offered.

He was still chuckling. "Thanks, honey, but I have tooth powder and I'll use the water in the canteen. God! Perrier water!"

"Well, I had to have water, but I wasn't able to snitch a canteen," she explained reasonably. "Believe me, I'd much rather have had a canteen. I had to wrap all the bottles in cloth so they wouldn't clink against each other or break."

It seemed completely logical to her, but it set him off

again. He sat with his shoulders hunched and shaking, holding his head between his hands and laughing until tears streamed down his face. After he had stopped, he brushed his own teeth, but he kept making little choking noises that told Jane he was still finding the situation extremely funny. She was lighthearted, happy that she had made him laugh.

She felt her blouse and found it stiff, but dry. "You can have your shirt back," she told him, turning her back to take it off. "Thanks for the loan."

"Is yours dry?"

"Completely." She pulled his shirt off and dropped it on her backpack, and hurriedly began to put her blouse on. She had one arm in a sleeve when he swore violently. She jumped, startled, and looked over her shoulder at him.

His face was grim as he strode rapidly over to her. His expression had been bright with laughter only a moment before, but now he looked like a thundercloud. "What happened to your arm?" he snapped, catching her elbow and holding her bruised arm out for his inspection. "Why didn't you tell me you'd hurt yourself?"

Jane tried to grab the blouse and hold it over her bare breasts with her free arm, feeling horribly vulnerable and exposed. She had been trying for a nonchalant manner while changing, but her fragile poise was shattered by his closeness and his utter disregard for her modesty. Her cheeks reddened, and in self-defense she looked down at her badly bruised arm.

"Stop being so modest," he growled irritably when she fumbled with the blouse. "I told you, I've already seen you without any clothes." That was embarrassingly true, but it didn't help. She stood very still, her face burning, while he gently examined her arm.

"That's a hell of a bruise, honey. How does your arm feel?"

"It hurts, but I can use it," she said stiffly.

"How did it happen?"

"In a variety of ways," she said, trying to hide her embarrassment behind a bright manner. "This bruise right here is where you hit me on the arm after sneaking into my bedroom and scaring me half to death. The big, multi-colored one is from falling down that bluff yesterday morning. This little interesting welt is where a limb swung back and caught me—"

"Okay, I get the idea." He thrust his fingers through his hair. "I'm sorry I bruised you, but I didn't know who you were. I'd say we were more than even on that score, anyway, after that kick you gave me."

Jane's dark chocolate eyes widened with remorse. "I didn't mean to, not really. It was just a reflex. I'd done it before I thought. Are you okay? I mean, I didn't do any permanent damage, did I?"

A small, unwilling grin tugged at his lips as he remembered the torment of arousal he'd been enduring on her account. "No, everything's in working order," he assured her. His gaze dropped to where she clutched her blouse to her chest, and his clear amber eyes darkened to a color like melted gold. "Couldn't you tell that when we were standing in the stream kissing?"

Jane looked down automatically, then jerked her gaze back up in consternation when she realized where she was looking. "Oh," she said blankly.

Grant slowly shook his head, staring at her. She was a constant paradox, an unpredictable blend of innocence and contrariness, of surprising prudery and amazing boldness. In no way was she what he'd expected. He was beginning to enjoy every moment he spent with her, but acknowledging that made him wary. It was his responsibility to get her out of Costa Rica, but he would compromise his own effectiveness if he allowed himself to become involved with her. Worrying over her could cloud his judgment. But, damn, how much could a man stand? He wanted her, and the wanting increased with every moment. In some curious way he felt lighter, happier. She certainly kept him on his toes! He was either laughing at her or contemplating beating her, but he was never bored or impatient in her company. Funny, but he couldn't remember ever laughing with a woman before. Laughter, especially during the past few years, had been in short supply in his life.

A chattering monkey caught his attention, and he looked up. The spots of sunlight darting through the shifting layers of trees reminded him that they were losing traveling time. "Get your blouse on," he said tersely, swinging away from her to sling his backpack on. He buckled it into place, then swung her pack onto his right shoulder. The rifle was slung over his left shoulder. By that time, Jane had jerked her blouse on and buttoned it up. Rather than stuffing it in her pants, she tied the tails in a knot at her waist as she had with Grant's shirt. He was already starting off through the jungle.

"Grant! Wait!" she called to his back, hurrying after him.

"You'll have to stay with me," he said unfeelingly, not slackening his pace.

Well, did he think she couldn't? Jane fumed, panting along in his path. She'd show him! And he could darn well act macho and carry both packs if he wanted; she wasn't going to offer to help! But he wasn't acting macho, she realized, and that deflated some of her indignation. He actually was that strong and indefatigable.

Compared to the harrowing day before, the hours passed quietly, without sight of another human being. She followed right on his heels, never complaining about the punishing pace he set, though the heat and humidity were even worse than the day before, if that were possible. There wasn't any hint of a breeze under the thick, smothering canopy. The air was still and heavy, steamy with an almost palpable thickness. She perspired freely, soaking her clothes and making her long for a real bath. That dousing in the stream the day before had felt refreshing, but didn't really qualify as bathing. Her nose wrinkled. She probably smelled like a goat.

Well, so what, she told herself. If she did, then so did he. In the jungle it was probably required to sweat.

They stopped about midmorning for a break, and Jane tiredly accepted the canteen from him. "Do you have any salt tablets?" she asked. "I think I need one."

"You don't need salt, honey, you need water. Drink up."

She drank, then passed the canteen back to him. "It's nearly empty. Let's pour the Perrier into it and chuck the empty bottles."

He nodded, and they were able to discard three bottles. As he got ready to start out again, Jane asked, "Why are you in such a hurry? Do you think we're being followed?"

"Not followed," he said tersely. "But they're looking for us, and the slower we move, the better chance they have of finding us."

"In this?" Jane joked, waving her hand to indicate the enclosing forest. It was difficult to see ten feet in any direction.

"We can't stay in here forever. Don't underrate Turego; he can mobilize a small army to search for us. The minute we show our faces, he'll know it."

"Something should be done about him," Jane said strongly. "Surely he's not operating with the sanction of the government?"

"No. Extortion and terrorism are his own little side-lines. We've known about him, of course, and occasionally fed him what we wanted him to know."

"We?" Jane asked casually.

His face was immediately shuttered, as cold and blank as a wall. "A figure of speech." Mentally, he swore at himself for being so careless. She was too sharp to miss anything. Before she could ask any more questions, he began walking again. He didn't want to talk about his past, about what he had been. He wanted to forget it all, even in his dreams.

ABOUT NOON THEY stopped to eat, and this time they had to resort to the field rations. After a quick glance at what she was eating, Jane didn't look at it at all, just put it in her mouth and swallowed without allowing herself to taste it too much. It wasn't really that bad; it was just so awfully bland. They each drank a bottle of Perrier, and Jane insisted that they take another yeast pill. A roll of thunder announced the daily downpour, so Grant quickly found them shelter under a rocky out-cropping. The opening was partially blocked by bushes, making it a snug little haven.

They sat watching the deluge for a few minutes; then

Grant stretched out his long legs, leaning back to prop himself on his elbow. "Explain this business of how your father disinherited you as a form of protection."

Jane watched a small brown spider pick its way across the ground. "It's very simple," she said absently. "I wouldn't live with around-the-clock protection the way he wanted, so the next best thing was to remove the incentive for any kidnappers."

"That sounds a little paranoid, seeing kidnappers behind every tree."

"Yes," she agreed, still watching the spider. It finally minced into a crevice in the rock, out of sight, and she sighed. "He is paranoid about it, because he's afraid that next time he wouldn't get me back alive again."

"Again?" Grant asked sharply, seizing on the implication of her words. "You've been kidnapped before?"

She nodded. "When I was nine years old."

She made no other comment and he sensed that she wasn't going to elaborate, if given a choice. He wasn't going to allow her that choice. He wanted to know more about her, learn what went on in that unconventional brain. It was new to him, this overwhelming curiosity about a woman; it was almost a compulsion. Despite his relaxed position, tension had tightened his muscles. She was being very matter-of-fact about it, but instinct told him that the kidnapping had played a large part in the formation of the woman she was now. He was on the verge of discovering the hidden layers of her psyche.

"What happened?" he probed, keeping his voice casual.

"Two men kidnapped me after school, took me to an abandoned house and locked me in a closet until Dad paid the ransom."

The explanation was so brief as to be ridiculous; how could something as traumatic as a kidnapping be condensed into one sentence? She was staring at the rain now, her expression pensive and withdrawn.

Grant knew too much about the tactics of kidnappers, the means they used to force anxious relatives into paying the required ransom. Looking at her delicate profile, with the lush provocativeness of her mouth, he felt something savage well up in him at the thought that she might have been abused.

"Did they rape you?" He was no longer concerned about maintaining a casual pose. The harshness of his tone made her glance at him, vague surprise in her exotically slanted eyes.

"No, they didn't do anything like that," she assured him. "They just left me in that closet…alone. It was dark."

And to this day she was afraid of the dark, of being alone in it. So that was the basis for her fear. "Tell me about it," he urged softly.

She shrugged. "There isn't a lot more to tell. I don't know how long I was in the closet. There were no other houses close by, so no one heard me scream. The two men just left me there and went to some other location to negotiate with my parents. After a while I became convinced that they were never coming back, that I was going to die there in that dark closet, and that no one would ever know what had happened to me."

"Your father paid the ransom?"

"Yes. Dad's not stupid, though. He knew that he wasn't likely to get me back alive if he just trusted the kidnappers, so he brought the police in on it. It's lucky he did. When the kidnappers came back for me, I overheard them making their plans. They were just going to kill me and dump my body somewhere, because I'd seen them and could identify them." She bent her head, studying the ground with great concentration, as if to somehow divorce herself from what she was telling him. "But there were police sharpshooters surrounding the house. When the two men realized that they were trapped, they decided to use me as a hostage. One of them grabbed my arm and held his pistol to my head, forcing me to walk in front of them when they left the house. They were going to take me with them, until it was safe to kill me."

Jane shrugged, then took a deep breath. "I didn't plan it, I swear. I don't remember if I tripped, or just fainted for a second. Anyway, I fell, and the guy had to let go of me or be jerked off balance. For a second the pistol wasn't pointed at me, and the policemen fired. They killed both men. The...the man who had held me was shot in the chest and the head, and he fell over on me. His blood splattered all over me, on my face, my hair...." Her voice trailed away.

For a moment there was something naked in her face, the stark terror and revulsion she'd felt as a child; then, as he had seen her do when he'd rescued her from the snake, she gathered herself together. He watched as she defeated the fear, pushed the shadows away. She smoothed her expression and even managed a glint of humor in her eyes as she turned to look at him. "Okay, it's your turn. Tell me something that happened to you."

Once he'd felt nothing much at all; he'd accepted the chilled, shadowed brutality of his life without thought. He still didn't flinch from the memories. They were part of him, as ingrained in his flesh and blood, in his very being, as the color of his eyes and the shape of his body. But when he looked into the uncommon innocence of Jane's eyes, he knew that he couldn't brutalize her mind with even the mildest tale of the life he'd known. Somehow she had kept a part of herself as pure and crystalline as a mountain stream, a part of childhood forever unsullied. Nothing that had happened to her had touched the inner woman, except to increase the courage and gallantry that he'd seen twice now in her determined efforts to pull herself together and face forward again.

"I don't have anything to tell," he said mildly.

"Oh, sure!" she hooted, shifting herself on the ground until she was sitting facing him, her legs folded in a boneless sort of knot that made him blink. She rested her chin in her palm and surveyed him, so big and controlled and capable. If this man had led a normal life, she'd eat her boots, she told herself, then quickly glanced down at the boots in question. Right now they had something green and squishy on them. Yuck. They'd have to be cleaned before even a goat would eat them. She returned her dark gaze to Grant and studied him with the seriousness of a scientist bent over a microscope. His scarred face was hard, a study of planes and angles, of bronzed skin pulled tautly over the fierce sculpture of his bones. His eyes were those of an eagle, or a lion; she couldn't quite decide which. The clear amber color was brighter, paler, than topaz, almost like a yellow diamond, and like an eagle's, the eyes saw everything. They were guarded, expressionless; they hid an almost unbearable burden of experience and weary cynicism.

"Are you an agent?" she asked, probing curiously.

Somehow, in those few moments, she had discarded the idea that he was a mercenary. Same field she thought, but a different division.

His mouth quirked. "No."

"Okay, let's try it from another angle. Were you an agent?"

"What sort of agent?"

"Stop evading my questions! The cloak-and-dagger sort of agent. You know, the men in overcoats who have forty sets of identification."

"No. Your imagination is running wild. I'm too easily identifiable to be any good undercover."

That was true. He stood out like a warrior at a tea party. Something went quiet within her, and she knew. "Are you retired?"

He was quiet for so long that she thought he wasn't going to answer her. He seemed to be thinking of something else entirely. Then he said flatly, "Yeah, I'm retired. For a year now."

His set, blank face hurt her, on the inside. "You were a...weapon, weren't you?"

There was a terrible clarity in his eyes as he slowly shifted his gaze to her. "Yes," he said harshly. "I was a weapon."

They had aimed him, fired him, and watched him destroy. He would be matchless, she realized. Before she'd even known him, when she'd seen him gliding into her darkened bedroom like a shadow, she'd realized how lethal he could be. And there was something else, something she could see now. He had retired himself, turned his back and walked away from that grim, shadowed life. Certainly his superiors wouldn't have wanted to lose his talents.

She reached out and placed her hand on his, her fingers slim and soft, curling around the awesome strength of his. Her hand was much smaller made with a delicacy that he could crush with a careless movement of his fingers, but implicit in her touch was the trust that he wouldn't turn that strength against her. A deep breath swelled the muscled planes of his chest. He wanted to take her right then, in the dirt. He wanted to stretch her out and pull her clothes off, bury himself in her. He wanted more of her touch, all of her touch, inside and out. But the need for her satiny female flesh was a compulsion that he couldn't satisfy with a quick possession, and there wasn't time for more. The rain was slowing and would stop entirely at any moment. There was a vague feeling marching up and down his spine that told him they couldn't afford to linger any longer.

But it was time she knew. He removed his hand from hers, lifting it to cup her chin. His thumb rubbed lightly over her lips. "Soon," he said, his voice guttural with need, "you're going to lie down for me. Before I take you back to your daddy, I'm going to have you, and the way I feel now, I figure it's going to take a long time before I'm finished with you."

Jane sat frozen, her eyes those of a startled woodland animal. She couldn't even protest, because the harsh desire in his voice flooded her mind and her skin with memories. The day before, standing in the stream, he'd kissed her and touched her with such raw sexuality that, for the first time in her life, she'd felt the coiling, writhing tension of desire in herself. For the first time she'd wanted a man, and she'd been shocked by the unfamiliarity of her own body. Now he was doing it to her again, but this time he was using words. He'd stated his intentions bluntly, and images began forming in her mind of the two of them lying twined together, of his naked, magnificent body surging against her.

He watched the shifting expressions that flitted across her face. She looked surprised, even a little shocked, but she wasn't angry. He'd have understood anger, or even amusement; that blank astonishment puzzled him. It was as if no man had ever told her that he wanted her. Well, she'd get used to the idea.

The rain had stopped, and he picked up the packs and the rifle, settling them on his shoulders. Jane followed him without a word when he stepped out from beneath the rocky outcropping into the already increasing heat. Steam rose in wavering clouds from the forest floor, immediately wrapping them in a stifling, humid blanket.

She was silent for the rest of the afternoon, lost in her thoughts. He stopped at a stream, much smaller than the one they'd seen the day before, and glanced at her. "Care for a bath? You can't soak, but you can splash."

Her eyes lit up, and for the first time that afternoon a smile danced on her full lips. He didn't need an answer to know how she felt about the idea. Grinning, he searched out a small bar of soap from his pack and held it out to her. "I'll keep watch, then you can do the same for me. I'll be up there."

Jane looked up the steep bank that he'd indicated. That was the best vantage point around; he'd have a clear view of the stream and the surrounding area. She started to ask if he was going to watch her, too, but bit back the question. As he'd already pointed out, it was too late for modesty. Besides, she felt infinitely safer knowing that he'd be close by.

He went up the bank as sure-footedly as a cat, and

Jane turned to face the stream. It was only about seven feet wide, and wasn't much more than ankle-deep. Still, it looked like heaven. She hunted her lone change of underwear out of her pack, then sat down to pull off her boots. Glancing nervously over her shoulder to where Grant sat, she saw that he was in profile to her, but she knew that he would keep her in his peripheral vision. She resolutely undid her pants and stepped out of them. Nothing was going to keep her from having her bath… except maybe another snake, or a jaguar, she amended.

Naked, she gingerly picked her way over the stony bottom to a large flat rock and sat down in the few inches of water. It was deliciously cool, having run down from a higher altitude, but even tepid water would have felt good on her overheated skin. She splashed it on her face and head until her hair was soaked. Gradually she felt the sweaty stickiness leave her hair, until the strands were once more silky beneath her fingers. Then she took the small bar of soap out from under her leg, where she'd put it for safekeeping, and rubbed it over her body. The small luxury made her feel like a new woman, and a sense of peace crept into her. It was only a simple pleasure, to bathe in a clear, cool stream, but added to it was her sense of nakedness, of being totally without restrictions. She knew that he was there, knew that he was watching her, and felt her breasts grow tight.

What would it be like if he came down from that bank and splashed into the water with her? If he took the blanket from his pack and laid her down on it? She closed her eyes, shivering in reaction, thinking of his hard body pressing down on her, thrusting into her. It had been so many years, and the few experiences she'd had with Chris hadn't taught her that she could be a creature of wanting, but with Grant she wasn't the same woman.

Her heart beat heavily in her breast as she rinsed herself by cupping water in her palms and pouring it over her. Standing up, she twisted the water out of her hair, then waded out. She was trembling as she pulled on her clean underwear, then dressed distastefully in her stained pants and shirt. "I'm finished," she called, lacing up her boots.

He appeared soundlessly beside her. "Sit in the same place where I sat," he instructed, placing the rifle in her hands. "Do you know how to use this?"

The weapon was heavy, but her slim hands looked capable as she handled it. "Yes. I'm a fairly good shot." A wry smile curved her lips. "With paper targets and clay pigeons, anyway."

"That's good enough." He began unbuttoning his shirt, and she stood there in a daze, her eyes on his hands. He paused. "Are you going to guard me from down here?"

She blushed. "No. Sorry." Quickly she turned and scrambled up the bank, then took a seat in the exact spot where he'd sat. She could see both banks, but at the same time there was a fair amount of cover that she could use if the need arose. He'd probably picked this out as the best vantage point without even thinking about it, just automatically sifting through the choices and arriving at the correct one. He might be retired, but his training was ingrained.

A movement, a flash of bronze, detected out of the corner of her eye, told her that he was wading into the stream. She shifted her gaze a fraction so she wouldn't be able to see him at all, but just the knowledge that he was as naked as she had been kept her heart pounding erratically. She swallowed, then licked her lips, forcing herself to concentrate on the surrounding jungle, but the compulsion to look at him continued.

She heard splashing and pictured him standing there like a savage, bare and completely at home.

She closed her eyes, but the image remained before her. Slowly, totally unable to control herself, she opened her eyes and turned her head to look at him. It was only a small movement, a fraction of an inch, until she was able to see him, but that wasn't enough. Stolen glances weren't enough. She wanted to study every inch of him, drink in the sight of his powerful body. Shifting around, she looked fully at him, and froze. He was beautiful, so beautiful that she forgot to breathe. Without being handsome, he had the raw power and grace of a predator, all the terrible beauty of a hunter. He was bronzed all over, his tan a deep, even brown. Unlike her, he didn't keep his back turned in case she looked; he had a complete disregard for modesty. He was taking a bath; she could look or not look, as she wished.

His skin was sleek and shiny with water, and the droplets caught in the hair on his chest glittered like captured diamonds. His body hair was dark, despite the sun-streaked blondness of his head. It shadowed his chest, ran in a thin line down his flat, muscled stomach, and bloomed again at the juncture of his legs. His legs were as solid as tree trunks, long and roped with muscle; every movement he made set off ripples beneath his skin. It was like watching a painting by one of the old masters come to life.

He soaped himself all over, then squatted in the water to rinse in the same manner she had, cupping his palms to scoop up the water. When he was rinsed clean, he stood and looked up at her, probably to check on her, and met her gaze head-on. Jane couldn't look away, couldn't pretend that she hadn't been staring at him with an almost painful appreciation. He stood very still in the stream, watching her as she watched him, letting her take in every detail of his body. Under her searching gaze, his body began to stir, harden, growing to full, heavy arousal.

"Jane," he said softly, but still she heard him. She was so attuned to him, so painfully sensitive to every move and sound he made, that she would have heard him if he'd whispered. "Do you want to come down here?"

Yes. Oh, God, yes, more than she'd ever wanted anything. But she was still a little afraid of her own feelings, so she held back. This was a part of herself that she didn't know, wasn't certain she could control.

"I can't," she replied, just as softly. "Not yet."

"Then turn around, honey, while you still have a choice."

She quivered, almost unable to make the required movement, but at last her muscles responded and she turned away from him, listening as he waded out of the water. In less than a minute he appeared noiselessly at her side and took the rifle from her hands. He had both packs with him. Typically, he made no further comment on what had just happened. "We'll get away from the water and set up camp. It'll be night pretty soon."

Night. Long hours in the dark tent, lying next to him. Jane followed him, and when he stopped she helped him do the work they had done the night before, setting up the tent and hiding it. She didn't protest at the cold field rations, but ate without really tasting anything. Soon she was crawling into the tent and taking off her boots, waiting for him to join her.

When he did, they lay quietly side by side, watching as the remaining light dimmed, then abruptly vanished.

Tension hummed through her, making her muscles tight. The darkness pressed in on her, an unseen monster that sucked her breath away. No list of compulsive questions leaped to her lips tonight; she felt oddly timid, and it had been years since she'd allowed herself to be timid about anything. She no longer knew herself.

"Are you afraid of me?" he asked, his voice gentle.

Just the sound of his voice enabled her to relax a little. "No," she whispered.

"Then come here and let me keep the dark away from you."

She felt his hand on her arm, urging her closer, then she was enfolded in arms so strong that nothing could ever make her afraid while they held her. He cradled her against his side, tucking her head into the hollow of his shoulder. With a touch so light that it could have been the brush of a butterfly's wings, he kissed the top of her head. "Good night, honey," he whispered.

"Good night," she said in return.

Long after he was asleep, Jane lay in his arms with her eyes open, though she could see nothing. Her heart was pounding in her chest with a slow, heavy rhythm, and her insides felt jittery. It wasn't fear that kept her awake, but a churning emotion that shifted everything inside her. She knew exactly what was wrong with her. For the first time in too many years, everything was right with her.

She'd learned to live her life with a shortage of trust. No matter that she'd learned to enjoy herself and her freedom; there had always been that residual caution that kept her from letting a man get too close. Until now she'd never been strongly enough attracted to a man for the attraction to conquer the caution.... Until now. Until Grant. And now the attraction had become something much stronger. The truth stunned her, yet she had to accept it: she loved him. She hadn't expected it, though for two days she had felt it tugging at her. He was harsh and controlled, bad-tempered, and his sense of humor was severely underdeveloped, but he had gently washed the snake's blood from her, held her hand during the night, and had gone out of his way to make their trek easier for her. He wanted her, but he hadn't taken her because she wasn't ready. She was afraid of the dark, so he held her in his arms. Loving him was at once the easiest and most difficult thing she'd ever done.

CHAPTER SEVEN

ONCE AGAIN HE awoke to find her cuddled on top of him, but this time it didn't bother him that he had slept peacefully through the night. Sliding his hands up her back, he accepted that his normally keen instincts weren't alarmed by her because there was absolutely no danger in her except perhaps the danger of her driving him crazy. She managed to do that with every little sway of her behind. Reveling in the touch of her all along his body, he moved his hands down, feeling her slenderness, the small ribs, the delicate spine, the enticing little hollow at the small of her back, then the full, soft mounds of her buttocks. He cupped his palms over them, kneading her with his fingers. She muttered and shifted against him, brushing at a lock of hair that had fallen into her face. Her eyelashes fluttered, then closed completely once more.

He smiled, enjoying the way she woke up. She did it by slow degrees, moaning and grousing while still more asleep than awake, frowning and pouting, and moving against him as if trying to sink herself deeper into him so she wouldn't have to wake up at all. Then her eyes opened, and she blinked several times, and as quickly as that the pout faded from her lips and she gave him a slow smile that would have melted stone.

"Good morning," she said, and yawned. She stretched,

then abruptly froze in place. Her head came up, and she stared at him in stupefaction. "I'm on top of you," she said blankly.

"Again," he confirmed.

"Again?"

"You slept on top of me the night before last, too. Evidently my holding you while you sleep isn't enough; you think you have to hold me down."

She slithered off him, sitting up in the tent and straightening her twisted, wrinkled clothing. Color burned in her face. "I'm sorry. I know it can't have been very comfortable for you."

"Don't apologize. I've enjoyed it," he drawled. "If you really want to make it up to me, though, we'll reverse positions tonight."

Her breath caught and she stared at him in the dim light, her eyes soft and melting. Yes. Everything in her agreed. She wanted to belong to him; she wanted to know everything about his body and let him know everything about hers. She wanted to tell him, but she didn't know how to put it into words. A crooked smile crossed his face; then he sat up and reached for his boots, thrusting his feet into them and lacing them up. Evidently he took her silence for a refusal, because he dropped the subject and began the task of breaking camp.

"We have enough food for one more meal," he said as they finished eating. "Then I'll have to start hunting."

She didn't like that idea. Hunting meant that he'd leave her alone for long stretches of time. "I don't mind a vegetarian diet," she said hopefully.

"Maybe it won't come to that. We've been gradually working our way out of the mountains, and unless

I miss my guess we're close to the edge of the forest. We'll probably see fields and roads today. But we're going to avoid people until I'm certain it's safe, okay?"

She nodded in agreement.

Just as he'd predicted, at midmorning they came abruptly to the end of the jungle. They stood high on a steep cliff, and stretched out below them was a valley with cultivated fields, a small network of roads, and a cozy village situated at the southern end. Jane blinked at the suddenly brilliant sunlight. It was like stepping out of one century into another. The valley looked neat and prosperous, reminding her that Costa Rica was the most highly developed country in Central America, despite the thick tangle of virgin rain forest at her back.

"Oh," she breathed. "Wouldn't it be nice to sleep in a bed again?"

He grunted an absent reply, his narrowed eyes sweeping the valley for any sign of abnormal activity. Jane stood beside him, waiting for him to make his decision.

It was made for them. Abruptly he grabbed her arm and jerked her back into the sheltering foliage, dragging her to the ground behind a huge bush just as a helicopter suddenly roared over their heads. It was flying close to the ground, following the tree line; she had only a glimpse of it before it was gone, hidden by the trees. It was a gunship, and had camouflage paint.

"Did you see any markings?" she asked sharply, her nails digging into his skin.

"No. There weren't any." He rubbed his stubbled jaw. "There's no way of telling who it belonged to, but we can't take any chances. Now we know that we can't just walk across the valley. We'll work our way down, and try to find more cover."

If anything, the terrain was even more difficult now. They were at the edge of a volcanic mountain range, and the land had been carved with a violent hand. It seemed to be either straight up, or straight down. Their pace was agonizingly slow as they worked their way down rocky bluffs and up steep gorges. When they stopped to eat, they had covered less than one-fourth the length of the valley, and Jane's legs ached as they hadn't since the wild run through the jungle the first day.

Right on schedule, just as they finished eating, they heard the boom of thunder. Grant looked around for shelter, considering every outcropping of rock. Then he pointed. "I think that's a cave up there. If it is we'll be in high cotton."

"What?" Jane asked, frowning.

"Sitting pretty," he explained. "Luxurious accommodations, in comparison to what we've had."

"Unless it's already occupied."

"That's why you're going to wait down here while I check it out." He moved up the fern covered wall of the gorge, using bushes and vines and any other toehold he could find. The gorge itself was narrow and steep, enclosing them on all four sides. Its shape gave a curious clarity to the calls of the innumerable birds that flitted among the trees like living Christmas decorations, all decked out in their iridescent plumage. Directly overhead was a streak of sky, but it consisted of rolling black clouds instead of the clear blue that she'd seen only moments before.

Grant reached the cave, then immediately turned and waved to her. "Come on up; it's clear! Can you make it?"

"Have I failed yet?" she quipped, starting the climb, but she'd had to force the humor. The desolation had been growing in her since they'd seen the valley. Knowing that they were so close to civilization made her realize that their time together was limited. While they had been in the forest, the only two people locked in a more primitive time, she'd had no sense of time running out. Now she couldn't ignore the fact that soon, in a few days or less, their time together would end. She felt as if she'd already wasted so much time, as if the golden sand had been trickling through her fingers and she'd only just realized what she held. She felt panic-stricken at the thought of discovering love only to lose it, because there wasn't enough time to let it grow.

He reached his hand down and caught hers, effortlessly lifting her the last few feet. "Make yourself comfortable; we could be here awhile. This looks like the granddaddy of all storms."

Jane surveyed their shelter. It wasn't really a cave; it was little more than an indentation in the face of the rock, about eight feet deep. It had a steeply slanting ceiling that soared to ten or eleven feet at the opening of the cave, but was only about five feet high at the back. The floor was rocky, and one big rock, as large as a love seat and shaped like a peanut, lay close to the mouth of the cave. But it was dry, and because of its shallowness it wasn't dark, so Jane wasn't inclined to find fault with it.

Given Grant's eerie sense of timing, she wasn't surprised to hear the first enormous raindrops begin filtering through the trees just as he spread out the tarp at the back of the cave. He placed it behind the big rock, using its bulk to shelter them. She sat down on the tarp and drew her legs up, wrapping her arms around them and resting her chin on her knees, listening to the sound of the rain as it increased in volume.

Soon it was a din and the solid sheets of water that obscured their vision heightened the impression that they were under a waterfall. She could hear the crack of lightning, feel the earth beneath her shake from the enormous claps of thunder. It was dark now, as the rain blotted out what light came through the thick canopy. She could barely see Grant, who was standing just inside the mouth of the cave with his shoulder propped against the wall, occasionally puffing on a cigarette.

Chills raced over her body as the rain cooled the air. Hugging her legs even tighter for warmth, Jane stared through the dimness at the broad, powerful shoulders outlined against the gray curtain of rain. He wasn't an easy man to get to know. His personality was as shadowy as the jungle, yet just the sight of that muscular back made her feel safe and protected. She knew that he stood between her and any danger. He had already risked his life for her on more than one occasion, and was as matter-of-fact about it as if being shot at were an everyday occurrence. Perhaps it was for him, but Jane didn't take it so lightly.

He finished his cigarette and fieldstripped it. Jane doubted that anyone would track them here through the rain, but it was second nature to him to be cautious. He went back to his calm perusal of the storm, standing guard while she rested.

Something shifted inside her and coiled painfully in her chest. He was so alone. He was a hard, lonely man, but everything about him drew her like a magnet, pulling at her heart and body.

Her eyes clouded as she watched him. When this

was over he'd walk away from her as if these days in the jungle had never existed. This was all routine for him. What she could have of him, all that she could ever have of him, was the present, too few days before this was over. And that just wasn't enough.

She was cold now, chilled to her bones. The unceasing, impenetrable curtain of rain carried a damp coldness with it, and her own spirits chilled her from the inside. Instinctively, like a sinuous cat seeking heat, she uncoiled from the tarp and went up to him, gravitating to his certain warmth and comfort. Silently she slid her arms around his taut waist and pressed her face into the marvelous heat of his chest. Glancing down at her, he lifted an eyebrow in mild inquiry. "I'm cold," she muttered, leaning her head on him and staring pensively at the rain.

He looped his arm around her shoulder, holding her closer to him and sharing his warmth with her. A shiver ran over her; he rubbed his free hand up her bare arm, feeling the coolness of her skin. Of its own accord his hand continued upward, stroking her satiny jaw, smoothing the dark tangle of hair away from her face. She was in a melancholy mood, this funny little cat, staring at the rain as if it would never stop, her eyes shadowed and that full, passionate mouth sad.

Cupping her chin in his hand, he tilted her face up so he could study her quiet expression. A small smile curved the corners of his hard mouth. "What's wrong, honey? Rain making you feel blue?" Before she could answer, he bent his head and kissed her, using his own cure.

Jane's hands went to his shoulders, clinging to him for support. His mouth was hard and demanding and oh so sweet. The taste of him, the feel of him, was just what she wanted. Her teeth parted, allowing the slow probing of his tongue. Deep inside her, fire began to curl, and she curled too, twining against him in an unconscious movement that he read immediately.

Lifting his mouth from hers just a little, he muttered, "Honey, this feels like an offer to me."

Her dark eyes were a little dazed as she looked up at him. "I think it is," she whispered.

He dropped his arms to her waist and wrapped them around her, lifting her off her feet, bringing her level with him. She wound her arms around his neck and kissed him fervently, lost in the taste and feel of his mouth, not even aware he'd moved until he set her down to stand on the tarp. The dimness at the back of the cave hid any expression that was in his eyes, but she could feel his intent amber gaze on her as he began calmly unbuttoning her shirt. Jane's mouth went dry, but her own shaking fingers moved to his chest and began opening his shirt in turn.

When both garments were hanging open, he shrugged out of his and tossed it on the tarp, never taking his eyes from her. Tugging his undershirt free of his pants, he caught the bottom of it and peeled it off over his head. He tossed it aside, too, completely baring his broad, hairy chest. As it had the day before, the sight of his half-naked body mesmerized her. Her chest hurt; breathing was incredibly difficult. Then his hard, hot fingers were inside her shirt, on her breasts, molding them to fit his palms. The contrast of his heated hands on her cool skin made her gasp in shocked pleasure. Closing her eyes, she leaned into his hands, rubbing her nipples against his calloused palms. His chest lifted on a deep, shuddering breath.

She could feel the sexual tension emanating from him in waves. Like no other man she'd known, he made her acutely aware of his sexuality, and equally aware of her own body and its uses. Between her legs, an empty throb began to torment her, and she instinctively pressed her thighs together in an effort to ease the ache.

As slight as it was, he felt her movement. One of his hands left her breast and drifted downward, over her stomach and hips to her tightly clenched thighs. "That won't help," he murmured. "You'll have to open your legs, not close them." His fingers rubbed insistently at her and pleasure exploded along her nerves. A low moan escaped from her lips; then she swayed toward him. She felt her legs parting, allowing him access to her tender body. He explored her through her pants, creating such shock waves of physical pleasure that her knees finally buckled and she fell against him, her bare breasts flattening against the raspy, hair-covered expanse of his chest.

Quickly he set her down on the tarp and knelt over her, unzipping her pants and pulling them down her legs, his hands rough and urgent. He had to pause to remove her boots, but in only moments she was naked except for the shirt that still hung around her shoulders. The damp air made her shiver, and she reached for him. "I'm cold," she complained softly. "Get me warm."

She offered herself to him so openly and honestly that he wanted to thrust into her immediately, but he also wanted more. He'd had her nearly naked in his arms before. In the stream, that wisp of wet silk had offered no protection, but he hadn't had the time to explore her as he'd wanted. Her body was still a mystery to him; he wanted to touch every inch of her, taste her and enjoy the varying textures of her skin.

Jane's eyes were wide and shadowed as he knelt over her, holding himself away from her outstretched arms. "Not just yet, honey," he said in a low, gravelly voice. "Let me look at you first." Gently he caught her wrists and pressed them down to the tarp above her head, making her round, pretty breasts arch as if they begged for his mouth. Anchoring her wrists with one hand, he slid his free hand to those tempting, gently quivering mounds.

A small, gasping sound escaped from Jane's throat. Why was he holding her hands like that? It made her feel incredibly helpless and exposed, spread out for his delectation, yet she also felt unutterably safe. She could sense him savoring her with his eyes, watching intently as her nipples puckered in response to the rasp of his fingertips. He was so close to her that she could feel the heat of his body, smell the hot, musky maleness of his skin. She arched, trying to turn her body into that warmth and scent, but he forced her flat again.

Then his mouth was on her, sliding up the slope of her breast and closing hotly on her nipple. He sucked strongly at her, making waves of burning pleasure sweep from her breast to her loins. Jane whimpered, then bit her lip to hold back the sound. She hadn't known, had never realized, what a man's mouth on her breasts could do to her. She was on fire, her skin burning with an acute sensitivity that was both ecstatic and unbearable. She squirmed, clenching her legs together, trying to control the ache that threatened to master her.

His mouth went to her other breast, the rasp of his

tongue on her nipple intensifying an already unbearable sensation. He swept his hand down to her thighs, his touch demanding that she open herself to him. Her muscles slowly relaxed for him, and he spread her legs gently. His fingers combed through the dark curls that had so enticed him before, making her body jerk in anticipation; then he covered her with his palm and thoroughly explored the soft, vulnerable flesh between her legs. Beneath his touch, Jane began to tremble wildly. "Grant," she moaned, her voice a shaking, helpless plea.

"Easy," he soothed, blowing his warm breath across her flesh. He wanted her so badly that he felt he would explode, but at the same time he couldn't get enough of touching her, of watching her arch higher and higher as he aroused her. He was drunk on her flesh, and still trying to satiate himself. He took her nipple in his mouth and began sucking again, wringing another cry from her.

Between her legs a finger suddenly penetrated, searching out the depths of her readiness, and shock waves battered her body. Something went wild inside her, and she could no longer hold her body still. It writhed and bucked against his hand, and his mouth was turning her breasts into pure flame. Then his thumb brushed insistently over her straining, aching flesh, and she exploded in his arms, blind with the colossal upheaval of her senses, crying out unconsciously. Nothing had ever prepared her for this, for the total, mindshattering pleasure of her own body.

When it was over, she lay sprawled limply on the tarp. He undid his pants and shoved them off, his eyes glittering and wild. Jane's eyes slowly opened and she stared up at him dazedly. Grasping her legs, he lifted them high and spread them; then he braced himself over her and slowly sank his flesh into hers.

Jane's hands clenched on the tarp, and she bit her lips to keep from crying out as her body was inexorably stretched and filled. He paused, his big body shuddering, allowing her the time to accept him. Then suddenly it was she who couldn't bear any distance at all between them, and she surged upward, taking all of him, reaching up her arms to pull him close.

She never noticed the tears that ran in silvered streaks down her temples, but Grant gently wiped them away with his rough thumbs. Supporting his weight on his arms, sliding his entire body over her in a subtle caress, he began moving with slow, measured strokes. He was so close to the edge that he could feel the feathery sensation along his spine, but he wanted to make it last. He wanted to entice her again to that satisfying explosion, watch her go crazy in his arms.

"Are you all right?" he asked in a raw, husky tone, catching another tear with his tongue as it left the corner of her eye. If he were hurting her, he wouldn't prolong the loving, though he felt it would tear him apart to stop.

"Yes, I'm fine," she breathed, stroking her hands up the moving, surging muscles of his back. Fine... What a word for the wild magnificence of belonging to him. She'd never dreamed it could feel like this. It was as if she'd found a half of herself that she hadn't even known was missing. She'd never dreamed that she could feel like this. Her fingers clutched mindlessly at his back as his long, slow movements began to heat her body.

He felt her response and fiercely buried his mouth against the sensitive little hollow between her throat and collarbone, biting her just enough to let her feel

his teeth, then licking where he'd bitten. She whimpered, that soft, uncontrollable little sound that drove
him crazy, and he lost control. He began driving into her
with increasing power, pulling her legs higher around
him so he could have more of her, all of her, deeper and
harder, hearing her little cries and going still crazier.
There was no longer any sense of time, or of danger,
only the feel of the woman beneath him and around
him. While he was in her arms he could no longer feel
the dark, icy edges of the shadows in his mind and soul.

IN THE AFTERMATH, like that after a storm of unbeliev-
able violence, they lay in exhausted silence, each reluctant to speak for fear it would shatter the fragile
peace. His massive shoulders crushed her, making it
difficult for her to breathe, but she would gladly have
spent the rest of her life lying there. Her fingers slowly
stroked the sweat-darkened gold of his hair, threading
through the heavy, live silk. Their bodies were reluctant to leave each other, too. He hadn't withdrawn from
her; instead, after easing his weight down onto her, he'd
nestled closer and now seemed to be lightly dozing.

Perhaps it had happened too quickly between them,
but she couldn't regret it. She was fiercely happy that
she'd given herself to him. She'd never been in love before, never wanted to explore the physical mysteries of
a man and a woman. She'd even convinced herself that
she just wasn't a physical person, and had decided to
enjoy her solitary life. Now her entire concept of herself had been changed, and it was as if she'd discovered
a treasure within herself. After the kidnapping she had
withdrawn from people, except for the trusted precious
few who she had loved before: her parents, Chris, a cou-

ple of other friends. And even though she had married Chris, she had remained essentially alone, emotionally withdrawn. Perhaps that was why their marriage had failed, because she hadn't been willing to let him come close enough to be a real husband. Oh, they had been physically intimate, but she had been unresponsive, and eventually he had stopped bothering her. That was exactly what it had been for her: a bother. Chris had deserved better. He was her best friend, but only a friend, not a lover. He was much better off with the warm, responsive, adoring woman he'd married after their divorce.

She was too honest with herself to even pretend that any blame for their failed marriage belonged to Chris. It had been entirely her fault, and she knew it. She'd thought it was a lack in herself. Now she realized that she did have the warm, passionate instincts of a woman in love—because she was in love for the first time. She hadn't been able to respond to Chris, simply because she hadn't loved him as a woman should love the man she marries.

She was twenty-nine. She wasn't going to pretend to a shyness she didn't feel for the sake of appearance. She loved the man who lay in her arms, and she was going to enjoy to the fullest whatever time she had with him. She hoped to have a lifetime; but if fate weren't that kind, she would not let timidity cheat her out of one minute of the time they did have. Her life had been almost snuffed out twenty years ago, before it had really begun. She knew that life and time were too precious to waste.

Perhaps it didn't mean to Grant what it did to her, to be able to hold and love like this. She knew intuitively that his life had been much harder than hers, that he'd seen things that had changed him, that had stolen the laughter from his eyes. His experiences had hardened him, had left him extraordinarily cautious. But even if he were only taking the shallowest form of comfort from her, that of sexual release, she loved him enough to give him whatever he needed from her, without question. Jane loved as she did everything else, completely and courageously.

He stirred, lifting his weight onto his forearms and staring down at her. His golden eyes were shadowed, but there was something in them that made her heart beat faster, for he was looking at her the way a man looks at the woman who belongs to him. "I've got to be too heavy for you."

"Yes, but I don't care." Jane tightened her arms about his neck and tried to pull him back down, but his strength was so much greater than hers that she couldn't budge him.

He gave her a swift, hard kiss. "It's stopped raining. We have to go."

"Why can't we stay the night here? Aren't we safe?"

He didn't answer, just gently disengaged their bodies and sat up, reaching for his clothes, and that was answer enough. She sighed, but sat up to reach for her own clothes. The sigh became a wince as she became aware of the various aches she'd acquired by making love on the ground.

She could have sworn that he wasn't looking at her, but his awareness of his surroundings was awesome. His head jerked around, and a slight frown pulled his dark brows together. "Did I hurt you?" he asked abruptly.

"No, I'm all right." He didn't look convinced by her

reassurance. When they descended the steep slope to the floor of the gorge, he kept himself positioned directly in front of her. He carried her down the last twenty feet, hoisting her over his shoulder despite her startled, then indignant, protests.

It was a waste of time for her to protest, though; he simply ignored her. When he put her down silently and started walking, she had no choice but to follow.

Twice that afternoon they heard a helicopter, and both times he pulled her into the thickest cover, waiting until the sound had completely faded away before emerging. The grim line of his mouth told her that he didn't consider it just a coincidence. They were being hunted, and only the dense cover of the forest kept them from being caught. Jane's nerves twisted at the thought of leaving that cover; she wasn't afraid for just herself now, but for Grant, too. He put himself in jeopardy just by being with her. Turego wanted her alive, but Grant was of no use to him at all.

If it came to a choice between Grant's life and giving Turego what he wanted, Jane knew that she would give in. She'd have to take her chances with Turego, though it would be impossible now to catch him off guard the way she had the first time. He knew now that she wasn't a rich man's flirtatious, charming plaything. She'd made a fool of him, and he wouldn't forget.

Grant stepped over a large fallen tree and turned back to catch her around the waist and lift her over it with that effortless strength of his. Pausing, he pushed her tangled hair back from her face, his touch surprisingly gentle. She knew how lethal those hands could be. "You're too quiet," he muttered. "It makes me think you're up to something, and that makes me nervous."

"I was just thinking," she defended herself.

"That's what I was afraid of."

"If Turego catches us…"

"He won't," Grant said flatly. Staring down at her, he saw more now than just an appealing, sloe-eyed woman. He knew her now, knew her courage and strength, her secret fears and her sunny nature. He also knew her temper, which could flare or fade in an instant. Sabin's advice had been to kill her quickly rather than let Turego get his hands on her; Grant had seen enough death to accept that as a realistic option at the time. But that was before he had known her, tasted her and felt the silky texture of her skin, watched her go wild beneath him. Things had changed now. He had changed—in ways that he neither welcomed nor trusted, but had to acknowledge. Jane had become important to him. He couldn't allow that, but for the time being he had to accept it. Until she was safe, she could be his, but no longer. There wasn't any room in his life for permanency, for roots, because he still wasn't certain that he'd ever live in the sunshine again. Like Sabin, he'd been in the shadows too long. There were still dark spots on his soul that were revealed in the lack of emotion in his eyes. There was still the terrible, calm acceptance of things that were too terrible to be accepted.

If things had gone as originally planned, they would have gotten on that helicopter and she would be safely home by now. He would never have really known her; he would have delivered her to her father and walked away. But instead, they had been forced to spend days with only each other for company. They had slept side by side, eaten together, shared moments of danger and of humor. Perhaps the laughter was the more intimate, to him; he'd known danger many times with many people, but humor was rare in his life. She had made him laugh, and in doing so had captured a part of him.

Damn her for being the woman she was, for being lively and good-natured and desirable, when he'd expected a spoiled, sulky bitch. Damn her for making men want her, for making him want her. For the first time in his life he felt a savage jealousy swelling in his heart. He knew that he would have to leave her, but until then he wanted her to be his and only his. Remembering the feel of her body under his, he knew that he would have to have her again. His golden eyes narrowed at the feeling of intense possessiveness that gripped him. An expression of controlled violence crossed his face, an expression that the people who knew him had learned to avoid provoking. Grant Sullivan was dangerous enough in the normal way of things; angered, he was deadly. She was his now, and her life was being threatened. He'd lost too much already; his youth, his laughter, his trust in others, even part of his own humanity. He couldn't afford to lose anything else. He was a desperate man trying to recapture his soul. He needed to find again even a small part of the boy from Georgia who had walked barefoot in the warm dirt of plowed fields, who had learned survival in the mysterious depths of the great swamp. What Vietnam had begun, the years of working in intelligence and operations had almost completed, coming close to destroying him as a man.

Jane and her screwball brand of gallantry were the source of the only warmth he'd felt in years.

He reached out and caught her by the nape of her neck, his strong fingers halting her. Surprised, she turned an inquiring glance at him, and the small smile that had begun forming on her lips faded at the fierce expression he couldn't hide.

"Grant? Is something wrong?"

Without thinking, he used the grip he had on her neck to pull her to him, and kissed her full lips, still faintly swollen from the lovemaking they'd shared in the cave. He took his time about it, kissing her with slow, deep movements of his tongue. With a small sound of pleasure she wound her arms around his neck and lifted herself on tiptoe to press more fully against him. He felt the soft juncture of her thighs and ground himself against her, his body jolting with desire at the way she automatically adjusted herself to his hardness.

She was his, as she'd never belonged to any other man.

Her safety hinged on how swiftly he could get her out of the country, for he sensed Turego closing in on them. That man would never give up, not while the microfilm was still missing. There was no way in hell, Grant vowed, that he would allow Turego ever to touch Jane again. Lifting his mouth from hers, he muttered in a harsh tone, "You're mine now. I'll take care of you."

Jane rested her head against his chest. "I know," she whispered.

CHAPTER EIGHT

THAT NIGHT CHANGED forever the way Jane thought of the darkness. The fear of being alone in the dark would probably always remain with her, but when Grant reached out for her, it stopped being an enemy to be held at bay. It became instead a warm blanket of safety that wrapped around them, isolating them from the world. She felt his hands on her and forgot about the night.

He kissed her until she was clinging to him, begging him wordlessly for release from the need he'd created in her. Then he gently stripped her and himself, then rolled to his back, lifting her astride him. "I hurt you this morning," he said, his voice low and rough. "You control it this time; take only as much as you're comfortable with."

Comfort didn't matter; making love with him was a primitive glory, and she couldn't place any limits on it. She lost control, moving wildly on him, and her uninhibited delight snapped the thin thread of control he was trying to maintain. He made a rough sound deep in his throat and clasped her to him, rolling once again until she was beneath him. The wildly soaring pleasure they gave each other wiped her mind clear of everything but him and the love that swelled inside of her. There was no darkness. With his passion, with the driving need of his body, he took her out of the darkness. When she fell asleep in his arms, it was without once having thought of the impenetrable darkness that surrounded them.

The next morning, as always, she awoke slowly, moving and murmuring to herself, snuggling against the wonderfully warm, hard body beneath her, knowing even in her sleep that it was Grant's. His hands moved down her back to cup and knead her buttocks, awakening her fully. Then he shifted gently onto his side, holding her in his arms and depositing her on her back. Her eyes fluttered open, but it was still dark, so she closed them again and turned to press her face against his neck.

"It's almost dawn, honey," he said against her hair, but he couldn't force himself to stop touching her, to sit up and put on his clothing. His hands slipped over her bare, silky skin, discovering anew all the places he'd touched and kissed during the night. Her response still overwhelmed him. She was so open and generous, wanting him and offering herself with a simplicity that took his breath away.

She groaned, and he eased her into a sitting position, then reached out to unzip the flap of the tent and let in a faint glimmer of light. "Are you awake?"

"No," she grumbled, leaning against him and yawning.

"We have to go."

"I know." Muttering something under her breath, she found what she presumed to be her shirt and began trying to untangle it. There was too much cloth, so she stopped in frustration and handed it to him. "I think this is yours. It's too big to be mine."

He took the shirt, and Jane scrambled around until she found her own under the blanket they'd been lying on. "Can't you steal a truck or something?" she asked, not wanting even to think about another day of walking.

He didn't laugh, but she could almost feel the way the corners of his lips twitched. "That's against the law, you know."

"Stop laughing at me! You've had a lot of specialized training, haven't you? Don't you know how to hot-wire an ignition?"

He sighed. "I guess I can hot-wire anything we'd be likely to find, but stealing a vehicle would be like advertising our position to Turego."

"How far can we be from Limon? Surely we could get there before Turego would be able to search every village between here and there?"

"It'd be too risky, honey. Our safest bet is still to cut across to the east coast swamps, then work our way down the coast. We can't be tracked in the swamp." He paused. "I'll have to go into the village for food but you're going to stay hidden in the trees."

Jane drew back. "Like hell."

"Damn it, don't you realize that it's too dangerous for you to show your face?"

"What about your face? At least I have dark hair and eyes like everyone else. Don't forget, that soldier saw you, and your pilot friend no doubt told them all about you, so they know we're together. That long blond mane of yours is pretty unusual around here."

He ran his hand through his shaggy hair, faintly surprised at how long it was. "It can't be helped."

She folded her arms stubbornly. "You're not going anywhere without me."

Silence lay between them for a moment. She was beginning to think she'd won a surprisingly easy victory when he spoke, and the even, almost mild tone of his voice made chills go up her spine, because it was the most implacable voice she'd ever heard. "You'll do what I say, or I'll tie and gag you and leave you here in the tent."

Now it was her turn to fall silent. The intimacy that had been forged between them had made her forget that he was a warrior first, and her lover second. Despite the gentle passion with which he made love to her, he was still the same man who had knocked her out and thrown her over his shoulder, carrying her away into the jungle. She hadn't held a grudge against him for that, after the reception she'd given him, but this was something else entirely. She felt as if he were forcibly reminding her of the original basis of their relationship, making her acknowledge that their physical intimacy had not made her an equal in his eyes. It was as if he'd used her body, since she had so willingly offered it, but saw no reason to let that give her any influence over him.

Jane turned away from him, fumbling with her shirt and finally getting it straight. She wouldn't let him see any hint of hurt in her eyes; she'd known that the love she felt was completely one-sided.

His hand shot out and pulled the shirt away from her. Startled, she looked at him. "I have to get dressed. You said we need to—"

"I know what I said," he growled, easing her down onto the blanket. The lure of her soft body, the knowledge that he'd hurt her and her characteristic chin-up attempt to keep him from seeing it, all made it impossible for him to remember the importance of moving on. The core of ice deep inside his chest kept him from whispering to her how much she meant to him. The remoteness bred into him by years of living on the edge of death hadn't yet been overcome; perhaps it never would be. It was still vital to him to keep some small significant part of himself sealed away, aloof and cold. Still, he couldn't let her draw away from him with that carefully blank expression on her face. She was his, and it was time she came to terms with the fact.

Putting his hands on her thighs, he spread them apart and mounted her. Jane caught her breath, her hands going up to grab at his back. He slowly pushed into her, filling her with a powerful movement that had her body arching on the blanket.

He went deep inside her, holding her tightly to him. Her inner tightness made him almost groan aloud as wild shivers of pleasure ran up his spine. Shoving his hand into her hair, he turned her head until her mouth was under his, then kissed her with a violence that only hinted at the inferno inside him. She responded to him immediately. Her mouth molded to his and her body rose to meet his thrusts in increasingly ecstatic undulations. He wanted to immerse himself in her, go deeper and deeper until they were bonded together, their flesh fused. He held her beneath him, their bodies locked together in total intimacy. He reveled in the waves of intensifying pleasure that made them clutch at each other, straining together in an effort to reach the peak of their passion. When he was inside her, he no longer felt the need to isolate himself. She was taking a part of him that he hadn't meant to offer, but he couldn't stop it. It was as if he'd gotten on a roller coaster and there was no way to get off until it reached the end of the line. He'd just have to go along for the ride, and he meant to wring every moment of pleasure he could from the short time that he had her all to himself.

Jane clung to his shoulders, driven out of her senses by the pounding of his body. He seemed to have lost all control; he was wild, almost violent, his flesh so heated that his skin burned her palms. She was caught up in the depth of his passion, writhing against him and begging for more. Then, abruptly, her pleasure crested, and he ground his mouth against hers to catch her mindless cries. Her hot flare of ecstasy caught him in its explosion, and he began shuddering as the final shock waves jolted through his body. Now it was she who held him, and when it was over he collapsed on her, his eyes closed and his chest heaving, his body glistening with sweat.

Her fingers gently touched the shaggy, dark gold threads of his hair, pushing them away from his forehead. She didn't know what had triggered his sudden, violent possession, but it didn't matter. What mattered was that, despite everything, he needed her in a basic way that he didn't welcome, but couldn't deny. That wasn't what she wanted, but it was a start. Slowly she trailed her hand down his back, feeling the powerful muscles that lay under his supple bronzed skin. The muscles twitched then relaxed under her touch, and he grew heavier as the tension left him.

"Now we really have to go," he murmured against her breast.

"Ummm." She didn't want to stir; her limbs were heavy, totally relaxed. She could happily have lain there for the rest of the day, dozing with him and waking to make love again. She knew that the peace wouldn't last; in a moment he stirred and eased their bodies apart.

They dressed in silence, except for the rustling of their clothing, until she began lacing her boots on her feet. He reached out and tilted her chin then, his thumb rubbing over her bottom lip. "Promise me," he demanded, making her look at him. "Tell me that you're going to do what I say, without an argument. Don't make me tie you up."

Was he asking for obedience, or trust? Jane hesitated, then went with her instincts. "All right," she whispered. "I promise."

His pupils dilated, and his thumb probed at the corner of her lips. "I'll take care of you," he said, and it was more than a promise.

They took down the tent; then Jane got out the meager supply of remaining food. She emptied the last of the Perrier into his canteen, disposed of the bottles, and broke in two the granola bar that she'd been saving. That and a small can of grapefruit was their breakfast, and the last of their food.

The morning was almost gone, and the heat and humidity had risen to almost unbearable levels, when Grant stopped and looked around. He wiped his forehead on his sleeve. "We're almost even with the village. Stay here, and I'll be back in an hour or so."

"How long is 'or so'?" she asked politely, but the sound of her teeth snapping together made him grin.

"Until I get back." He took the pistol out of its holster and extended it to her. "I take it you know how to use this, too?"

Jane took the weapon from his hand, a grim expression on her mouth. "Yes. After I was kidnapped, Dad insisted that I learn how to protect myself. That included a course in firearms, as well as self-defense classes." Her slim hand handled the gun with respect, and reluctant expertise. "I've never seen one quite like this. What is it?"

"A Bren 10 millimeter," he grunted.

Her eyebrows lifted. "Isn't it still considered experimental?"

He shrugged. "By some people. I've used it for a while; it does what I want." He watched her for a moment, then a frown drew his brows together. "Could you use it, if you had to?"

"I don't know." A smile wobbled on her mouth. "Let's hope it doesn't come to that."

He touched her hair, hoping fervently that she never had to find the answer to his question. He didn't want anything ever to dim the gaiety of her smile. Bending, he kissed her roughly, thoroughly, then without a word blended into the forest in that silent, unnerving way of his. Jane stared at the gun in her hand for a long moment, then walked over to a fallen tree and carefully inspected it for animal life before sitting down.

She couldn't relax. Her nerves were jumpy, and though she didn't jerk around at every raucous bird call or chattering monkey, or even the alarming rustles in the underbrush, her senses were acutely, painfully attuned to the noises. She had become used to having Grant close by, his mere presence making her feel protected. Without him, she felt vulnerable and more alone than she had ever felt before.

Fear ate at her, but it was fear for Grant, not herself. She had walked into this with her eyes open, accepting the danger as the price to be paid, but Grant was involved solely because of her. If anything happened to him, she knew she wouldn't be able to bear it, and she was afraid. How could he expect to walk calmly into a small village and not be noticed. Everything about him drew attention, from his stature to his shaggy blond hair and those wild, golden eyes. She knew how single-mindedly Turego would search for her, and since Grant had been seen with her, his life was on the line now just as much as hers.

By now Turego must know that she had the microfilm. He'd be both furious and desperate; furious because she'd played him for a fool, and desperate because she could destroy his government career. Jane twisted her fingers together, her dark eyes intent. She thought of destroying the microfilm, to ensure that it would never fall into the hands of Turego or any hostile group or government—but she didn't know what was on it, only that it was supremely important. She didn't want to destroy information that her own country might need. Not only that, but she might need it as a negotiating tool. George had taught her well, steeped her in his cautious, quicksilver tactics, the tactics that had made him so shadowy that few people had known of his existence. If she had her back to the wall, she would use every advantage she had, do whatever she had to—but she hoped it wouldn't come to that kind of desperation. The best scenario would be that Grant would be able to smuggle her out of the country. Once she was safe in the States, she'd make contact and turn the microfilm over to the people who should have it. Then she could concentrate on chasing Grant until he realized that he couldn't live without her. The worst scenario she could imagine would be for something to happen to Grant. Everything in her shied away even from the thought.

He'd been hurt too much already. He was a rough,

hardened warrior, but he bore scars, invisible ones inside as well as the ones that scored his body. He'd retired, trying to pull himself away, but the wasteland mirrored in his eyes told her that he still lived partially in the shadows, where sunlight and warmth couldn't penetrate.

A fierce protectiveness welled up inside her. She was strong; she'd already lived through so much, overcome a childhood horror that could have crippled her emotionally. She hadn't allowed that to clip her wings, had learned instead to soar even higher, reveling in her freedom. But she wasn't strong enough to survive a world without Grant. She had to know that he was alive and well, or there would be no more sunshine for her. If anyone dared harm him...

Perspiration curled the hair at her temples and trickled between her breasts. Sighing, she wondered how long she had been waiting. She wiped her face and twisted her hair into a knot on top of her head to relieve herself of its hot weight on the back of her neck. It was so hot! The air was steamy, lying on her skin like a wet, warm blanket, making it difficult to breathe. It had to rain soon; it was nearing the time of day when the storms usually came.

She watched a line of ants for a time, then tried to amuse herself by counting the different types of birds that flitted and chirped in the leafy terraces above her head. The jungle teemed with life, and she'd come to learn that, with caution, it was safe to walk through it—not that she wanted to try it without Grant. The knowledge and the experience were his. But she was no longer certain that death awaited her behind every bush. The animal life that flourished in the green depths was generally shy, and skittered away from the approach of man. It was true that the most dangerous animal in the jungle was man himself.

Well over an hour had passed, and a sense of unease was prickling her spine. She sat very still, her green and black clothing mingling well with the surrounding foliage, her senses alert.

She saw nothing, heard nothing out of the ordinary, but the prickling sensation along her spine increased. Jane sat still for a moment longer, then gave in to the screaming of her instincts. Danger was near, very near. Slowly she moved, taking care not to rustle even a leaf, and crawled behind the shelter of the fallen tree's roots. They were draped in vines and bushes that had sprung to life already, feeding off the death of the great plant. The heaviness of the pistol she held reminded her that Grant had had a reason for leaving it with her.

A flash of movement caught her attention, but she turned only her eyes to study it. It was several long seconds before she saw it again, a bit of tanned skin and a green shape that was not plant or animal, but a cap. The man was moving slowly, cautiously, making little noise. He carried a rifle, and he was headed in the general direction of the village.

Jane's heart thudded in her breast. Grant could well meet him face-to-face, but Grant might be surprised, while this man, this guerrilla, was expecting to find him. Jane didn't doubt that normally Grant would be the victor, but if he were overtaken from behind he could be shot before he had a chance to act.

The distinctive beating of helicopter blades assaulted the air, still distant, but signaling the intensified search. Jane waited while the noise of the helicopter faded, hoping that its presence had alerted Grant. Surely it had; he was far too wary not to be on guard. For that, if nothing else, she was grateful for the presence of the helicopters.

She had to find Grant before he came face-to-face with one of the guerrillas and before they found her. This lone man wouldn't be the only one searching for her.

She had learned a lot from Grant these past few days, absorbing the silent manner in which he walked, his instinctive use of the best shelter available. She slid into the jungle, moving slowly, keeping low, and always staying behind and to the side of the silent stalker. Terror fluttered in her chest, almost choking her, but she reminded herself that she had no choice.

A thorny vine caught her hair, jerking it painfully, and tears sprang to her eyes as she bit her lip to stifle a reflexive cry of pain. Trembling, she freed her hair from the vine. Oh, God, where was Grant? Had he been caught already?

Her knees trembled so badly that she could no longer walk at a crouch. She sank to her hands and knees and began crawling, as Grant had taught her, keeping the thickest foliage between herself and the man, awkwardly clutching the pistol in her hand as she moved.

Thunder rumbled in the distance, signaling the approach of the daily rains. She both dreaded and prayed for the rain. It would drown out all sound and reduce visibility to a few feet, increasing her chances for escape—but it would also make it almost impossible for Grant to find her.

A faint crackle in the brush behind her alerted her, but she whirled a split second too late. Before she could bring the pistol around, the man was upon her, knocking the gun from her grip and twisting her arm up behind her, then pushing her face into the ground. She gasped, her breath almost cut off by the pressure of his knee on her back. The moist, decaying vegetation that littered the forest floor was ground into her mouth. Twisting her head to one side, Jane spat out the dirt. She tried to wrench her arm free; he cursed and twisted her arm higher behind her back, wringing an involuntary cry of pain from her.

Someone shouted in the distance, and the man answered, but Jane's ears were roaring and she couldn't understand what they said. Then he roughly searched her, slapping his free hand over her body and making her face turn red with fury. When he was satisfied that she carried no other weapons, he released her arm and flipped her onto her back.

She started to surge to her feet, but he swung his rifle around so close that the long, glinting barrel was only a few inches from her face. She glanced at it, then lifted her eyes to glare at her captor. Perhaps she could catch him off guard. "Who are you?" she demanded in a good imitation of a furious, insulted woman, and swatted the barrel away as if it were an insect. His flat, dark eyes briefly registered surprise, then wariness. Jane scrambled to her feet and thrust her face up close to his, letting him see her narrowed, angry eyes. Using all the Spanish she knew, she proceeded to tell him what she thought of him. For good measure she added all the ethnic invective she'd learned in college, silently wondering at the meaning of everything she was calling the soldier, who looked more stunned by the moment.

She poked him repeatedly in the chest with her finger, advancing toward him, and he actually fell back a few paces. Then the other soldier, the one she'd spotted before, joined them, and the man pulled himself together.

"Be quiet!" he shouted.

"I won't be quiet!" Jane shouted in return, but the other soldier grabbed her arms and tied her wrists. Incensed, Jane kicked out behind her, catching him on the shin with her boot. He gave a startled cry of pain, then whirled her around and drew his fist back, but at the last moment stayed his blow. Turego probably had given orders that she wasn't to be hurt, at least until he'd gotten the information he wanted from her.

Shaking her tangled hair away from her eyes, Jane glared at her captors. "What do you want? Who are you?"

They ignored her, and pushed her roughly ahead of them. With her arms tied behind her, her balance was off, and she stumbled over a tangled vine. She couldn't catch herself, and pitched forward with a small cry. Instinctively one of the soldiers grabbed for her. Trying to make it look accidental, she flung out one of her legs and tangled it through his, sending him crashing into a bush. She landed with a jolt on a knotted root, which momentarily stunned her and made her ears ring.

He came out of nowhere. One moment he wasn't there; the next he was in the midst of them. Three quick blows with the side of his hand to the first soldier's face and neck had the man crumpling like a broken doll. The soldier who Jane had tripped yelled and tried to swing his rifle around, but Grant lashed out with his boot, catching the man on the chin. There was a sickening thud; the man's head jerked back, and he went limp.

Grant wasn't even breathing hard, but his face was

set and coldly furious as he hauled Jane to her feet and roughly turned her around. His knife sliced easily through the bonds around her wrists. "Why didn't you stay where I left you?" he grated. "If I hadn't heard you yelling—"

She didn't want to think about that. "I did stay," she protested. "Until those two almost walked over me. I was trying to hide, and to find you before you ran straight into them!"

He gave her an impatient glance. "I would've handled them." He grabbed her wrist and began dragging her after him. Jane started to defend herself, then sighed. Since he so obviously had handled them, what could she say? She concentrated instead on keeping her feet under her and dodging the limbs and thorny vines that swung at her.

"Where are we going?"

"Be quiet."

There was a loud crack, and Grant knocked her to the ground, covering her with his body. Winded, at first Jane thought that the thunder of the approaching storm had startled him; then her heart convulsed in her chest as she realized what the noise had been. Someone was shooting at them! The two soldiers hadn't been the only ones nearby. Her eyes widened to dark pools; they were shooting at Grant, not at her! They would have orders to take her alive. Panic tightened her throat, and she clutched at him.

"Grant! Are you all right?"

"Yeah," he grunted, slipping his right arm around her and crawling with her behind the shelter of a large mahogany tree, dragging her like a predator carrying off its prey. "What happened to the Bren?"

"He knocked it out of my hand...over there." She waved her hand to indicate the general area where she'd lost the gun. Grant glanced around, measuring the shelter available to him and swearing as he decided it was too much of a risk.

"I'm sorry," Jane said, her dark eyes full of guilt.

"Forget it." He unslung the rifle from his shoulder, his motions sure and swift as he handled the weapon. Jane hugged the ground, watching as he darted a quick look around the huge tree trunk. There was a glitter in his amber eyes that made her feel a little in awe of him; at this moment he was the quintessential warrior, superbly trained and toned, coolly assessing the situation and determining what steps to take.

Another shot zinged through the trees, sending bark flying only inches from Grant's face. He jerked back, then swiped at a thin line of blood that trickled down from his cheekbone, where a splinter had caught him.

"Stay low," he ordered, his tone flat and hard. "Crawl on your belly through those bushes right behind us, and keep going no matter what. We've got to get out of here."

She'd gone white at the sight of the blood ribboning down his face, but she didn't say anything. Controlling the shaking of her legs and arms, she got down on her stomach and obeyed, snaking her way into the emergent shrubs. She could feel him right behind her, directing her with his hand on her leg. He was deliberately keeping himself between her and the direction from which the shots had come, and the realization made her heart squeeze painfully.

Thunder rumbled, so close now that the earth shuddered from the shock waves. Grant glanced up. "Come on, rain," he muttered. "Come on."

It began a few minutes later, filtering through the leaves with a dripping sound, then rapidly intensifying to the thunderous deluge that she'd come to expect. They were soaked to the skin immediately, as if they'd been tossed into a waterfall. Grant shoved her ahead of him, heedless now of any noise they made, because the roar of the rain obliterated everything else. They covered about a hundred yards on their hands and knees, then he pulled her upright and brought his mouth close to her ear. "Run!" he yelled, barely making himself heard over the din of the pummeling rain.

Jane didn't know how she could run but she did. Her legs were trembling, she was dizzy and disoriented, but somehow her feet moved as Grant pulled her through the forest at breakneck speed. Her vision was blurred; she could see only a confused jumble of green, and the rain, always the rain. She had no idea where they were going, but trusted Grant's instincts to guide them.

Suddenly they broke free of the jungle's edge, where man had cut back the foliage in an attempt to bring civilization to a small part of the tropical rain forest. Staggering across fields turned into a quagmire by the rain, Jane was held upright only by Grant's unbreakable grip on her wrist. She fell to her knees once and he dragged her for a few feet before he noticed. Without a word he scooped her up and tossed her over his shoulder, carrying her as effortlessly as ever, showing no trace of the exhaustion she felt.

She closed her eyes and hung on, already dizzy and now becoming nauseated as her stomach was jolted by his hard shoulder. Their surroundings had become a nightmare of endless gray water slapping at them, wrapping them in a curtain that obliterated sight and sound. Terror lay in her stomach in a cold, soggy lump, triggered by the sight of the blood on Grant's face. She couldn't bear it if anything happened to him, she simply couldn't.... He lifted her from his shoulder, propping her against something hard and cold. Jane's fingers spread against the support, and dimly she recognized the texture of metal. Then he wrenched open the door of the ancient pickup truck and picked her up to thrust her into the shelter of the cab. With a lithe twist of his body he slid under the wheel, then slammed the door.

"Jane," he bit out, grabbing her shoulder in a tight grip and shaking her. "Are you all right? Are you hit?"

She was sobbing, but her eyes were dry. She stretched out a trembling hand to touch the red streak that ran down his rain-wet face. "You're hurt," she whispered; he couldn't hear her over the thunder of the rain pounding on the metal top of the old truck, but he read her lips and gathered her in his arms, pressing hard, swift kisses to her dripping hair.

"It's just a scratch, honey," he reassured her. "What about you? Are you okay?"

She managed a nod, clinging to him, feeling the incredible warmth of his body despite the soggy condition of his clothes. He held her for a moment, then pulled her arms from around his neck and put her on the other side of the truck. "Sit tight while I get this thing going. We've got to get out of here before the rain stops and everyone comes out."

He bent down and reached under the dash of the truck, pulling some wires loose.

"What are you doing?" Jane asked numbly.

"Hot-wiring this old crate," he replied, and gave her a quick grin. "Pay close attention, since you've been so insistent that I do this. You may want to steal a truck someday."

"You can't see to drive in this," she said, still in that helpless, numb tone of voice, so unlike her usual cheerful matter-of-fact manner. A frown drew his brows together, but he couldn't stop to cradle her in his arms and reassure her that everything was going to be all right. He wasn't too sure of that himself; all hell had broken loose, reminding him how much he disliked being shot at—and now Jane was a target as well. He hated this whole setup so much that a certain deadly look had come into his eyes, the look that had become legend in the jungles and rice paddies of Southeast Asia.

"I can see well enough to get us out of here."

He put two wires together, and the engine coughed and turned over, but didn't start. Swearing under his breath, he tried it again, and the second time the engine caught. He put the old truck in gear and let up on the clutch. They lurched into motion with the old vehicle groaning and protesting. The rain on the windshield was so heavy that the feeble wipers were almost useless, but Grant seemed to know where he was going.

Looking around, Jane saw a surprisingly large number of buildings through the rain, and several streets seemed to branch away from the one they were on. The village was a prosperous one, with most of the trappings of civilization, and it looked somehow incongruous existing so close to the jungle.

"Where are we going?" she asked.

"South, honey. To Limon, or at least as far as this crate will carry us down the road."

CHAPTER NINE

LIMON. THE NAME sounded like heaven, and as she clung to the tattered seat of the old truck, the city seemed just as far away. Her dark eyes were wide and vulnerable as she stared at the streaming windshield, trying to see the road. Grant gave her a quick look, all he could safely spare when driving took so much of his attention. Keeping his voice calm, he said, "Jane, scoot as far into the corner as you can. Get your head away from the back window. Do you understand?"

"Yes." She obeyed, shrinking into the corner. The old truck had a small window in back and smaller windows on each side, leaving deep pockets of protection in the corners. A broken spring dug into the back of her leg, making her shift her weight. The upholstery on this side of the seat was almost nonexistent, consisting mostly of miscellaneous pieces of cloth covering some of the springs. Grant was sitting on a grimy patch of burlap. Looking down, she saw a large hole in the floorboard beside the door.

"This thing has character," she commented, regaining a small portion of her composure.

"Yeah, all of it bad." The truck skewed sideways on a sea of mud, and Grant gave all his attention to steering the thing in a straight line again.

"How can you tell where we're going?"

"I can't. I'm guessing." A devilish grin twisted his lips, a sign of the adrenaline that was racing through his system. It was a physical high, an acute sensitivity brought on by pitting his wits and his skills against the enemy. If it hadn't been for the danger to Jane, he might even have enjoyed this game of cat and mouse. He risked another quick glance at her, relaxing a little as he saw that she was calmer now, gathering herself together and mastering her fear. The fear was still there, but she was in control.

"You'd better be a good guesser," she gasped as the truck lurched sickeningly to the side. "If you drive us off a cliff, I swear I'll never forgive you!"

He grinned again and shifted his weight uncomfortably. He leaned forward over the wheel. "Can you get these packs off? They're in the way. And keep down!"

She slithered across the seat and unbuckled the backpacks, pulling them away from him so he could lean back. How could she have forgotten her pack? Stricken that she'd been so utterly reckless with it, she drew the buckles through the belt loops of her pants and fastened the straps.

He wasn't paying any attention to her now, but was frowning at the dash. He rapped at a gauge with his knuckle. "Damn it!"

Jane groaned. "Don't tell me. We're almost out of gas!"

"I don't know. The damned gauge doesn't work. We could have a full tank, or it could quit on us at any time."

She looked around. The rain wasn't as torrential as it had been, though it was still heavy. The forest pressed closely on both sides of the road, and the village was out of sight behind them. The road wasn't paved, and the truck kept jouncing over the uneven surface, forcing her to cling to the seat to stay in it—but it was a road and the truck was still running along it. Even if it quit that minute, they were still better off than they had been only a short while before. At least they weren't being shot at now. With any luck Turego would think they were still afoot and continue searching close by, at least for a while. Every moment was precious now, putting distance between them and their pursuers.

Half an hour later the rain stopped, and the temperature immediately began to climb. Jane rolled down the window on her side of the truck, searching for any coolness she could find. "Does this thing have a radio?" she asked.

He snorted. "What do you want to listen to, the top forty? No, it doesn't have a radio."

"There's no need to get snippy," she sniffed.

Grant wondered if he'd ever been accused of being "snippy" before. He'd been called a lot of things, but never that; Jane had a unique way of looking at things. If they had met up with a jaguar, she probably would have called it a "nice kitty"! The familiar urge rose in him, making him want to either throttle her or make love to her. His somber expression lightened as he considered which would give him the most pleasure.

The truck brushed against a bush that was encroaching on the narrow road. Jane ducked barely in time to avoid being slapped in the face by the branches that sprang through the open window, showering them with the raindrops that had been clinging to the leaves.

"Roll that window up," he ordered, concern making his voice sharp. Jane obeyed and sat back in the corner again. Already she could feel perspiration beading on her face, and she wiped her sleeve across her forehead. Her hand touched her hair, and she pushed the heavy mass away from her face, appalled at the tangled ringlets she found. What she wouldn't give for a bath! A real bath, with hot water and soap and shampoo, not a rinsing in a rocky stream. And clean clothes! She thought of the hairbrush in her pack, but she didn't have the energy to reach for it right now.

Well, there was no sense in wasting her time wishing for something she couldn't have. There were more important issues at hand. "Did you get any food?"

"In my pack."

She grabbed the pack and opened it, pulling out a towel-wrapped bundle of bread and cheese. That was all there was, but she wasn't in the mood to quibble about the limited menu. Food was food. Right now, even field rations would have been good.

Leaning over, she took his knife from his belt and swiftly sliced the bread and cheese. In less than a minute, she'd made two thick cheese sandwiches and returned the knife to its sheath. "Can you hold the sandwich and drive, or do you want me to feed you?"

"I can manage." It was awkward, wrestling with the steering wheel and holding the sandwich at the same time, but she would have to slide closer to him to feed him, and that would expose her head in the back window. The road behind them was still empty, but he wasn't going to take any chances with her welfare.

"I could lie down with my head in your lap and feed you," she suggested softly, and her dark eyes were sleepy and tender.

He jerked slightly, his entire body tensing. "Honey,

if you put your head in my lap, I might drive this crate up a tree. You'd better stay where you are."

Was it only yesterday that he'd taken her so completely in that cave? He'd made her his, possessed her and changed her, until she found it difficult to remember what it had been like before she'd known him. The focus of her entire life had shifted, redirected itself onto him.

What she was feeling was plainly revealed in her eyes, in her expressive face. A quick glance at her had him swallowing to relieve an abruptly dry throat, and his hands clenched on the wheel. He wanted her, immediately; he wanted to stop the truck and pull her astride him, then bury himself in her inner heat. The taste and scent of her lingered in his mind, and his body still felt the silk of her skin beneath his. Perhaps he wouldn't be able to get enough of her to satisfy him in the short time they had remaining, but he was going to try, and the trying would probably drive him crazy with pleasure.

They wolfed down the sandwiches, then Jane passed him the canteen. The Perrier was flat, but it was still wet, and he gulped it thirstily. When he gave the canteen back to her, she found herself gulping, too, in an effort to replenish the moisture her body was losing in perspiration. It was so hot in the truck! Somehow, even trekking through the jungle hadn't seemed this hot, though there hadn't been even a hint of breeze beneath the canopy. The metal shell of the truck made her feel canned, like a boiled shrimp. She forced herself to stop drinking before she emptied the canteen, and capped it again.

Ten minutes later the truck began sputtering and coughing; then the engine stopped altogether, and Grant coasted to a stop, as far to one side of the narrow road as he could get. "It lasted almost two hours," he said, opening the door and getting out.

Jane scrambled across the truck and got out on his side, since he'd parked so close to the edge that her door was blocked by a tree. "How far do you think we got?"

"Thirty miles or so." He wound a lock of her hair around his forefinger and smiled down at her. "Feel up to a walk?"

"A nice afternoon stroll? Sure, why not?"

He lowered his head and took a hard kiss from her mouth. Before she could respond he'd drawn away and pushed her off the road and into the shelter of the forest again. He returned to the truck, and she looked back to see him obliterating their footprints; then he leaped easily up the low bank and came to her side. "There's another village down the road a few more miles; I hoped we'd make it so we could buy more gas, but—" He broke off and shrugged at the change of plans. "We'll follow the road and try to get to the village by nightfall, unless they get too close to us. If they do, we'll have to go back into the interior."

"We're not going to the swamp?"

"We can't," he explained gently. "There's too much open ground to cover, now that they know we're in the area."

A bleak expression came and went in her eyes so fast that he wasn't certain he'd seen it. "It's my fault. If I'd just hidden from them, instead of trying to find you…"

"It's done. Don't worry about it. We just have to adjust our plans, and the plan now is to get to Limon as fast as we can, any way we can."

"You're going to steal another truck?"

"I'll do whatever has to be done."

Yes, he would. That knowledge was what made her feel so safe with him; he was infinitely capable, in many different areas. Even wearily following him through the overgrown tangle of greenery made her happy, because she was with him. She didn't let herself think of the fact that they would soon part, that he'd casually kiss her goodbye and walk away, as if she were nothing more than another job finished. She'd deal with that when it happened; she wasn't going to borrow trouble. She had to devote her energies now to getting out of Costa Rica, or at least to some trustworthy authorities, where Grant wouldn't be in danger of being shot while trying to protect her. When she'd seen the blood on his face, some vital part inside of her had frozen knowing that she couldn't survive if anything happened to him. Even though she'd been able to see that he wasn't badly hurt, the realization of his vulnerability had frightened her. As strong as he was, as vital and dangerous, he was a man, and therefore mortal.

They heard only one vehicle on the road, and it was moving toward the village where they'd stolen the truck. The sun edged downward, and the dim light in the forest began to fade. Right before the darkness became total, they came to the edge of a field, and down the road about half a mile they could see the other village spread out. It was really more of a small town than a village; there were bright electric lights, and cars and trucks were parked on the streets. After days spent in the jungle, it looked like a booming metropolis, a cornerstone of civilization.

"We'll stay here until it's completely dark, then go into town," Grant decided, dropping to the ground and stretching out flat on his back. Jane stared at the twinkling lights of the town, torn between a vague uneasiness and an eagerness to take advantage of the comforts a town offered. She wanted a bath, and to sleep in a bed, but after so much time spent alone with Grant, the thought of once more being surrounded by other people made her wary. She couldn't relax the way Grant did, so she remained on her feet, her face tense and her hands clenched.

"You might as well rest, instead of twitching like a nervous cat."

"I am nervous. Are we going on to Limon tonight?"

"Depends on what we find when we get into town."

She glared down at him in sudden irritation. He was a master at avoiding straight answers. It was so dark that she couldn't make out his features; he was only a black form on the ground, but she was certain that he was aware of her anger, and that the corner of his mouth was turning up in that almost-smile of his. She was too tired to find much humor in it, though, so she walked away from him a few paces and sat down, leaning her head on her drawn-up knees and closing her eyes.

There wasn't even a whisper of sound to warn her, but suddenly he was behind her, his strong hands massaging the tight muscles of her shoulders and neck. "Would you like to sleep in a real bed tonight?" he murmured in her ear.

"And take a real bath. And eat real food. Yes, I'd like that," she said, unaware of how wistful her tone was.

"A town this size probably has a hotel of some sort, but we can't risk going there, not looking the way we do. I'll try to find someone who takes in boarders and won't ask many questions."

Taking her hand, he pulled her to her feet and draped

his arm over her shoulder. "Let's go, then. A bed sounds good to me, too."

Walking across the field, ever closer to the beckoning lights, Jane became more conscious of how she looked, and she pushed her fingers through her tangled hair. She knew that her clothes were filthy, and that her face was probably dirty. "No one is going to let us in," she predicted.

"Money has a way of making people look past the dirt."

She glanced up at him in surprise. "You have money?"

"A good Boy Scout is always prepared."

In the distance, the peculiarly mournful wail of a train whistle floated into the air, reinforcing the fact that they'd left the isolation of the rain forest behind. Oddly, Jane felt almost nakedly vulnerable, and she moved closer to Grant. "This is stupid, but I'm scared," she whispered.

"It's just a mild form of culture shock. You'll feel better when you're in a tub of hot water."

They kept to the fringes of the town, in the shadows. It appeared to be a bustling little community. Some of the streets were paved, and the main thoroughfare was lined with prosperous looking stores. People walked and laughed and chatted, and from somewhere came the unmistakable sound of a jukebox, another element of civilization that jarred her nerves. The universally known red-and-white sign of a soft drink swung over a sidewalk, making her feel as if she had emerged from a time warp. This was definitely culture shock.

Keeping her pushed behind him, Grant stopped and carried on a quiet conversation with a rheumy-eyed old man who seemed reluctant to be bothered. Finally Grant thanked him and walked away, still keeping a firm grip on Jane's arm. "His sister-in-law's first cousin's daughter takes in boarders," he told her, and Jane swallowed a gasp of laughter.

"Do you know where his sister-in-law's first cousin's daughter lives?"

"Sure. Down this street, turn left, then right, follow the alley until it dead-ends in a courtyard."

"If you say so."

Of course he found the boardinghouse easily, and Jane leaned against the white adobe wall that surrounded the courtyard while he rang the bell and talked with the small, plump woman who answered the door. She seemed reluctant to admit such exceedingly grimy guests. Grant passed her a wad of bills and explained that he and his wife had been doing field research for an American pharmaceutical company, but their vehicle had broken down, forcing them to walk in from their camp. Whether it was the money or the tale of woe that swayed Señora Trejos, her face softened and she opened the grill, letting them in.

Seeing the tautness of Jane's face, Señora Trejos softened even more. "Poor lamb," she cooed, ignoring Jane's dirty state and putting her plump arm around the young woman's sagging shoulders. "You are exhausted, no? I have a nice cool bedroom with a soft bed for you and the señor, and I will bring you something good to eat. You will feel better then?"

Jane couldn't help smiling into the woman's kind dark eyes. "That sounds wonderful, all of it," she managed in her less-than-fluent Spanish. "But most of all, I need a bath. Would that be possible?"

"But of course!" Señora Trejos beamed with pride.

"Santos and I, we have the water heated by the tank. He brings the fuel for the heating from San Jose."

Chatting away, she led them inside her comfortable house, with cool tiles on the floors and soothing white walls. "The upstairs rooms are taken," she said apologetically. "I have only the one room below the stairs, but it is nice and cool, and closer to the conveniences."

"Thank you, Señora Trejos," Grant said. "The downstairs room will more than make us happy."

It did. It was small, with bare floors and plain white walls, and there was no furniture except for the wood framed double bed, a cane chair by the lone, gracefully arched window, and a small wooden washstand that held a pitcher and bowl. Jane gazed at the bed with undisguised longing. It looked so cool and comfortable, with fat fluffy pillows.

Grant thanked Señora Trejos again; then she went off to prepare them something to eat, and they were alone. Jane glanced at him and found that he was watching her steadily. Somehow, being alone with him in a bedroom felt different from being alone with him in a jungle. There, their seclusion had been accepted. Here there was the sensation of closing out the world, of coming together in greater intimacy.

"You take the first turn at the bath," he finally said. "Just don't go to sleep in the tub."

Jane didn't waste time protesting. She searched the lower floor, following her nose, until she found Señora Trejos happily puttering about the kitchen. "Pardon, señora," she said haltingly. She didn't know all the words needed to explain her shortage of a robe or anything to wear after taking a bath, but Señora Trejos caught on immediately. A few minutes later Jane had a plain white nightgown thrust into her hands and was shown to the señora's prized bathroom.

The bathroom had cracked tile and a deep, old-fashioned tub with curved claw feet, but when she turned on the water it gushed out in a hot flood. Sighing in satisfaction, Jane quickly unbuckled the backpack from her belt and set it out of the way, then stripped off her clothes and got into the tub, unwilling to wait until it was full. The heat seeped into her sore muscles and a moan of pleasure escaped her. She would have liked to soak in the tub for hours, but Grant was waiting for his own bath, so she didn't allow herself to lean against the high back and relax. Quickly she washed away the layers of grime, unable to believe how good it felt to be clean again. Then she washed her hair, sighing in relief as the strands came unmatted and once again slipped through her fingers like wet silk.

Hurrying, she wrapped her hair in a towel and got her safety razor out of the backpack. Sitting on the edge of the tub, she shaved her legs and under her arms, then smoothed moisturizer into her skin. A smile kept tugging at her mouth as she thought of spending the night in Grant's arms again. She was going to be clean and sweet-smelling, her skin silky. After all, it wasn't going to be easy to win a warrior's love, and she was going to use all the weapons at her disposal.

She brushed her teeth, then combed out her wet hair and pulled the white nightgown over her head, hoping that she wouldn't meet any of Señora Trejos's other boarders on the short trip back to her room. The señora had told her to leave her clothes on the bathroom floor, that she would see that they were washed, so Jane got the backpack and hurried down the hall to the room where Grant waited.

He had closed the shutters over the arched window and was leaning with one shoulder propped against the wall, declining to sit in the single chair. He looked up at her entrance, and the inky pupils at the center of his golden irises expanded until there was only a thin ring of amber circling the black. Jane paused, dropping the pack beside the bed, feeling abruptly shy, despite the tempestuous lovemaking she'd shared with this man. He looked at her as if he were about to pounce on her, and she found herself crossing her arms over her breasts, aware that her nakedness was fully apparent beneath the thin nightgown. She cleared her throat, her mouth suddenly dry. "The bathroom is all yours."

He straightened slowly, not taking his eyes from her. "Why don't you go on to bed?"

"I'd rather wait for you," she whispered.

"I'll wake you up when I come to bed." The intensity of his gaze promised her that she wasn't going to sleep alone that night.

"My hair... I have to dry my hair."

He nodded and left the room, and Jane sat down on the chair weakly, shaking inside from the way he'd looked at her. Bending over, she rubbed her hair briskly, then began to brush it dry. It was so thick and long that it was still damp when Grant came back into the room and stood silently, watching her as she sat bent over, her slender arms curving as she drew the brush through the dark mass. She sat up, tossing her head to fling her hair back over her shoulders, and for a moment they simply stared at each other.

They had made love before, but now sensual awareness was zinging between them like an electric current. Without even touching each other, they were both becoming aroused, their heartbeats quickening, their skin growing hot.

He had shaved, probably using the razor she'd left in the bathroom. It was the first time she'd seen him without several days' growth of beard, and the clean, hard lines of his scarred face made her breath catch. He was naked except for a towel knotted around his lean waist, and as she watched he pulled the towel free and dropped it to the floor. Reaching behind him, he locked the door. "Are you ready for bed?"

"My hair...isn't quite dry."

"Leave it," he said, coming toward her.

The brush dropped to the floor as he caught her hand and pulled her up. Instantly she was in his arms, lifted off her feet by his fierce embrace. Their mouths met hungrily, and her fingers tangled in his water-darkened hair, holding him to her. His mouth was fresh and hot, his tongue thrusting deep into her mouth in a kiss that made her whimper as currents of desire sizzled her nerves.

He was hard against her, his manhood pushing against her softness, his hands kneading her hips and rubbing her over him. Jane pulled her mouth free, gasping, and dropped her head to his broad shoulder. She couldn't contain the wild pleasure he was evoking, as if her body were out of control, already reaching for the peak that his arousal promised. She'd been quite content to live celibately for years, the passion in her unawakened until she met Grant. He was as wild and beautiful and free as the majestic jaguars that melted silently through the tangled green jungle. The wildness in him demanded a response, and she was helpless to restrain it. He didn't have to patiently build her passion; one kiss and she trembled against him, empty and aching and ready for him, her breasts swollen and painful, her body growing wet and soft.

"Let's get this thing off you," he whispered, pulling at the nightgown and easing it up. Reluctantly she released him, and he pulled the gown over her head, dropping it over the chair; then she was back in his arms, and he carried her to the bed.

Their naked bodies moved together, and there was no more waiting. He surged into her, and she cried out a little from the delicious shock of it. Catching the small cry with his mouth, he lifted her legs and placed them around his waist, then began to move more deeply into her.

It was like the night before. She gave no thought to anything but the man with shoulders so broad that they blocked out the light. The bed was soft beneath them, the sheets cool and smooth, and the rhythmic creak of the springs in time with his movements was accompanied by the singing of insects outside the window. Time meant nothing. There was only his mouth on hers, his hands on her body, the slow thrusts that went deep inside her and touched off a wildfire of sensation, until they strained together in frenzied pleasure and the sheets were no longer cool, but warm from their damp, heated flesh.

Then it was quiet again, and he lay heavily on her, drawing in deep breaths while her hands moved over his powerful back. Her lips trembled with the words of love that she wanted to give him, but she held them back. All her instincts told her that he wouldn't want to know, and she didn't want to do anything to spoil their time together.

Perhaps he had given her something anyway, if not his love, something at least as infinitely precious. As her sensitive fingertips explored the deep valley of his spine, she wondered if he had given her his baby. A tremor of pleasure rippled down her body, and she held him closer, hoping that her body would be receptive to his seed.

He stirred, reaching out to turn off the lamp, and in the darkness he moved to lie beside her. She curled against his side, her head on his shoulder, and after a moment he gave a low chuckle.

"Why don't you just save time and get on top of me now?" he suggested, scooping her up and settling her on his chest.

Jane gave a sigh of deep satisfaction, stretching out on him and looping her arm around his neck. With her face pressed against his throat she was comfortable and safe, as if she'd found a sheltering harbor. "I love you," she said silently, moving her lips without sound against his throat.

THEY WOKE WITH the bright early morning sun coming through the slats of the shutters. Leaving Jane stretching and grousing on the bed, Grant got up and opened the shutters, letting the rosy light pour into the room. When he turned, he saw the way the light glowed on her warm-toned skin, turning her nipples to apricot, catching the glossy lights in her dark hair. Her face was flushed, her eyes still heavy with sleep.

Suddenly his body throbbed, and he couldn't bear to be separated from her by even the width of the small room. He went back to the bed and pulled her under him, then watched the way her face changed as he slowly eased into her, watched the radiance that lit her. Something swelled in his chest, making it difficult for him to breathe, and as he lost himself in the soft depths of her body he had one last, glaringly clear thought: she'd gotten too close to him, and letting her go was going to be the hardest thing he'd ever done.

HE DRESSED, PULLING on the freshly washed clothes that one of Señora Trejos's daughters had brought, along with a tray of fruit, bread and cheese. Jane flushed wildly when she realized that Señora Trejos must have brought a tray to them the night before, then discreetly left when she heard the sounds they had been making. A quick glance at Grant told her that he'd had the same thought, because the corner of his mouth was twitching in amusement.

The señora had also sent along a soft white off-the-shoulder blouse, and Jane donned it with pleasure, more than glad to discard her tattered black shirt. After selecting a piece of orange from the tray, she bit into the juicy fruit as she watched him pull his dark green undershirt over his head.

"You're going to be pretty noticeable in those camouflage fatigues," she said, poking a bit of the orange into his mouth.

"I know." He quickly kissed her orange-sticky lips. "Put the shirt in your pack and be ready to go when I get back."

"Get back? Where are you going?"

"I'm going to try to get some sort of transport. It won't be as easy this time."

"We could take the train," she pointed out.

"The rifle would be a mite conspicuous, honey."

"Why can't I go with you?"

"Because you're safer here."

"The last time you left me, I got into trouble," she felt obliged to remind him.

He didn't appreciate the reminder. He scowled down at her as he reached for a spear of melon. "If you'll just keep your little butt where I tell you to, you'll be fine."

"I'm fine when I'm with you."

"Damn it, stop arguing with me!"

"I'm not arguing. I'm pointing out some obvious facts! You're the one who's arguing!"

His eyes were yellow fire. He bent down until they were almost nose to nose, his control under severe stress. His teeth were clenched together as he said, evenly spacing the words out, "If you make it home without having the worst spanking of your life, it'll be a miracle."

"I've never had a spanking in my life," she protested.

"It shows!"

She flounced into the chair and pouted. Grant's hands clenched; then he reached for her and pulled her out of the chair, hauling her up to him for a deep, hard kiss. "Be good, for a change," he said, aware that he was almost pleading with her. "I'll be back in an hour—"

"Or so!" she finished in unison with him. "All right, I'll wait! But I don't like it!"

He left before he completely lost his temper with her, and Jane munched on more of the fruit, terribly grateful for something fresh to eat. Deciding that he'd meant only for her to stay in the house, not in the room, she first got everything ready for them to leave, as he'd instructed, then sought out the señora and had a pleasant chat with her. The woman was bustling around the kitchen preparing food for her boarders, while two of her daughters diligently cleaned the house and did a mountain of laundry. Jane had her arms deep in a bowl of dough when Grant returned.

He'd gone first to their room, and when he found her in the kitchen there was a flicker of intense relief in his eyes before he masked it. Jane sensed his presence and looked up, smiling. "Is everything arranged?"

"Yes. Are you ready?"

"Just as soon as I wash my hands."

She hugged the señora and thanked her, while Grant leaned in the doorway and watched her. Did she charm everyone so effortlessly? The señora was beaming at her, wishing her a safe journey and inviting her back. There would always be a room for the lovely young señora and her husband in the Trejos house!

They collected their packs, and Grant slung the rifle over his shoulder. They risked attracting attention because of it, but he didn't dare leave it behind. With any luck they would be on a plane out of Costa Rica by nightfall, but until they were actually on their way he couldn't let his guard down. The close call the day before had been proof of that. Turego wasn't giving up; he stood to lose too much.

Out in the alley, Jane glanced up at him. "What exactly did you arrange?"

"A farmer is going into Limon, and he's giving us a ride."

After the adventure of the last several days that seemed almost boringly tame, but Jane was happy to be bored. A nice, quiet ride, that was the ticket. How good it would be not to feel hunted!

As they neared the end of the alley, a man stepped suddenly in front of them. Grant reacted immediately, shoving Jane aside, but before he could swing the rifle around there was a pistol in his face, and several more men stepped into the alley, all of them armed, all of them with their weapons pointed at Grant. Jane stopped breathing, her eyes wide with horror. Then she recognized the man in the middle, and her heart stopped. Was Grant going to die now, because of her?

She couldn't bear it. She had to do something, anything.

"Manuel!" she cried, filling her voice with joy. She ran to him and flung her arms around him. "I'm so glad you found me!"

CHAPTER TEN

IT WAS A NIGHTMARE. Grant hadn't taken his narrowed gaze off her, and the hatred that glittered in his eyes made her stomach knot, but there was no way she could reassure him. She was acting for all she was worth, clinging to Turego and babbling her head off, telling him how frightened she'd been and how this madman had knocked her out and stolen her away from the plantation, all the while clinging to Turego's shirt as if she couldn't bear to release him. She had no clear idea of what she was going to do, only that somehow she had to stay unfettered so she could help Grant, and to do that she had to win Turego's trust and soothe his wounded vanity.

The entire situation was balanced on a knife edge; things could go in either direction. Wariness was in Turego's dark eyes, as well as a certain amount of cruel satisfaction in having cornered his prey. He wanted to make her suffer for having eluded him, she knew, yet for the moment she was safe from any real harm, because he still wanted the microfilm. It was Grant whose life was threatened, and it would take only a word from Turego for those men to kill him where he stood. Grant had to know it, yet there wasn't even a flicker of fear in his expression, only the cold, consuming hatred of his glare as he stared at Jane. Perhaps it was that, in the end, that eased Turego's suspicions somewhat. He would never relax his guard around her again, but Jane could only worry about one thing at a time. Right now, she had to protect Grant in any way she could.

Turego's arm stole around her waist, pulling her tightly against him. He bent his head and kissed her, a deeply intimate kiss that Jane had to steel herself not to resist in any way, even though she shuddered at having to endure the touch and taste of him. She knew what he was doing; he was illustrating his power, his control, and using her as a weapon against Grant. When he lifted his head, a cruel little smile was on his handsome mouth.

"I have you now, *chiquita*," he reassured her in a smooth tone. "You are quite safe. This...madman, as you called him, will not bother you again, I promise. I am impressed," he continued mockingly, inclining his head toward Grant. "I have heard of you, señor. Surely there can be only one with the yellow eyes and scarred face, who melts through jungles like a silent cat. You are a legend, but it was thought that you were dead. It has been a long time since anything was heard of you."

Grant was silent, his attention now on Turego, ignoring Jane as if she no longer existed. Not a muscle moved; it was as if he'd turned to stone. He wasn't even breathing. His utter stillness was unnerving, yet there was also the impression of great strength under control, a wild animal waiting for the perfect moment to pounce. Even though he was only one against many, the others were like jackals surrounding a mighty tiger; the men who held their weapons trained on him were visibly nervous.

"Perhaps it would be interesting to know who now

pays you for your services. And there are others who would like very much to have an opportunity to question you, yes? Tie him, and put him in the truck," Turego ordered, still keeping his arm around Jane. She forced herself not to watch as Grant was roughly bound and dragged over to a two ton military-type truck, with a canvas top stretched over the back. Instead she gave Turego her most dazzling smile and leaned her head on his shoulder.

"I've been so frightened," she whispered.

"Of course you have, *chiquita*. Is that why you resisted my men when they found you in the forest yesterday?"

She might have known he was too sharp to simply believe her! She let her eyes widen incredulously. "Those were your men? Well, why didn't they say so? They were shoving me around, and I was afraid they wanted to…to attack me. I had managed to slip away from that crazy man; I'd have made it, too, if it hadn't been for all the noise your men made! They led him right to me!" Her voice quivered with indignation.

"It is over; I will take care of you now." He led her to the truck and assisted her into the cab, then climbed in beside her and gave terse instructions to the driver.

That was exactly what she was afraid of, being taken care of by Turego, but for the moment she had to play up to him and somehow convince him that she was totally innocent of her escape from under the noses of his guards. He hadn't gotten where he was by being a gullible idiot; though she'd successfully fooled him the first time, the second time would be much more difficult.

"Where are we going?" she asked innocently, leaning against him. "Back to the plantation? Did you bring any of my clothes with you? He brought me this blouse this morning," she said, plucking at the soft white fabric, "but I'd really like to have my own clothes."

"I have been so worried about you that I did not think of your clothes, I confess," Turego lied smoothly. His hard arm was around her shoulders, and Jane smiled up at him. He was unnaturally handsome, with perfect features that would have done better on a statue than a man, though perhaps Turego wasn't quite human. He didn't show his age; he looked to be in his twenties, though Jane knew that he was in his early forties. Emotion hadn't changed his face; he had no wrinkles, no attractive crinkles at the corners of his eyes, no signs that time or life had touched him. His only weakness was his vanity; he knew he could force himself on Jane at any time, but he wanted to seduce her into giving herself willingly to him. She would be another feather in his cap; then, once he had the microfilm, he could dispose of her without regret.

She had only the microfilm to protect her, and only herself to protect Grant. Her mind raced, trying to think of some way she could free him from his bonds, get some sort of weapon to him. All he needed was a small advantage.

"Who is he? You seem to know him."

"He hasn't introduced himself? But you have spent several days alone with him, my heart. Surely you know his name."

Again she had to make a split second decision. Was Grant's real name commonly known? Was Grant his real name, anyway? She couldn't take the chance. "He told me that his name is Joe Tyson. Isn't that his real name?" she asked in an incredulous voice, sitting up to turn the full force of her brown eyes on him, blinking as if in astonishment.

Oddly, Turego hesitated. "That may be what he calls himself now. If he is who I think he is, he was once known as the Tiger."

He was uneasy! Grant was tied, and there were ten guns on him, but still Turego was made uneasy by his presence! Did that slight hesitation mean that Turego wasn't certain of Grant's real name and didn't want to reveal his lack of knowledge—or was the uncertainty of a greater scope? Was he not entirely certain that Grant was the Tiger? Turego wouldn't want to make himself look foolish by claiming to have captured the Tiger, only to have his prisoner turn out to be someone much less interesting.

Tiger. She could see how he had gained the name, and the reputation. With his amber eyes and deadly grace, the comparison had been inevitable. But he was a man, too, and she'd slept in his arms. He'd held her during the long hours of darkness, keeping the night demons away from her, and he'd shown her a part of herself that she hadn't known existed. Because of Grant, she felt like a whole person, capable of love and passion, a warm, giving woman. Though she could see what he had been, the way she saw him now was colored by love. He was a man, not a supernatural creature who melted through the dark, tangled jungles of the world. He could bleed, and hurt. He could laugh, that deep, rusty laugh that caught at her heart. After Grant, she felt contaminated just by sitting next to Turego.

She gave a tinkling laugh. "That sounds so cloak-and-daggerish! Do you mean he's a spy?"

"No, of course not. Nothing so romantic. He is really just a mercenary, hiring himself out to anyone for any sort of dirty job."

"Like kidnapping me? Why would he do that? I mean, no one is going to pay any ransom for me! My father doesn't even speak to me, and I certainly don't have any money of my own!"

"Perhaps something else was wanted from you," he suggested.

"But I don't have anything!" She managed to fill her face and voice with bewilderment, and Turego smiled down at her.

"Perhaps you have it and are not aware of it."

"What? Do you know?"

"In time, love, we shall find out."

"No one tells me anything!" she wailed, and lapsed into a pout. She allowed herself to hold the pout for about thirty seconds, then roused to demand of him again, like an impatient child, "Where are we going?"

"Just down this street, love."

They were on the very fringes of the town, and a dilapidated tin warehouse sat at the end of the street. It was in sad shape, its walls sagging, the tin roof curled up in several places, sections of it missing altogether in others. A scarred blue door hung crookedly on its hinges. The warehouse was their destination, and when the truck stopped beside the blue door and Turego helped Jane from the cab, she saw why. There were few people about, and those who were in the vicinity quickly turned their eyes away and scurried off.

Grant was hauled out of the back of the truck and shoved toward the door; he stumbled and barely caught his balance before he would have crashed headlong against the building. Someone chuckled, and when

Grant straightened to turn his unnerving stare on his captors, Jane saw that a thin trickle of blood had dried at the corner of his mouth. His lip was split and puffy. Her heart lurched, and her breath caught. Someone had hit him while he had his hands tied behind his back! Right behind her first sick reaction came fury, raw and powerful, surging through her like a tidal wave. She shook with the effort it took to disguise it before she turned to Turego again.

"What are we going to do here?"

"I just want to ask a few questions of our friend. Nothing important."

She was firmly escorted into the building, and she gasped as the heat hit her in the face like a blow. The tin building was a furnace, heating the air until it was almost impossible to breathe. Perspiration immediately beaded on her skin, and she felt dizzy, unable to drag in enough oxygen to satisfy her need.

Evidently Turego had been using the warehouse as a sort of base, because there was equipment scattered around. Leaving Grant under guard, Turego led Jane to the back of the building, where several small rooms connected with each other, probably the former offices. It was just as hot there, but a small window was opened and let in a measure of fresh air. The room he took her to was filthy, piled with musty smelling papers and netted with cobwebs. An old wooden desk, missing a leg, listed drunkenly to one side, and there was the unmistakable stench of rodents. Jane wrinkled her nose fastidiously. "Ugh!" she said in completely honest disgust.

"I apologize for the room," Turego said smoothly, bestowing one of his toothpaste-ad smiles on her. "Hopefully, we won't be here long. Alfonso will stay with you while I question our friend about his activities, and who hired him to abduct you."

What he meant was that she was also under guard. Jane didn't protest, not wanting to arouse his suspicions even more, but her skin crawled. She was very much afraid of the form his "questioning" would take. She had to think of something fast! But nothing came to mind, and Turego tilted her chin up to kiss her again. "I won't be long," he murmured. "Alfonso, watch her carefully. I would be very upset if someone stole her from me again."

Jane thought she recognized Alfonso as one of the guards who had been at the plantation. When Turego had gone, closing the door behind him, Jane gave Alfonso a slow glance from under lowered lashes and essayed a tentative smile. He was fairly young and good-looking. He had been warned against her, but still he couldn't help responding to her smile.

"You were a guard at the plantation?" she asked in Spanish.

He gave a reluctant nod.

"I thought I recognized you. I never forget a good-looking man," she said with more enthusiasm than precision, her pronunciation mangled just enough to bring a hint of amusement to Alfonso's face. She wondered if he knew what Turego was up to, or if he had been told some fabrication about protecting her.

Whatever he had been told, he wasn't inclined toward conversation. Jane poked around the room, looking for anything to use as a weapon, but trying not to be obvious about it. She kept straining her ears for any sound from the warehouse, her nerves jumping. What was Turego doing? If he harmed Grant...

How long had it been? Five minutes? Ten? Or less than that? She had no idea, but suddenly she couldn't stand it any longer, and she went to the door. Alfonso stretched his arm in front of her, barring her way.

"I want to see Turego," she said impatiently. "It's too hot to wait in here."

"You must stay here."

"Well, I won't! Don't be such a stuffed shirt, Alfonso; he won't mind. You can come with me, if you can't let me out of your sight."

She ducked under his arm and had the door open before he could stop her. With a muffled oath he came after her, but Jane darted through the door and the connecting offices. Just as she entered the main warehouse she heard the sickening thud of a fist against flesh, and the blood drained from her face.

Two men held Grant between them, holding him up by his bound arms, while another stood before him, rubbing his fist. Turego stood to the side, a small, inhuman smile on his lips. Grant's head sagged forward on his chest, and drops of blood spotted the floor at his feet.

"This silence will gain you nothing but more pain, my friend," Turego said softly. "Tell me who hired you. That is all I want to know, for now."

Grant said nothing, and one of the men holding him grabbed a fistful of hair, jerking his head up. Just before Alfonso took her arm, Jane saw Grant's face, and she jerked free, driven by a wild strength.

"Turego!" she cried shrilly, drawing everyone's attention to her. Turego's brows snapped together over his nose.

"What are you doing here? Alfonso, take her back!"

"No!" she yelled, pushing Alfonso away. "It's too hot

back there, and I won't stay! Really, this is too much! I've had a miserable time in that jungle, and I thought when you rescued me that I'd be comfortable again, but no, you drag me to this miserable dump and leave me in that grungy little room. I insist that you take me to a hotel!"

"Jane, Jane, you don't understand these things," Turego said, coming up to her and taking her arm. "Just a few moments more and he will tell me what I want to know. Aren't you interested in knowing who hired him?" He turned her away, leading her back to the offices again. "Please be patient, love."

Jane subsided, letting herself be led docilely away. She risked a quick glance back at Grant and his captors, and saw that they were waiting for Turego's return before resuming the beating. He was sagging limply in their grasp, unable even to stand erect.

"You are to stay here," Turego said sternly when they reached the office again. "Promise me, yes?"

"I promise," Jane said, turning toward him with a smile on her face; he never saw the blow coming. She caught him under the nose with the bridge of her hand, snapping his head back and making blood spurt. Before he could yell with pain or surprise, she slammed her elbow into his solar plexus and he doubled over with an agonized grunt. As if in a well-choreographed ballet, she brought her knee up under his unprotected chin, and Turego collapsed like a stuffed doll. Jane cast a quick thought of thanks to her father for insisting that she take all of those self-defense classes, then bent down and quickly jerked the pistol from Turego's holster.

Just as she started through the doorway again, a shot

reverberated through the tin building, and she froze in horror. "No," she moaned, then launched herself toward the sound.

WHEN JANE HAD hurled herself into Turego's arms, Grant had been seized by a fury so consuming that a mist of red had fallen over his vision, but he'd been trained to control himself, and that control had held, even though he had been on the edge of madness. Then the mist had cleared, and cold contempt had taken its place. Hell, what had he expected? Jane was a survivor, adept at keeping her feet. First she had charmed Turego, then Grant had stolen her from Turego and she'd charmed him as effortlessly as she had put Turego under her spell. Now Turego was back, and since he had the upper hand, it was a case of So long, Sullivan. He even felt a sort of bitter admiration for the way she had so quickly and accurately summed up the situation, then known exactly the tone to set to begin bringing Turego back to heel.

Still, the sense of betrayal was staggering, and nothing would have pleased him at that moment as much as to get his hands on her. Damn her for being a lying, treacherous little bitch! He should have known, should have suspected that her patented look of wide-eyed innocence was nothing but a well-rehearsed act.

The old instincts, only partially shelved, suddenly returned in full force. Forget about the bitch. He had to look out for himself first, then see to her. She was curling in Turego's arms like a cat, while Grant knew that his own future was nonexistent unless he did some fast thinking.

Part of the thinking was done for him when Turego

put two and two together and came up with an accurate guess about Grant's identity. A year had been far too short a time for people in the business to even begin forgetting him. After he'd disappeared, his absence had probably made his reputation grow to legendary proportions. Well, let Turego think that he was after the missing microfilm, too; Grant felt no compunction about using Jane in any way he could. She'd not only used him, she'd had him dancing to her tune like a puppet on a fancy little string. If he hadn't agreed to bring her out of Costa Rica, he would have wished the joy of her on Turego, and gotten himself out any way he could. But he'd taken the job, so he had to finish it—if he came out of this alive. When he got his hands on her again she'd find that there would be no more kid-glove treatment.

Turego was curious. With his hands tied behind his back, supported between two of the hired goons, Grant found out just how curious.

"Who hired you? Or are you an independent now?"

"Naw, I'm still a Protestant," Grant said, smiling smoothly. At a nod from Turego, a fist crashed into his face, splitting his lip and filling his mouth with blood. The next blow was into his midsection, and he'd have jackknifed if it hadn't been for the cruel support of his twisted arms.

"Really, I don't have the time for this," Turego murmured. "You are the one known as the Tiger; you aren't a man who works for nothing."

"Sure I am; I'm a walking charity."

The fist landed on his cheekbone, snapping his head back. This guy was a real boxer; he placed his blows with precision. The face a couple of times, then the ribs and kidneys. Pain sliced through Grant until his stomach heaved. He gasped, his vision blurred even though his mind was still clear, and he deliberately let all his weight fall on his two supporters, his knees buckling.

Then he heard Jane's voice, petulant and demanding, as he'd never heard it before, followed by Turego's smooth reassurances. The men's attention wasn't on him; he sensed its absence, like a wild animal acutely sensitive to every nuance. He sagged even more, deliberately putting stress on the bonds around his wrists, and fierce satisfaction welled in him as he felt them slip on his right hand.

He had powerful hands, hands that could destroy. He used that power against the cord that bound him, extending his hand to the fullest and stretching the cord, then relaxing and letting the cord slip even lower. Twice he did that, and the cord dropped around his fingers in loose coils.

Looking about through slitted eyes, he saw that no one was paying much attention to him, not even the boxer, who was absently rubbing his knuckles and waiting for Turego to return from wherever he'd gone. Jane was nowhere in sight, either. Now was the time.

The two men holding him were off guard; he threw them away from him like discarded toys. For a split second everyone was disconcerted, and that split second was all he needed. He grabbed a rifle and kicked its butt up under the chin of the soldier he'd taken it from, sending him staggering backward. He whirled, lashing out with his feet and the stock of the rifle. The soldiers really didn't have much of a chance; they didn't have a fraction of the training he'd had, or the years of experience. They didn't know how to react to an attacker who struck and whirled away before anyone could move. Only one managed to get his rifle up, and he fired wildly, the bullet zinging far over Grant's head. That soldier was the last one standing; Grant took him out with almost contemptuous ease. Then he hesitated only the barest moment as he waited for movement from any of them, but there was none. His gaze moved to the door at the far end of the warehouse, and a cold, twisted smile touched his bruised and bloody lips. He went after Jane.

SHE'D NEVER KNOWN such terror; even her fear of the dark was nothing compared to the way she felt now. She couldn't move fast enough; her feet felt as if they were slogging through syrup. Oh, God, what if they'd killed him? The thought was too horrible to be borne, yet it swelled in her chest until she couldn't breathe. No, she thought, no, no, no!

She burst through the door, the pistol in her hand, half-crazed with fear and ready to fight for her man, for her very life. She saw a confused scene of sprawled men and her mind reeled, unable to comprehend why so many were lying there. Hadn't there been only one shot?

Then an arm snaked around her neck, jerking her back and locking under her chin. Another arm reached out, and long fingers clamped around the hand that held the pistol, removing it from her grip.

"Funny thing, sweetheart, but I feel safer when you're unarmed," a low voice hissed in her ear.

At the sound of that voice, Jane's eyes closed, and two tears squeezed out from under the lids. "Grant," she whispered.

"Afraid so. You can tell me how glad you are to see me later; right now we're moving."

He released his arm lock about her neck, but when she tried to turn to face him, he caught her right arm and pulled it up behind her back, not so high that she was in pain, but high enough that she would be if he moved it even a fraction of an inch higher. "Move!" he barked, thrusting her forward, and Jane stumbled under the force of the motion, wrenching her arm and emitting an involuntary cry.

"You're hurting me," she whimpered, still dazed and trying to understand. "Grant, wait!"

"Cut the crap," he advised, kicking open the door and shoving her out into the searing white sunlight. The transport truck was sitting there, and he didn't hesitate. "Get in. We're going for a ride."

He opened the door and half lifted, half threw Jane into the truck, sending her sprawling on the seat. She cried out, her soft cry knifing through him, but he told himself not to be a fool; she didn't need anyone to look after her. Like a cat, she always landed on her feet.

Jane scrambled to a sitting position, her dark eyes full of tears as she stared at his battered, bloody face in both pain and horror. She wanted to reassure him, tell him that it had all been an act, a desperate gamble to save both their lives, but he didn't seem inclined to listen. Surely he wouldn't so easily forget everything they'd shared, everything they'd been to each other! Still, she couldn't give up. She'd lifted her hand to reach out for him when a movement in the door beyond them caught her eye, and she screamed a warning.

"Grant!"

He whirled, and as he did Turego lifted the rifle he held and fired. The explosive crack of sound split the air, but still Jane heard, felt, sensed the grunt of pain that Grant gave as he dropped to one knee and lifted the pistol. Turego lunged to one side, looking for cover, but the pistol spat fire, and a small red flower bloomed high on Turego's right shoulder, sending him tumbling back through the door.

Jane heard someone screaming, but the sound was high and far away. She lunged through the open door of the truck, falling to her hands and knees on the hot, rocky ground. Grant was on his knees, leaning against the running board of the truck, his right hand clamped over his upper left arm, and bright red blood was dripping through his fingers. He looked up at her, his golden eyes bright and burning with the fire of battle, fierce even in his swollen and discolored face.

She went a little mad then. She grabbed him by his undershirt and hauled him to his feet, using a strength she'd had no idea she possessed. "Get in the truck!" she screamed, pushing him in the door. "Damn it, get in the truck! Are you trying to get yourself killed?"

He winced as the side of the seat smashed into his bruised ribs; Jane was shoving at him and screaming like a banshee, tears streaming down her face. "Would you shut up!" he yelled, painfully pulling himself inside.

"Don't you tell me to shut up!" she screamed, pushing him until he moved over. She slapped the tears from her cheeks and climbed into the truck herself. "Get out of the way so I can get this thing started! Are there any keys? Where are the keys? Oh, damn!" She dove head-first under the steering wheel, feeling under the dash and pulling wires out frantically.

"What're you doing?" Grant groaned, his mind reeling with pain.

"I'm hot-wiring the truck!" she sobbed.

"You're tearing the damned wiring out!" If she was trying to disable their only transportation, she was doing a good job of it. He started to yank her out from under the steering wheel when suddenly she bounced out on her own, jamming the clutch in and touching two wires together. The motor roared into life, and Jane slammed the door on her side, shoved the truck into gear and let out on the clutch. The truck lurched forward violently, throwing Grant against the door.

"Put it in low gear!" he yelled, pulling himself into a sitting position and getting a tighter grip on the seat.

"I don't know where the low gear is! I just took what I could find!"

Swearing, he reached for the gear shift, the pain in his wounded arm like a hot knife as he closed his hand over the knob. There was nothing he could do about the pain, so he ignored it. "Put the clutch in," he ordered. "I'll change gears. Jane, put the damned clutch in!"

"Stop yelling at me!" she screamed, jamming in the clutch. Grant put the truck in the proper gear and she let out on the clutch; this time the truck moved more smoothly. She put her foot on the gas pedal, shoving it to the floor, and slung the heavy truck around a corner, sending its rear wheels sliding on the gravel.

"Turn right," Grant directed, and she took the next right.

The truck was lunging under her heavy urging, its transmission groaning as she kept her foot down on the gas pedal.

"Change gears!"

"Change them yourself!"

"Put in the clutch!"

She put in the clutch, and he geared up. "When I

tell you, put in the clutch, and I'll change the gears, understand?"

She was still crying, swiping at her face at irregular intervals. Grant said, "Turn left," and she swung the truck in a turn that sent a pickup dodging to the side of the road to avoid them.

The road took them out of town, but they were only a couple of miles out when Grant said tersely, "Pull over." Jane didn't question him; she pulled over to the side of the road and stopped the truck.

"Okay, get out." Again she obeyed without question, jumping out and standing there awkwardly as he eased himself to the ground. His left arm was streaked with blood, but from the look on his face Jane knew that he wasn't about to stop. He shoved the pistol into his belt and slung the rifle over his shoulder. "Let's go."

"Where are we going?"

"Back into town. Your boyfriend won't expect us to double back on him. You can stop crying," he added cruelly. "I didn't kill him."

"He's not my boyfriend!" Jane spat, whirling on him.

"Sure looked like it from where I was."

"I was trying to catch him off guard! One of us had to stay free!"

"Save it," he advised, his tone bored. "I bought your act once, but it won't sell again. Now, are you going to walk?"

She decided that there was no use trying to reason with him now. When he'd calmed down enough to listen, when she'd calmed down enough to make a coherent explanation, then they'd get this settled. As she turned away from him, she looked in the open door of the truck and caught a glimpse of something shoved in the far corner of the floor. Her backpack! She crawled up in the truck and leaned far over to drag the pack out from under the seat; in the excitement, it had been totally overlooked and forgotten.

"Leave the damned thing!" Grant snapped.

"I need it," she snapped in return. She buckled it to her belt-loop again.

He drew the pistol out of his belt and Jane swallowed, her eyes growing enormous. Calmly he shot out one of the front tires of the truck, then stuck the pistol back into his belt.

"Why did you do that?" she whispered, swallowing again.

"So it'll look as if we were forced to abandon the truck."

He caught her upper arm in a tight grip and pulled her off the road. Whenever he heard an engine he forced her to the ground and they lay still until the sound had faded. Her blouse, so white and pretty only an hour or so before, became streaked with mud and torn in places where the thorns caught it. She gave it a brief glance, then forgot about it.

"When will Turego be after us again?" she panted.

"Soon. Impatient already?"

Grinding her teeth together, she ignored him. In twenty more minutes they approached the edge of the town again, and he circled it widely. She wanted to ask him what he was looking for, but after the way he'd just bitten her head off, she kept silent. She wanted to sit down to wash his bruised face, and bandage the wound in his arm, but she could do none of those things. He didn't want anything from her now.

Still, what else could she have done? There was no

way she could have known he was going to be able to escape. She'd had to use the best plan she had at the time.

Finally they slipped into a ramshackle shed behind an equally ramshackle house and collapsed on the ground in the relatively cool interior. Grant winced as he inadvertently strained his left arm, but when Jane started toward him, he gave her a cold glare that stopped her in her tracks. She sank back to the ground and rested her forehead on her drawn-up knees. "What are we going to do now?"

"We're getting out of the country, any way we can," he said flatly. "Your daddy hired me to bring you home, and that's what I'm going to do. The sooner I turn you over to him, the better."

CHAPTER ELEVEN

AFTER THAT JANE sat quietly, keeping her forehead down on her knees and closing her eyes. A cold desolation was growing inside her, filling her, thrusting aside anxiety and fear. What if she could never convince him that she hadn't betrayed him? With the life he'd led, it was probably something that he'd had to guard against constantly, so he wasn't even surprised by betrayal. She would try again to reason with him, of course; until he actually left her, she wouldn't stop trying. But…what if he wouldn't listen? What would she do then? Somehow she just couldn't imagine her future without Grant. The emotional distance between them now was agonizing, but she could still lift her head and see him, take comfort in his physical proximity. What would she do if he weren't there at all?

The heat and humidity began building, negating the coolness of the shade offered by the old, open-sided shed, and in the distance thunder rumbled as it announced the approach of the daily rain. A door creaked loudly, and soon a stooped old woman, moving slowly, came around the side of the house to a small pen where pigs had been grunting occasionally as they lay in the mud and tried to escape the heat. Grant watched her, his eyes alert, not a muscle moving. There wasn't any real danger that she would see them; weeds and bushes grew out of control, over waist-high, between the house and the shed, with only a faint little-used path leading to the shed. The pigs squealed in loud enthusiasm when the old woman fed them, and after chatting fondly to them for a moment she laboriously made her way back into the shack.

Jane hadn't moved a muscle, not opening her eyes even when the pigs had begun celebrating the arrival of food. Grant looked at her, a faint puzzlement creeping into the coldness of his eyes. It was unlike her to sit so quietly and not investigate the noise. She knew it was the pigs, of course, but she hadn't looked up to see what was making them squeal so loudly, or even when the old woman had begun talking to them. She was normally as curious as a cat, poking her nose into everything whether it concerned her or not. It was difficult to tell, the way she had her head down, but he thought that she was pale; the few freckles he could see stood out plainly.

An image flashed into his mind of Turego bending his head to press his mouth to Jane's, and the way Jane had stood so quiescently to accept that kiss. Rage curled inside him again, and his fists knotted. Damn her! How could she have let that slime touch her?

The thunder moved closer, cracking loudly, and the air carried the scent of rain. Wind began to swirl, darting through the shed and bringing with it welcome coolness. The air was alive, almost shining with the electrical energy it carried. The small creatures began to take shelter, birds winging back and forth in an effort to find the most secure perch to wait out the storm.

During the rain would be a good time to leave, as everyone else would take shelter until it was over, but his body ached from the beating he'd received, and his left arm was still sullenly oozing blood. They were in no immediate danger here, so he was content to rest. Night would be an even better time to move.

The rain started, going from a sprinkle to a deluge in less than a minute. The ground wasn't able to soak up that enormous amount of water, and a small stream began to trickle through the shed. Grant got up, stifling a groan as his stiff body protested, and found a seat on top of a half-rotten vegetable crate. It gave a little, but held his weight.

Jane still hadn't moved. She didn't look up until the moisture began to dampen the seat of her pants; then her head lifted and she realized that a river was beginning to flow around her. She didn't look at Grant, though she moved away from the water, shifting to the side. She sat with her back to him and resumed her earlier posture, with her knees drawn up, her arms locked around her legs, and her head bent down to rest on her knees.

Grant knew how to wait; patience was second nature to him. He could hold a position all day long, if necessary, ignoring physical discomfort as if it didn't exist. But the silence and lack of motion in the shed began to grate on his nerves, because it wasn't what he'd learned to expect from Jane. Was she planning something?

Eventually the rain stopped, and the steamy heat began to build again. "Are we going to sit here all day?" Jane finally asked fretfully, breaking her long silence.

"Might as well. I don't have anything better to do. Do you?"

She didn't answer that, or ask any more questions, realizing that he wasn't in the mood to tell her anything. She was so hungry that she was sick, but there wasn't any food in her pack, and she wasn't about to complain to him. She dropped her head back to her knees and tried to seek refuge in a nap; at least then she could forget how miserable she was.

She actually managed to sleep, and he woke her at twilight, shaking her shoulder. "Let's go," he said, pulling her to her feet. Jane's heart stopped because just for that moment his touch was strong but gentle, and she had the crazy hope that he'd cooled down and come to his senses while she was napping. But then he dropped her arm and stepped away from her, his face hard, and the hope died.

She followed him like a toy on a string, right in his footsteps, stopping when he stopped, always the same distance behind him. He went boldly into the center of town, walking down the streets as if no one at all was looking for him, let alone a small army. Several people looked at them oddly, but no one stopped them. Jane supposed they did look strange: a tall blond man with a bruised, swollen face and a rifle carried easily in one hand, followed by a woman with wild tangled hair, dirty clothes and a backpack buckled to her belt and swinging against her legs as she walked. Well, everything seemed strange to her, too. She felt as if they'd gotten lost in a video game, with crazy neon images flashing at her. After a moment she realized that the images were real; a street sign advertising a cantina flashed its message in neon pink and blue.

What was he doing? They were attracting so much notice that Turego would have to hear of it if he asked any questions at all. For all Grant knew, Turego could have the local law enforcement looking for them under trumped-up charges; Turego certainly had enough authority to mobilize any number of people in the search. It was as if Grant wanted Turego to find them.

He turned down a side street and paused outside a small, dimly lit cantina. "Stay close to me, and keep your mouth shut," he ordered tersely, and entered.

It was hot and smoky in the small bar, and the strong odor of alcohol mixed with sweat permeated the air. Except for the waitress, a harried looking girl, and two sultry prostitutes, there were no other women there. Several men eyed Jane, speculation in their dark eyes, but then they looked at Grant and turned back to their drinks, evidently deciding that she wasn't worth the trouble.

Grant found them space at a small table at the back, deep in the shadows. After a while the waitress made it over to them, and without asking Jane her preference, Grant ordered two tequilas.

Jane stopped the waitress. "Wait—do you have lime juice?" At the young woman's nod, she heaved a sigh of relief. "A glass of lime juice, instead of the tequila, please."

Grant lit a cigarette, cupping his hands around the flame. "Are you on the wagon or something?"

"I don't drink on an empty stomach."

"We'll get something to eat later. This place doesn't run to food."

She waited until their drinks were in front of them before saying anything else to him. "Isn't it dangerous for us to be here? Any of Turego's men could have seen us walking down the street."

His eyes were narrow slits as he stared at her through the blue smoke of his cigarette. "Why should that worry you? Don't you think he'd welcome you back with open arms?"

Jane leaned forward, her own eyes narrowed. "Listen to me. I had to buy time, and I did it the only way I could think of. I'm sorry I didn't have time to explain it to you beforehand, but I don't think Turego would have let me call 'time out' and huddle with you! If he'd tied me up, too, there would have been no way I could help you!"

"Thanks, honey, but I can do without your sort of help," he drawled, touching his left eye, which was puffy and red.

Anger seared her; she was innocent, and she was tired of being treated like Benedict Arnold. She thought of pouring the lime juice in his lap, but her stomach growled and revenge took a distant second place to putting something in her empty stomach, even if it was just fruit juice. She sat back in her chair and sipped, wanting to make the juice last as long as possible.

The minutes crawled by, and Jane began to feel a twitch between her shoulder blades. Every second they sat there increased the danger, gave Turego a better chance of finding them. The abandoned truck wouldn't fool him for long.

A man slipped into the chair beside her and Jane jumped, her heart flying into her throat. He gave her only a cursory glance before turning his attention to Grant. He was a nondescript character, his clothing worn, his face covered by a couple of days' growth of beard, and his smell of stale alcohol made Jane wrinkle her nose. But then he said a few words to Grant, so quietly that she couldn't understand them, and it all clicked into place.

Grant had advertised their presence not because he

wanted Turego to find them, but because he wanted someone else to find them. It had been a gamble, but it had paid off. He was no longer in the business, but he was known, and he'd trusted his reputation to pull in a contact. This man was probably just a peripheral character, but he would have his uses.

"I need transport," Grant said. "Within the hour. Can you manage it?"

"Sí," the man said, slowly nodding his head for emphasis.

"Good. Have it sitting behind the Blue Pelican exactly one hour from now. Put the keys under the right seat, get out, and walk away."

The man nodded again. "Good luck, amigo."

That hard, lopsided smile curved Grant's lips. "Thanks. I could use some about now."

The man blended in with the crowd, then was gone. Jane slowly twirled the glass of juice between her palms, keeping her eyes on the table. "Now that you've made your contact, shouldn't we get out of here?"

Grant lifted the tequila to his mouth, his strong throat working as he swallowed the sharp tasting liquid. "We'll wait a while longer."

No, it wouldn't do to follow the other man too closely. George had always told her how important it was to make contact without seeming to. The man had taken a chance by walking up to them so openly, but then, Grant had taken a chance by making himself so available. It had probably been clear that the situation was desperate, though Grant looked as if he was thinking about nothing more important than going to sleep. He was sprawled in his chair, his eyes half-closed, and if

Jane hadn't noticed that he kept his left hand on the rifle she would have thought that he was totally relaxed.

"Do you suppose we could find a bathroom?" she asked, keeping her tone light.

"In here? I doubt it."

"Anywhere."

"Okay. Are you finished with that?" He downed the rest of his tequila, and Jane did the same with her lime juice. Her skin was crawling again; she felt that tingling on the back of her neck, and it intensified as she stood up.

They threaded their way through the tangle of feet and tables and chairs to the door, and as soon as they stepped outside Jane said, "I think we were being watched."

"I know we were. That's why we're going in the opposite direction of the Blue Pelican."

"What on earth is the Blue Pelican? How do you know so much about this town? Have you been here before?"

"No, but I keep my eyes open. The Blue Pelican is the first cantina we passed."

Now she remembered. It was the cantina with the flashing neon sign, the one that had given her such an intense feeling of unreality.

They were walking down the small side street into a yawning cave of darkness. The street wasn't paved, and there were no sidewalks, no streetlights, not even one of the incongruous neon signs to lend its garish light. The ground was uneven beneath her boots, and the sour smell of old garbage surrounded her. Jane didn't think; her hand shot out, and she grabbed Grant's belt.

He hesitated, then resumed walking without saying

anything. Jane swallowed, belatedly realizing that she could have found herself sailing over his shoulder again, as she had the first time she'd grabbed him from behind. What would she do if she no longer had him to cling to in the dark? Stand around wringing her hands? She'd already come a long way from the child who had sat in a terrified stupor for days, and perhaps it was time for one step more. Slowly, deliberately, Jane released her grip on his belt and let her arm drop to her side.

He stopped and looked around at her, darkness shrouding his features. "I don't mind you holding on to my belt."

She remained silent, feeling his reluctant curiosity, but unable to give him any explanation. All her milestones had been inner ones, attained only by wrenching effort, and this wasn't something she could easily talk about. Not even the frighteningly expensive child psychologist to whom her parents had taken her had been able to draw her out about the kidnapping. Everyone knew about the nightmares she'd had, and her abrupt, unreasonable fear of the dark, but she'd never told anyone the details of her experience. Not her parents, not even Chris, and he'd been her best friend long before he'd been her husband. In all the years since the kidnapping, she'd told only one person, trusted only one person enough. Now there was a distance between them that she'd tried to bridge, but he kept pushing her away. No matter how she wanted to throw herself into his arms, she had to stand alone, because soon she might have no choice in the matter.

The fear of being alone in the dark was nothing compared to the fear that she might be alone for the rest of her life.

He wove a crazy path through the town, crisscrossing, backtracking, changing their route so many times that Jane completely lost her sense of direction. She chugged along doggedly, staying right on his heels. He stopped once, and stood guard while Jane sneaked in the back of the local version of a greasy spoon. The plumbing was pre-World War II, the lighting was a single dim bulb hanging from the ceiling, and the carcass of an enormous cockroach lay on its back in the corner, but she wasn't in the mood to quibble. At least the plumbing worked, and when she turned on the water in the cracked basin a thin, lukewarm stream came out. She washed her hands and, bending over, splashed water on her face. There was no towel, so she wiped her hands on her pants and left her face to dry naturally.

When she tiptoed out of the building, Grant stepped from the shadows where he had concealed himself and took her arm. They weren't far from the Blue Pelican, as it turned out; when they turned the corner, she could see the blue-and-pink sign flashing. But Grant didn't walk straight to it; he circled the entire area, sometimes standing motionless for long minutes while he waited, and watched.

At last they approached the old Ford station wagon that was parked behind the cantina, but even then he was cautious. He raised the hood and used his cigarette lighter to examine the motor. Jane didn't ask what he was looking for, because she had the chilling idea that she knew. He closed the hood as quietly as possible, evidently reassured.

"Get in, and get the keys out from under the seat."

She opened the door. The dome light didn't come on, but that was to be expected. Doing a little checking on her own, she peered over the back of the seat, holding her breath in case there was actually someone there. But the floorboard was empty, and her breath hissed out of her lungs in relief.

Leaning over, she swept her hand under the seat, searching for the keys. The other door opened, and the car swayed under Grant's weight. "Hurry," he snapped.

"I can't find the keys!" Her scrabbling fingers found a lot of dirt, a few screws, a scrap of paper, but no keys. "Maybe this isn't the right car!"

"It'll have to do. Check again."

She got down on the floor and reached as far under the seat as she could, sweeping her hands back and forth. "Nothing. Try under yours."

He leaned down, extending his arm to search under his seat. Swearing softly, he pulled out a single key wired to a small length of wood. Muttering under his breath about damned people not being able to follow simple instructions, he put the key in the ignition and started the car.

Despite its age, the engine was quiet and smooth. Grant shifted into gear and backed out of the alley. He didn't turn on the headlights until they were well away from the Blue Pelican and the well-lit main street.

Jane leaned back in the musty smelling seat, unable to believe that at last they seemed to be well on their way. So much had happened since that morning that she'd lost her sense of time. It couldn't be late; it was probably about ten o'clock, if that. She watched the road for a while, hypnotized by the way it unwound just ahead of the reach of their headlights, tired but unable to sleep. "Are we still going to Limon?"

"Why? Is that what you told your lover?"

Jane sat very still, clenching her teeth against the anger that shook her. All right, she'd try one more time. "He isn't my lover, and I didn't tell him anything. All I was trying to do was to stay untied until I could catch one of them off guard and get his gun." She spat the words out evenly, but her chest was heaving as she tried to control her anger. "Just how do you think I got the pistol that you took away from me?"

She felt that was a point that he couldn't ignore, but he did, shrugging it away. "Look, you don't have to keep making explanations," he said in a bored tone. "I'm not interested—"

"Stop the car!" she shouted, enraged.

"Don't start pitching one of your fits," he warned, slanting her a hard look.

Jane dived for the steering wheel, too angry to care if she caused them to crash. He pushed her off with one hand, cursing, but Jane ducked under his arm and caught the wheel, wrenching it violently toward her. Grant hit the brake, fighting to keep the car under control with one hand while he held Jane off with the other. She caught the wheel again and pulled it, and the car jolted violently as it hit the shoulder of the road.

Grant let go of her and wrestled with the car as it slewed back and forth on the narrow road. He braked sharply, finally bringing the car to a complete halt so he could give his full attention to Jane, but even before the car had completely stopped she threw the door open and jumped out. "I'll get myself out of Costa Rica!" she yelled, slamming the door.

He got out of the car. "Jane, come back here," he warned as she started walking off.

"I'm not going another mile with you, not another inch!"

"You're going if I have to hog-tie you," he said, coming after her, his stride measured.

She didn't stop. "That's your remedy for everything, isn't it?" she sneered.

Without warning, he sprinted. He moved so fast that Jane didn't have time to run. She gave a startled cry, twisting away as he reached her; his outstretched hand caught her blouse and Jane jerked as he stopped her. It was doubly infuriating to find herself so easily caught, and with a fresh burst of rage she threw herself away from him, twisting and doubling her lithe body, trying to break his grip.

He caught her wildly flailing arm and pinned it to her side. "Damn, woman, why do you have to do everything the hard way?" he panted.

"Let...go!" she shouted, but he wrapped his arms around her, holding her arms pinned down. She kicked and shrieked, but he was too strong; there was nothing she could do as he carried her back to the car.

But he had to release her with one arm so he could open the car door, and when he did she twisted violently, at the same time lifting her feet. The combination of the twist and the sudden addition of weight broke his grip, and she slid under his arm. He grabbed for her again, his fingers hooking in the low neckline of the blouse. The fabric parted under the strain, tearing away from her shoulders.

Tears spurted from Jane's eyes as she scrambled to cover her breasts, holding the ruined cloth over them. "Now look what you've done!" Turning away from him, she burst into sobs, her shoulders shaking.

The raw, hard sobs that tore from her throat were so violent that he dropped his outstretched arms. Wearily he rubbed his face. Why couldn't she cry with sedate little sniffles, instead of these sobs that sounded as if she had been beaten? Despite everything that had happened, he wanted to take her in his arms and hold her head to his chest, stroke her dark hair and whisper that everything was going to be all right.

She whirled on him, wiping her face with one hand and clutching the ruined blouse to her breasts with the other. "Think about a few things!" she said hoarsely. "Think about how I got that pistol. And think about Turego. Remember when he came up behind you with the rifle, and I warned you? Did you notice, before you shot him, that his face was bloody? Do you remember the way his nose was bleeding? Do you think it was the altitude that made his nose bleed? You big, stupid, boneheaded jackass!" she bellowed, so beside herself with fury that she was shaking her fist under his nose. "Damn it, can't you tell that I love you?"

Grant was as still as stone, not a muscle moving in his face, but he felt winded, as if he'd just taken a huge blow in the chest. Everything hit him at once, and he staggered under the weight of it. She was right. Turego's face had been bloody, but he hadn't thought anything about it at the time. He'd been so damned angry and jealous that he hadn't been thinking at all, only reacting to what had looked like betrayal. Not only had she done some quick thinking to avoid being tied up, she'd charged to his rescue as soon as she could, and when he remembered the way she'd looked when she came through that door, so white and wild—Turego's goons were probably lucky that he'd gotten free first. She loved him! He stared down at her, at the small fist that was waving dangerously close to his nose. She was utterly magnificent, her hair a wild tangle around her shoulders, her face filled with a temper that burned out of control, yelling at him like some banshee. She clutched that ridiculous scrap of cloth to her breasts with the hand that wasn't threatening his profile. Indomitable. Courageous. Maddening. And so damned desirable that he was suddenly shaking with need.

He caught her fist and jerked her to him, holding her to him so tightly that she gasped, his face buried against her hair.

She was still struggling against him, beating at his back with her fists and crying again. "Let me go! Please, just let me go."

"I can't," he whispered, and caught her chin, turning her face up to him. Fiercely he ground his mouth down on hers and, like a cornered cat, she tried to bite him. He jerked his head back, laughing, a wild joy running through him. The torn blouse had fallen away, and her naked breasts were flattened against him, their soft fullness reminding him of how good it felt when she wasn't fighting him. He kissed her again, roughly, and cupped her breast in his palm, rubbing his thumb over the velvet nipple and making it tighten.

Jane whimpered under the onslaught of his mouth, but her temper had worn itself out, and she softened against him, suddenly aware that she'd gotten through to him. She wanted to hold on to her anger, but she couldn't hold a grudge. All she could do was kiss him back, her arms sliding up to lock around his neck. His hand burned her breast, his thumb exciting her acutely sensitive skin and beginning to tighten the coil of desire deep in her loins. He had no need to hold her still for his kisses now, so he put his other hand on her bottom and urged her against him, demonstrating graphically that she wasn't the only one affected.

He lifted his mouth from hers, pressing his lips to her forehead. "I swear, that temper of yours is something," he whispered. "Do you forgive me?"

That was a silly question; what was she supposed to say, considering that she was hanging around his neck like a Christmas ornament? "No," she said, rubbing her face into the hollow of his throat, seeking his warm, heady male scent. "I'm going to save this to throw up at you the next time we have a fight." She wanted to say "for the rest of our lives," but though his arms were hard around her, he hadn't yet said that he loved her. She wasn't going to dig for the words, knowing that he might not be able to say them and mean it.

"You will, too," he said, and laughed. Reluctantly his arms loosened, and he reached up, removing her arms from his neck. "I'd like to stay like this, but we need to get to Limon." He looked down at her breasts, and a taut look came over his battered face. "When this is over with, I'm going to take you to a hotel and keep you in bed until neither of us can walk."

They got back in the car, and Jane removed the remnants of the blouse, stuffing it in the backpack and pulling on Grant's camouflage shirt that she'd put in the pack that morning. It would have wrapped around her twice, and the shoulder seams hung almost to her elbows. She rolled the sleeves up as far as they would go, then gathered the long tails and tied them at her waist. Definitely not high fashion, she thought, but she was covered.

The Ford rolled into Limon in the early hours of the morning, and though the streets were nearly deserted, it was obvious that the port was a well-populated city of medium size. Jane's hands clenched on the car seat. Were they safe, then? Had Turego been fooled by the abandoned truck?

"What now?"

"Now I try to get in touch with someone who can get us out tonight. I don't want to wait until morning."

So he thought Turego's men were too close for safety. Was it never going to end? She wished they had remained in the jungle, hidden so deeply in the rain forest that no one would ever have found them.

Evidently Grant had been in Limon before; he negotiated the streets with ease. He drove to the train station, and Jane gave him a puzzled look. "Are we going to take the train?"

"No, but there's a telephone here. Come on."

Limon wasn't an isolated jungle village, or even a tiny town at the edge of the forest; it was a city, with all of the rules of a city. He had to leave the rifle in the back of the station wagon, but he stuck the pistol into his boot. Even without his being obviously armed, Jane thought there was no chance at all of them going anywhere without being noticed. They both looked as if they'd come fresh from a battle, which, in effect, they had. The ticket agent eyed them with sharp curiosity, but Grant ignored him, heading straight for a telephone. He called someone named Angel, and his voice was sharp as he demanded a number. Hanging up, he fed more coins into the slot, then dialed another number.

"Who are you calling?" Jane whispered.

"An old friend."

The old friend's name was Vincente, and intense satisfaction was on Grant's face when he hung up. "They're pulling us out of here. In another hour we'll be home free."

"Who's 'they'?" Jane asked.

"Don't ask too many questions."

She scowled at him, then something else took her attention. "While we're here, could we clean up a little? You look awful."

There was a public bathroom—empty, she was thankful to see—and Grant washed his face while Jane brushed her hair out and quickly pulled it back into a loose braid. Then she wet a towel and painstakingly cleaned the wound on Grant's arm; the bullet hadn't penetrated, but the graze was deep and ugly. After washing it with a strong smelling soap, she produced a small first-aid kit from her backpack.

"One of these days I'm going to see what all's in that thing," Grant growled.

Jane uncapped a small bottle of alcohol and poured it on the graze. He caught a sharp breath, and said something extremely explicit. "Don't be such a baby," Jane scolded. "You didn't make this much fuss when you were shot."

She smeared an antibiotic cream on the wound, then wrapped gauze snugly around his arm and tied the ends together. After replacing the kit, she made certain the pack was still securely buckled to her belt-loop.

Grant opened the door, then abruptly stepped back and closed it again. Jane had been right behind him, and the impact of their bodies made her stagger. He caught her arm, keeping her from falling. "Turego and a few of his men just came into the station." He looked around, his eyes narrowed and alert. "We'll go out a window."

Her heart pounding, Jane stared in dismay at the row of small, high windows that lined the restroom. They were well over her head. "I can't get up there."

"Sure you can." Grant bent down and grasped her around the knees, lifting her until she could reach the windows. "Open one, and go through it. Quick! We only have a minute."

"But how will you get up—"

"I'll make it! Jane, get through that window!"

She twisted the handle and shoved the window open. Without giving herself time to think about how high above the ground on the other side it might be, she grasped the bottom edge of the frame and hauled herself through, jumping into the darkness and hoping she didn't kill herself on a railroad tie or something. She landed on her hands and knees in loose gravel, and she had to bite back a cry of pain as the gravel cut her palms. Quickly she scrambled out of the way, and a moment later Grant landed beside her.

"Are you all right?" he asked, hauling her to her feet.

"I think so. No broken bones," she reported breathlessly.

He started running along the side of the building, dragging her behind him. They heard a shot behind them, but didn't slow down or look back. Jane stumbled and was saved from falling only by his grip on her hand. "Can't we go back for the Ford?" she wailed.

"No. We'll have to get there on foot."

"Get where?"

"To the pickup point."

"How far is that?"

"Not too far."

"Give it to me in yards and miles!" she demanded

He dodged down a street and pulled her into the deep shadows of an alley. He was laughing. "Maybe a mile," he said, and kissed her, his mouth hard and hungry, his tongue finding hers. He hugged her fiercely.

"Whatever you did to Turego, honey, he looks like hell."

"I think I broke his nose," she admitted.

He laughed again. "I think you did, too. It's swollen all over his face. He won't forget you for a long time!"

"Never, if I have anything to do with it. We're going to tell the government about that man," she vowed.

"Later, honey. Right now, we're getting out of here."

CHAPTER TWELVE

A HELICOPTER CAME in low and fast, and settled lightly on its runners, looking like a giant mosquito. Grant and Jane ran across the small field, bent low against the wind whipped up by the rotors, which the pilot hadn't cut. Behind them people were pouring out of their houses to see what the uproar was about. Jane began to giggle, lightheaded with the triumph of the moment; by the time Grant boosted her into the helicopter, she was laughing so hard she was crying. They'd done it! Turego couldn't catch them now. They would be out of the country before he could mobilize his own helicopters to search for them, and he wouldn't dare pursue them across the border.

Grant flashed her a grin, telling her that he understood her idiotic laughter. He shouted, "Buckle up!" at her, then levered himself into the seat beside the pilot and gave him the thumbs-up sign. The pilot nodded, grinned, and the helicopter rose into the night. Grant put on the headset that would allow him to talk to the pilot, but there wasn't one in the back. Jane gave up trying to hear what they were saying and gripped the sides of her seat, staring out through the open sides of the helicopter. The night air swirled around her, and the world stretched out beyond the small craft. It was the first time she'd ever been in a helicopter, and it was a totally different sensation from being in a jet. She felt adrift in the velvet darkness, and she wished that it wasn't night, so she could see the land below.

The flight didn't take long, but when they set down, Jane recognized the airport and reached up to grab Grant's shoulder. "We're in San Jose!" she yelled, anxiety filling her voice. This was where it had all begun. Turego had plenty of men in the capitol!

Grant took off the headset. The pilot cut the rotors, and the noise began to decrease. They shook hands, and the pilot said, "Nice to see you again! Word filtered down that you were in the area, and that we should give you any assistance you asked for. Good luck. You'd better run. You have just enough time to get on that flight."

They jumped to the asphalt and began running toward the terminal. "What flight is that?" Jane panted.

"The flight to Mexico City that's leaving in about five minutes."

Mexico City! That sounded more like it! The thought lent her strength.

The terminal was almost deserted at that time of night, because the flight for Mexico City had already boarded. The ticket clerk stared at them as they approached, reminding Jane once again of how they looked. "Grant Sullivan and Jane Greer," Grant said tersely. "You're holding our tickets."

The clerk had regained his composure. "Yes, sir, and the plane," he returned in perfect English, handing over two ticket folders. "Ernesto will take you directly aboard."

Ernesto was an airport guard, and he led the way, running. Grant held Jane's hand to make certain she kept up with them. She had a fleeting thought about the pistol stuck in his boot, but they bypassed all check-points. Grant certainly had connections, she thought admiringly.

The jet was indeed waiting, and the smiling stewardess welcomed them aboard as calmly as if there was nothing unusual about them. Jane wanted to giggle again; maybe they didn't look as outlandish as she felt they did. After all, camouflage clothing was all the rage in the States. So what if Grant was sporting an almost black eye, a puffy lip and a bandage on his arm? Maybe they looked like journalists who had had a rough time in the field.

As soon as they were seated, the plane began rolling. As they buckled their seat belts, Grant and Jane exchanged glances. It was well and truly over now, but they still had some time together. The next stop was Mexico City, an enormous international city with shops, restaurants…and hotels. Her body longed for a bed, but even deeper than her weariness ran the tingling awareness that Grant would be in that bed with her. He lifted the armrest between their seats and pulled her over so her head nestled into the hollow of his shoulder. "Soon," he murmured against her temple. "In a couple of hours we'll be in Mexico. Home free."

"I'm going to call Dad as soon as we get there, so he and Mom will stop worrying." Jane sighed. "Do you have anyone to call? Does your family know where you were?"

His eyes took on that remote look. "No, they don't know anything about what I do. I'm not close to my family, not anymore."

That was sad, but Jane supposed that when someone was in the business Grant had been in, it was safer for his family not to be close to him. She turned her face into his neck and closed her eyes, holding tightly to him in an effort to let him know that he wasn't alone anymore. Had his nights been spent like hers, lying awake in bed, so achingly alone that every nerve in her body cried out against it?

She slept, and Grant did, too, exhaustion finally sweeping over him as he allowed his bruised body to relax. With her in his arms, it was easy to find the necessary relaxation. She nestled against him as trustingly as a child, but he could never forget that she was a woman, as fierce and elemental as wind or fire. She could have been the spoiled debutante he'd expected. It was what she should have been, and no one would have thought the less of her for being the product of her environment— no one expected her to be any more than that. But she'd risen above that, and above the crippling trauma of her childhood, to become a woman of strength and humor and passion.

She was a woman in whose arms a wary, battered, burnt-out warrior could sleep.

The sky was turning pearl pink with dawn when they landed in Mexico City. The terminal was teeming with people scurrying to catch early flights, a multitude of languages and accents assailing the air. Grant hailed a cab, which took them on a hair-raising ride through traffic that made every moment an exercise in survival—or it would have been hair-raising if Jane had had the energy to care. After what she'd been through, the Mexico City traffic looked mundane.

The city was beautiful at dawn, with its wide avenues and fragrant trees; and the white of the buildings glowed rosily in the early morning sun. The sky was already a deep blue bowl overhead, and the air carried that velvet feel that only the warmer climes achieved. Despite the odor of exhaust fumes she could smell the sweetness of orange blossoms, and Grant was warm beside her, his strong leg pressed against hers.

The desk clerk in the pristine white, high-rise hotel was reluctant to give them a room without a reservation. His black eyes kept wandering to Grant's bruised face as he rattled off excuses in rapid-fire Spanish. Grant shrugged, reached into his pocket and peeled off a couple of bills from a roll. The clerk suddenly smiled; that changed everything. Grant signed them in, and the clerk slid a key across the desk. After taking a few steps, Grant turned back. "By the way," he said easily, "I don't want any interruptions. If anyone calls or asks, we aren't here. *¿Comprende?* I'm dead tired, and I get irritable if I'm jerked out of a sound sleep."

His voice was full of silky, lazy menace, and the clerk nodded rapidly.

With Grant's arm draped across her shoulders, they walked over to the bank of elevators. He punched the button for the nineteenth floor, and the doors slid silently shut. Jane said dazedly, "We're safe."

"Having trouble believing it?"

"I'm going to get that man. He's not going to get off scot-free!"

"He won't," Grant drawled. "He'll be taken care of, through channels."

"I don't want 'channels' to take care of him! I want to do it myself!"

He smiled down at her. "You're a bloodthirsty little wench, aren't you? I almost think you enjoyed this."

"Only parts of it," she replied, giving him a slow smile.

Their room was spacious, with a terrace for sunning, a separate sitting area with a dining table and a stunningly modern bath. Jane poked her head into it and withdrew with a beatific smile on her face. "All the modern conveniences," she crowed.

Grant was studying the in-house registry for room service. Picking up the phone, he ordered two enormous breakfasts, and Jane's mouth watered at the thought. It had been almost twenty-four hours since they'd eaten. While they were waiting for their food, she began the process of making a phone call to Connecticut. It took about five minutes for the call to go through, and Jane sat with the receiver gripped tightly in her hand, taut with the need to hear her parents' voices.

"Mom? Mom, it's Jane! I'm all right—don't cry, I can't talk to you if you're crying," Jane said, and wiped away a few tears herself. "Put Dad on the line so I can tell him what's going on. We'll blubber together just as soon as I get home, I promise." She waited a few moments, smiling mistily at Grant, her dark eyes liquid.

"Jane? Is it really you?" Her father's voice boomed across the line.

"Yes, it really is. I'm in Mexico City. Grant got me out; we just flew in a few minutes ago."

Her father made a choked sound, and Jane realized that he was crying, too, but he controlled himself. "Well, what now?" he demanded. "When are you going to be here? Where are you going from there?"

"I don't know," she said, lifting her brows at Grant and taking the receiver from her ear. "Where are we going next?"

He took the phone from her. "This is Sullivan. We'll probably be here for a couple of days, getting some paperwork straightened out. We came in here without being checked for passports, but I'll have to make some calls before we can get into the States. Yes, we're okay. I'll let you know as soon as I find out something."

When he hung up, he turned to find Jane surveying him with pursed lips. "How did we get here without being checked for passports?"

"A few people turned their heads, that's all. They knew we were coming through. I'll report our passports as being lost, and get duplicates from the American Embassy. No big deal."

"How did you manage to set all that up so quickly? I know this wasn't the original plan."

"No, but we had some inside help." Sabin had been as good as his word, Grant reflected. All the old contacts had been there, and they had all been notified to give him whatever he needed.

"Your...former business associates?" Jane hazarded a guess.

"The less you know, the better. You pick up on this too damned quickly. Like hot-wiring that truck. Had you ever done it before?"

"No, but I watched you do it the first time," she explained, her eyes full of innocence.

He grunted. "Don't waste your time giving me that wide-eyed look."

A tap on the door and a singsong voice announced that room service had arrived in record time. Grant checked through the fish-eye viewer, then unbolted the door and let the young boy in. The aroma of hot coffee filled the room, and Jane's mouth started watering. She hovered over the boy as he set the food out on the table.

"Look at this," she crooned. "Fresh oranges and melon. Toast. Apricot Danish. Eggs. Butter. Real coffee!"

"You're drooling," Grant teased, giving the boy a generous tip, but he was just as ravenous, and between them they destroyed the array of food. Every crumb was gone and the pot of coffee was empty before they looked at each other and smiled.

"I feel almost human again," Jane sighed. "Now for a hot shower!"

She began unlacing her boots, pulling them off and sighing in relief as she wiggled her toes. Glancing at him, she saw that he was watching her with that lopsided smile that she loved so much. Her heart kicked into time and a half rhythm. "Aren't you going to shower with me?" she asked innocently, sauntering into the bathroom.

She was already under the deliciously warm spray of water, her head tilted up so it hit her directly in the face, when the shower door slid open and he joined her. She turned, wiping the moisture from her eyes, a smile ready on her lips, but the smile faded when she saw the mottled bruises on his rib cage and abdomen. "Oh, Grant," she whispered, reaching out to run her fingers lightly over the dark, ugly splotches. "I'm so sorry."

He gave her a quizzical look. He was sore and stiff, but nothing was broken and the bruises would fade. He'd suffered much worse than this, many times. Of course, if Turego had been able to carry the beating as far as he'd wanted, Grant knew that he probably would have died of internal injuries. But it hadn't happened, so he didn't worry about it. He caught her chin, turning her face up to him. "We're both covered with bruises, honey, in case you haven't noticed. I'm okay." He covered her mouth with his, tasting her sweetness with his tongue, easing her against him.

Their wet, naked bodies created a marvelous friction against each other, heating them, tightening the coil of desire. The rather boring process of soaping and rinsing became a lingering series of strokes, her hands slipping over the muscles and intriguing hardness of his body, his finding the soft curves and slopes of hers, the enticing depths. He lifted her off her feet and bent her back over his arm, kissing her breasts and sucking at her nipples until they were hard and reddened, tasting the freshness of newly soaped skin and the sweetness of her flesh that no soap could ever disguise. Jane writhed against him, her legs twining with his, and heat fogged his mind as he thrust himself against the juncture of her thighs.

She wanted him, wanted him, wanted him. Her body ached and burned. The bed was suddenly too far away. Her legs parted, lifting to wrap around his waist, and with a hoarse cry he pinned her to the wall. She shuddered as he drove into her, going as deep as he could with a single, powerful thrust, as if any distance at all between them was far too much. Digging his fingers into her hair, he pulled her head back and kissed her, his mouth wild and rough, the kiss deep, his tongue twining with hers, the water beating down on them. The power of his thrusts made her consciousness dim, but she clung to him, whimpering, begging him not to stop. He couldn't have stopped, couldn't even have slowed, his body demanding release inside her. The red mists that clouded his mind blocked out everything but the hot ecstasy of the way her body sheathed him, so softly, so tightly.

She cried out again and again as the almost unbearable waves of pleasure crashed over her. She clung tightly to his shoulders, trembling and shivering, the velvet clasp of her body driving him to the edge. He poured himself into her, heaving against her, feeling that he was dying a little, and yet so intensely alive that he almost screamed from the conflict.

They barely made it to the bed. Drying off had taken all their energy, and Jane was so weak she could barely walk. Grant was shaking in every muscle of his big body. They tumbled onto the bed, not caring that their wet hair soaked the pillows.

Grant reached out for her. "Crawl up here," he rumbled, hauling her on top of him. Blissfully, her eyes closing, she made herself comfortable on the hard expanse of his chest. He adjusted her legs, parting them, and her lashes fluttered open as he eased into her. A purr of pleasure escaped her lips, but she was so sleepy, so tired… "Now we can sleep," he said, his lips moving on her hair.

THE ROOM WAS hot when they awoke, the Mexican sun broiling through the closed curtains. Their skin was stuck together with perspiration and made a wet, sucking noise as Grant lifted her off him. He got up and turned the air-conditioning on full blast, and stood for a moment with the cold air hitting his naked body. Then he came back to the bed and turned her onto her back.

They scarcely left the bed that day. They made love, napped and woke to make love again. She couldn't get enough of him, nor he, it seemed, of her. There was no sense of urgency now to their lovemaking, only a deep reluctance to be parted from each other. He taught her the unlimited reaches of her own sensuality, tasting her all over, making love to her with his mouth until she was shivering and shuddering with pleasure, mindless, helpless. She told him that she loved him. She couldn't keep the words unsaid, not now, when she'd already told him anyway and soon the world would intrude on them again.

Night came, and finally they left the room. Walking hand in hand in the warm Mexican night, they sought out some shops that were open late. Jane bought a pink sundress that made her tanned skin look like honey, a pair of sandals and new underwear. Grant wasn't much on shopping, so she blithely picked out jeans, loafers and a white polo shirt for him. "You might as well change," she instructed, pushing him toward the dressing room. "We're going out to eat tonight."

There wasn't any talking her out of it, either. It wasn't until he was seated across from her in a dimly lit restaurant with a bottle of wine between them that he realized this was the first time in years that he'd been with a woman in a strictly social setting. They had nothing to do but eat and talk, sip the wine, and think about what they were going to do when they got back to the hotel. Even after he'd retired, he'd kept to himself on the farm, sometimes going for weeks without seeing another human being. When the need for supplies had forced him to go into town, he'd gone straight there and back, a lot of times without speaking to anyone. He hadn't been able to stand anyone else around him. But now he was relaxed, not even thinking about the strangers surrounding him, accepting their presence but not noticing them, because his mind and his senses were on Jane.

She was radiant, incandescent with energy. Her dark eyes shone; her tanned skin glowed; her laughter sparkled. Her breasts thrust against the bodice of the sundress, her nipples puckered by the coolness of the restaurant, and desire began to stir inside him again. They didn't have much more time together; soon they would be back in the States, and his job would be finished. It was too soon, far too soon. He hadn't had his fill yet of the taste of her, the wild sweetness of her body beneath him, or the way her laughter somehow eased all the knots of tension inside him.

They went back to the hotel, and back to bed. He made love to her furiously, trying to sate himself, trying to hoard enough memories to hold him during the long, empty years ahead. Being alone was a habit deeply ingrained in him; he wanted her, but couldn't see taking her back to the farm with him, and there was no way he could fit into her world. She liked having people around her, while he was more comfortable with a wall at his back. She was outgoing, while he was controlled, secretive.

She knew, too, that it was almost over. Lying on his chest, with the darkness wrapped around them like a blanket, she talked. It was a gift that she gave him, the tales of her childhood, where she'd gone to school, her food and music preferences, what she liked to read. Because she talked, he found it easier to return the favor, his voice low and rusty as he told her about the white-haired young boy he'd been, his skin burned dark by the hot, south Georgia summers, running wild in the swamp. He'd learned to hunt and fish almost as soon as he'd learned how to walk. He told her about playing football during high school, chasing after the cheerleaders, getting drunk and raising hell, then trying to sneak into the house so his mother wouldn't catch him.

Her fingers played in the hair on his chest, aware that silence had fallen because he'd reached the point in his story where his life had changed. There were no more easy tales of growing up.

"Then what happened?" she whispered.

His chest rose and fell. "Vietnam happened. I was drafted when I was eighteen. I was too damned good at sneaking through jungles, so that's where they put me. I went home, once, for R & R, but the folks were just the same as always, while I was nothing like what I had been. We couldn't even talk to each other. So I went back."

"And stayed?"

"Yeah. I stayed." His voice was flat.

"How did you get into the secret agent business, or whatever you call it?"

"Covert activities. High risk missions. The war ended, and I came home, but there was nothing for me to do. What was I going to do, work in a grocery store, when I'd been trained to such an edge that people would be taking their lives in their hands to walk up to me and ask the price of eggs? I guess I'd have settled down eventually, but I didn't want to hang around to find out. I was embarrassing the folks, and I was a stranger to them anyway. When an old colleague contacted me, I took him up on his offer."

"But you're retired now. Did you go back to Georgia?"

"Just for a few days, to let them know where I'd be. I couldn't settle there; too many people knew me, and I wanted to be left alone. So I bought a farm close to the mountains in Tennessee, and I've been hibernating there ever since. Until your dad hired me to fetch you home."

"Have you ever married? Been engaged?"

"No," he said, and kissed her. "That's enough questions. Go to sleep."

"Grant?"

"Hmmm?"

"Do you think he's really given up?"

"Who?"

"Turego."

Amusement laced his voice. "Honey, I promise you, he'll be taken care of. Don't worry about it. Now that you're safe and sound, steps can be taken to neutralize him."

"You're using some ominous sounding phrases. What do 'taken care of' and 'neutralize' mean?"

"That he's going to be spending some time in those gracious Central American jails that everyone hears so much about. Go to sleep."

She obeyed, her lips curved in a contented smile, his arms securely around her. Someone had pulled strings again. It could have been her father, or the mysterious "friend" of Grant's who kept arranging things, or possibly Grant had intimidated someone at the embassy. However it happened, the next afternoon they had passports. They could have taken the next flight to Dallas, but instead they spent another night together, making love in that king-size bed, the door securely bolted. She didn't want to leave. As long as they were still in Mexico City, she could pretend that it wasn't over, that the job wasn't finished. But her parents were waiting for her, and Grant had his own life to go back to. She had to find another job, as well as take care of the little chore that had gotten her into so much trouble to begin with. There was no way they could stay in Mexico.

Still, tears burned the back of her eyes when they boarded the jet that would take them to Dallas. She knew that Grant had booked separate flights for them from Dallas; she was going on to New York, and he was flying to Knoxville. Their goodbyes would be said in the vast, busy Dallas-Ft. Worth airport, and she couldn't stand it. If she didn't get a tight hold on herself she'd be squalling like a baby, and he wouldn't want that. If he wanted more of her than what he'd already had, he'd have asked her, because she'd made it more than obvious that she was willing to give him whatever he wanted. But he hadn't asked, so he didn't want her. She'd known that this time would come, and she'd accepted it, taken the risk, grabbed for what happiness she could get. Pay up time had come.

She controlled her tears. She read the airline magazine; and was even able to comprehend what she was reading. For a while she held his hand, but she released it when the in-flight meal was served. She ordered a gin and tonic, gulped it down, then ordered another.

Grant eyed her narrowly, but she gave him a bright, glittering smile, determined not to let him see that she was shattering on the inside.

Too soon, far too soon, they landed at Dallas and filed out of the plane through the portable tunnel. Jane clutched the dirty, battered backpack, for the first time realizing that his boots and fatigues were in it along with her clothing. "I need your address," she chattered brightly, nervously. "To mail your clothes to you. Unless you want to buy a bag in the airport shop, that is. We have plenty of time before our flights."

He checked his watch. "You have twenty-eight minutes, so we'd better find your gate. Do you have your ticket?"

"Yes, it's right here. What about your clothes?"

"I'll be in touch with your father. Don't worry about it."

Yes, of course; there was the matter of payment for dragging her out of Costa Rica. His face was hard and expressionless, his amber eyes cool. She held out her hand, not noticing how it was shaking. "Well, goodbye, then. It's—" She broke off. What could she say? It's been nice meeting you? She swallowed. "It's been fun."

He looked down at her extended hand, then back up at her, disbelief edging into the coolness of his eyes. He said slowly, "The hell you say," caught her hand, and jerked her into his arms. His mouth was hot, covering hers, his tongue curling slowly into her mouth as if they weren't surrounded by curiously gawking people. She clung to him, shaking.

He set her away from him. His jaw was clenched. "Go on. Your folks are waiting for you. I'll be in touch in a few days." The last slipped out; he'd intended this to be the final break, but her dark eyes were so lost and full of pain, and she'd kissed him so hungrily, that he couldn't stop the words. One more time, then. He'd give himself one more time with her.

She nodded, drawing herself up. She wasn't going to break down and cry all over him. He almost wished she would cry, because then he'd have an excuse to hold her again. But she was stronger than that. "Goodbye," she said, then turned and walked away from him.

She barely saw where she was going; people blurred in her vision, and she stubbornly blinked her eyes to keep the tears back. Well, she was alone again. He'd said he'd be in touch, but she knew he wouldn't. It was over. She had to accept that and be grateful for the time she'd had. It had been obvious from the first that Grant Sullivan wasn't a man to be tied down.

Someone touched her arm, the touch warm and strong, a man's touch. She stopped, wild hope springing into her breast, but when she turned she found that it wasn't Grant who had stopped her. The man had dark hair and eyes, and his skin was dark, his features strongly Latin. "Jane Greer?" he asked politely.

She nodded, wondering how he'd known her name and recognized her. His grip tightened on her arm. "Would you please come with me," he said, and though his voice remained polite, it was an order, not a question.

Alarm skittered through her, jerking her out of her misery. She smiled at the man and swung the backpack by its straps, catching him on the side of the head with it and sending him staggering. From the solid 'thunk' it made, she knew Grant's boots had hit him.

"Grant!" she screamed, her voice slicing through the bustle of thousands of people. "Grant!"

The man caught himself and lunged for her. Jane began running back in the direction she'd come from, dodging around people. Up ahead she saw Grant coming through the crowd like a running back, shoving people out of his path. The man caught up with her, catching her arm; then Grant was there. People were screaming and scattering, and the airport guards were running toward them. Grant sent the man sprawling, then grabbed Jane's arm and ran for the nearest exit, ducking past the milling crowds and ignoring the shouts to stop.

"What the hell's going on?" he roared, jerking her out into the bright Texas sunlight. The humid heat settled over them.

"I don't know! That man just came up to me and asked if my name was Jane Greer; then he caught my arm and told me to come with him, so I hit him in the head with the backpack and started screaming."

"Makes perfect sense to me," he muttered, flagging a cab and putting her in it, then crawling in beside her.

"Where to, folks?" the cabdriver asked.

"Downtown."

"Any particular place downtown?"

"I'll tell you where to stop."

The driver shrugged. As they pulled away from the curb there seemed to be a lot of people spilling out of the terminal, but Jane didn't look back. She was still shaking. "It can't be Turego again, can it?"

Grant shrugged. "It's possible, if he has enough money. I'm going to make a phone call."

She'd thought she was safe, that they were both safe. After the two peaceful days spent in Mexico, the sudden fear seemed that much sharper and more acrid. She couldn't stop trembling.

They didn't go all the way into Dallas. Grant instructed the driver to drop them at a shopping mall. "Why a shopping mall?" Jane asked, looking around.

"There are telephones here, and it's safer than standing in a phone booth on the side of a street." He put his arm around her and hugged her briefly to him. "Don't look so worried, honey."

They went inside and found a bank of pay telephones, but it was a busy day and all the lines were in use. They waited while a teenager argued extensively with her mother about how late she could stay out that night, but at last she hung up and stormed away, evidently having lost the argument. Grant stepped in and commandeered the telephone before anyone else could reach it. Standing close by him, Jane watched as he dropped in the coins, punched in a number, then dropped in more coins. He leaned casually against the fieldstone nook that housed the telephone, listening to the rings on the other end.

"Sullivan," he finally drawled when the phone was answered. "She was nearly grabbed in DFW." He listened a moment; then his eyes flicked to Jane. "Okay, I got it. We'll be there. By the way, that was a dumb move. She could've killed the guy." He hung up, and his lips twitched.

"Well?" Jane demanded.

"You just belted an agent."

"An agent? You mean, one of your friend's men?"

"Yeah. We're taking a little detour. You're going to be debriefed. It was left up to some other people to pick you up, and they decided to pick you up after we'd parted company, since I'm no longer in the business and this doesn't officially concern me. Sabin will pin their ears back."

"Sabin? Is he your friend?"

He was smiling down at her. "He's the one." He stroked her cheekbone very gently with the backs of his fingers. "And that's a name you're going to forget, honey. Why don't you call your parents and let them know that you won't be in tonight? It'll be tomorrow; you can call them again when we know something definite."

"Are you going, too?"

"I wouldn't miss it." He grinned a little wolfishly, already anticipating Kell's reaction to Jane.

"But where are we going?"

"Virginia, but don't tell your parents that. Just tell them that you missed your flight."

She reached for the phone, then stopped. "Your friend must be pretty important."

"He's got some power," Grant understated.

So, they must know about the microfilm. Jane punched in her credit card number. She'd be glad to get the whole thing over with, and at least Grant was going to be with her one more day. Just one more day! It was a reprieve, but she didn't know if she'd have the strength for another goodbye.

CHAPTER THIRTEEN

THE VIRGINIA COUNTRYSIDE around the place was quiet and serene, the trees green, the flowering shrubs well-tended. It looked rather like her father's Connecticut estate. Everyone was polite, and several people greeted Grant, but Jane noticed that even the ones who spoke to him did so hesitantly, as if they were a little wary of him.

Kell's office was right where it had always been, and the door still had no name on it. The agent who had escorted them knocked quietly. "Sullivan is here, sir."

"Send them in."

The first thing Jane noticed was the old-fashioned charm of the room. The ceilings were high; the mantel was surely the original one that had been built with the house over a hundred years before. Tall glass doors behind the big desk let in the late-afternoon sun. They also placed the man behind the desk in silhouette, while anyone who came in the door was spotlighted by the blazing sun, something George had told her about. He rose to his feet as they entered, a tall man, maybe not quite as tall as Grant, but lean and hard with a whipcord toughness that wasn't maintained by sitting behind a desk.

He stepped forward to greet them. "You look like hell, Sullivan," he said, and the two men shook hands;

then he turned his eyes on her, and for the first time Jane felt his power. His eyes were so black that there was no light in them at all; they absorbed light, drawing it into the depths of the irises. His hair was thick and black, his complexion dark, and there was an intense energy about him that seared her.

"Ms. Greer," he said, holding out his hand.

"Mr. Sabin," she returned, calmly shaking his hand.

"I have a very embarrassed agent in Dallas."

"He shouldn't be," Grant drawled behind her. "She let him off easy."

"Grant's boots were in the pack," Jane explained. "That's what stunned him so badly when I hit him in the head."

There was the first hint in Sabin's eyes that Jane wasn't quite what he'd expected. Grant stood behind her, his arms calmly folded, and waited.

Sabin examined her open expression, the catlike slant of her dark eyes, the light dusting of freckles across her cheekbones. Then he quickly glanced at Grant, who was planted like the Rock of Gibraltar behind her. He could question her, but he had the feeling that Grant wouldn't let her be harrassed in any way. It wasn't like Sullivan to get involved, but he was out of the business now, so the old rules didn't apply. She wasn't a great beauty, but there was a lively charm about her that almost made Sabin want to smile. Maybe she'd gotten close to Sullivan. Sabin didn't trust that openness, however, because he knew more about her now than he had in the beginning.

"Ms. Greer," he began slowly, "did you know that George Persall was—"

"Yes, I did," Jane interrupted cheerfully. "I helped him sometimes, but not often, because he liked to use different methods every time. I believe this is what you want." She opened the backpack and began digging in it. "I know it's in here. There!" She produced the small roll of film, placing it on his desk.

Both men looked thunderstruck. "You've just been carrying it around?" Sabin asked in disbelief.

"Well, I didn't have a chance to hide it. Sometimes I put it in my pocket. That way Turego could search my room all he wanted and he'd never find anything. All of you spy types try to make everything too complicated. George always told me to keep it simple."

Grant began to chuckle. He couldn't help it; it was funny. "Jane, why didn't you tell me you had the microfilm?"

"I thought it would be safer for you if you didn't know about it."

Again Sabin looked thunderstruck, as if he couldn't believe anyone would actually feel the need to protect Grant Sullivan. As Kell was normally the most impassive of men, Grant knew that Jane had tilted him off balance, just as she did everyone she met. Sabin coughed to cover his reaction.

"Ms. Greer," he asked cautiously, "do you know what's on the film?"

"No. Neither did George."

Grant was laughing again. "Go ahead," he told Sabin. "Tell her about the film. Or, better yet, show her. She'll enjoy it."

Sabin shook his head, then picked up the film and pulled it out, unwinding it. Grant produced his cigarette lighter, leaned forward, and set the end of the film on fire. The three watched as the flames slowly ate up the length of celluloid until it burned close to Sabin's fingers and he dropped it into a large ashtray. "The film," Sabin explained, "was a copy of something we don't want anyone else to know. All we wanted was for it to be destroyed before anyone saw it."

With the stench of burning plastic in her nostrils, Jane silently watched the last of the film curl and crumble. All they'd wanted was for it to be destroyed, and she'd hauled it through a jungle and across half a continent— just to hand it over and watch it burn. Her lips twitched; she was afraid of making a scene, so she tried to control the urge. But it was irresistible; it rolled upward, and a giggle escaped. She turned, looking at Grant, and between them flashed the memory of everything they'd been through. She giggled again, then they were both laughing, Jane hanging on to his shirt because she was laughing so hard her knees had gone limp.

"I fell down a cliff," she gasped. "We stole a truck… shot another truck… I broke Turego's nose…all to watch it burn!"

Grant went into another spasm of laughter, holding his sore ribs and bending double. Sabin watched them clinging to each other and laughing uproariously. Curiosity seized him. "Why did you shoot a truck?" he asked; then suddenly he was laughing, too.

An agent paused outside the door, his head tilted, listening. No, it was impossible. Sabin never laughed.

THEY LAY IN bed in a hotel in the middle of Washington, D.C., pleasantly tired. They had made love as soon as the door was locked behind them, falling on the bed and removing only the necessary clothing. But that had been hours before, and now they were completely nude, slipping gradually into sleep.

Grant's hand moved up and down her back in a lazy pattern. "Just how involved were you in Persall's activities?"

"Not very," she murmured. "Oh, I knew about them. I had to know, so I could cover for him if I had to. And he sometimes used me as a courier, but not very often. Still, he talked to me a lot, telling me things. He was a strange, lonely man."

"Was he your lover?"

She lifted her head from his chest, surprised. "George? Of course not!"

"Why 'of course not'? He was a man, wasn't he? And he was in your bedroom when he died."

She paused. "George had a problem, a medical one. He wasn't capable of being anyone's lover."

"So that part of the report was wrong, too."

"Deliberately. He used me as a sort of shield."

He put his hand in her hair and held her for his kiss. "I'm glad. He was too old for you."

Jane watched him with wise, dark eyes. "Even if he hadn't been, I wasn't interested. You might as well know, you're the only lover I've ever had. Until I met you, I'd never…wanted anyone."

"And when you met me…?" he murmured.

"I wanted." She lowered her head and kissed him, wrapping her arms around him, slithering her body over his until she felt his hardening response.

"I wanted, too," he said, his words a mere breath over her skin.

"I love you." The words were a cry of pain, launched by desperation, because she knew this was definitely the last time unless she took the chance. "Will you marry me?"

"Jane, don't."

"Don't what? Tell you that I love you? Or ask you to marry me?" She sat up, moving her legs astride him, and shook her dark hair back behind her shoulders.

"We can't live together," he explained, his eyes turning dark gold. "I can't give you what you need, and you'd be miserable."

"I'll be miserable anyway," she said reasonably, striving for a light tone. "I'd rather be miserable with you than miserable without you."

"I'm a loner. Marriage is a partnership, and I'd rather go it alone. Face it, honey. We're good together in bed, but that's all there is."

"Maybe for you. I love you." Despite herself, she couldn't keep the echo of pain out of her voice.

"Do you? We were under a lot of stress. It's human nature to turn to each other. I'd have been surprised if we hadn't made love."

"Please, spare me your combat psychology! I'm not a child, or stupid! I know when I love someone, and damn it, I love you! You don't have to like it, but don't try to talk me out of it!"

"All right." He lay on his back, looking up into her angry eyes. "Do you want me to get another room?"

"No. This is our last night together, and we're going to spend it together."

"Even if we're fighting?"

"Why not?" she dared.

"I don't want to fight," he said, lunging up and twisting. Jane found herself on her back, blinking up at him in astonishment. Slowly he entered her, pushing her legs high. She closed her eyes, excitement spiraling through her. He was right; the time was far better spent making love.

She didn't try again to convince him that they had a future together. She knew from experience just how hardheaded he was; he'd have to figure it out for himself. So she spent her time loving him, trying to make certain that he never forgot her, that no other woman could begin to give him the pleasure that she did. This would be her goodbye.

Late in the night she leaned over him. "You're afraid," she accused softly. "You've seen so much that you're afraid to let yourself love anyone, because you know how easily a world can be wrecked."

His voice was tired. "Jane, let it be."

"All right. That's my last word, except for this: if you decide to take a chance, come get me."

She crept out of bed early the next morning and left him sleeping. She knew that he was too light a sleeper not to have awakened some time during the shower she took, or while she was dressing, but he didn't roll over or in any way indicate that he was awake, so she preserved the pretence between them. Without even kissing him, she slipped out the door. After all, they'd already said their goodbyes.

At the sound of the door closing Grant rolled over in the bed, his eyes bleak as he stared at the empty room.

JANE AND HER parents fell into each other's arms, laughing and crying and hugging each other exuberantly. Her return called for a family celebration that lasted hours, so it was late that night before she and her father had any time alone. Jane had few secrets from her father; he was too shrewd, too realistic. By silent, instinctive agreement, they kept from her mother the things that would upset her, but Jane was like her father in that she had an inner toughness.

She told him how the entire situation in Costa Rica had come about, and even told him about the trek through the rain forest. Because he was shrewd, he picked up on the nuances in her voice when she mentioned Grant.

"You're in love with Sullivan, aren't you?"

She nodded, sipping her glass of wine. "You met him. What did you think about him?" The answer was important to her, because she trusted her father's judgment of character.

"I thought him unusual. There's something in his eyes that's almost scary. But I trusted him with my daughter's life, if that tells you what you want to know, and I'd do so again."

"Would you mind having him in the family?"

"I'd welcome him with open arms. I think he could keep you in one place," James said grumpily.

"Well, I asked him to marry me, but he turned me down. I'm going to give him a while to stew over it; then I'm going to fight dirty."

Her father grinned, the quick, cheerful grin that his daughter had inherited. "What are you planning?"

"I'm going to chase that man like he's never been chased before. I think I'll stay here for a week or two; then I'm going to Europe."

"But he's not in Europe!"

"I know. I'll chase him from a distance. The idea is

for him to know how much he misses me, and he'll miss me a lot more when he finds out how far away I am."

"But how is he going to find out?"

"I'll arrange that somehow. And even if it doesn't work, a trip to Europe is never a waste!"

IT WAS ODD how much he missed her. She'd never been to the farm, but sometimes it seemed haunted by her. He'd think he heard her say something and turn to find no one there. At night... God, the nights were awful! He couldn't sleep, missing her soft weight sprawled on top of him.

He tried to lose himself in hard physical work. Chores piled up fast on a farm, and he'd been gone for two weeks. With the money he'd been paid for finding Jane, he was able to free the farm from debt and still have plenty left over, so he could have hired someone to do the work for him. But the work had been therapy for him when he'd first come here, still weak from his wounds, and so tightly drawn that a pinecone dropping from a tree in the night had been enough to send him diving from the bed, reaching for his knife.

So he labored in the sun, doing the backbreaking work of digging new holes for the fence posts, putting up new sections of fencing, patching and painting the barn. He reroofed the house, worked on the old tractor that had come with the farm; and thought about doing more planting the next spring. All he'd planted so far was a few vegetables for himself, but if he was going to own a farm, he might as well farm it. A man wouldn't get rich at it, not on this scale, but he knew how to do it. Working the earth gave him a measure of peace, as if it put him in contact with the boy he'd once been, before war had changed his life.

In the distance loomed the mountains, the great, misty mountains where the ghosts of the Cherokee still walked. The vast slopes were uninhabited now, but then, only a few hardy souls other than the Cherokee had ever called the mountains home. Jane would like the mountains. They were older, wreathed in silvery veils, once the mightiest mountain range on earth, but worn down by more years than people could imagine. There were places in those mountains where time stood still.

The mountains, and the earth, had healed him, and the process had been so gradual that he hadn't realized he was healed until now. Perhaps the final healing had come when Jane had shown him how to laugh again.

He had told her to let it be, and she had. She had left in the quiet morning, without a word, because he'd told her to go. She loved him; he knew that. He'd pretended that it was something else, the pressure of stress that had brought them together, but even then he'd known better, and so had she.

Well, hell! He missed her so badly that he hurt, and if this wasn't love, then he hoped he never loved anyone, because he didn't think he could stand it. He couldn't get her out of his mind, and her absence was an empty ache that he couldn't fill, couldn't ease.

She'd been right; he was afraid to take the chance, afraid to leave himself open to more hurt. But he was hurting anyway. He'd be a fool if he let her get away.

But first there were old rifts to try to heal.

He loved his parents, and he knew they loved him, but they were simple people, living close to the earth, and he'd turned into someone they didn't recognize.

His sister was a pretty, blond woman, content with her job at the local library, her quiet husband, and her three children. It had been a couple of years since he'd even seen his nephew and two nieces. When he'd stopped by the year before to tell his parents that he'd retired and had bought a farm in Tennessee, they'd all been so uncomfortable that he'd stayed for only a few hours, and had left without seeing Rae, or the kids.

So he drove down to Georgia, and stood on the weathered old porch, knocking on the door of the house where he'd grown up. His mother came to the door, wiping her hands on her apron. It was close to noon; as always, as it had been from the time he could remember, she was cooking lunch for his father. But they didn't call it lunch in this part of the country; the noon meal was dinner, and the evening meal was supper.

Surprise lit her honey-brown eyes, the eyes that were so like his, only darker. "Why, son, this is a surprise. What on earth are you knocking for? Why didn't you just come in?"

"I didn't want to get shot," he said honestly.

"Now, you know I don't let your daddy keep a gun in the house. The only gun is that old shotgun, out in the barn. What makes you say a thing like that?" Turning, she went back to the kitchen, and he followed. Everything in the old frame house was familiar, as familiar to him as his own face.

He settled his weight in one of the straight chairs that were grouped around the kitchen table. This was the table he'd eaten at as a boy. "Mama," he said slowly, "I've been shot at so much that I guess I think that's the normal way of things."

She was still for a moment, her head bent; then she

resumed making her biscuits. "I know, son. We've always known. But we didn't know how to reach you, how to bring you back to us again. You was still a boy when you left, but you came back a man, and we didn't know how to talk to you."

"There wasn't any talking to me. I was still too raw, too wild. But the farm that I bought, up in Tennessee… it's helped."

He didn't have to elaborate, and he knew it. Grace Sullivan had the simple wisdom of people who lived close to the land. She was a farm girl, had never pretended to be anything else, and he loved her because of it.

"Will you stay for dinner?"

"I'd like to stay for a couple of days, if I won't be messing up any plans."

"Grant Sullivan, you know your daddy and I don't have any plans to go off gallivanting anywhere."

She sounded just like she had when he had been five years old and had managed to get his clothes dirty as fast as she could put them on him. He remembered how she'd looked then, her hair dark, her face smooth and young, her honey-gold eyes sparkling at him.

He laughed, because everything was getting better, and his mother glanced at him in surprise. It had been twenty years since she'd heard her son laugh. "That's good," he said cheerfully. "Because it'll take me at least that long to tell you about the woman I'm going to marry."

"What!" She whirled on him, laughing, too. "You're pulling my leg! Are you really going to get married? Tell me about her!"

"Mama, you'll love her," he said. "She's nuts."

HE'D NEVER THOUGHT that finding her would be so hard. Somehow he'd thought that it would be as simple as calling her father and getting her address from him, but he should have known. With Jane, nothing was ever as it should be.

To begin with, it took him three days to get in touch with her father. Evidently her parents had been out of town, and the housekeeper either hadn't known where Jane was, or she'd been instructed not to give out any information. Considering Jane's circumstances, he thought it was probably the latter. So he cooled his heels for three days until he was finally able to speak to her father, but that wasn't much better.

"She's in Europe," James explained easily enough. "She stayed here for about a week, then took off again."

Grant felt like cursing. "Where in Europe?"

"I don't really know. She was vague about it. You know Jane."

He was afraid that he did. "Has she called?"

"Yes, a couple of times."

"Mr. Hamilton, I need to talk to her. When she calls again, would you find out where she is and tell her to stay put until I get in touch?"

"That could be a couple of weeks. Jane doesn't call regularly. But if it's urgent, you may know someone who knows exactly where she is. She did mention that she's talked to a friend of yours…let's see, what was his name?"

"Sabin," Grant supplied, grinding his teeth in rage.

"Yes, that's it. Sabin. Why don't you give him a call? It may save you a lot of time."

Grant didn't want to call Kell; he wanted to see him

face-to-face and strangle him. Damn him! If he'd re-
cruited Jane into that gray network...!

He was wasting time and money chasing over the
country after her, and his temper was short when he
reached Virginia. He didn't have the clearance to go in,
so he called Kell directly. "Sullivan. Clear me through.
I'll be there in five minutes."

"Grant—"

Grant hung up, not wanting to hear it over the phone.

Ten minutes later he was leaning over Kell's desk.
"Where is she?"

"Monte Carlo."

"Damn it!" he yelled, pounding his fist on the desk.
"How could you drag her into this?"

"I didn't drag her," Kell said coolly, his dark eyes
watchful. "She called me. She said she'd noticed something funny and thought I might like to know. She was
right; I was highly interested."

"How could she call you? Your number isn't exactly
listed."

"I asked her the same thing. It seems she was standing beside you when you called me from Dallas."

Grant swore, rubbing his eyes. "I should have known.
I should have been expecting it after she hot-wired that
truck. She watched me do it, just once, then did it herself the next time."

"If it's any consolation, she didn't get it exactly right.
She remembered the numbers, but not the right order.
She told me I was the fifth call she'd placed."

"Oh, hell. What kind of situation is she in?"

"A pretty explosive one. She's stumbled across a high
rolling counterfeiter. He has some high quality plates

of the pound, the franc and several denominations of our currency. He's setting up the deal now. Some of our comrades are very interested."

"I can imagine. Just what does she think she can do?"

"She's going to try to steal the plates."

Grant went white. "And you were going to let her?"

"Damn it, Grant!" Kell exploded. "It's not a matter of letting her and you know it! The problem is stopping her without tipping the guy off and sending him so deep underground we can't find him. I've got agents tiptoeing all around her, but the guy thinks he's in love with her, and his buyer has watchdogs sniffing around, and we simply can't snatch her without blowing the whole thing sky-high!"

"All right, all right. I'll get her out of it."

"How?" Kell demanded.

"I'll get the plates myself, then jerk her out of there and make damned certain she never calls you again!"

"I would deeply appreciate it," Kell said. "What are you going to do with her?"

"Marry her."

Something lightened in Kell's dark face, and he leaned back in his chair, looping his hands behind his head. "Well, I'll be damned. Do you know what you're getting into? That woman doesn't think like most people."

That was a polite way of saying it, but Kell wasn't telling him anything he didn't already know. Within moments of meeting her, Grant had realized that Jane was just a little unorthodox. But he loved her, and she couldn't get into too much trouble on the farm.

"Yeah, I know. By the way, you're invited to the wedding."

JANE SMILED AT FELIX, her eyes twinkling at him. He was such a funny little guy; she really liked him, despite the fact that he was a counterfeiter and was planning to do something that could really damage her country. He was slightly built, with shy eyes and a faint stutter. He loved to gamble, but had atrocious luck; that is, he'd had atrocious luck until Jane had started sitting beside him. Since then he'd been winning regularly, and he was now devoted to her.

Despite everything she was having fun in Monte Carlo. Grant was being slow coming around, but she hadn't been bored. If she had trouble sleeping, if she sometimes woke to find her cheeks wet, that was something she had to accept. She missed him. It was as if part of herself were gone. Without him there was no one she could trust, no one in whose arms she could rest.

It was a dangerous tightrope she was walking, and the excitement of it helped keep her from settling into depression. The only thing was, how much longer was it going to last? If she saw that Felix was finally going to make up his mind who to sell to, she would be forced to do something—fast—before the plates got into the wrong hands.

Felix was winning again, as he had every night since he'd met Jane. The elegant casino was buzzing, and the chandeliers rivaled in brilliance the diamonds that were roped about necks and dripping from ears. The men in their formal evening wear, the women in their gowns and jewels, casually wagering fortunes on the roll of the dice or the turn of a card, all created an atmosphere that was unequaled anywhere in the world. Jane fit into it easily, slim and graceful in her black silk gown, her shoulders and back bare. Jet earrings dangled to her shoulders, and her hair was piled on top of her head in a careless, becoming twist. She wore no necklace, no bracelets, only the earrings that touched the glowing gold of her skin.

Across the table Bruno was watching them closely. He was becoming impatient with Felix's dithering, and his impatience was likely to force her hand.

Well, why not? She'd really waited as long as she could. If Grant had been interested, he'd have shown up before now.

She stood and bent down to kiss Felix on the forehead. "I'm going back to the hotel," she said, smiling at him. "I have a headache."

He looked up, dismayed. "Are you really ill?"

"It's just a headache. I was on the beach too long today. You don't have to leave; stay and enjoy your game."

He began to look panicky, and she winked at him. "Why don't you see if you can win now without me? Who knows, it may not be me at all."

He brightened, the poor little man, and turned back to his game with renewed fervor. Jane left the casino and hurried back to the hotel, going straight to her room. She always allowed for being followed, because she sensed that she always was. Bruno was a very suspicious man. Swiftly she stripped off her gown, and she was reaching into the closet for a dark pair of pants and a shirt when a hand closed over her mouth and a a muscular arm clamped around her waist.

"Don't scream," a low, faintly raspy voice said in her ear, and her heart jumped. The hand left her mouth, and Jane turned in his arms, burying her face against his neck, breathing in the delicious, familiar male scent of him.

"What are you doing here?" she breathed.

"What do you think I'm doing here?" he asked irritably, but his hands were sliding over her nearly naked body, reacquainting himself with her flesh. "When I get you home, I just may give you that spanking I've threatened you with a couple of times. I get you away from Turego, and as soon as my back is turned you plunge right back into trouble."

"I'm not in trouble," she snapped.

"You couldn't prove it by me. Get dressed. We're getting out of here."

"I can't! There are some counterfeit plates that I've got to get. My room is being watched, so I was going to climb out the window and work my way around to Felix's room. I have a pretty good idea where he's hidden them."

"And you say you're not in trouble."

"I'm not! But really, Grant, we've got to get those plates."

"I've already got them."

She blinked, her brown eyes owlish. "You do? But... how? I mean, how did you know—never mind. Kell told you, didn't he? Well, where did Felix have them hidden?"

She was enjoying this. He sighed. "Where do you think he had them?"

"In the ceiling. I think he pushed up a square of the ceiling and hid the plates in there. It's really the only good hiding place in the room, and he isn't the type to put them in a safety deposit box in a bank, which is where I'd have put them."

"No, you wouldn't," he said, annoyed. "You'd have put them in the ceiling, just like he did."

She grinned. "I was right!"

"Yes, you were right." And he probably never should have told her. Turning her around, he gave her a pat on the bottom. "Start packing. Your little friend is probably the nervous sort who checks his hidey-hole every night before he goes to bed, and we want to be long gone before he does."

She dragged down her suitcases and started throwing clothes into them. He watched her, sweat popping out on his brow. She looked even better than he remembered, her breasts ripe and round, her legs long and shapely. He hadn't even kissed her. He caught her arm, swinging her around and catching her close to him. "I've missed you," he said, and lowered his mouth to hers.

Her response was instantaneous. She rose on tiptoe, moving against him, her arms coiled around his neck and her fingers deep in his hair. He'd had a haircut, and the dark blond strands slipped through her fingers to fall back in place, shaped perfectly to his head. "I've missed you, too," she whispered when he released her mouth.

His breathing was ragged as he reluctantly let her go. "We'll finish this when we have more time. Jane, would you please put on some clothes?"

She obeyed without question, pulling on green silk trousers and a matching green tunic. "Where are we going?"

"Right now? We're driving to the beach and turning the plates over to an agent. Then we're going to catch a flight to Paris, London and New York."

"Unless, of course, Bruno is waiting just outside the

door, and instead we end up sailing across the Mediterranean."

"Bruno isn't waiting outside the door. Would you hurry?"

"I'm finished."

He picked up the suitcases and they went downstairs, where he checked her out. It all went like clockwork. There was no sign of Bruno, or any of the men she had dubbed "Bruno's goons." They turned the plates over to the promised agent and drove to the airport. Jane's heart was thudding with a slow, strong, powerful beat as Grant slipped into the seat beside her and buckled himself in. "You know, you never did actually tell me what you're doing here. You're retired, remember? You're not supposed to be doing things like this."

"Don't play innocent," he advised, giving her a look from molten gold eyes. "I saw your fine hand in this from the beginning. It worked. I came after you. I love you; I'm taking you to Tennessee; and we're going to be married. But you'd better remember that I'm onto your tricks now, and I know you're too slick for your own good. Did I leave anything out?"

"No," Jane said, settling back in her seat. "I think you have everything covered."

* * * * *

TEARS OF THE RENEGADE

CHAPTER ONE

IT WAS LATE, already after eleven o'clock, when the broad-shouldered man appeared in the open French doors. He stood there, perfectly at ease, watching the party with a sort of secret amusement. Susan noticed him immediately, though she seemed to be the only one who did so, and she studied him with faint surprise because she'd never seen him before. She would have remembered if she had; he wasn't the sort of man that anyone forgot.

He was tall and muscular, his white dinner jacket hugging his powerful shoulders with just enough precision to proclaim exquisite tailoring, yet what set him apart wasn't the almost dissolute sophistication that sat so easily on him; it was his face. He had the bold look of a desperado, an impression heightened by the level dark brows that shadowed eyes of a pale, crystalline blue. Lodestone eyes, she thought, feeling their effect even though he wasn't looking at her. A funny little quiver danced down her spine, and her senses were suddenly heightened—the music was more vibrant, the colors more intense, the heady perfume of the early spring night stronger. Every instinct within her was abruptly awakened as she stared at the stranger with a sort of primitive recognition. Women have always known which men are dangerous, and this man radiated danger.

It was there in his eyes, the self-assurance of a man who was willing to take risks, and willing to accept the consequences. An almost weary experience had hardened his features, and Susan knew, looking at him, that he would be a man no one would lightly cross. Danger rode those broad shoulders like a visible mantle. He wasn't quite…civilized. He looked like a modern-day pirate, from those bold eyes to the short, neatly trimmed dark beard and moustache that hid the lines of his jaw and upper lip; but she knew that they would be strong lines. Her eyes traveled to his hair, dark and thick and vibrant, styled in a casual perfection that most men would have paid a fortune to obtain, just long enough to brush his collar in the back with a hint of curl.

At first no one seemed to notice him, which was surprising, because to Susan he stood out like a tiger in a roomful of tabbies. Then, gradually, people began to look at him, and to her further astonishment a stunned, almost hostile silence began to fall, spreading quickly over the room, a contagious pall that leaped from one person to another. Suddenly uneasy, she looked at her brother-in-law, Preston, who was the host and almost within touching distance of the newly arrived guest. Why didn't he welcome the man? But instead Preston had gone stiff, his face pale, staring at the stranger with the same sort of frozen horror one would eye a cobra coiled at one's feet.

The tidal wave of silence had spread to include the entire huge room now, even the musicians on the raised dais falling silent. Under the glittering prisms of the chandeliers, people were turning, staring, shock rippling over their faces. A shiver of alarm went down Susan's slender back; what was going on? Who was he? Something awful was going to happen. She sensed it, saw Preston tensing for a scene, and knew that she wasn't going to let it happen. Whoever he was, he was a guest of the Blackstones, and no one was going to be rude to him, not even Preston Blackstone. Instinctively she moved, stepping into the middle of the scene, murmuring "Excuse me" to people as she slipped past them. All attention turned to her as if drawn by a magnet, for her movement was the only movement in the room. The stranger turned his gaze on her, too; he watched her, and he waited, those strange lodestone eyes narrowing as he examined the slim, graceful woman whose features were as pure and serene as a cameo, clothed in a fragile cream silk dress that swirled about her ankles as she walked. A three-strand pearl choker encircled her delicate throat; with her soft dark hair drawn up on top of her head and a few tendrils curling about her temples, she was a dream, a mirage, as illusive as angel's breath. She looked as pure as a Victorian virgin, glowingly set apart from everyone else in the room, untouched and untouchable; and, to the man who watched her approach, an irresistible challenge.

Susan was unaware of the male intent that suddenly gleamed in the depths of his pale blue eyes. She was concerned only with avoiding the nastiness that had been brewing, something she didn't understand but nevertheless wanted to prevent. If anyone had a score to settle with this man, they could do it at another time and in another place. She nodded a silent command to the band as she walked, and obediently the music began again, hesitantly at first, then gaining in volume.

By that time, Susan had reached the man, and she held her hand out to him. "Hello," she said, her low, musical voice carrying effortlessly to the people who listened openly, gaping at her. "I'm Susan Blackstone; won't you dance with me?"

Her hand was taken in long, hard fingers, but there was no handshake. Instead, her hand was simply held, and a slightly rough thumb rubbed over the back of her fingers, feeling the softness, the slender bones. A level brow quirked upward over the blue eyes that were even more compelling at close range, for now she could see that the pale blue was ringed by deep midnight. Staring into those eyes, she forgot that they were simply standing there while he held her hand until he used his grip on her to pull her into his embrace as he swung her into a dance, causing the skirt of her dress to wrap about his long legs as they moved.

At first he simply held her, his strength moving her across the dance floor with such ease that her feet barely touched down. No one else was dancing, and Susan looked at several people, her level gaze issuing a quiet, gentle command that was obeyed without exception. Slowly they were joined by other dancers, and the man looked down at the woman he held in his arms.

Susan felt the strength in the hand on her lower back as the fingers slowly spread and exerted a gentle pressure that was nevertheless inexorable. She found herself closer to him, her breasts lightly brushing against his hard chest, and she suddenly felt overwarm, the heat from his body enveloping her. The simple, graceful steps he was using in the dance were abruptly difficult to follow, and she forced herself to concentrate to keep from stepping on his toes.

A quivering, spring-loaded tension began coiling in her stomach, and her hand trembled in his. He squeezed her fingers warmly and said into her ear, "Don't be afraid; I won't hurt you."

His voice was a soft, deep rumble, as she had known it would be, and again that strange little shiver rippled through her. She lifted her head and found how close he had been when one of the soft curls at her temple became entangled in his beard, then slid free. She was almost dazed when she found herself looking directly at the chiseled strength of his lips, and she wondered with raw hunger if his mouth would be firm or soft, if he would taste as heady as he looked. With an inner groan, she jerked her thoughts away from the contemplation of how he would taste, what it would be like to kiss him. It was difficult to move her gaze higher, but she managed it, then wished that she hadn't; staring into those unusual eyes was almost more than her composure could bear. Why was she reacting like a teenager? She was an adult, and even as a teenager she had been calm, nothing like the woman who now found herself quaking inside at a mere glance.

But she was seared by that glance, which surveyed, approved, asked, expected and...knew. He was one of those rare men who knew women, and were all the more dangerous for their knowledge. She responded to the danger alarm that all women possess by lifting her head with the innate dignity that characterized her every movement, and met that bold look. She said quietly, "What an odd thing to say," and she was proud that her voice hadn't trembled.

"Is it?" His voice was even softer than before, deeper,

increasingly intimate. "Then you can't know what I'm thinking."

"No," she said, and left it at that, not picking up on the innuendo that she knew was there.

"You will," he promised, his tone nothing now but a low rasp that touched every nerve in her body. As he spoke, the arm about her waist tightened to pull her closer, not so close that she would have felt obliged to protest, but still she was suddenly, mutely aware of the rippling muscles in his thighs as his legs moved against hers. Her fingers clenched restlessly on his shoulder as she fought the abrupt urge to slide them inside his collar, to feel his bare skin and discover for herself if her fingers would be singed by the fire of him. Shocked at herself, she kept her eyes determinedly on the shoulder seam of his jacket and tried not to think of the strength she could feel in the hand that clasped hers, or in the one that pressed so lightly on the small of her back…lightly; but she had the sudden thought that if she tried to move away from him, that hand would prevent the action.

"Your shoulders look like satin," he murmured roughly; before she could guess his intentions, his head dipped and his mouth, warm and hard, touched the soft, bare curve of her shoulder. A fine madness seized her and she quivered, her eyes drifting shut. God, he was making love to her on the dance floor, and she didn't even know his name! But everything in her was responding to him, totally independent of her control; she couldn't even control her thoughts, which kept leaping ahead to more dangerous subjects, wondering how his mouth would feel if it kept sliding down her body….

"Stop that," she said, to herself as well as to him, but her voice was lacking any element of command; instead it was soft and shivery, the way she felt. Her skin felt as if it were on fire, but voluptuous shivers almost like a chill kept tickling her spine.

"Why?" he asked, his mouth making a sleek glissade from her shoulder to the sensitive hollow just before her ear.

"People are watching," she murmured weakly, sagging against him as her body went limp from the flaming delight that went off like a rocket inside her. His arm tightened about her waist to hold her up, but the intensified sensations of being pressed to him only made her that much weaker. She drew a ragged breath; locked against him as she was, there was no mistaking the blatant male arousal of his body, and she lifted stunned, drowning eyes to him. He was watching her through narrowed eyes, the intense, laser quality of his gaze burning into her. There was no embarrassment or apology in his expression; he was a man, and reacted as such. Susan found, to her dazed astonishment, that the deeply feminine center of her didn't want an apology. She wanted instead to drop her head to his shoulder and collapse into his lean, knowledgeable hands; but she was acutely aware not only of the people watching him, but also that if she followed her very feminine inclination, he was likely to respond by carrying her away like a pirate stealing a lady who had taken his fancy. No matter how he made her feel, this man was still a stranger to her.

"I don't even know who you are," she gasped quietly, her nails digging into his shoulder.

"Would knowing my name make any difference?" He blew gently on one of the tendrils that lay on her temple, watching the silky hair lift and fall. "But if it makes you feel better, sweetheart, we're keeping it in the family."

He was teasing, his teeth glistening whitely as he smiled, and Susan caught her breath, holding it for a moment before she could control her voice again. "I don't understand," she admitted, lifting her face to him.

"Take another deep breath like that, and it won't matter if you understand or not," he muttered, making her searingly aware of how her breasts had flattened against the hard planes of flesh beneath the white jacket. His diamond-faceted gaze dipped to the softness of her mouth as he explained, "I'm a Blackstone, too, though they probably don't claim me."

Susan stared at him in bewilderment. "But I don't know you. Who are you?"

Again those animal-white teeth were revealed in a wicked grin that lifted the corners of his moustache. "Haven't you heard any gossip? The term 'black sheep' was probably invented especially for me."

Still she stared at him without comprehension, the graceful line of her throat vulnerable to his hungry scrutiny as she kept her head lifted the necessary inches to look at him. "But I don't known of any black sheep. What's your name?"

"Cord Blackstone," he replied readily enough. "First cousin to Vance and Preston Blackstone; only son of Elias and Marjorie Blackstone; born November third, probably nine months to the day after Dad returned from his tour of duty in Europe, though I never could get Mother to admit it," he finished, that wicked, fascinating grin flashing again like a beacon on a dark night. "But what about you, sweetheart? If you're a Blackstone, you're not a natural one. I'd remember any blood relative who looked like you. So, which of my esteemed cousins are you married to?"

"Vance," she said, an echo of pain shadowing her delicate features for a moment. It was a credit to her strength of will that she was able to say evenly, "He's dead, you know," but nothing could mask the desolation that suddenly dimmed the luminous quality of her eyes.

The hard arms about her squeezed gently. "Yes, I'd heard. I'm sorry," he said with rough simplicity. "Damn, what a waste. Vance was a good man."

"Yes, he was." There was nothing more that she could say, because she still hadn't come to terms with the senseless, unlikely accident that had taken Vance's life. Death had struck so swiftly, taken so much from her, that she had automatically protected herself by keeping people at a small but significant distance since then.

"What happened to him?" the silky voice asked, and she was a little stunned that he'd asked. Didn't he even know how Vance had died?

"He was gored by a bull," she finally replied. "In the thigh…a major artery was torn. He bled to death before we could get him to a hospital." He had died in her arms, his life seeping away from him in a red tide, yet his face had been so peaceful. He had fixed his blue eyes on her and kept them there, as if he knew that he was dying and wanted his last sight on earth to be of her face. There had been a serene, heartbreaking smile on his lips as the brilliance of his gaze slowly dimmed and faded away forever….

Her fingers tightened on Cord Blackstone's shoulder, digging in, and he held her closer. In an odd way, she felt some of the pain easing, as if he had buffered it with his big, hard body. Looking up, she saw a reflection in those pale eyes of his own harsh memories, and with a flash of intuition she realized that he was a man who had seen violent deaths before, who had held someone, a friend perhaps, in his arms while death approached and conquered. He understood what she had been through. Because he understood, the burden was abruptly easier to bear.

Susan had learned, over the years, how to continue with everyday things even in the face of crippling pain. Now she forced herself away from the horror of the memory and looked around, recalling herself to her duties. She noticed that far too many people were still standing around, staring at them and whispering. She caught the bandleader's eye and gave another discreet nod, a signal for him to slide straight into another number. Then she let her eyes linger on her guests, singling them out in turn, and under the demand in her clear gaze the dance floor began to fill, the whispers to fade, and the party once more resumed its normal noise level. There wasn't a guest there who would willingly offend her, and she knew it.

"That's a neat trick," he observed huskily, having followed it from beginning to end, and his voice reflected his appreciation. "Did they teach that in the finishing school you attended?"

A little smile played over her soft mouth before she glanced up at him, allowing him to divert her. "What makes you think I went to a finishing school?" she challenged.

His bold gaze slipped down the front of her gown to seek out and visually touch her rounded breasts. "Because you're so obviously...finished. I can't see anything that Mother Nature left undone." His hard, warm fingers slid briefly down her back. "God, how soft your skin is," he finished on a whisper.

A faint flush colored her cheeks at the husky note of intimacy that had entered his voice, though she was pleased in a deeply feminine way that he had noticed the texture of her skin. Oh, he was dangerous, all right, and the most dangerous thing about him was that he could make a woman take a risk even knowing how dangerous he was.

After a moment when she remained silent, he prodded, "Well? Am I right or not?"

"Almost," she admitted, lifting her chin to smile at him. There was a soft, glowing quality to her smile that lit her face with gentle radiance, and his heavy-lidded eyes dropped even more in a signal that someone who knew him well would have recognized immediately. But Susan didn't know him well, and she was unaware of how close she was skating to thin ice. "I attended Adderley's in Virginia for four months, until my mother had a stroke and I left school to care for her."

"No point in wasting any more money for them to gild the lily," he drawled, letting his eyes drift over her serene features, then down her slender, graceful throat to linger once again, with open delight, on her fragrant, silky curves. Susan felt an unexpected heat flood her body at this man's undisguised admiration; he looked as if he wanted to lean down and bury his face between her breasts, and she quivered with the surprising longing to have him do just that. He was more than dangerous; he was lethal!

She had to say something to break the heady spell

that was enveloping her, and she used the most immediate topic of conversation. "When did you arrive?"

"Just this afternoon." The curl of his lip told her that
he knew what she was doing, but was allowing her to
get away with it. Lazily he puckered his lips and blew
again at the fine tendril of dark hair that entranced
him as it lay on the fragile skin of her temple, where
the delicate blue veining lay just under the translucent
skin. Susan felt her entire body pulsate, the warm scent
of his breath affecting her as strongly as if he'd lifted
his hand and caressed her. Almost blindly she looked
at him, compelling herself to concentrate on what he
was saying, but the movement of those chiseled lips was
even more enticing than the scent of him.

"I heard that Cousin Preston was having a party," he
was saying in a lazy drawl that had never lost its Southern music. "So I thought I'd honor old times by insult-
ing him and crashing the shindig."

Susan had to smile at the incongruity of describing
this elegant affair as a "shindig," especially when he
himself was dressed as if he had just stepped out of a
Monte Carlo casino...where he would probably be more
at home than he was here. "Did you used to make a habit
of crashing parties?" she murmured.

"If I thought it would annoy Preston, I did," he replied, laughing a little at the memories. "Preston and
I have always been on opposite sides of the fence," he
explained with a careless smile that told her how little
the matter bothered him. "Vance was the only one I ever
got along with, but then, he never seemed to care what
kind of trouble I was in. Vance wasn't one to worship
at the altar of the Blackstone name."

That was true; Vance had conformed on the surface

to the demands made on him because his name was Blackstone, but Susan had always known that he did so with a secret twinkle in his eyes. Sometimes she didn't think that her mother-in-law, Imogene, would ever forgive Vance for his mutiny against the Blackstone dynasty when he married Susan, though of course Imogene would never have been so crass as to admit it; a Blackstone didn't indulge in shrewish behavior. Then Susan felt faintly ashamed of herself, because Vance's family had treated her with respect.

Still, she felt a warm sense of comradeship with this man, because he had known Vance as she had, had realized his true nature, and she gave him a smile that sparked a glow in her own deep blue eyes. His arms tightened around her in an involuntary movement, as if he wanted to crush her against him.

"You've got the Blackstone coloring," he muttered, staring at her. "Dark hair and blue eyes, but you're so soft there's no way in hell you could be a real Blackstone. There's no hardness in you at all, is there?"

Puzzled, she stared back at him with a tiny frown puckering her brow. "What do you mean by hardness?"

"I don't think you'd understand if I told you," he replied cryptically, then added, "were you handpicked to be Vance's wife?"

"No." She smiled at the memory. "He picked me himself."

He gave a silent whistle. "Imogene will never recover from the shock," he said irreverently, and flashed that mocking grin at her again.

Despite herself, Susan felt the corners of her mouth tilting up in an answering smile. She was enjoying herself, talking to this dangerous, roguish man with the strangely compelling eyes, and she was surprised because she hadn't really enjoyed herself in such a long time…since Vance's death, in fact. There had been too many years and too many tears between her smiles, but suddenly things seemed different; she felt different inside herself. At first, she'd thought that she'd never recover from Vance's death, but five years had passed, and now she realized that she was looking forward to life again. She was enjoying being held in this man's strong arms and listening to his deep voice…and yes, she enjoyed the look in his eyes, enjoyed the sure feminine knowledge that he wanted her.

She didn't want to examine her reaction to him; she felt as if she had been dead, too, and was only now coming alive, and she wanted to revel in the change, not analyze it.

She was in danger of drowning in sensation, and she recognized the inner weakness that was overtaking her, but felt helpless to resist it. He must have sensed, with a primal intuition that was as alarming as the aura of danger that surrounded him, that she was close to surrendering to the temptation to play with fire. He leaned down and nuzzled his mouth against the delicate shell of her ear, sending every nerve in her body into delirium. "Go outside with me," he enticed, dipping his tongue into her ear and tracing the outer curve of it with electrifying precision.

Susan's entire body reverberated with the shock of it, but his action cleared her mind of the clouds of desire that had been fogging it. Totally flustered, her cheeks suddenly pink, she stopped dead. "Mr. Blackstone!"

"Cord," he corrected, laughing openly now. "After all, we're at least kissing cousins, wouldn't you say?"

She didn't know what to say, and fortunately she was saved from forming an answer that probably wouldn't have been coherent anyway, because Preston chose that moment to intervene. She had been vaguely aware, as she circled the room in Cord's arms, that Preston had been watching every move his cousin made, but she hadn't noticed him approaching. Putting his hand on Susan's arm, he stared at his cousin with frosty blue eyes. "Has he said anything to upset you, Susan?"

Again she was thrown into a quandary. If she said yes, there would probably be a scene, and she was determined to avoid that. On the other hand, how could she say no, when it would so obviously be a lie? A spark of genius prompted her to reply with quiet dignity, "We were talking about Vance."

"I see." It was perfectly reasonable to Preston that, even after five years, Susan should be upset when speaking of her dead husband. He accepted her statement as an explanation instead of the red herring it was, and gave all of his attention to his cousin, who was standing there totally relaxed, a faintly bored smile on his lips.

"Mother is waiting in the library," Preston said stiffly. "We assume you have some reason for afflicting us with your company."

"I do." Cord agreed easily with Preston's insult, still smiling as he ignored the red flag being waved at him. He lifted one eyebrow. "Lead the way. Somehow, I don't trust you at my back."

Preston stiffened, and Susan forestalled the angry outburst she saw coming by placing her hand lightly on Cord's arm and saying, "Let's not keep Mrs. Blackstone waiting."

As she had known he would, Preston shifted his attention to her. "There's no reason for you to come along, Susan. You might as well stay here with the guests."

"I'd like to have her there." Cord had instantly contradicted his cousin, and in a manner that made Susan certain he'd spoken merely to irritate Preston. "She's family, isn't she? She might as well hear it all firsthand, rather than the watered-down and doctored version that she'd get from you and Imogene."

For a moment Preston looked as if he would debate the point; then he turned abruptly and walked away. Preston was a Blackstone; he might want to punch Cord in the mouth, but he wouldn't make a public scene. Cord following him at a slight distance, his hand dropping to rest lightly on Susan's waist. He grinned down at her. "I wanted to make sure you didn't get away from me."

Susan was a grown woman, not a teenager. Moreover, she was a woman who for five years had managed large and varied business concerns with cool acumen; she was twenty-nine years old, and she told herself that she should long ago have passed out of the blushing stage. Yet this man, with the dashing air of a rake and those bold, challenging eyes, could make her blush with a mere glance. Excitement such as she had never felt before was racing through her, setting her heart pounding, and she actually felt giddy. She knew what love was like, and it wasn't this. She had loved Vance, loved him so strongly that his death had nearly destroyed her, so she realized at once that this wasn't the same emotion. This was primitive attraction, heady and feverish, and it was based entirely on sex. Vance Blackstone had been Love; Cord Blackstone meant only Lust.

But recognizing it for what it was didn't lessen its

impact as she walked sedately beside him, so vibrantly aware of the hand on her back that he might as well have been touching her naked body. She wasn't the type for an affair. She was a throwback to the Victorian era, as Vance had once teased her by saying. She had been lovingly but strictly brought up, and she was the lady that her mother had meant her to be, from the top of her head down to her pink toes. Susan had never even thought of rebelling, because she was by nature exactly what she was: a lady. She had known love and would never settle for less than that, not even for the heady delights offered by the black sheep of the Blackstone family.

Just before they entered the library where Imogene waited, Cord leaned down to her. "If you won't go outside with me, then I'll take you home and we can neck on the front porch like teenagers."

She flashed him an indignant glance that made him laugh softly to himself, but she was prevented from answering him because at that moment they passed through the door and she realized that he had perfectly timed his remark. He had a genius for throwing people off balance, and he had done it again; despite herself, she felt the heat of intensified color in her face.

Imogene regarded her thoughtfully for a moment, her gray eyes sharpening for a fraction of a second as her gaze flickered from Susan to Cord, then back to Susan's flushed face. Then she controlled her expression, and the gray eyes resumed their normal cool steadiness. "Susan, do you feel well? You look flushed."

"I became a little warm during the dancing." Susan was aware that once again she was throwing out a statement that would be regarded as an answer, but was in fact only a smoke screen. If she didn't watch it, Cord

Blackstone would turn her into a world-class liar before the night was out!

The tall man beside her directed her to a robin's egg blue love seat and sprawled his graceful length beside her, earning himself a glare—which rolled right off of his toughened hide—from both Preston and Imogene. Smiling at his aunt, he drawled a greeting. "Hello, Aunt Imogene. How's the family fortune?"

He was good at waving his own red flags, Susan noticed. Imogene settled back in her chair and coolly ignored the distraction. "Why have you come back?"

"Why shouldn't I come back? This is my home, remember? I even own part of the land. I've been roaming around for quite a while now, and I'm ready to put down my roots. What better place for that than home? I thought I'd move into the cabin on Jubilee Creek."

"That shack!" Preston's voice was full of disdain.

Cord shrugged. "You can't account for tastes. I prefer shacks to mausoleums." He grinned, looking around himself at the formal furniture, the original oil paintings, the priceless vases and miniatures that adorned the shelves. Though called a library, the room actually contained few books, and all of them had been bought, Susan sometimes suspected, with an eye on the color of the dust jackets to make certain the books harmonized with the color scheme of the room.

Preston eyed his cousin with cold, silent hatred for a moment, an expanse of time which became heavy with resentment. "How much will it cost us?"

From the corner of her eye, Susan could see the lift of that mocking eyebrow. "Cost you for what?"

"For you to leave this part of the country again."

Cord smiled, a particularly wolfish smile that should

have warned Preston. "You don't have enough money, Cousin."

Imogene lifted her hand, forestalling Preston's heated reply. She had a cooler head and was better at negotiating than her son was. "Don't be foolish...or hasty," she counseled. "You *do* realize that we're prepared to offer you a substantial sum in exchange for your absence?"

"Not interested," he said lazily, still smiling.

"But a man with your...lifestyle must have debts that need settling. Then there's the fact that I have many friends who owe me for favors, and who could be counted on to make your stay unpleasant, at the least."

"Oh, I don't think so, Aunt Imogene." Cord was utterly relaxed, his long legs stretched out before him. "The first surprise in store for you is that I don't need the money. The second is that if any of your 'friends' decide to help you by making things difficult for me, I have friends of my own who I can call on, and believe me, my friends make yours look like angels."

Imogene sniffed. "I'm sure they do, considering."

For the first time Susan felt compelled to intervene. Fighting upset her; she was quiet and naturally peaceful, but with an inner strength that allowed her to throw herself into the breach. Her gentle voice immediately drew everyone's attention, though it was to her mother-in-law that she spoke. "Imogene, look at him; look at his clothes." She waved her slender hand to indicate the man lounging beside her. "He's telling the truth. He doesn't need any money. And I think that when he mentions his friends, he isn't talking about back-alley buddies."

Cord regarded her with open, if somewhat mocking, admiration. "At last, a Blackstone with perception, though of course you weren't born to the name, so maybe that explains it. She's right, Imogene, though I'm sure you don't like hearing it. I don't need the Blackstone money because I have money of my own. I plan to live in the cabin because I like my privacy, not because I can't afford any better. Now, I suggest that we manage to control our differences, because I intend to stay here. If you want to air the family dirty laundry, then go ahead. It won't bother me; you'll be the only one to suffer from that."

Imogene gave a curious little sigh. "You've always been difficult, Cord, even when you were a child. My objection to you is based on your past actions, not on you personally. You've dragged your family through enough mud to last for four lifetimes, and I find that hard to forgive, and I find it equally as hard to trust you to behave with some degree of civility."

"It's been a long time," he said obliquely. "I've spent a lot of time in Europe, and too long in South America; it makes a man appreciate his home."

"Does it? I wonder. Forgive me if I suspect an ulterior motive, but then, your past gives me little choice. Very well, we'll call a truce...for the time being."

"A truce." He winked at her, and to Susan's surprise, Imogene blushed. So he had that effect on every female! But he was a fool if he believed that Imogene would go along with a truce. She might appear to give in, but that was *all* it was: appearance. Imogene never gave in; she merely changed tactics. If she couldn't bribe or threaten him, then she would try other measures, though for the moment Susan couldn't think of anything else that could be brought to bear on the man.

He was rising to his feet, his hand under Susan's

elbow, urging her up also. "You've been away from
your guests long enough," he told Imogene politely.
"I give you my solemn promise that I won't cause any
scandals tonight, so relax and enjoy yourself." Pulling
Susan along with him like a puppy, he crossed the floor
to Imogene and bent down to kiss his aunt. Imogene
sat perfectly still under the touch of his lips, though her
color rose even higher. Then he straightened, his eyes
dancing. "Come along, Susan," he commanded.

"Just a moment," Preston intervened, stepping before them. Imogene might have called a truce, but Preston hadn't. "We've agreed to no open hostilities; we
haven't agreed to associate with you. Susan isn't going
anywhere with you."

"Oh? I think that's up to the lady. Susan?" Cord
turned to her, making his wishes known by the curl of
his fingers on her arm.

Susan hesitated. She wanted to go with Cord. She
wanted to laugh with him, to see the wicked twinkle in
his eyes, feel the magic of being held in his arms. But
she couldn't trust him, and for the first time in her life,
she didn't trust herself. Because she wanted so badly to
go with him, she had to deny him. Slowly, regretfully,
she shook her head. "No. I think it would be better if I
didn't go with you."

His blue eyes narrowed, and suddenly they were
no longer laughing, but wore the sheen of anger. He
dropped his hand from her arm. "Perhaps you're right,"
he said coldly, and left her without another word.

The silence in the library was total, the three occu-
pants motionless. Then Imogene sighed again. "Thank
heavens you didn't go with him, dear. He's charming,
I know, but beneath all of that charm, he hates this en-

tire family. He'll do anything, *anything,* he can to harm us. You don't know him, but it's in your best interest if you avoid him." Having delivered her graceful warning, Imogene shrugged. "Ah, well, I suppose we'll have to suffer through this until he gets bored and drifts off to hunt other amusements. He was right about one thing, the wretch; I do have to get back to my guests." She rose and left the room, her mist-gray gown swaying elegantly about her feet as she walked. Imogene was still a beautiful woman; she hardly looked old enough to be the mother of the man who stood beside Susan. Imogene didn't age; she endured.

After a moment, Preston took Susan's hand, his ingrained sense of courtesy taking control of him again. His confrontation with his cousin had been the only occasion when Susan could remember seeing Preston be anything but polite, even when he was disagreeing with someone. "Let's relax for a moment before we rejoin them. Would you like a drink?" he suggested.

"No, thank you." Susan allowed him to seat her on the love seat again, and she watched as he poured himself a neat whiskey and sat down beside her, a small frown puckering his brow as he regarded the glass in his hand. Something was on his mind; she knew his mannerisms as well as she knew her own. She waited, not pushing him. She and Preston had become close since Vance's death, and she felt strongly affectionate toward him. He looked so much like Vance, so much like all the Blackstones, with his dark hair and blue eyes and lopsided smile. Preston lacked Vance's sense of humor, but he was a formidable opponent in business. He was stubborn; slower than Vance to react, but more determined when he did.

"You're a lovely woman, Susan," he said abruptly.

Startled, she stared at him. She knew she looked good tonight; she had debated over wearing the cream silk dress, for her tastes since Vance's death had been somber, but she had remembered that the medieval color of mourning had been white, not black, and only she knew when she put on the white dress that she did so with a small but poignant remnant of grief. She had dressed for Vance tonight, wearing the pearls that he had given her, spraying herself with his favorite perfume. But for a few mad moments she had gloried in the knowledge that she looked good, not for Vance's sake, but because of the admiration she had seen in another pair of eyes, strange lodestone eyes. What would have happened if she had gone with Cord Blackstone tonight, instead of playing it safe?

Preston's eyes softened as he looked at her. "You're no match for him. If you let him, he'll use you to hurt us; then he'll leave you on the trash pile and walk away without looking back. Stay away from him; he's poison."

Susan regarded him steadily. "Preston, I'm a woman, not a child; I'm capable of making my own decisions. I can see why you wouldn't like your cousin, since he's so totally different from you. But he hasn't done anything to harm me, and I won't snub him."

He gave a rueful smile at her firm, reasonable tone. "I've heard that voice in enough board meetings over the past five years to know you've dug in your heels and won't budge without a good reason. But you don't know what he's like. You're a lady; you've never been exposed to the sort of things that are commonplace to him. He's lived the life of an alley cat, not because he had no choice, no way out, but because he preferred that type of life. He broke his mother's heart, making her so ashamed of him that he wasn't welcome in her home."

"Exactly what did he do that was so terrible?" Deliberately, she kept her tone light, not wanting Preston to see how deeply she was interested in the answer, how deeply she was disturbed by Cord Blackstone.

"What didn't he do?" Sarcasm edged Preston's answer. "Fights, drinking, women, gambling...but the final straw was the scandal when he was caught with Grant Keller's wife."

Susan choked. Grant Keller was dignity personified, and so was his wife. Preston looked at her and couldn't prevent a grin. "Not this Mrs. Keller; the former Mrs. Keller was entirely different. She was thirty-six, and Cord was twenty-one when they left town together."

"That was a long time ago," Susan pointed out.

"Fourteen years, but people have long memories. I saw Grant Keller's face when he recognized Cord tonight, and he looked murderous."

Susan was certain there was more to the story, but she was reluctant to pry any deeper. The old scandal in no way explained Preston's very personal hatred for Cord. For right now, though, she was suddenly very tired and didn't want to pursue the subject. All the excitement that had lit her up while she was dancing with Cord had faded. Rising, she smoothed her skirt. "Will you take me home? I'm exhausted."

"Of course," he said immediately, as she had known he would. Preston was entirely predictable, always solicitous of her. At times, the cushion of gallantry that protected her gave her a warm sense of security, but at other times she felt restricted. Tonight, the feeling of restriction deepened until she felt as if she were being smothered. She wanted to breathe freely, to be unobserved.

It was only a fifteen-minute drive to her home, and soon she was blessedly alone, sitting on the dark front porch in the wooden porch swing, listening to the music of a Southern night. She had waited until Preston left before she came out to sit in the darkness, her right foot gently pushing her back and forth to the accompanying squeak of the chains that held the swing. A light breeze rustled through the trees and kissed her face, and she closed her eyes. As she often did, she tried to summon up Vance's face, to reassure herself with the mental picture of his violet-blue eyes and lopsided grin, but to her alarm, the face that formed wasn't his. Instead she saw pale blue eyes above the short black beard of a desperado; they were the reckless eyes of a man who dared anything. A shiver ran down her spine as she recalled the touch of his warm mouth on her shoulder, and her skin tingled as if his lips were still pressed there.

Thank heavens she had had the good sense to ask Preston to bring her home instead of going with that man as he had asked. Preston was at least safe, and Cord Blackstone had probably never heard the word.

CHAPTER TWO

THE BLACKSTONE SOCIAL circle ranged in a sort of open arc from Mobile to New Orleans, with the Gulfport-Biloxi area as the center of their far-flung web of moneyed and blue-blooded acquaintances. With such a wide area and so many friends of such varied interests, Susan was amazed that the sole topic of conversation seemed to be Cord Blackstone's return. She lost count of the number of women, many of them married, who drilled her on why he was back, how long he was staying, whether he was married, whether he had been married, and endless variations on those questions, none of which she could answer. What could she tell them? That she had danced two dances with him and gotten drunk on his smile?

She hadn't seen him since the night of his return, and she made a point of not asking about him. She told herself that it was best to leave well enough alone and let her interest in him die a natural death. All she had to do was do nothing and refuse to feed the strange attraction. It wasn't as if he were chasing her all over south Mississippi; he hadn't called, hadn't sought her out as she had half feared, half wanted him to do.

But her resolution to forget about him was stymied at every turn; even Preston seldom talked of anything except his cousin. She decided that all Cord had to do to irritate Preston was to breathe. Through Preston, she learned that Cord was working on the old cabin at Jubilee Creek, replacing the roof and the sagging old porch, putting in new windows. Preston had tried to find out where Cord had borrowed the money to repair the cabin, and found instead, to his chagrin, that there was no loan involved. Cord was paying for everything in cash, and had opened a sizable checking account at the largest bank in Biloxi. Preston and Imogene spent hours speculating on how he had acquired the money, and what his purpose was in returning to Mississippi. Susan wondered why they found it so hard to accept that he had simply returned home. As people grew older, it wasn't unusual for them to want to return to the area where they had grown up. It seemed silly to her that they attached such sinister motives to his smallest action, but then she realized that she was guilty of the same thing. She'd all but convinced herself that, if she had allowed him to drive her home that night, he would have taken her to bed over any protests she might have made...if any.

If any. That was the hard part for her to accept. Would she have made any protest, even a token one? What had happened to her? One moment her life had been as serene as a quiet pool on a lazy summer day, and she had been satisfied, except for the hollowness left by Vance's death. Then Cord Blackstone had walked in out of the night and everything had shifted, the world had been thrown out of kilter. Now, suddenly, she wanted to run away, or at least smash something...do anything, anything at all, that was totally out of character.

And it was all because of Cord. He was a man who lived by his own rules, a man who lived recklessly and dangerously, but with a vital intensity that made every other man seem insipid when compared to him. By contrast, she was a field mouse who was comfortable only with security, yet now the very security that she had always treasured was chafing at her. The priorities that she had set for herself now seemed valueless in comparison with the wild freedom that Cord enjoyed.

She had been a quiet child, then a quiet girl, never according her parents any of the worries that most parents had concerning their children. Susan's personality was serene, naturally kind and courteous, and the old-fashioned, genteel upbringing she'd had merely reinforced those qualities. By both nature and practice she was a lady, in every sense of the word.

Her life hadn't been without pain or difficulty. Without resentment, she had left school to help care for her mother when a stroke left the older woman partially paralyzed. Another stroke later was fatal, and Susan quietly supported her father during his grief. Her father remarried within the year, with Susan's blessing, and retired to South Florida; she remained in New Orleans, which had been her father's last teaching post, and reorganized her life. She took a secretarial job and dated occasionally, but never seriously, until Vance Blackstone saw her gracing her desk at work and decided right then that she should be gracing his home. Vance hadn't swept her off her feet; he had gently gained her confidence, gradually increasing the frequency of their dates until she was seeing no one but him; then he had proposed marriage by giving her one perfect rosebud with an exquisite diamond ring nestled in the heart of it.

Imogene hadn't been thrilled that her son had selected his wife from outside the elite circle of their social group, but not even Imogene could really find fault with Susan. Susan was, as everyone phrased it, "a perfect lady." She was accepted as Vance's wife, and for three years she had been blessed with happiness. Vance was a considerate lover and husband, and he never let her forget that she was the most important thing in his life, far more important than the Blackstone empire and traditions. He demonstrated his faith in her by leaving everything to her in his will, including control of his share of the family businesses. Devastated by his sudden death, the terms of the will had meant nothing to Susan. Nothing was important to her without Vance.

But time passed, and time healed. Imogene and Preston, at first furious when they learned that she intended to oversee her share of the businesses instead of turning them over to Preston as they had expected, had gradually forgotten their anger as Susan handled herself well, both privately and publicly. She wasn't a woman on an ego trip, nor was she prone to make irresponsible decisions. She had both feet firmly on the ground...or she *had* had, until another Blackstone had entered her life.

As the days passed, she told herself over and over how silly she was being. Why moon over a man who hadn't shown the slightest interest in her since the night they had met? He had just been trying to irritate Preston by playing up to her, that was all. But as soon as that thought registered in her mind, a memory would surface, that of a hard, aroused male body pressing against her, and she knew that Cord hadn't been playing.

She couldn't get his face out of her mind. Odd that she hadn't noticed the family resemblance, but for all the blue eyes and dark hair, nothing about Cord had seemed familiar to her. When she looked at Preston, she was always reminded strongly of Vance; Cord Blackstone resembled no one but himself, with his black brigand's beard and wicked eyes. His personality overshadowed the similarities of coloring and facial structure.

Stop thinking about him! she told herself sternly one night as she dressed to attend a party with Preston. She had been looking at herself in the mirror, checking to see if her dress fit as it should, and had suddenly found herself wondering if Cord would like the dress, if he would find her attractive in it. With rare irritation, she whirled away from the mirror. She had to get him out of her mind! It had been almost three weeks since she'd met him, and it was obvious that she was in a tizzy over nothing, because in those three weeks he'd made no effort to see her again.

It was just as well; they were totally unsuited. She was a gentle spring shower; he was thunder and lightning. She had let a simple flirtation go to her head, and it was time she realized that there was nothing to it.

Glancing out a window at the gloomy sky, she reached into the closet for a coat. The capricious weather of the Gulf states had reminded everyone that it was still only March, despite the balmy weather they had been enjoying for most of the month. The temperature would be close to freezing before she came home, so she chose the warmest coat she owned, as well as wearing a long-sleeved dress.

Preston was always exactly on time, so Susan went down a few minutes early to chat with her cook and housekeeper, Emily Ferris. "I'll be leaving in a few minutes; why don't you go home early today?" she suggested.

"I might at that." Emily looked out the window, watching the wind whip the giant oak tree at the edge of the yard. "This is the kind of day that makes me want to wrap up in a blanket and sleep in front of a fire. Do you have a coat?" she asked sternly, looking at Susan's slender form.

Susan laughed. "Yes, I have a coat." Emily watched over her like a mother hen, but mothering came naturally to Emily, who had five children of her own. The youngest had left the nest a year ago, and since then, Susan had received the full intensity of Emily's protection. She didn't mind; Emily was as steady as a rock, and had been in Susan's employ since she had married Vance. It was in Emily's arms that Susan had wept her most violent tears after Vance's death.

"I'll leave the heat on, so the house won't be cold when you come in," Emily promised. "Where're you going tonight?"

"To the Gages'. I believe William is planning to run for governor next year, and he's lining up support and campaign contributors."

"Hummph," Emily snorted. "What does a Gage know about politics? Don't tell me that Preston's going to support him?"

Susan lifted one elegant eyebrow. "You know Preston; he's very cautious. He'll have to look at every candidate before he makes up his mind." She knew from experience that every politician in the state would be burying the Blackstones under an avalanche of invitations. Susan had tried to stay out of politics, but Imogene and Preston were heavily courted, and Preston invariably asked her to accompany him whenever he attended a party with either political overtones or undertones.

She heard the doorbell at the precise instant the clock

chimed the hour, and with a smile she went to greet Preston.

He helped her with her coat, arranging the collar snugly around her throat.

"It's getting really cold," he muttered. "So much for spring."

"Don't be so impatient." She smiled. "It's still only March. It's just that these last few weeks spoiled everyone, but you knew it couldn't last."

It began to rain as they drove to the Gages' house, a slow, sullen rain that turned the late afternoon into night. Preston was a careful, confident driver, and he made the thirty-mile drive in good time. Caroline Gage met them at the door. "Preston, Susan, I'm glad you could come! Would you like a drink before dinner? William's playing bartender in the den."

Despite Caroline's easy manner, Susan caught a hint of tension in the older woman's expression and wondered if Caroline wasn't enthusiastic about her husband's foray into politics. Following Preston into the den, she found the room already crowded with friends and acquaintances, the usual social crowd. Preston was promptly hailed by William Gage, and with a smile for Susan he allowed himself to be drawn aside.

Susan refused anything to drink, since she hadn't eaten anything, and wandered around talking to her friends. She was popular with both men and women, and it took her quite a while to make a circle of the room. It was almost time for dinner and she glanced at her hostess, frowning when she saw Caroline watching the door, anxiety clearly evident on her face. Was some special guest late?

The doorbell chimed and Caroline paled, but didn't

pause as she went to greet her late-arriving guests. Susan watched the door curiously, waiting to see who it was; Caroline was usually unflappable, and it must be someone really important to have her so on edge.

Her brows rose when George and Olivia Warren came into the room; the Warrens were part of the social hierarchy, but Caroline had been friends with them for years. Cheryl Warren followed them, her ash-blond hair a mass of carefully disarranged curls, her svelte body outlined in a formfitting black dress...and behind her, towering over her, his bearded face sardonic, was Cord Blackstone.

So that was why Caroline was nervous! She'd known that Cord would be with Cheryl Warren, and she was on pins and needles at having Cord and Preston in the same room.

She needn't have worried, Susan thought, glancing at Preston. He wouldn't like it, but neither would he make a scene in someone else's home. If Cord just behaved himself, the evening would go smoothly, though she was acutely aware that Cord would behave himself only if it suited his own purposes.

But, surprisingly, he was a perfect gentleman throughout the long dinner. He was politely attentive to Cheryl, a fact which made Susan's stomach knot. She tried not to look at him, and told herself wryly that she shouldn't have been surprised to see him with another woman...any other woman. He was a man who would always have a female companion. She *was* surprised, however, by the jealousy that jolted her whenever she heard Cheryl's clear laughter, or caught the dark murmur of Cord's voice under the noise of the general chatter.

Caroline had cleared the large living room for dancing, and after dinner she put a stack of easy-listening albums on the stereo, keeping the volume low so her guests could dance or talk as they wished. Susan danced a few dances and talked with her friends, wishing that Preston would cut the evening short and take her home, but he was effectively caught in a group of men earnestly talking politics, and she knew that it would be hours before he was free. She sighed and absently watched the slow-moving couples swaying to the music, then stiffened as her gaze accidentally locked with Cord's pale, glittering eyes. Cheryl was held securely in his strong arms, but he wasn't paying any attention to her as he stared at Susan over Cheryl's bare shoulder. He didn't smile; his gaze slid down her body in a leisurely journey, then returned to her face, staring at her as if he could pierce her thoughts. She paled and looked away. Why had he done that? He'd made it plain by his silence these past three weeks that their flirtation hadn't meant anything to him; why look at her now as if he meant to drag her away to his lair? How *could* he look at her like that, when he held Cheryl in his arms?

Susan pushed her thoughts away by entering into a conversation about vacation cruises, and kept her back turned to the center of the room. It was a tactical error, but one she didn't realize until she felt the fine hairs on the back of her neck standing on end, the age-old warning of danger nearby, and she knew that Cord was behind her. She tensed, waiting for the contact that she knew was coming. His hand touched her waist at the same time that his dark, husky voice said above her head, "Dance with me."

A variation of the same tune, she thought dazedly, allowing herself to be turned and taken into his arms.

Taken...that was the operative word. She felt taken, as if the simple closing of his arms around her had sealed her off from the rest of the world, drawn her deeply and irrevocably under his spell. She was crazy to dance so close to the flame, knowing that she would be burned, but she felt helpless to resist the temptation of his company. As his arms brought her close to his body, the virile scent of his subtle cologne, mingled with the intoxicating smell of his male flesh, went straight to her head and she all but staggered. His hand was burning through the fabric of her dress and scorching her skin; her breasts throbbed and tightened in mindless response, completely out of her control, and she closed her eyes at the powerful surge of desire. Her heart was thumping heavily in her chest, almost painfully, sending her blood zinging through her veins like electrical charges.

There seemed to be nothing to say, so she didn't try to make conversation. She simply followed his lead, intensely aware of the fluid strength of his body, the animal grace of his movements. His warm breath was caressing her temple like the fragrant spring breezes that she loved, and without thinking she opened her eyes, lifting her misty, dreaming gaze to meet the laser intensity of his.

Something hard and frightening was in his gaze, but it was swiftly masked before she could read it. The hard planes of his face were taut, as if he were under some sort of strain. He muttered, "I've tried to stay away from you."

"You've succeeded." Confused, she wondered what he meant. *He* was the dangerous one, not she. Why should he want to stay away? She was the one who should be running for safety, and the fact that she wasn't had her almost in a panic.

"I haven't succeeded at all," he said flatly. The arm at her waist tightened until she was pressed into his body, his hard thighs sliding against her, making his desire firmly obvious. Susan pulled in a wavering breath as her fingers tightened on his shoulder. He dipped his head until his mouth was against her ear, his voice a low rumble. "I want to make love to you. You're responsible for this, sweetheart, and I'm all yours."

The words should have frightened her, but she was beyond fright, already oblivious to anything beyond this man. Her senses had narrowed, sharpened, until he was the only person in the room who was in focus. Everyone else was blurred, distant, and she danced with him in an isolated glow. She closed her eyes again at the thrill that electrified her from head to toe.

He swore softly under his breath. "You look as if I'm making love to you right now. You're driving me out of my mind, sweetheart."

He *was* making love to her, with his words, with every brush of his body against hers as they moved in time with the music. And if he was tortured, so was she. She had been utterly chaste since Vance's death, not even kissing another man, but now she felt as if Cord possessed her in the most basic sense of the word.

"Cheryl came with me, so I'll take her home," he said, placing his lips against her temple as he talked. "But we're going to have to talk. Will you be at home tomorrow afternoon?"

Dazedly, she tried to recall if she had made any plans for the next day; nothing came to mind. It didn't matter; even if she had, she would cancel them. "Yes, I'll be there." Her voice sounded odd, she noted dimly, as if she hadn't any strength.

"I have some business to take care of tomorrow, so I can't nail down an exact time when I'll be there, but I *will* be there," he promised.

"Do you know where I live?"

She could feel his lips curving in a smile. "Of course I know where you live. I made a point of finding out the day after I met you."

The song ended, and she automatically moved away from him, but his arm tightened around her waist. He grinned, his teeth flashing whitely in the darkness of his beard. "You're going to have to shield me for a few more minutes."

A delicate rise of color tinted her cheeks. "We shouldn't dance. That would only…prolong the situation."

"We'll find a corner to stand in." A twinkle danced in the glittering depths of his eyes. "We'll have to stand; I'm incapable of sitting down right now."

She felt her blush deepen, and he chuckled as he moved with her to the edge of the room. She was aware deep inside herself that her heightened color wasn't from embarrassment, but from a primal excitement. She wasn't shocked that he was aroused; she was proud!

He positioned himself with his back to everyone else, his broad shoulders effectively blocking her view of the room. His eyes roamed slowly, intently over her face, as if he were trying to read something in the serenity of her expression. "Did you come with Preston?" he asked abruptly.

"Yes." Suddenly she wanted to launch into an explanation of why she was there in Preston's company, but she left the words unsaid and let her simple reply stand on its own. Preston was her brother-in-law, and she was fond of him; she wouldn't apologize for being with him.

The magnetic power of Cord's eyes was frightening; tiny prisms of light seemed caught in them, holding her gaze captive. Her breath caught in her throat and hung there, swelling her lungs, as she waited for him to release her from his spell. "Am I horning in between you and Preston?" he finally asked in not much more than a whisper. "Are you involved with him?"

The breath that she'd been holding was released on her soft answer. "No."

A smile lifted one corner of his hard mouth. "Good. I just wanted to know if I have any competition. It wouldn't stop me, but I like to know what I'm up against."

No, he didn't have any competition—in any sense. He stood out like a cougar among sheep. The thought of him turning his single-minded attention on her was alarming, but at the same time, she already knew that she wouldn't say the words necessary to turn him away. She knew that she should run like crazy, but her body refused to obey the dictates of common sense.

A tiny frown flickered across his brow as he stared down at her, as if he had seen something that he hadn't expected. He couldn't be wary of her, or alarmed by her femininity; he had known far too many women for there to be any mysteries left for him. Perhaps he was surprised to find himself flirting with her, because she certainly wasn't his type. Perhaps he was looking at her quiet face, her becoming but unspectacular dress, and wondering if he'd temporarily lost his mind. Then the frown was gone, and he smiled faintly as he brushed her cheek with the tips of his fingers. "Tomorrow, sweetheart."

"Yes."

Susan both dreaded and longed for the next day to arrive, but with outward calm and practiced self-discipline, she made it through the remainder of the evening with her usual dignity, chatted normally with Preston on the drive back home, and even went through her nightly routine without missing a beat. Once she was in bed, however, lying alone in the darkened room, she couldn't keep her thoughts from swinging dizzily around Cord, picturing his saturnine face, his incredible lodestone eyes, the black beard that was as soft as a child's hair.

He had a black magic that went to her head like the finest champagne, but how could she be so foolish as to let herself be drawn into the whirlpool of his masculine charm? She'd be sucked so far under the dark waters that she'd have no control over herself or her life; she'd be his plaything, as other women had been, toys that interested him intensely for a short while before they were discarded in favor of a new and more intriguing amusement. Could she really let herself become one of his toys? She'd known real love with Vance, a love that had endowed their physical union with a deep and satisfying richness. Having known that, how could she settle for anything less?

Her mind, her heart, the very core of her being—all said no. Her body, however, lying warm and quivering, yearning for the touch of his strong, lean hands, rebelled against the commonsense strictures of her mind. She was learning now how primitive and powerful desire could be, how disobedient the flesh could be to the demands of conscience. Her soft, feminine body had instinctively recognized the touch of a master, a man who knew far too many ways to bring pleasure to her.

She lay awake for several long, tormented hours, but at last her quietly indomitable will won out over her fevered, longing body. She was not now, never had been, and never would be, the type to indulge in a shallow affair, no matter how physically attractive a man was. If he wanted her company for something other than sex, then she would be happy to be his friend, but the thought of sex without love was abhorrent to her. Making love with Vance had been spiritual and emotional, as well as physical, and her knowledge of the heights had left her dissatisfied with the lower peaks that could be scaled without love.

Not once, during the dark hours, did she have any doubts about the nature of the relationship that Cord wanted with her. He'd told her bluntly that he wanted to make love to her; she sensed that he was always that honest about his desires. His honesty wasn't the courageous openness of honor, but merely his lack of concern over what anyone else thought or had to say about him. He was already an outlaw; why worry about ruining his reputation further?

If only the forbidden weren't always so enticing! Her mind darted and leaped around his image, held so clearly in her memory. He was wickedly attractive; even talking to him gave her the sense of playing with fire. She had to admit that Cord had certainly captured her imagination, but it was nothing more than that, surely, except for his obvious physical charm. The ways of the wicked have always held a fascination for those who walk the bright and narrow path of morality.

But that bright and narrow path was where she belonged, where life had placed her, where she was happy. The shadows where Cord Blackstone stood weren't for her, no matter how intriguing the weary knowledge in his crystalline eyes.

She slept little, but woke feeling calm and rested. Her inner surety of self often masked such physical weaknesses as tiredness or minor illness; her features might be pale, but there was always a certain calmness that overlay any signs of strain. It was Sunday, so she dressed and drove her eight-year-old blue Audi over to Blackstone House to attend church with Imogene and Preston, as she had always done. To her relief, Preston didn't mention that Cord had been at the party the night before; he was too interested in relating to Imogene the details of William Gage's infant political career. Susan commented little, entering the conversation only when she was addressed directly. She sat quietly through the church service, accepted Imogene's invitation to lunch, and maintained her mood of strong reserve all through the meal. Her in-laws didn't try to draw her out of her relative quiet; they had learned to accept her occasional silences as they accepted her smiles. Susan didn't run to a comforting shoulder to unburden herself whenever something troubled her; they might never know what made her deep blue eyes so pensive, and they didn't ask.

They had just finished lunch and were moving into the den when Mrs. Robbins, the housekeeper, appeared with a visitor at her elbow. "Someone to see you, ma'am," she told Imogene, and went about her business. Mrs. Robbins had been with the Blackstones for five years, but she had evidently not heard the rumors and wild tales that had circulated about Cord Blackstone, because there hadn't been a flicker of recognition in the woman's features as she admitted him.

Susan's eyes swept over his face, and she surprised a look of irritation that drew his level brows together in a brief frown when he saw her. Then the frown was gone, and he crossed the room with his easy grace to kiss Imogene, bending down to touch his lips to her cool, ageless cheek. Once again that astonishing color pinkened Imogene's face, though her voice was as controlled as always when she spoke. "Hello, Cord. We've just finished lunch, or I'd invite you to eat with us. Would you like something to drink?"

"Thank you. Whiskey, neat." His mobile lips quirked at the ironclad Southern manners that demanded she offer him food and drink, even when he knew that she despised him. Watching him, Susan surprised herself by reading exactly the thoughts that were only hinted at in his expression. She would have thought that Cord would be more difficult to read.

He chose one of the big, brown leather armchairs, and accepted the short, wide glass of amber liquid that Imogene extended to him, murmuring his thanks in a low voice. Totally at ease, he stretched his long legs out before him and sipped the whiskey.

The room was totally silent, except for the rhythmic ticking of the antique clock perched on the massive oak mantel. Cord seemed to be the only one who was comfortable with the silence. Preston was becoming increasingly red in the face, and Imogene fidgeted with her skirt before she caught herself and commanded her hands to lie calmly in her lap. Susan didn't fidget, but she felt as if her heart were going to bruise itself against the cage of her ribs. How could he have this effect on her by simply walking into the room? It was insane!

He was dressed with fine disregard for the capricious March weather, wearing only impeccable black slacks, creased to a razor's edge, and a thin blue silk shirt through which she could see his darkly tanned flesh and the curling black hair on his chest. Her eyes drank in the details of him, even as she tried not to look at him. For the first time, she noticed the small gold band that he wore on the little finger of his right hand, and she wondered if it was a woman's wedding band. The thought jolted her. What woman had been so important to him that he would wear her ring?

Behind her, Preston had evidently reached the end of his patience. "Did you have a reason for coming here?" he asked bluntly.

A level brow rose in mocking query. "Do you have a reason for being so suspicious?"

Preston didn't even notice the way his words had been turned back on him, but Susan did, and she lifted her head just a fraction of an inch, only a small movement, but one that signaled to people who knew her well that she wasn't pleased. Preston and Imogene knew, and Preston gave her a look that was abruptly apologetic. He had opened his mouth to apologize aloud, a concession that Susan knew didn't come easily to him, when Cord cut smoothly across him.

"Of course I have a reason for coming, and I'm glad that you're smart enough to know that you aren't going to like hearing it. I wouldn't enjoy knowing that I have an idiot for a cousin."

Cord was being deliberately argumentative, Susan

realized, and her eyes narrowed just a tiny bit as she stared at him, but she didn't say anything.

Again silence reigned, as Preston and Imogene seemed to stiffen, waiting. After a moment's surprise, Susan realized that both of them seemed to know what Cord was getting at, and she looked from her in-laws back to Cord's faintly amused expression. He let the quietness draw itself out until the room fairly reverberated with tension; then he negligently crossed one booted foot over the other.

With an air of idle musing, he said, "I know you've probably thought that I've spent the past few years bumming around the world, but I've been gainfully employed most of the time since I left Mississippi. I work for an oil company, as a sort of troubleshooter." His pale eyes gleamed with amusement as he watched the parade of astonishment marching across the features of his cousin and aunt. He didn't look at Susan at all.

"I...smooth things out for them," he continued silkily. "I don't have a title; I have contacts, and methods. I'm surprisingly good at my job, because I don't take no for an answer."

Imogene was the first to recover, and she favored Cord with a polite smile. "I appreciate that you're very well suited for your job, but why are you telling us about it?"

"I just wanted you to understand my position. Look at it as honor among thieves, if you prefer. Now, let's get down to business."

"We don't have any business with you," Preston interjected.

Cord flicked an impatient glance over him. "The Blackstones own a lot of land in Alabama, southern

Mississippi, and Louisiana. I inherited my share of it, so I should know. But the land that I'm interested in isn't part of my inheritance; if it was, I wouldn't be here now. I know that several oil companies have approached you in the last ten years for permission to drill in the ridges, but you've turned them all down. Newer surveys have indicated that the reserves of oil or gas in the ridges could be much larger than originally projected. I want to lease the ridges for my company."

"No," said Preston without hesitation. "Mother and Vance and I talked it over when we were first approached years ago. We don't want any drilling on Blackstone property."

"For what reason, other than a vague idea that it's too moneygrubbing for a blue-blooded old Southern family like the Blackstones?"

Susan sat very still, nothing in the room escaping her attention. A cold chill was lacing itself around her body, freezing her in place. The ridges weren't exactly ridges; they were only ripples in the earth, clothed in thick stands of pine. She liked the ridges, liked the peacefulness of them, the sweet smell of pure earth and pine. But why was Cord asking Imogene and Preston about them? Didn't he know?

"It was nothing as silly as that," Imogene explained calmly. "We simply didn't feel that the chances of a significant oil find were great enough to justify disturbing the ridges. There aren't any roads into them except for that one Jeep track; trees would have to be cut, roads made. I've seen the messes that drilling sites make."

"Things have changed in the last ten years," Cord replied, carrying the glass of whiskey to his lips. "A lot more care is taken not to disturb any area, and, as

I said, it looks as if there's a lot more oil in the ridges than anyone thought at first."

Preston laughed. "Thank you for the information. We'll think about it; we might decide to allow drilling in the ridges after all. But I don't think we'll use your company."

A slow, satisfied smile began to move Cord's lips. "I think you will, cousin. Or you can face criminal charges."

Susan didn't know what he was talking about, but she knew that he had led Preston to exactly that point. He had played the scene as he had wanted it, knowing what Preston's reaction would be, and knowing all the time that he held all the aces. Cord Blackstone had a streak of ruthlessness in him, and her chill deepened.

Preston had gone pale. Of course, she thought absently. Cord wouldn't have made a statement like that without being very sure of himself. She noted that Imogene was also as white and still as a china doll, so Imogene also knew what was going on.

"What are you saying?" Preston asked hoarsely.

"My inheritance." Cord smiled lazily. "I'm a Blackstone, remember? I own stock in all the Blackstone companies. The funny thing is, I haven't been receiving my share of any of the profits. Nothing has been deposited into my accounts at any of the banks we use. I didn't have to dig very deep before I found some papers that had my signature forged on them." He took another sip of whiskey, slowly tightening the screws. He knew he had them. "I believe forgery and theft are still against the law. And we aren't talking about pin money, either, are we? You didn't think I'd ever come back, so you and Aunt Imogene have been steadily lining your own pockets with my money. Not exactly an honorable thing to do, is it?"

Imogene looked as if she would faint. Preston had been turned into stone. Cord looked at them, totally satisfied with the effect he'd had. He smiled again. "Now, about those leases."

Susan stood, her movements slow and graceful, drawing all attention to her. She felt curiously removed from them, as if she were swathed in protective layers of cotton. Somehow she wasn't surprised, or even shocked, to learn that Preston and Imogene had been taking profits that were legally Cord's. It was a stupid thing to do, as well as illegal, but they had a different view of things. To them, what belonged to one Blackstone belonged to all of them. It was a feudal outlook, but there it was. The most trouble she'd ever had with Imogene had been when Vance died and it became known that he'd left everything to Susan, instead of returning it to the family coffers. That was the one mistake Cord had made, in assuming that Vance had left his mother and brother in control of his share. It was an uncharacteristic mistake, and one that he had made because he was a Blackstone himself, with all of their inborn arrogance.

"You're bullying the wrong people," she told Cord remotely, her low voice cutting through the layers of tension and hostility. She felt the lash of his suddenly narrowed gaze, but she didn't flinch under it. "If Preston and Imogene are guilty, then so am I, by association if not actual knowledge. But they can't get you the leases to the ridges. The ridges belong to me."

CHAPTER THREE

SHE DIDN'T REMEMBER driving home. She'd walked out, not even pausing to get her coat, but hadn't felt the cold in her detachment. The house was empty, when she got home, without any welcoming smells emanating from the kitchen, because Sunday was Emily's day off. Susan knew that she'd find something in the refrigerator already prepared, if she was hungry, but she didn't think she'd be able to eat again that day.

She changed clothes, carefully hanging the garments in the closet, then immediately took off the casual clothing she'd just put on. She needed a hot bath, something to take away the coldness that had nothing to do with her skin, but was rather a great lump inside her chest. She threw some sweet herbs into the hot water and eased into the tub, feeling the heat begin to soothe away her stress.

Why did she feel so stunned? Preston had warned her that Cord was ruthless; why hadn't she believed him? It wasn't even what he had done, as much as the way he had done it. He had a right to punish Preston and Imogene for taking what was, essentially, his birthright. If he had wanted to trade that for the leases to the ridges, that was also his right. But he had played with them, leading them step-by-step to the point where they would feel the shock the worst, and he had enjoyed the effect his words had had on them. There was obviously no love lost between them, but Susan didn't believe in inflicting unnecessary pain. Cord had wanted them to squirm.

When the water had cooled, she let it out and dried herself, sighing as she dressed again in the dark brown slacks and white shirt she'd chosen. The bath had helped, but she still felt that inner chill. She checked the thermostat and found that it was set at a comfortable level, but she didn't feel comfortable. She lit a fire under the logs that had already been placed in the fireplace in the den, then wandered into the kitchen to put on a pot of coffee.

The fire was catching when she went back into the den, and she sat for long, increasingly peaceful moments, staring at the licking blue and orange flames. There was nothing as calming as a fire on a cold day. She thought about the needlepoint she was doing, but discarded the idea of working on it. She didn't want to sew; sewing left her mind free to wander, and she wanted to wipe the day from her mind, occupy her thoughts with something else. She got up and went over to the bookshelves, then began to run her finger across the spines of the books, considering and rejecting as she read the titles. Before she could choose a book, the doorbell chimed, then was followed promptly by a hard knock that rattled the door.

She knew instinctively who it was, but her steps didn't falter as she went to the door and opened it.

He was leaning against the door frame, his breath misting in the cold air. His blue eyes were leaping with a strange anger. "I didn't want you involved in this," he snapped.

Susan stepped back and waved him into the house.

He had made some concession to the weather, after all, she noted, as he shrugged out of the lightweight jacket he wore. She took it from him and hung it neatly in the coat closet. She was calm, as if the shock of seeing his cruelty had freed her from the dizzying spell of his sensuality. Her heartbeat was slow and steady, her breathing regular.

"I've just put on a pot of coffee. Would you like some?"

His mouth thinned into a hard line. "Aren't you going to offer me whiskey, try to get me drunk so it'll be easier to handle me?"

Did he think that was why Imogene had offered him something to drink? She started to ask him, then shut her mouth, because it was possible that he was right. Imogene could have offered coffee, because there was always a fresh pot made after every meal. And neither Imogene nor Preston drank very much, beyond what was required socially.

Instead she treated his question literally. "I don't have any whiskey in the house, because I don't drink it. If you want something alcoholic, you'll have to settle for wine. Not only that, I think it would be difficult to get you drunk, and that being drunk would make you harder to handle, rather than easier."

"You're right about that; I make a mean drunk. Coffee will do fine," he said tersely, and followed her as she went into the kitchen. Without looking, she knew that he was examining her home, seeing the warmth and comfort of it, so different from the formal perfection of Blackstone House. Her rooms were large and airy, with a lot of windows; the floors were natural wood, polished to a high gloss. A profusion of plants, happy in the warmth and light, gave the rooms both color and coziness.

He watched as she took two brown earthenware mugs from the cabinet and poured the strong, hot coffee into them. "Cream or sugar?" she asked, and he shook his head, taking the cup from her.

"There's a fire lit in the den; let's go in there. I was cold when I got home," she said by way of explanation, leading the way into the other room.

She curled up in her favorite position, in a corner of the love seat that sat directly before the fire, but he propped himself against the mantel as he drank his coffee. Again he looked at his surroundings, taking in her books, the needlepoint she'd been working on, the television and stereo system perched in place on the built-in shelves. He didn't say anything, and she wondered if he used silence as a weapon, forcing others to make the first move. But she wasn't uncomfortable, and she felt safe in her own home. She drank her coffee and watched the fire, content to wait.

He placed the mug on the mantel with a thud, and Susan looked up. "Would you like more coffee?" she offered.

"No."

The flat refusal, untempered by the added "thank you" that politeness demanded, signaled that he was ready for the silence to end. Susan mentally braced herself, then set her cup aside and said evenly, "I suppose you want to talk about leasing the ridges."

He uttered an explicit Anglo-Saxon phrase that brought her to her feet, her cheeks flaming, ready to show him the door. He reached out and caught her arm, swinging her around and hauling her up against his body in a single movement that stunned her with its swiftness. He wrapped his left arm around her waist, anchoring her to him, while he cupped her chin in his right hand. He turned her face up, and she saw the male intent in his eyes, making her shiver.

She wasn't afraid of him, yet the excitement that was racing along her body was very like fear. The false calm she'd been enjoying had shattered at the first move he'd made, and now her heart was shifting into double time, reacting immediately to his touch. He wouldn't hurt her; she wasn't afraid of that. It was her own unwilling but powerful attraction to him that made her uneasy, that brought her hands up to press against his chest as he bent closer to her.

"Stop," she whispered, turning her head aside just in time, making his lips graze her soft cheek. His grip on her chin tightened, and he brought her mouth back around, holding her firmly, but instead of taking her lips he let his mouth wander to her ear, where his teeth nibbled sharply on the lobe. Susan caught her breath, then forgot to let it out as the warm slide of his lips went down the column of her throat and nuzzled her open collar aside, to find and press the soft, tender hollow just below her collarbone. She felt his tongue lick out and taste her flesh, and her breath rushed from her lungs.

"Cord, no," she protested frantically, alarmed by the tingling warmth that coursed through her body, spreading like wildfire from the touch of his mouth on her. Her pushing hands couldn't budge him. All she succeeded in doing was making herself deeply aware of the powerful muscles that layered his chest and shoulders, of the wild animal strength of him.

"Susan, honey, don't tell me no," he murmured insistently into the fragrant softness of her shoulder, before licking and kissing his way up her throat. Her fingers dug into his shoulder as every tiny flick of his tongue sent her nerves into twitching ecstasy. He finally lifted his head and hovered over her, their lips barely separated, their breaths mingling. "Kiss me," he demanded, his voice harsh, his eyes narrowed and intent.

Her body was quaking in his arms, her flesh fevered and aching for greater closeness with him, but her alarm equaled her physical need. The look in his pale eyes was somehow both cold and fiery, as if his body were responding to her but his actions were deliberately planned. Horrified, she realized that he knew exactly what his touch did to her, and if she didn't stop him soon, she would be beyond stopping him. He'd actually done so little, only kissing her shoulder, but she could feel the hardened readiness of his body and the tension that coiled in his muscles. He was a fire waiting to consume her, and she was afraid that she didn't know how to fight him.

"No, I can't—" she began, and that was all the chance he needed. His mouth closed on hers, and Susan melted almost instantaneously, her body telegraphing its need for him even though her mind rebelled. Her lips and teeth parted to allow the intrusion of his tongue; her hands slid up to lock around his neck, her fingers clenching in the thickness of his hair. As a first kiss, it was devastating. She was already at such a high level of awareness of him that the growing heat of the kiss was inevitable. She gave in without protest to the increasing pressure of his arms as he gathered her even closer to the heated need of his body.

The warning voice of caution was fragmented into a

thousand helpless little pieces, useless against the overwhelming maleness of him. Too many sensations were attacking a body that had been innocent of sensuality for five long years, turning her thoughts into chaos, her body into a dizzying maelstrom of need.

She'd never before been so aware of a man's kiss as a forerunner to and an imitation of the act of sexual possession, but the slow penetration and withdrawal of his tongue sent shudders of pure desire reverberating through her. Mindlessly she rose on tiptoe, and he reacted to the provocation of her movement, his hands sliding down her back to curve over and cup the roundness of her buttocks, his fingers kneading her soft flesh as he lifted her still more, molding her to him so precisely that they might as well have been naked for all the protection their clothing afforded her from the secrets of his body. A moan, so low that it was almost a vibration rather than a sound, trembled in the air, and after a moment Susan realized with shock that it was coming from her throat.

No.

The denial was, at first, only a forlorn whisper in her own mind, without force, but some portion of her brain heard and understood, accepted that she couldn't allow herself to sample the lustful delights this man offered her. With the age-old wisdom of women, she knew that she couldn't offer herself casually, though he would take her casually. It would be nothing to him; a moment of pleasure, good but unimportant and swiftly forgotten. Susan, being the woman she was, would have to offer her heart before she could offer her body, and though she was dangerously attracted to him, she was still heart whole.

No! The word echoed in her mind again, stronger this time, and she tensed in his arms, oblivious now to the seduction of his mouth. The protest still hadn't been voiced aloud, she realized, and with an effort she pulled her mouth free of his. She was suspended in his arms, her toes dangling above the floor while he cupped her hips to his in a position of intimacy, but her stiffened arms held her head and shoulders slightly away from him. She met his glittering diamond eyes evenly. "No."

His lips were red and sensuously swollen from their kiss, and she knew that hers must look the same. His dark beard had been so soft that she hadn't been aware of any prickles, and a rebellious tingle of desire made her want to nuzzle her face against that softness. To deny herself, she said again, "No."

His mouth quirked, amusement shining like a ray of sunshine across his face. "If people learn through repetition, then I have that word engraved on my brain."

Under any other circumstances she would have laughed, but her nerves were too raw to permit humor. She increased the pressure of her hands against his heavy shoulders, desperately trying to ignore the heat of his flesh searing her through the thin silk of his shirt. "Put me down. Please."

He obeyed, slowly, and his obedience was almost as provocative as his sensual attack. He let her slide with excruciating slowness down the hard length of his body, turning her release into an extended caress that touched her from her knees to her shoulders. She almost faltered, almost let her hands leave his shoulders to slide up and clasp around his neck again. Alarmed, determined, she stepped back as soon as her feet touched the floor, and with a wry smile, he let her go.

"You weren't so wary of me last night," he teased, but he watched sharply as she carefully placed herself out of his reach.

That was nothing less than the truth, so she agreed. "No, I wasn't."

"Do I look more dangerous in daylight?"

Yes, infinitely so, because now she'd seen a ruthlessness in him that she hadn't realized was there. Susan regarded him seriously, not even tempted to smile. She could try to put him off with vague excuses, but they wouldn't work with this man. He was still watching her with the deceptive laziness of a cat watching a mouse, letting it go just so far before lashing out with a paw and snatching it back. She sighed, the sound gentle in the room. "I don't think I could trust anyone who did what you did today."

He straightened from his negligent stance, his eyes narrowing. "I only went as far as I had to go. If they'd agreed to lease the ridges, the threat wouldn't have been made."

She shook her head, sending her dark hair swirling in a soft, fragrant cloud around her face. "It was more than that. You set it up, deliberately antagonized both Imogene and Preston from the moment you walked in the door, pushing them so hard that you *knew* they wouldn't lease the ridges to you, *knew* you were going to hit them with your threats. You led them to it, and you gloated every inch of the way."

She stopped there, not voicing the other suspicion that was clouding her mind. Even without really knowing him, she felt as if she knew enough about him to realize that he seldom made mistakes; he was simply too smart, too cunning. But he had either made a mistake in not completely investigating the ownership of the ridges, or he had known all along that she was the owner, and hoped to use his threat against Imogene and Preston as a means of forcing her to sign the leases. It was common knowledge in the area how close she was to her in-laws; even an outsider could have discovered that. Cord might not have the means of threatening her personally, but he would see right away that she was vulnerable through her regard for her husband's family. And even worse than that, she had another suspicion: Was he bent on seducing her for some murky plan of revenge, or as a less than honorable means of securing the lease on the ridges? Either way, his attention to her was suddenly open to question, and she shrank from the thought.

He was still watching her with that unsettling stare. "Guilty as charged. I enjoyed every minute of making the slimy little bastard squirm."

Shaken by the relish in his tone, she winced. "It was cruel and unnecessary."

"Cruel, maybe," he drawled. "But it was damned necessary!"

"In what way? To feed your need for revenge?"

It had been a shot in the dark, but she saw immediately that it had been dead on target. The look he gave her was almost violent; then he turned and took the poker in his hand, bending down to rearrange the burning logs in the fireplace, expending his flare of anger on them. Straightening, he returned the poker to its place and stood with his head down, staring into the hypnotically dancing fire.

"I have my reasons," he said harshly.

She waited, but the moments stretched out and she

saw that he wasn't going to explain himself. He saw no need to justify himself to her; the time had long passed when he needed anyone's approval of his actions.

The question had to be asked, so she braced herself and asked it. "What are you going to do about the money Preston owes you, now that you know he doesn't control the ridges?"

He gave her a hard, glinting look. "I haven't decided."

Chilled by the speculation in his eyes, Susan resumed her seat, an indefinable sadness overwhelming her. Had she really expected him to trust her? He probably trusted no one, keeping his thoughts locked behind iron barricades.

It had to be due to a streak of hidden perversity inside her that, even though she'd rejected the idea of having an affair with him, now she was hurt because she thought he might have an ulterior motive for pursuing her. If she had any brains at all, she'd not only keep the mental distance between them, she'd widen it. He'd made a pass at her, but she couldn't attach any importance to it; he probably made passes at a lot of women. If his kisses were anything, they were a subtle means of revenge. She was a Blackstone by name, and automatically included in his target area. Besmirching the reputation of Vance Blackstone's widow would be a scheme likely to appeal to Cord, if he wanted the Blackstones to squirm.

Because she couldn't stand the horror of the thought, her tone was abrupt when she spoke again. "I can't give you an answer about the ridges. I won't say no, but I can't say yes, either. I'll have an independent geological survey made, as well as gather several opinions about

more immersed in the daily details of running a corporation with a myriad of interests, and Preston had long
ago gotten in the habit of talking everything over with
her. He had the training, but she was quick and knowledgeable, and had good instincts about business. After
Vance's death, taking over his office had been a means
of keeping her sanity, but before long she'd found herself enjoying the work, enjoying the flood of information on which decisions were based.

She arrived early, but Preston was even earlier. Having seen his car in the parking lot, she went straight to
his office, knocking softly on his door. Their mutual
secretary hadn't arrived yet, and the building echoed
with sounds not usually heard during the busy days.

He looked up at the interruption, and a welcoming
smile eased the shadow of worry that had darkened
his face. "Come on in. I've already put the coffee on."

"I could do with an extra jolt of caffeine," Susan
sighed, heading straight for the coffeepot.

They sipped the hot brew in companionable silence
for several minutes, then Susan put her cup down.
"What are we going to do?"

He made no pretense of misunderstanding. "I went
over the old books last night, trying to nail down exactly
how much we owe him. It's a lot, Susan." He rubbed
his forehead wearily.

"You're going to try to replace the money, aren't
you?"

He nodded. "What else can I do? The hell of it is, we
don't have that much ready cash right now. We've invested heavily in research that won't pay off for another
couple of years, but you know that as well as I do. I'm
not going to touch anything that you have an interest

in; Mother and I agreed on that last night. We're going to liquidate some of our personal assets—"

"Preston Blackstone!" she scolded gently. "Did you think I wouldn't be willing to help you?"

"Of course not, honey, but it wouldn't be fair to you. Mother and I did this, and we knew that we were taking a chance. We gambled that Cord wouldn't come back until we'd been able to replace the money, and we lost." He shrugged, his blue eyes full of wry acceptance of his own mistake. "It didn't seem so wrong at the time. We didn't use the money for anything personal; every cent of it was invested back into the corporation, but I don't suppose that would make any difference in a court of law. I still forged his signature on some papers."

"Will you be able to raise enough?" He might protest, but if they couldn't cover the amount they owed Cord, then she would insist on helping them. She didn't want to do anything to jeopardize the corporation, so she agreed that its assets shouldn't be touched, but Vance had left her a lot of personal assets that could easily be liquidated, including some highly valuable property. She also had the ridges, she realized with a sudden start. How badly did Cord want them? Badly enough to take the land in exchange for not pressing charges against Imogene and Preston? Two could play his game!

"I have an idea," she said slowly, not giving Preston time enough to answer her question. "I have something he wants; perhaps we could make a trade."

Preston was a smart man, and he knew her well; he leaned back in his chair, his blue eyes narrowing as he stared at her and sorted out the options and details in his mind. He didn't waste time on unnecessary questions. "You're talking about the ridges. You know that even if you lease the ridges to him, he can still file charges, don't you? He might swear that he wouldn't, but I don't think his word of honor is worth much. Not only that, you'd be giving in to his blackmail."

"Not quite," she said, thinking her way through the situation. "I'll have to have those surveys made, and estimate the worth of an oil lease on the ridges, but if he accepts the leases as restitution for the amount you owe him, then he doesn't have a case any longer, does he?"

Preston looked thunderstruck. "My God, you're talking about letting him have the oil leases for free? Do you have any idea what a rich field could be worth?"

"Millions, I'd imagine, or he wouldn't be so determined to have it."

"A lot more than what we owe him! He'd jump at the deal, but you'd be losing a fortune. No, there's no way I can let you do that."

"There's no way you can stop me," she reminded him, giving him a tender smile. She'd gladly give up a fortune to keep her family intact and safe. Preston had his faults, as did Imogene, but she knew that they'd never turn their backs on her, no matter what happened. They weren't easy people to know—the stiff-necked Blackstone pride and arrogance was present in abundance in both of them—but they also had a loyalty that went all the way to the bone. When she married Vance Blackstone, she had been taken into the family and guaranteed its protection. Preston had been a lifesaver for her when Vance died, pushing his own grief for his brother aside to comfort her and protect her to the best of his ability. Even Imogene, whose proud head had never lowered even on the day of Vance's funeral, had helped Susan by showing her a gritty courage and determination that wouldn't falter.

Preston's frustration was evident in his eyes as he glared at her. "I don't like it when you use that soft, sweet tone of voice. That means you've dug in your heels and won't budge, doesn't it?"

A sound in the outer office alerted them to the arrival of their secretary, Beryl Murphy. Knowing that they both had a lot of paperwork to handle, Susan got to her feet and used that excuse to escape to her own office, even though she knew Preston wanted to try to talk her out of letting Cord have the ridges. Blue fire was in his gaze as he watched her leave the office, but Beryl was already approaching with the first of the day's crises, and he groaned in momentary surrender.

Susan had a stack of reports left on her desk from the Friday before, and she dutifully began reading them, but before long she'd lost the thread of meaning as her mind worried at every angle of the deal she'd be offering Cord.

She really needed to know the monetary value of the oil leases on the ridges before making a deal, but on the other hand, she didn't want to wait before approaching Cord about it. Though he could file charges immediately, she didn't think he would; he would wait, as much to worry everyone as to make up his mind. He probably had already made up his mind, she realized with a burst of panic. Should she wait, or should she tell him right away about the deal? Finally she decided to approach him immediately, before he could take any legal action. If any formal charges were ever made, there would be no way of keeping them from becoming public knowledge, and that would hurt her in-laws enormously.

The realization that she would have to see him, that day if possible, sent a chill down her spine. Just the thought of being close to him again made her blood tumble madly through her veins, whether in dread or anticipation she couldn't say. The way he had kissed her the day before was still seared into her mind, and she couldn't get the taste of his mouth from her lips, or rub from her skin the lingering sensation of the soft brush of his moustache and beard. He was a dangerous animal, but he appealed to her on a primitive level that she had never before suspected existed within herself. She wanted him, and her body's longing made every meeting with him hazardous, because she wasn't certain of her mind's ability to retain control.

But how silky his beard was! Not bristly at all, but soft and sensuous. Was the hair all over his body as soft as that? An image of his nude form sprang into her mind, and a wave of heat washed over her, forcing her to take off the suit jacket she was still wearing.

My God, what was she thinking?

It was useless to entertain daydreams of him. Oh, he'd willingly use her sexually, but for reasons that had nothing to do with being attracted to her personally. Her feminine spirit couldn't take that, nor could her conscience allow her to so abandon her morals.

She got through the day, and somehow avoided Preston when he tried to pin her down at lunch. He didn't want her to sacrifice anything, and Imogene would also object. She'd have to stay one step ahead of both of them, and she meant to do that by seeing Cord as soon as possible. She made the necessary phone calls to get the geological survey in progress and grimly ignored

the thought that now she couldn't let any ecological
damage to the area matter.

By afternoon a weak sun was trying to break through
the cloud layer, and a brisk wind had sprung up. Would
Cord be working on the old cabin at Jubilee Creek? If
he wasn't, she had no idea where to find him. She'd deliberately tried not to listen to all the gossip about him
these past few weeks, and now she wished instead that
she'd absorbed every word; at least then she might have
an idea of where he was. She could ask Preston, but she
knew what fireworks that would set off, so she decided
simply to try her luck at Jubilee Creek.

She left early, because she wasn't certain of her memory of the location of the cabin. Secondary roads wound
through the region like grape runners, crisscrossing
each other and meandering in no particular direction,
it sometimes seemed. Vance had taken her to the Jubilee Creek area a few times, early in their marriage, but
that had been years ago.

Suddenly the sun brightened, as the wind pushed the
clouds away, and she squinted against the sudden glare
of sun on the wet highway. Reaching above the visor,
she grabbed her sunglasses and quickly slid them on.
Perhaps the sun was an omen; then she made a face at
herself at the frivolous thought. She didn't believe in
omens.

She was nervous, her stomach queasy at the thought
of dealing with him, and to take her mind off of it she
tried to concentrate on the passing scenery. The weather
might be chilly, but there were signs of spring after all,
even discounting the stubborn jonquils. Oak trees had
that fuzzy look conveyed by new leaves, and patches of
green grass were shooting up. In another week, two at

the most, color would be rioting over the land as shrubs and trees bloomed, and it couldn't happen soon enough for her. It was already what she counted as a late spring.

She almost missed the turn onto the narrow road that she thought was the correct one. It was only a roughly paved secondary road, without benefit of a painted centerline or graded shoulders. She slowed down, looking for the next turn, and just when she had almost decided that she'd taken the wrong road, she recognized the turn she was supposed to take. It was an unpaved lane that was really only two tracks, crowded on both sides by tall, monolithic pines and sweeping oaks that rapidly hid the secondary road from view. The lane made a long curve; then she found herself rattling across an old wooden bridge that spanned Jubilee Creek itself.

The rain had filled the broad, shallow creek, and the muddy water tumbled over the rocks and around the meandering curves as the creek snaked its way south to empty eventually into the Gulf. She could see the cabin now, a small structure dwarfed by three massive oaks behind it, capping the crest of a small rise. Even from where she was, it was evident that the porch that ran the length of the cabin was completely new, and as she drew closer she could see that the roof was also new, shingles replacing the rusted tin that had been there before.

She didn't know what kind of car he drove, but it didn't matter anyway, since there was no sign of any vehicle. Her heart sank. She slowed her own car to a stop in front of the cabin, staring at the curtainless windows in despair. Where could she find him?

She was just about to put the car in reverse when the door opened and he stepped onto the porch. Even from that distance she could see the icy glare of his eyes, and she knew that this wasn't going to be easy. She drew a deep breath to brace herself, then cut the ignition off and got out of the car.

Walking up the steps was like running a gauntlet; he leaned against the door frame and watched her in nerve-racking silence, his arms crossed over his chest. He looked huge, she noticed; perhaps it was his clothes. He wore only a pair of faded jeans and a black T-shirt, and scuffed brown boots on his feet. The short sleeves of the T-shirt revealed his brawny forearms, sprinkled with dark hair and corded with veins that pulsed with his hot, life-giving blood. From the way the thin cotton clung to his torso, she knew that the image she'd had of his nude body had been remarkably accurate, and her mouth went dry. He was lean and hard and muscular, and his chest looked like a wall.

His glacial eyes swept her from her neat spectator pumps to her head, where her dark hair had been swept into a simple chignon. "Slumming?" he drawled sarcastically.

She controlled the quiver that wanted to weaken her legs, and ignored his opening salvo. "I want to make a deal with you," she said firmly.

Amusement, and a savage satisfaction, glinted in his eyes. He stepped away from the door and waved her inside with an exaggerated bow. "Come inside, lady, and let's hear what you have to offer."

CHAPTER FOUR

THEIR STEPS ECHOED hollowly as she entered the cabin and he followed, closing the door behind them. The smell of newly cut wood struck her nostrils, and fine particles of sawdust floated through the air. Through an open door she could see a couple of sawhorses with a length of wood lying across them, and she realized that she had interrupted his work. She wanted to apologize, but the words refused to leave her thickened throat. To give herself time to recover, she looked around the empty cabin; despite the improvements, it still had an atmosphere of being old and still felt incredibly solid anyway. The new windows, large and airtight, let the light in but kept the damp chill out. An enormous fireplace, laid with logs but unlit, gave the promise of cozy fires. The open door to the right of the fireplace indicated the only other room, and except for it, she could see all of the cabin from where she stood. Beneath her feet, the floor was pine, treated and polished, then left alone to glow with its natural golden color. In spite of her nervousness she was charmed by the old cabin, as if she could feel at peace here.

He stepped past her and leaned down to strike a match and touch it to the old newspaper in the fireplace. It flamed with tongues of blue, which quickly caught the kindling, and soon the fire was licking at the big logs. "I don't feel the cold much while I'm working," he said by way of explanation. "But since you've interrupted me…"

"I'm sorry," she murmured, feeling incredibly awkward.

There was nowhere to sit, but he looked perfectly comfortable as he wedged one strong shoulder against the mantel and gave her a sardonic look. "Okay, lady, you wanted to talk turkey. Talk."

He wasn't going to give an inch. She didn't waste time pleading with him to be reasonable; she lifted her chin and plunged in. "Have you filed charges yet?"

"I haven't had time today," he responded lazily. "I've been working here."

"I… I want to make you an offer, if you'll agree not to file charges."

His ice-blue eyes sharpened and raked down her slim, tense body. "Are you offering yourself?"

The thought jolted her, and she wondered what would happen if she said yes. Would he take her now, on the bare floor? But she said, "No, of course not," in a low voice that disguised her reaction.

"Pity." Nonchalantly, he surveyed her again. "That was the one offer you could have made that might interest me. It might have been fun to see if you get mussed up when you're having sex. I doubt it, though. You're probably starched all the way through."

Susan curled her fingers into her palms, and only then did she notice how cold her hands were. "I'm offering you the lease on the ridges."

He straightened, his hard mouth curving in amusement. "Let me remind you that that was my original offer. But I've thought about it since then, and I've changed my mind. And didn't you tell me yesterday that you couldn't be blackmailed into selling me the lease?"

She stepped closer, to get nearer the fire as much as to read his eyes better. "I'm not offering to sell you the lease—I'll *give* you the lease, as restitution for the amount owed to you by Preston and Imogene."

He laughed, throwing back his dark head on the rich sound. "Do you have any idea how much money you're talking about?"

Preston had asked her the same thing, and her answer was still the same. "More than what they owe you. I realize that. I'm asking you to accept the lease as restitution."

He stopped laughing, and his eyes narrowed on her. "Why should you pay their debts? Why should I let them off scot-free?"

"They're my family," was all she could offer by way of explanation.

"Family, hell! They're pit vipers, sugar, and I should know better than anyone else. I don't want *you* to pay; I want *them* to pay."

"Like you said last night, you want them to squirm."

"Exactly."

"You're turning down an oil lease worth a fortune just for your petty sense of revenge?" she cried.

Anger darkened his face. "Easy there, lady," he said softly. "You're pushing me."

Susan swept an agitated hand across her brow. "You need pushing! How can you be so stubborn?" He wasn't going to agree, and desperation clawed through her stomach. "Why won't you take the lease as payment?"

He grinned, but it wasn't from amusement; his grin was one of grinding rage and grim anticipation. "Because if I accept the lease under those conditions, then I no longer have a case against them, as you well know. Did Preston talk you into this? Well, it won't work. I'll pay you for the lease, and I'll pay you well, but I won't let Preston hide behind your skirt. It's no deal."

Tears stung her eyes as he turned away from her to kick the burning logs into better position. She clutched at his arm, feeling his warm flesh, the steeliness of the muscles underneath. "Please!" she begged.

He swung around, looming over her, the red flames of the fire reflected in his pale eyes and making them glow like a devil's. "Damn you!" he spat from between his clenched teeth. "Don't you dare beg for them!"

Wildly she reached out with her other hand and grasped the fabric of his T-shirt, trying to shake him, but unable to budge him. She had to make him understand! How could he destroy his own family, his own blood? The thought was so horrible that she couldn't stand it. She had to do something, anything, to convince him how wrong and futile revenge was. "Don't do this, please!" she cried frantically. "I *am* begging you—"

"Stop it!" he ordered, his deeper, darker voice completely overriding hers. He jerked her hands off him and held her, his long fingers wrapped around her upper arms. Anger made his fingers bite into her soft flesh, and she gasped, twisting in an effort to free herself. Immediately his grip relaxed, and she jerked away. In the silence that fell between them, her breathing was swift and audible as she gulped in air, her breasts rising and falling. His eyes dropped to the soft mounds as they moved, lingered for a long, heart-stopping moment, and when he finally looked back up to her face, black fury had filled his gaze. "You begged…for *him*.

Get out of here. You can tell him that his little scheme didn't work. Go on, go back to him, and to his bed."

Susan came apart under the tension and the lash of his words. She, who never lost control, whose nature was serene and peaceful, suddenly found herself flying at him, thrusting her face up close to his and yelling, "It was *my* scheme, not his! He tried to talk me out of it! You fool! You're so wrapped up in the past, in your sick need for revenge, that you can't even see how self-destructive you are! If this is how you were fourteen years ago, no wonder you were run out of town—mmmmph!"

He had reached out, his hard hands closing on her waist, and had jerked her against him with enough force to knock the breath out of her. She threw her head back, gasping, and his mouth came down, attacking, fastening on hers, forcing her lips to part and mold themselves to his. There was nothing gentle or seductive in his kiss this time; he forced her response, his arms locking around her and holding her to him, one hand going up her back to fasten in her hair and hold her head back for him to drink as he willed from her mouth. Dazed, dizzied by his sudden sensual attack, she made on effort to wrench away from him.

He kissed her again and again, his tongue making forays that brought her onto her tiptoes, straining against him, forgetting the anger between them, forgetting the reason she was there. The feel of him, so hard and warm, so strong, was all she wanted in the world, the source of every comfort she could imagine. His kisses became deeper, longer, sweet-tart with the passion that turned their embrace into pure fire. His hand went under her jacket, sweeping up to close over her breast with a sure touch that didn't allow her to deny him the right to touch her so intimately. Her blouse was opened so roughly that she was dimly surprised when the buttons didn't fly off; then his hand was inside, sliding between her bra and the soft, satiny flesh beneath it, her nipple stabbing into his rough palm.

She whimpered into his mouth as his hand stroked and kneaded, his demanding man's touch swamping her with a sensual delight that turned her body into pure molten need. Her breasts were very sensitive, and his expertise made them harden with desire, turned the velvet nipple into a taut, throbbing point. She was throbbing everywhere, her entire body pulsating, her own hands digging into the deep valley along his spine, then pulling frantically at his T-shirt until it came free of his pants and she could slide her hands under it, running her palms up the damp, muscled expanse of his back. He quivered under her touch, telling her without words that he was as aroused as she. He had the raw, musky smell of sweat mingled with his own potent masculinity; and she wanted to spend the rest of her life locked in his hard arms, breathing in that scent. It was mad, but oh, it was sweet.

When he released her and stepped back, she was as shocked as if a bucket of icy water had been hurled in her face. Disoriented, lost without the heat of his body, the hard security of his arms, she stared up at him with bewildered blue eyes grown so huge that they dominated her face.

He wasn't unaffected; he was breathing hard, and color was high in his face. When he looked at her open blouse and his pupils dilated, she swayed on her feet, thinking for a moment that he was going to return to her. Then he thrust a rough hand through his hair, ruffling the silky strands. "Is this Plan Two to get me to agree to your deal?"

Susan stepped back, her face losing its color. "Do you really believe that?" she choked, anguish twisting her insides.

"It seems possible enough. You don't have the guts to admit that you want me; you have to cling to your spotless, genteel reputation. But if you sacrifice yourself to me to save your family, why, then you're a noble martyr, and you get to enjoy the sin without sinning. I admit, it sounds like something out of a Victorian novel, but that's what you make me think of."

"A coward," she said painfully.

A hard smile twisted his mouth. "Exactly."

She stood poised, uncertain if she should go or try again to convince him not to press charges against her family. She badly wanted to leave; she was afraid that if he threw any more harsh words against her, her dignity and self-control would be totally destroyed and she'd begin crying, and she didn't want that. She swallowed to force control on her voice, and said quietly, "Please reconsider. How can you turn down a fortune? You know what those ridges are worth if the geologists are right, and what the lease would normally cost you."

"You're offering to save my company a fortune," he pointed out coolly. "I wouldn't get any of the money personally. What's in it for me?"

Confused, she stared at him. How stupid of her! Her great plan had been to offer him personal gain, and he had let her make a complete fool of herself before reminding her that giving the lease to him would benefit the company he worked for, not him personally. Mortified, she turned and walked quickly to the door, wanting nothing more than to leave. A deep chuckle followed her, and as she opened the door and stepped onto the porch, he called, "But it was a good try!"

Susan kept her pace steady as she went to the car, trying not to run even though she wanted to get away from him as fast as she could. What a colossal blunder she'd made! And how he must be laughing at her! When she thought of the way she'd returned his kisses, she blushed, then turned pale. Good Lord, how could he think she was anything but cheap, after she'd virtually offered herself to him? He'd thought that she was just part of the deal, and she couldn't blame him for that; what else could he think, when she'd kissed him back so hungrily?

When she pulled into her own driveway and saw Imogene's Cadillac in front of the house, she groaned aloud. The last thing she felt like right then was facing Imogene's drilling; she wanted to take a long bath and pamper herself in an effort to soothe her ragged nerves. She knew that Preston would have called Imogene and talked to her about Susan's ploy, and now Imogene was here to discover how things had gone. Why couldn't she have waited just a few hours more?

There would be no easy way to dash Imogene's hopes, and the strain was evident in Susan's face as she entered the house and walked to the den, where she knew her mother-in-law would be waiting. The older woman rose to her feet when Susan entered, and her shrewd gray eyes examined every nuance of expression in Susan's face. "He turned you down, didn't he?" It wasn't like Imogene to give in to defeat, but now her discouragement gave a leaden cast to her eyes, dulled her voice.

He'd turned her down in more ways than one, Susan thought wearily. Her mental and physical fatigue muted her voice as she sank down in one of the chairs. "Yes."

"I knew he would." Imogene sighed and resumed her seat, her patrician face stiff with effort. "It would be too easy to let you pay; it's Preston and me that he's after."

Remembering the cool contempt in his eyes when he had looked at her, Susan couldn't agree fully with Imogene. A hard knot of pain formed in her chest; why did it have to be like that? When she remembered the intense magic of their first two meetings, she wanted to weep at the harsh words that had passed between them since then. She felt as if she had lost something precious, without ever having held it in her hands. He was a hard man, yet inexplicably she wanted to get closer to him, to get to know him, learn his moods and his laughter as well as his anger, delve into his protected personality until she found some inner core of tenderness. When he had kissed her the first time, it had been with a tender consideration for her soft flesh. But today… Susan raised her fingers and touched her lips, still a little swollen and sensitive from his hard kisses. He hadn't been gentle today; he had been angry, and he had punished her for daring to try to protect Preston.

Suddenly she realized that Imogene had followed the telltale gesture with knowing eyes, and she blushed.

Imogene sat upright. "Susan! He's interested in you, isn't he? How perfect! Thank God," she said fervently.

Susan had expected a subtle scolding, not Imogene's almost rapturous joy. "What's perfect?" she asked in confusion.

"Don't you see? You're in a marvelous position to find out what he's planning and keep us informed; that way we can take steps to counteract anything he does. Why, you might even be able to talk him out of staying here!"

Stunned, she stared at Imogene, not quite able to believe what was being asked of her, what Imogene automatically assumed she would do, without protest. After all, she was family, and her first allegiance was to that family. It was the same sort of thinking that had allowed Imogene and Preston to use Cord's money illegally in the first place; it wasn't as much Cord's money as it was Blackstone money, and therefore available for their use.

She strove for an even tone. "He's not interested in me. If anything, I'm tarred with the same brush he's used to paint you and Preston."

Imogene waved that thought aside with a brisk movement of her hand. "Nonsense." She examined Susan critically, her gray eyes narrowed. "You're a lovely woman, though of course not his usual sort. It shouldn't be difficult for you to get around him."

"But I don't want to get around him!"

"Dear, you *must!* Don't you see that the only way we can protect ourselves is to know in advance what he's planning?"

Agitation tumbled Susan's insides with a restless hand, and she got to her feet, unable to sit still. "It's impossible," she blurted. "I'm not a…a slut. I can't sleep with him just to *spy* on him!"

Imogene looked affronted. "Of course you wouldn't, but I'm not asking that of you, Susan. All I'm asking is that you see him, talk to him, try to find out what he's planning. I realize that it may cost you a few kisses, but surely you're willing to give that in exchange for our protection."

A few kisses! Did Imogene really know so little about her own nephew? Susan shook her head slowly, denying the idea to herself, as well as to Imogene. "A few kisses isn't what he wants," she said, her voice muffled. And even if she went to bed with him, he still wouldn't divulge any secrets to her. All he wanted from her was a good time in bed, physical release, a momentary pleasure.

Imogene didn't give up easily; there was steel in her spine, in her character. Sitting very upright, her chin lifted proudly, she said firmly, "Then it's up to you to keep him under control. You're not a teenager, to be seduced in the backseat of a car to the theme of 'but everyone does it.' You can string him along."

If Susan had been less shocked, she would have laughed aloud, but as it was she stood frozen, staring at Imogene as if she were a stranger. What her mother-in-law was telling her to do struck her as little less than prostitution, and she felt chilled by the realization that Imogene had so little regard for her feelings, her morals. She was simply supposed to do whatever was asked of her.

"No," she refused in a low voice. "I can't... I *won't* do it."

A cold fire began snapping in Imogene's eyes. "Really? Do you care so little for me, for Preston, that you'll simply stand and watch while that wretch destroys us? We won't be in it by ourselves, you know. You'll suffer, too. If he decides to sue us for damages, he could bankrupt the company, and there would go the standard of living that you currently enjoy. People will talk about you just as they would about us; everyone will believe that you knew about the money from the beginning.

You've made a big show of 'working' at the company since Vance died, so people will assume that not only did you know about it, you approved."

Susan had seen Imogene in action before, and knew that few people could stand up to her when she lashed out with her lethal tongue, when she stared at someone with those cool, hard eyes. Most people gave in to her without even a hint of resistance. Vance had had the strength to soothe her, agree with her, and calmly go about his own business in his own way, smiling at her and charming her whenever she realized that he'd ignored her directions. Preston wasn't that often at variance with her, though he was a lot warmer, a lot more human. Because she had been challenged so seldom in her life, she didn't expect anyone to disobey her openly. The quiet determination Susan had shown in becoming Vance's wife, then in taking up the reins of his business interests at his death, should have told her that Susan wasn't like most people, but still she wasn't prepared for a refusal.

Susan stood very straight, very still, her expression calm, her dark blue eyes quiet and level. "Regardless of what anyone says, I'll know that I haven't done anything wrong, and that's what's important to me. I'll help you any way I can, except for that way. I'll sell everything I own, but I won't play the whore for you, and that's what you're asking me to do. You know as well as I do that Cord isn't a man who can be controlled by any woman."

Imogene got to her feet, her mouth tight. "I expected more loyalty from you than this. If you want to turn your back on us when we're in trouble, I can't stop you, but think very carefully about what you stand to lose."

"My self-respect," Susan said dryly.

Imogene didn't storm out of the house; she swept out, regally, in a cold rage. Susan stood at the window and watched her drive away, her chest tight with hurt and sadness because she hadn't wanted to damage the relationship she had with Imogene. Since she'd first met Vance's mother, she had carefully cultivated a closeness with the older woman, knowing how important the ties of family were to a marriage, and how much Vance had loved his mother despite her reserve. Imogene wasn't a villain, even though she was autocratic. When she loved, she loved deeply, and she'd fight to the death for those she cared about. Her blindness was her family; anything was acceptable to her if it protected her family. Until now Susan had been wrapped in that fierce blanket of protection, but now she felt that she'd been cast out as Cord had been cast out. Dues had to be paid if someone expected to benefit from that protection; conformity was expected, and a willingness to sacrifice oneself for the well-being of the whole. Cord had been cast out because he hadn't conformed, because he'd left the family open to gossip. His reputation hadn't been up to par, and he'd been forced out of the closed circle.

Had he felt like this? Susan wondered, running her hands up her chilled arms. Had he felt lost, betrayed? Had he been alarmed to be without the support that he'd known since birth? No, he hadn't been alarmed, not that man; instead he would have thought with grim delight of punishing them for turning their backs on him. Wasn't that what he was doing now?

Cord. Somehow all her thoughts these days returned to him, as if he had become the center of her world. She hadn't wanted him to, but since the moment he'd walked in from the night, he had eclipsed everyone else in her every waking thought, in her dreams, had invaded even her memory, so that she constantly had the taste of his mouth on her tongue, felt the hard warmth of his hands on her flesh. *I could love him!* she thought wildly, and shuddered in half fear, half excitement. Loving him would be the most dangerous thing she'd ever done in her life, yet she felt helpless to deny the effect he had on her. If it wasn't love yet, it had nevertheless gone beyond mere desire, and she was teetering on the edge of an emotional chasm. If she fell into it, she'd be forever lost.

The emotional strain that she was under was visible on her face the next morning when she walked into the office, later than usual for her because she'd spent a restless night, then overslept when she finally did manage to fall asleep. Because she felt so frazzled, she'd attempted to disguise her emotional state by hiding behind an image that was sterner than the one she usually projected. She'd pulled her soft dark hair back into a tight knot and applied makeup carefully, hoping to divert attention from the lost expression in her eyes. The dress she had chosen was sleekly sophisticated, a black silk tunic with narrow white vertical stripes, cinched about her slender waist with a thin black belt. It wasn't a dress that she wore often, because it had always seemed too stark for her, but today it suited her mood perfectly.

She told Beryl good morning, then went straight through to her office and closed the door, hoping to submerge herself in the reports that she hadn't finished the day before, because she'd been in such a hurry to see Cord. A wasted effort, she thought with a painful catch in her breath. Resolutely she pushed away the thought of her failure and picked up the first report, only to replace it when someone knocked firmly on her door.

Without waiting for an answer, Preston let himself in and sauntered over to ease himself into the chair opposite her desk. He sprawled in it and pressed his fingers together to form a steeple, over which he peered with blue eyes alive with curiosity. "What did you say to Mother?" he asked with relish. "I haven't seen her so angry in years."

Susan caught the grin that twitched at his mouth, and against her will she found herself smiling at him. Preston had a little bit of the devil in him at times, a puckish sense of humor that he seldom allowed to surface. Whenever he did, it made his eyes sparkle in a manner that reminded her strongly of Vance. Now was one of those times. Despite the pressure he was under, he was being eaten alive with curiosity, wondering what Susan could possibly have said to his mother to put her in such a snit.

She wasn't certain just how much to tell him, if anything. She decided to stall. "Did Imogene tell you that Cord turned down my offer of the ridges?"

He nodded. "I'm glad, too. I know it would've been the easy way, but I don't want you to pay for something that was our fault. You know that." He gave a graceful shrug. "Mother didn't agree; she thought that it would be worth it if we stopped any trouble before it began."

Yes, head off scandal, at any cost. Deciding to tell him the truth in the hope that he would support her, she took a deep breath and braced herself. "She wanted me to see Cord—play up to him—and try to find out what he was planning so you could counteract it. I refused."

Preston's eyes had widened, then narrowed as he

realized the scope of her simplified explanation. He swore softly. "Thank God for that! I don't want you around him. Mother shouldn't have suggested anything like that."

"She'd do anything to protect her family," Susan offered in Imogene's defense.

"Telling you to play up to Cord is like throwing a lamb to the wolves," he snapped. "You wouldn't have a chance. What in hell ever gave her the idea?"

A faint blush crept into Susan's cheeks, and she looked away from him. "She knows that he kissed me...."

Preston bolted upright in his chair. "He what?"

"He kissed me," she repeated steadily. Did Preston think that was something to be ashamed of?

He'd turned pale, and abruptly he surged to his feet, running his fingers through his neat hair in an uncharacteristic gesture. "I thought, the night he first showed up, that he was just playing up to you to get back at me. Is that all it is?"

Susan bit her lip; she honestly didn't know. Her body told her that Cord Blackstone's interest wasn't limited to her name, but her mind worried over the issue. A man's sexual instincts could be aroused even when he had another motive for seducing a woman, so she couldn't let herself be confused by the physical responses he'd shown. Yet, he'd responded to her from the very beginning... Just when her heart was beginning to beat faster in faint hope, she saw herself stretching out her hand to him, and heard herself saying, "I'm Susan Blackstone..." No, he'd known from the first that she was a Blackstone, married to either Vance or Preston. Unhappily, she looked up at Preston. "I don't know," she said miserably.

He began to pace around the room. "Susan, please, don't have anything else to do with him. Don't see him at all, unless you have to. You don't have any idea of the type of man he is."

"Yes, I do," she interrupted. "He's a hard, lonely man." How could he not be lonely? He might have built an emotional wall to guard him, but he was all alone behind it.

Preston gave her a derisive, unbelieving look. "My God, how can you be so naive? You've got to stop seeing good in everyone! Some people are bad all the way through. Will you promise me not to see him again, and protect yourself before he has a chance to really hurt you?"

There was a very real chance that *he* wouldn't want to see *her*, but suddenly she knew that if by some miracle he gave her another opportunity, she'd seize it with both hands. She wanted to be with him. She wanted to kiss him, to try to discover if what she felt for him was a fleeting sexual magic, or if the seeds of real love had been sown. For five years she'd grieved for Vance, and though her love for him would never die, neither would it grow. Vance was frozen in place in her heart, but he didn't occupy all of it. There was still so much love in her to give! She wanted to love again; she wanted to marry again, and bear children. Perhaps Cord wasn't the man who would be able to touch her heart, but she already knew that she had to take the chance. If she let the opportunity pass, she'd always wonder about it, and mourn for lost chances for the rest of her days.

She looked Preston in the eye. "I can't promise that."

He swore softly, and suddenly his shoulders hunched.

"All of these years," he muttered. "First you were Vance's wife, then his widow. I've waited, knowing you weren't over Vance, that you weren't ready to become involved with anyone else. Damn it, why does it have to be Cord?" The last sentence was a harsh cry, and his chest swelled with the fury inside him. He gave Susan a look so tortured that tears welled in her eyes.

She found herself on her feet, unable to calmly sit there while he bared his deepest secret to her. "Preston... I didn't know," she whispered.

His clear blue eyes were a little shiny, too. "I know," he said, taking a shuddering breath. "I made sure I kept it from you. What else could I do? Try to steal my brother's wife?"

"I'm sorry. I'm so sorry!" What else was there to say? Events couldn't be altered. Perhaps, if their lives had been allowed to go on undisturbed, she might one day have come to love Preston in the way he wanted, though she rather thought that instead she would always have seen him as Vance's brother, and looking at him would always have been like looking at a slightly altered photo of Vance. But the even tenor of her life had been disrupted from the moment she'd seen Cord, and crossing that dance floor to take his hand and shield him from the scene that had been brewing had forever altered her, in ways that she hadn't yet discovered.

"I know." He turned his head away, not wanting her to see the depth of his pain. He was a man of pride and patience, and his patience had gained him nothing. All he could do now was cling to his pride. He walked to the door and left, his shoulders square, his gait steady, but still Susan knew what the effort cost him, and her vision blurred as she watched him.

Would Cord be glad that, even involuntarily, he'd managed to hurt Preston? She winced at the thought. She'd certainly never tell him that Preston had hoped for a deeper relationship. What he'd told her today would go no further; it was the least she could do for someone she loved as much as she could, even though, for him, that wasn't enough.

CHAPTER FIVE

BY FRIDAY HER emotional turmoil had taken its toll on her, and the price she'd paid was evident in an even more slender waistline, and a fragility in her face that was startling. She and Imogene had made up, in a way. They had spoken to each other on the phone, never making reference to their difference of opinion, but their conversation had been stilted and brief. Imogene had simply asked her if she would be attending Audrey Gregg's Friday night fund-raising dinner for a local charity. Imogene had a prior commitment, and she wanted Susan to go, since Audrey was a very good friend. Susan had agreed, reluctant to face an evening of having to smile and pretend that everything was all right, but acknowledging her family duty. At least it wasn't formal, thank God. Audrey Gregg believed in keeping her guests entertained; there would be dancing, a generous buffet instead of a sit-down dinner, and probably a night-club act brought in from New Orleans.

Spring was tantalizing them again with marvelous weather, though only the day before it had been cold and overcast. Today the temperature had soared to eighty, and the forecasters had promised a mild night. With that in mind, Susan dressed in a floaty dress in varying shades of lavender and blue, with a wrap bodice that hugged and outlined her breasts. She was too tired and depressed to fool much with her hair, and simply brushed it back, securing it behind each ear with fila-gree combs. The sun was setting in a marvelous sky-scape of reds and gold and purples when she drove over to Audrey's house, and the natural beauty lifted her spirits somewhat. How could she keep frowning in the face of that magnificent sunset?

The brief lifting of her spirits lasted only until she glanced over the crowd at Audrey's and saw Cord, ca-sually sophisticated in gray flannel slacks and a blue blazer, dancing with Cheryl Warren. Cheryl again! Though Cheryl was a likable person, unexpectedly kind despite her chorus-girl looks, Susan felt an unwelcome sting of jealousy. It was just that Cheryl was so...so sexy, and so *together*. Her tall, leggy body was svelte, with a dancer's grace; her makeup was always a little dramatic, but always perfectly applied, and somehow right for her. Her ash-blond hair looked wonderful—loose and sexy, tousled.

Compared to Cheryl, Susan felt nondescript. Her simple hairstyle suddenly seemed childish, her makeup humdrum, her dress the common garden variety. She scolded herself for feeling that way, because she knew the dress was becoming to her and was perfectly styl-ish. It was just that Cord made her feel so insecure, so unsure of herself and what she wanted. Then she had to admit to herself that she did know what she wanted: She wanted Cord. But she couldn't have him; he was all wrong for her, and he didn't want her anyway.

Suddenly Preston was at her elbow, his strong hand guiding her to the buffet. With a pang, Susan realized that normally she would have been here with Pres-ton, but this time he hadn't even asked her. Cord had managed to drive a wedge between her and Preston, whose friendship she had depended on for so long. How pleased he would be if he only knew what he'd done!

Preston's blue eyes were worried as he looked down at her. "Relax for a minute," he advised. "You're wound up like a two-dollar watch."

"I know," she sighed, watching as he automatically filled a plate for her. He knew all her favorite foods, and he chose them without asking. When he had two laden plates in his hand, he nodded over to a group of empty chairs and they made their way across the room to claim them, with Susan stopping en route to fetch two glasses of champagne punch.

He watched as she nibbled on a fresh, succulent Gulf shrimp. "You're lovely," he said with the blunt honesty of people who know each other well. "But you look as if you're going to fly into a million pieces, and that isn't like you."

She managed a wry smile. "I know. You don't know how I wish I could do more than catnap. At least Imogene's speaking to me again."

He grinned. "I knew she wouldn't last long. She's been so restless, it was almost funny. Honey, if it's such a strain on you, why don't you take a vacation? Forget about all of this and get away from all of us for a while."

"I can't do that now." The look she gave him was worried. "I can't leave you not knowing if…if…"

"I know." He covered her hand with his, briefly applying pressure before removing his touch. "I'm handling it, so don't worry so much. In another week to ten days, I'll have the money repaid into Cord's account."

She bit her lip. She knew that he would have had to liquidate a lot of assets to raise that much money so quickly, and she felt guilty that he hadn't allowed her to help. Perhaps she hadn't known anything about it, but she had profited by the use of the money because it had made the company stronger.

By sheer willpower, she kept her gaze from straying too often to Cord as the minutes crawled past, but still she somehow always knew where he was. He'd stopped dancing with Cheryl, and she was surprised by the number of people who engaged him in conversation, despite how wary most of them still were of him. Why was he here? She couldn't imagine that Audrey Gregg had invited him, so he had to have come with someone else, probably Cheryl. Was he seeing Cheryl often?

For a while he stood alone, off to one side, slowly sipping a glass of amber liquid, his dark face blank of any expression, his eyes hooded. He was always alone, she thought painfully. Even when someone was talking with him, he had a quality about him that set him apart, as if he were surrounded by an invisible barrier. He'd probably had to become hard and aloof to survive, but now that very protection kept him from being close to another human being.

It was too stressful to watch him. To divert herself, she began talking to Preston, and resolutely kept her gaze away from Cord. Good friend that Preston was, he talked easily of many things, keeping her occupied. She knew that he had to be under a strain himself, even more so than she was, but he was handling it well, and his concern was all for her.

Suddenly Preston looked past her, his blue gaze sharpened and alert. "It's in the fan now," he muttered. "Grant Keller is about to tie into Cord."

Susan whirled, and gasped at the hostility of the

scene. Grant Keller was a picture of aggressive, bitter hatred, standing directly in front of Cord, his fists knotted and his jaw thrust out as he spat some indistinguishable words at the younger man. His handsome, aristocratic face was twisted with hate and fury. Cord, on the other hand, looked cool and bored, but there was an iciness in his eyes that warned Susan that he was on the verge of losing his temper. His stance was relaxed, and that too was a signal. He was perfectly balanced, ready to move in any direction.

Her breath caught in her chest. He'd never before seemed so aloof, so unutterably alone, with only his natural pride and arrogance to stand with him. Her heart was stabbed with pain, and she felt as if she were choking. He was a warrior who would die rather than run, standing by his own code, loyal to his own ideals. Oh, God, couldn't they see that only pain could force a man into such isolation? He'd been hurt enough! Then, out of the corner of her eye, Susan saw Mary Keller watching her husband, with distress and a wounded look evident on her quiet face.

Suddenly Susan was angry, with a fierce swell of emotion that drove away her depression, her tiredness. That old scandal had already caused enough trouble and pain, and now another woman was about to be hurt by it. Mary Keller had to sit there and watch her husband try to start a fight over another woman, something that couldn't be pleasant. And Cord…what about Cord? His youthful love affair had caused him to be driven away from his family, and the hard life that he'd lived since then had only isolated him more. Grant Keller was the wronged husband, true, but he wasn't the only one who had suffered. It was time for it to end, and she was going to see that it did!

People who had never seen Susan Blackstone angry were startled by the look on her face as she headed across the room, and a path was cleared for her. Her eyes were a stormy indigo, her cheeks hot with color, as she marched up to the two men and put her slender body gracefully between them. She was dwarfed by their size, but no one had any doubt that the situation had been swiftly defused. She was practically sparking with heat.

"Grant," she said with a sweetness that couldn't begin to disguise the fire in her eyes, "I'd like to talk to you, please. Alone. Now."

Surprised, he looked down at her. "What?" His tone indicated that he hadn't quite registered her presence.

Cord's hard hands clamped about her waist, and he started to move her to one side. She looked up, smiling at him over her shoulder. *"Don't...you...dare,"* she said, still sweetly. She looked back at Grant. "Grant. Outside." To make certain that he obeyed her, she took his arm and forcefully led him out of the room, hearing the buzz of gossip begin behind her like angry bees swarming.

"Are you crazy?" she demanded in a fierce whisper when they were out of earshot, dropping the older man's arm and whirling on him in a fury. "Haven't enough people already been hurt by that old scandal? It's *over!* It can't be undone, and everyone has paid for it. Let it die!"

"I can't," he returned just as fiercely. "It's burned into my head! I walked into my own home and found my wife in bed with *him*. Do you think he was ashamed?

He just glared at me, as if she were *his* wife, as if I had no right to be there!"

Yes, that sounded like Cord, able to stare down the devil himself. But she brushed all of that aside. "Maybe you have bad memories, but you're just going to have to handle them. Are you still in love with your first wife? Is that it? Do you want her back? You have Mary now, remember! Have you given her a thought? Have you thought of how she must feel right now, watching you start a fight over another woman? Why don't you just walk up and slap her in the face? I'm sure it wouldn't hurt her any worse than she's hurting right now."

He blanched, staring down at her. Perspiration broke out on his face, and he wiped his brow with a nervous hand. "My God, I hadn't thought," he stammered.

Susan poked him in the chest with her forefinger. "It's a dead issue," she said flatly. "I don't want to hear about it again. If anyone…*anyone*…wants to fight Cord over something that happened fourteen years ago, they're going to have to go over me first. Now, go back in there to your wife and try to make it up to her for what you've done!"

"Susan—" He broke off, staring at her pale, furious face as if he'd never seen her before. "I didn't mean—"

"I know," she said, relenting. "Go on now." She gave him a gentle push, and he sucked in a deep breath, obviously preparing himself to face a wife who had every right to be hurt, humiliated and angry. Susan stood where she was for a moment after he'd gone, drawing in her own deep breaths until she felt calm seep back into her body, replacing the furious rush of adrenaline that had sent her storming across the room to step between two angry men.

"That's a bad habit you've got." The deep drawl came from behind her, and she whirled, her breath catching, as Cord sauntered out of the shadows. Abruptly she shivered, no longer protected by her anger, as the cooling night air finally penetrated her consciousness. Quickly she cast a glance at the crowd of people visible through the patio doors, some of them dancing again, going about their own concerns. She had stepped in too soon for anything exciting to happen, so there wouldn't even be much gossip.

"They all know we're out here, but no one is going to intrude," he said cynically. "Not even Preston, the Boy Wonder." He touched the soft curve of her cheek with one finger, trailing it down to the graceful length of her throat. "Didn't your mother ever teach you that it's dangerous to get between two fighting animals?"

She shivered again, and when she tried to speak she found that her voice wouldn't work right; it was husky, strained. "I knew you wouldn't hurt me."

Again his finger moved, sliding with excruciating slowness over her collarbone, then stroking lightly over the sensitive hollow of her shoulder. Susan found that the touch of his finger, the hypnotic motion of it, somehow interfered with her breathing; the rhythm of her lungs was thrown off, and she was almost hyperventilating one moment, then holding her breath the next. She stared up at him, seeing his lips move as he spoke, but her attention was focused on his touch, and the words didn't make sense. She swallowed, licked her suddenly dry lips, and croaked, "I'm sorry. What—"

One corner of his mouth lifted in a strange almost-smile. "I said, you'd be a lot safer if you didn't trust me.

Then you'd stay away from me, and you wouldn't get burned. I can't decide about you, honey."

"What do you mean?" Why couldn't her voice be stronger? Why couldn't she manage more than that husky whisper?

His finger moved again, making a slow trek over to her other shoulder, touching her in a way that made her heart slam excitedly. She'd never noticed her shoulders being so sensitive, but he was doing things to her that were rocketing her into desire. "I can't decide whose side you're on," he murmured, watching both his finger and the way her breasts were heaving as she struggled to regulate her breathing. "You're either the best actress I've ever seen, or you're so innocent you should be locked up to keep you safe." Suddenly his pale eyes slashed upward, his gaze colliding with hers with a force that stunned her. "Don't step in front of me again. If Grant had accidentally hit you, I'd have killed him."

She opened her mouth to say something, but whatever was in her mind was forever lost when he trailed his finger downward to her breasts, stroking her cleavage, then exploring beneath the cloth of her bodice to flick over a velvet nipple. She caught a moan before it surfaced, gasping in air. With a slow, sure touch he put his hand inside her dress, cupping her in his palm with a bold caress, as sure of himself as if they weren't standing on the patio where any of fifty people could interrupt them at any time. He looked at her face, soft, drowning in sensuality, and suddenly he wondered if she looked the same whenever Preston touched her. She was either the most sensual woman he'd ever seen, or she was fantastic at faking it. At the thought of Preston, he removed his hand, leaving her dazed and floundering. "You'd better get back inside," he muttered; then he turned and walked away, disappearing into the night shadows, leaving her more alone than she'd felt since Vance's death.

Her body burned from his touch, yet she was shaking with something like a chill. It was like a fever, she thought dimly, burning hot and cold at the same time. He *was* a fever, consuming her, and she reached the horrified realization that the way she felt about him was no longer under her control. Without wanting to, she cared too much about him. She was playing Russian roulette with her emotions, but it was far too late to stop.

She stood there in the cool night for several minutes longer, then slipped quietly inside to rejoin the party. Preston came over and touched her arm gently. "Are you all right?" he asked with tender concern, and in his eyes she saw the love that he couldn't quite hide.

She was calm enough now to give him her most reassuring smile, one that made most people feel that everything was right with the world. "Yes, I'm fine."

"Grant and Mary have gone home. What'd you say to him? He looked like he was in shock when he came in, and he went straight to Mary."

She shook her head, still smiling. "Nothing, really. I just calmed him down."

His look said he didn't quite believe her, but he kissed her forehead lightly in tribute. It was inevitable that when Susan glanced around she saw Cord standing across the room, staring at her with cold, unreadable eyes, and a sad pain bloomed in her heart. He'd never trust her, she thought, and wished that it didn't mean so much to her.

Audrey Gregg found the opportunity to thank her for

averting a scene, and after that Susan made her excuses and drove herself home where she fell into bed in mental exhaustion, then got up ten minutes later to restlessly pace the house. Finally she turned on the television to watch an old Jerry Lewis and Dean Martin comedy, letting their antics clear her mind. She was engrossed in the movie, chuckling to herself, when the doorbell rang. Frowning, she glanced at the clock. It was almost midnight, the witching hour.

"Who is it?" she called through the door, tying the sash of her robe tighter.

"Cord."

She unlocked the dead bolt and opened the door to him. He straightened from his slouch against the door frame and walked inside. Her eyes dropped to the whiskey bottle he carried in his hand. A half-empty whiskey bottle.

"Are you drunk?" she asked warily.

"On my way." He smiled at her and took a drink from the bottle. "It's hard for me to get drunk, but champagne does it to me every time. Something about my chemistry. I'm just trying to finish it off with this."

"Why do you want to get drunk?" He was walking toward the den, and she followed him automatically. If he was drunk, or even high, he was certainly handling it well. His walk was steady, his speech clear. He sat down on the couch and stretched his long legs out before him, sighing as his muscles relaxed. Susan went over to the television and switched it off in the middle of a Jerry Lewis pratfall.

She repeated her question. "Why do you want to get drunk?"

"It just seems like the thing to do. A sort of tribute to the past."

"So you lift a glass…excuse me, a bottle…to auld lang syne."

"That's right." He drank again, then set the bottle down with a thud and pinned her with his glittering eyes. "Why did you have to get between us? I wanted to hit him. My God, how I wanted to hit him!"

"Another tribute to the past?" she asked sharply.

"To Judith," he corrected, smiling a little. "Do you know what he said? He came up to me and said, 'So the little whore didn't stay with you, either.' I should've broken his neck on the spot."

Susan hadn't heard the name before, but she knew that Judith had been Grant's first wife, the woman caught in bed with Cord. She sat down beside him and folded her robe around her legs, waiting. Her attitude was calm, her entire attention focused on him. People often talked to her, telling her things that they'd never tell anyone else, without really understanding what it was about her that inspired such trust. Susan didn't understand it herself, unless it was that she truly listened.

He leaned his head back, and his eyelids drooped to half-mast. "She was pure fire," he said softly. "A total mismatch for Grant Keller. She had red hair and slanted green eyes, just like a cat's. She sparkled. She liked to laugh and dance and have a good time, do all of the things that Grant was too stodgy to enjoy. He wasn't the type to go skinny-dipping at night, or dance in the streets during Mardi Gras. But, as far as I know, she was entirely faithful to him." He fell silent, staring into the past.

When several moments had passed, Susan prompted him. "Until you."

He glanced up and gave her a wry look that held a curious overtone of pain and guilt. "Until she met me," he agreed harshly. With a deft movement he seized the bottle and tipped it to his mouth. She watched in amazed fascination as his strong throat worked, and when he set the bottle down it was empty. He looked at it savagely. "There wasn't enough."

Warily, she wondered if he would still be able to say that when his body began to absorb the alcohol he'd just consumed, if he would be able to say anything at all.

A fine sheen of perspiration had broken out on his face, and he wiped it away with the back of his hand. "We'd been having an affair for almost a year before we were caught." His voice was gruff, strained. "I'd asked her over and over to divorce Grant, leave with me, but beneath all of that flash, Judith was strongly conventional. Her reputation meant a lot to her, and she adored her kids. She just couldn't break all her ties. She didn't have any choice after Grant found us together."

Susan swallowed, trying not to imagine the scene. What would it do to any of the three people involved in a triangle for a husband to walk in while his wife was in bed with her lover?

"She was crucified." He heaved himself off the couch and walked restlessly around the room, and what she saw on his face frightened her. "She didn't have a friend left; her own children wouldn't speak to her after Grant threw her out of the house. My dear aunt Imogene was the leader in ostracizing her. Preston doesn't know that I know what *he* did, because he made certain he wasn't in the group, but he organized a sort of mob scene; a group of teenage toughs danced around Judith one afternoon in the parking lot of a grocery store and called her 'Blackstone's Whore.' It sounds almost Victorian, doesn't it? I caught one of the kids that night and... ah, *persuaded* him to tell me who'd set it up. I hunted for Preston, but he flew the coop, and I couldn't find where he'd gone."

So that was why he hated Preston so fiercely! She could understand his bitterness, but still she stared at him, troubled. Couldn't he see that revenge so often has a backlash, punishing the avenger as cruelly as his victim?

His fists were knotted whitely at his sides, his lips drawn back over his teeth. Alarmed, Susan got up and went to him, putting her soft hands over his fists. He'd removed his tie, and his shirt was open at the throat, revealing the beginning curls of hair on his chest; her eyes were on a level with those curls, and for a moment she stared at them, entranced, before she jerked her thoughts away from the dangerous direction they were taking and looked upward.

"Where is she now?" she asked, having a vision of Judith in some sleazy bar somewhere, middle-aged and despairing.

"She's dead." His voice was soft now, almost gentle, as if he had to put some distance between himself and his memories. "My wife is dead, and that bastard called her a whore!"

Susan sucked in a quiet breath, shocked at what he'd just told her. His wife! "What happened?"

"They broke her spirit." He was breathing deeply, almost desperately, but his hands had unknotted, and now his fingers were twined with hers, holding her so tightly that he hurt her. His face was pulled into a grimace of pain. "We were married as soon as her divorce was final. But she was never Judith again, never the laughing, dancing woman I'd wanted so much. I wasn't enough to replace her children, her friends, and she just faded away from me."

"She had to love you, to risk all that she did," Susan said painfully.

"Yes, she loved me. She just wasn't strong enough not to have any regrets, not to let the hurt eat away at her. She came down with pneumonia, and she didn't want to fight it. She gave up, let go. And do you want to know the hell of it?" he ground out. "I didn't love her. I couldn't love her. She'd changed, and she wasn't anything like the woman I'd loved, but I stayed with her because she'd given up so much for me. Damn it, she deserved more than that! I did my best to make sure she never knew, and I hope she died thinking that I still loved her, but the feeling was long gone by then. I'm guilty, too, in what happened to Judith. As guilty as hell!"

His eyes were dry, burning like wildfire, and Susan realized that though he wasn't able to weep for his dead wife, he was about to fly apart before her. She forcibly tugged her hands away from his death grip and cupped his face in her palms, her cool, tender hands lying along his hot flesh like a benediction. His soft beard tickled her palms, and she stroked it gently. His eyes closed at her touch.

"She was a grown woman, and she made her choice when she decided to have an affair with you," she pointed out softly. "The stress was too much for her, but I can't see that it's any more your fault than it was hers." She wanted to ease his pain, do anything to take that look of suffering off his face. My God, he'd been little more than a boy, to bear so much!

He put his hands over hers and turned his face to nuzzle his lips into her left palm, then rubbed his cheek against her hand. His pent-up breath gusted out of him on a long, soft sigh, and his eyes opened.

"You're a dangerous woman," he murmured sleepily. "I didn't intend to tell you all of that."

Looking at him, Susan saw that the whiskey was hitting him hard and fast. Cautiously, she eased him back over to the couch, and he dropped heavily onto it, sighing as he relaxed. For a moment she stood indecisively, then made up her mind; he was in no condition to drive, so he would have to spend the night there. She knelt down and began removing his shoes.

"What're you doing?" he mumbled, his eyelids drooping even more.

"Taking off your shoes. I think you'd better stay here tonight, rather than risk driving home."

A faint smile quirked his lips. "What will people say?" he mocked; then his eyes closed and he sighed again, a peculiarly peaceful sound.

Susan shrugged at his question; what people would say if anyone knew he'd spent the night here was almost beyond her imagination, yet she really couldn't see that she had a choice. He was mentally and emotionally exhausted, as well as drunk, and if anyone chose to gossip about that, she couldn't stop them. She wouldn't risk his life for that. She completed her task and set his shoes neatly to one side, then swung his long legs up on the couch.

He grunted and adjusted his length to the supporting

cushions, dangling one leg off the side and swinging the other one over the back of the couch. Sprawled in that boneless position, he went to sleep as quietly and easily as a child.

Susan shook her head, unable to repress a smile. He'd told her that he was a mean drunk. Looking at him as he slept so peacefully made her doubt that. She went upstairs to get a pillow and blanket, returning to drape the blanket over him and place the pillow under his head. He didn't rouse at all, even when she lifted his head.

Lying alone in her own bed, she was aware of a deep feeling of contentment at just knowing he was under the same roof. The warm aching of her body told her that she wanted more from him than just his presence; she wanted the completion of his lovemaking. She wanted to be everything to him, every dream he'd ever had, every wish he'd ever made. She wanted to ease him and comfort him, and make him forget his black past. Knowing that he stood too much alone to allow anyone to mean that much to him didn't lessen the way she felt. How odd it was that, when she loved again, she loved someone so different from herself!

Yet Vance had been different. Unlike Cord, Vance had conformed, at least on the surface, but she had always known that Vance could have been a hard, dangerous man if anything or anyone had threatened those he loved. Circumstances had been different for Vance than they had for Cord, and that part of his personality had never developed, but the potential had been there. With Vance she had felt utterly protected, utterly loved, because she had sensed that he would have put himself between her and anything that threatened her, without counting the cost to himself.

The way I love Cord! she thought, shocked, her eyes wide in the darkness. It stunned her to think that she could be stirred to violence, but when she thought of the anger that had surged through her that night, she knew that she'd have done anything she could have to keep Grant Keller from punching Cord. She didn't fear for Cord; he was far too capable of taking care of himself. It was simply that she couldn't bear the idea of him suffering the least hurt. She would gladly have taken a punch on the jaw herself rather than let it land on Cord.

She fell asleep quickly and woke before her alarm clock went off. The sun coming in her window, bright and warm, told her that it was going to be another gorgeous spring day. Humming, she took a shower and put on fresh lacy underwear and chose a bright summer dress that reflected her rise in spirits. The pure white fabric, with its fragile lace trim and scattering of brightly colored spring flowers, made her feel as fresh as the new day, as full of hope. Still humming, she went downstairs and peeked into the den, where Cord still lay sprawled on the couch, sleeping heavily. He'd rolled over on his stomach, and his head was turned to the back of the couch, revealing only his tousled dark hair. Quietly she closed the door and went to the kitchen.

Emily was already there, quietly and efficiently making breakfast. When Susan entered, the older woman looked up with a smile. "Who's your guest?"

"Cord Blackstone," Susan replied, returning the smile and pouring herself a cup of fresh coffee. While the coffee cooled, she got the plates and silverware for setting the table.

"Cord Blackstone," Emily mused, her eyes softening. "My, my, it's been a long time since I've seen that boy. He even spent a few nights under my roof, when he was younger."

"He was drunk last night," Susan explained as she arranged the plates on the table, absently placing the napkins and silverware just so, moving them around by fractions of an inch until she was satisfied.

"I don't remember him as being much of a drinker, though of course that was a long time ago. I'm not saying that he couldn't put it away, but it just never seemed to affect him. My boy would be passed out, and Cord would be as steady on his feet as ever."

After pouring another cup of coffee, Susan carried it into the den and carefully placed it on the coffee table, then knelt in front of the couch. She put her hand on his blanket-covered shoulder, feeling the warmth of his flesh even through the fabric. "Cord, wake up."

She didn't have to shake him. At her touch, her voice, he rolled over, tangling himself in the blanket, and his eyelids lifted to reveal pale, glittering irises. He smiled, then yawned, stretching his arms over his head. "Good morning."

"Good morning," she replied, watching him with veiled concern. "Do you feel like having a cup of coffee?"

"H'mmmm," he said in a rumbling, early-morning voice, a noise that could have meant anything. He heaved himself into a sitting position, raking his fingers through his hair. He yawned again, then reached around her for the coffee, holding the cup to his mouth and cautiously sipping the steaming liquid. He closed his eyes as the caffeine seared its way to his stomach. "God, that's good! Do I smell bacon cooking?"

"If you think you can eat—"

He grinned, opening his eyes. "I told you, I don't have hangovers."

Susan couldn't help the laughter that bubbled out. "Yes, but you also told me that you're a mean drunk, and you weren't anything but a big pussycat! A big, *sleepy* pussycat!"

He reached out and caught her hand, his gaze on her radiant, laughing face. "It depends on my company when I'm drunk. I can be mean if I have to." He finished the coffee and set the cup down, then slid back into a reclining position, closing his eyes, her hand still held loosely in his.

She shook his shoulder with her free hand. "Don't go back to sleep! It's time for breakfast—"

Without opening his eyes he tugged on her hand, and Susan found herself on the couch with him, sprawled over him in a very undignified position. Her eyes widened to huge blue pools, and she began squirming in an effort to push her skirt down, but her efforts were hampered because her feet had somehow become tangled in the blanket and she couldn't get her legs straight.

He sucked in his breath sharply, and his hand caught in her hair, holding her still. "I'd rather have you for breakfast," he muttered huskily, his fingers exerting just enough pressure to ease her head forward slowly, an inch at a time, until he could put his mouth to hers. Susan quivered, her lips opening to his like a soft spring blossom, her mouth being filled with the coffee taste of his. Like a welcome, familiar friend, his tongue entered lazily and explored the tiny serrated edges of her teeth, the softness of her lips, the sensual curling of her tongue as it met his. His hand left her hair and moved down her back, searching out the slender curve of her spine, as slow and inexorable as the seasons.

Susan forgot about breakfast. She wound her arms around his neck, her hands clenching in his hair, meeting the open hunger of his kiss with her own. It was so sweet and good, and it was all she could ask of life, to be in his arms. She felt his hands on her body, experienced, calm hands, as they sleeked down her sides to the graceful curve of her waist, then down to the roundness of her hips. He cupped her buttocks, grasping, filling his hands with the smooth mounds and pressing her to him. The raw sexuality of his gesture left her reeling with pleasure, unable to rein in the hot sparks of desire that were shooting through her body. She was a woman, and he knew exactly what to do with her woman's body. With a few swift movements he had her skirt up, and his hands were under the material, burrowing under the elastic waistband of her panties to brand the coolness of her buttocks with the heat of his palms.

Susan moaned aloud, and the sound was taken into his mouth. He began nibbling at her flesh, his teeth catching her lower lip, the tender curve of her jaw, the delicate lobe of her ear. Her breath was rushing in and out of her lungs, her heart racing out of control. The feel of him was driving her mad, and she wanted to sink down on him in boneless need. Now he was biting at her neck, his teeth stinging her skin; then he soothed it with tiny licks of his tongue. Her hands had made fists in his hair, pulling at the thick, vital mane mindlessly. She wanted to give him everything, every part of her, blend the softness of her body with the hardness of his.

"Two minutes!" Emily sang out from the kitchen.

Susan heard the words, but they didn't make any

sense to her. Cord groaned, and his hands tightened on her buttocks in momentary denial; then he reluctantly withdrew his touch from her enticing curves. "I thought a two-minute warning was only in football," he grumbled, easing her to one side.

She sat up, dazed and aching with frustration, wondering why the narcotic of his touch had been so suddenly withdrawn from her feverish, addicted flesh. He looked at her face, so soft and vulnerable in her passion, and his jaw went rigid with the effort he had to make not to reach for her again. She was too much woman to be so prim and proper, and he was becoming increasingly fascinated by just how prim and proper she wasn't. She was forbidden fruit, and probably deceitful into the bargain, but logic had nothing to do with the way he wanted her.

Susan willed herself to be calm, forcing her shaky legs to support her when she stood, forcing her voice to a deceptive evenness. "You'll probably want to wash before eating," she murmured, and showed him the way to the downstairs bathroom. "Come through to the kitchen when you're finished."

But for all her surface serenity, it was several moments after she entered the kitchen before she had collected her thoughts. After staring blankly at the small table in the breakfast alcove, set with three places, a vase of cheerful shasta daisies in the center, she was overcome by the thought that for the first time in five years she would be sharing her breakfast with a man. And not just any man! She would be eating the first meal of the day with a man who made every other man of her acquaintance pale in comparison. A quiver of desire ran through her body again, and she blushed hotly at the thought that she would have let him take her a few moments ago, sprawled on the couch like a wanton, with Emily in the kitchen. Muttering an excuse about collecting his coffee cup, which she'd left in the den, she escaped for a few minutes of necessary solitude.

She had returned with the cup and had a refill of fresh, steaming coffee sitting by his plate when Cord paused in the doorway, assaulting her senses with his size, overpowering everything in her feminine house. He had an aura of hard vitality about him, and for a moment she could only stand and stare at him helplessly. It didn't make it any better to know that he affected every woman that way; not even Imogene was immune to him, and now Emily turned to greet him, a flush of pleasure pinkening her features. "Cord Blackstone, I swear, you're even handsomer than ever!"

He searched her face for only a second, his ice-blue eyes sharp; then he grinned and his white teeth flashed. "Mrs. Ferris!" Without pause, he moved across the kitchen to take her firmly in his arms and press a kiss on her flustered mouth, a warm and friendly kiss that had Susan envying Emily for even that small moment.

Emily was laughing and patting his cheek. "That beard! You look like an outlaw for sure! Sit down, sit down. I hope you still like your eggs over easy?"

"Yes, ma'am," he replied, his inbred Southern courtesy not allowing him to address her in any other manner. He seated Susan and Emily before taking his own chair, his long legs fitting under the table with difficulty, but Susan didn't mind the way their knees bumped. His presence at her breakfast table was as natural as if it were an ordinary occurrence, and the sun was shining for her after an absence of five years. She could feel

Emily's glance on her, but she couldn't control the radiance of her smile.

She wasn't the only one who was smiling; Emily was clucking around Cord, chattering at him and fussing over him, and he was eating it up with a look of pleasure that told Susan it had been a long time since he'd known the subtle delight of being cherished in the small, all-important ways. Susan didn't talk much, just listened to their conversation. She learned that Cord and Emily's eldest son had been inseparable companions during their teen years, and that Cord had eaten a lot of meals that Emily had cooked. Emily brought Cord up to date on Jack's life, but Susan noticed that Cord didn't divulge any information about himself. His past was a closed book; she realized that she didn't know anything about what he'd done or where he'd been since he'd left Mississippi, not even where he'd been immediately before returning.

She hated to see the meal end, but all too soon the table had been cleared and the kitchen cleaned, the last cup of coffee drunk. She walked with him to the door, her heart beating slowly, heavily. It was either bright sunlight or the darkest shadows, she realized painfully; there was no middle ground in loving him. She stopped in the middle of the foyer, her heart in her eyes as she looked at him.

CHAPTER SIX

His eyes were hooded and unreadable as he watched her, but his hand smoothed over her shoulder as if he couldn't prevent himself from touching her, his fingers heating the cool silk of her skin before sliding upward over her throat to cup her chin and lift her face. He hadn't said a word, but he didn't need to; the burning possession of his lips told her all she needed to know. With a silent gasp, she melted against him, her hands going up to lie along his jawline, where the silkiness of his beard tickled her palms.

He lifted his mouth and simply held her close for a moment. Susan kept her hands on his face, stroking her fingers lightly over his beard, drowning in the enjoyment of being cuddled by him. His strong, warm throat beckoned, and she stood on tiptoe to press a light kiss onto the skin above his collar. "What do you look like without a beard?" she asked dreamily, for no other reason than that her hands were on his beard and it was the first sentence that popped out.

He chuckled, a husky, male sound that rippled over her like warm water. "Like myself, I suppose. Why? Are you curious?"

"M'mmmm," she said, letting him interpret the sound as he chose. "How long have you worn a beard?"

"Just for this past winter, though I've had a moustache for several years. I was stranded for a week or so without any way of shaving, short of scraping my face with a dull knife, and I realized just how much time I wasted in scraping hair off my face when it promptly grew back, so I kept the beard."

She trailed one fingertip over his bearded chin. "Do you have a cleft chin? Or a dimple?"

Suddenly he laughed, pulling away from her. "Well, see for yourself," he teased, catching her hand and pulling her after him as he started up the stairs with a swift, leaping stride. "Where's your bathroom?"

Susan laughed too, and tried to stop him. "What're you doing? You're going too fast! I'll fall!"

He turned around and scooped her up in his arms, and kissed her so hard that her lips stung. Holding her securely against his chest, he opened doors until he found her bedroom, then walked into it and let her slide to the floor. He looked around at the completely feminine room, the lace curtains, the cream satin comforter on her bed, the delicately flowered wallpaper. His face changed, became curious, surprised. "Vance didn't sleep in here," he said. "This is a woman's room."

Susan swallowed, a little surprised at his perception. "This was our room," she admitted. "But I changed everything when he died. I couldn't sleep in here with everything the way it had been when he was alive, so I bought new furniture and had the room redone completely. Not even the carpet is the same."

"A different bed?" he asked, watching her narrowly.

Susan shivered. "Yes," she whispered. "Everything. New mattress, new sheets…everything."

"Good." The single word was a low growl of satisfaction, and his gaze was so heated that she rubbed her hands up her bare arms, feeling a little singed. He looked around and indicated a door, releasing her from his visual force field. "Is that the bathroom?"

"Yes, but why—"

"Because," he answered maddeningly, catching her hand and pulling her with him again, into the bathroom. He began unbuttoning his shirt, opening it down to his waist, then pulling the fabric free of his pants and finishing the job. He shrugged out of the shirt and handed it to her; she took it automatically, folding it over her arm.

"You aren't going to do that," she said in disbelief, having realized what he intended.

"Why not? Do you have a fresh blade for your razor? And I'll need a pair of scissors to start off."

"There's a small pair in the drawer there," she said, pointing. "Cord, wait. I wasn't hinting for you to shave off your beard."

"It'll grow back, if you don't like my naked face," he drawled, opening the drawer and taking out the scissors. "Why don't you just sit down and enjoy the show?"

Because there was nothing else to do, she closed the lid on the toilet and sat down, her eyes wide with fascination as she watched him snip the beard as short as he could get it with the scissors. He asked again for her razor, and she indicated the left-hand side of the built-in medicine cabinet. He extracted the razor, new blades, and shaving gel from the cabinet, then deftly changed blades.

He wet his face with warm water and worked the gel into a lather, covering his face with enough foamy white soap to make him look like a wicked Santa Claus. Susan almost winced when the razor sliced into his beard and left a smooth streak of skin in its path. Half of her was trembling with anticipation at seeing his face, but the other half of her hated to see the beard go; it had been so soft and silky, and made her skin tingle wherever it touched.

He went through the contortions that men put themselves through when shaving, arching his neck, tilting his head, and Susan sat spellbound. It was the first time she'd seen him without his shirt, and her eyes drifted down over his muscled torso. She'd known he was strong, but now she saw the layered muscles that covered him, and her mouth went dry. His broad shoulders gleamed under the light, the skin as taut and supple as a young boy's. With every movement he made the muscles in his back bunched and rippled, then relaxed, flexing in an endless ballet that riveted her attention. His spine ran in a deep hollow down the center of his back, inviting inquisitive fingers to stroke and probe.

Susan noticed that the rhythm of her breathing had been broken, and she wrenched her gaze away from his back. Determinedly she again looked in the mirror at the reflection of his face, and the complete concentration she saw there started an ache deep inside her. That frown was so completely male, and it had been so long since she'd seen it. Vance had frowned just like that. For five years her life had lacked something because she hadn't been able to sit in the bathroom and watch her man shave; a simple pleasure, but one of the lasting ones. Cord was giving her that pleasure again, as he had given her his presence at breakfast, and somehow the simple act of watching him shave was seducing her more completely than his heated kisses could have done.

Slowly her gaze dipped, and she inspected his mirrored image. His chest was covered by a tangle of black curls that looked as incredibly soft as his beard had been; she clenched her hands to prevent them from reaching out to touch him and verify the texture. His nipples were flat circles, small and dark, with tiny points in the center of them, and she wanted to put her mouth to them. The curve of his rib cage was laced by bands of muscle, and the solid wall of his abdomen rippled with power. The tiny ringlets of hair on his chest became a straight and silky line that ran down the middle of his stomach and disappeared into the waistband of his pants. He raised his arms and his torso stretched, giving her a glimpse of his taut, shallow navel, and the thin scar that began on the right side of it, angling down out of sight.

Susan almost strangled, and this time she couldn't stop her hands; they flew out, touching the scar, tracing it lightly. Now her fevered gaze roamed over him again, anxiously, and she found other marks of other battles. A small, silvered, puckered scar on his right shoulder had to be from a gunshot wound, and her spine prickled with fear for him. Another line ran from under his left breast, around under his arm, and ended below his left shoulder blade. Obviously he hadn't always ducked in time.

Suddenly she noticed that he was very still under her hands, and she let them fall to her side, swiftly looking away from him. She was aware of his slow movements as he splashed the remnants of lather from his face and patted it dry, but she couldn't look directly at him.

"There's nothing wrong with touching me," he growled harshly, dropping his words into the sudden canyon of silence. "Why did you stop?"

She swallowed. "I was afraid you'd think I was pry-ing. My God!" she burst out rawly. "What happened to you? All those scars..."

He gave a short, mirthless laugh. "Just a lot of hard living," he answered obliquely. "I was tossed off the lap of luxury a long time ago."

She glanced up at the harshness of his tone, and for the first time since he'd finished shaving, she saw his face. Her mouth went dry again.

She'd never before seen anyone who looked as hard and cool as he did. He'd left his moustache, thank God; she couldn't imagine his face without it. His jaw was lean and clearly cut, his chin square and impossibly stubborn. His lower lip had taken on a fullness that she hadn't noticed before, a new sensuality. He lacked the classic perfection of handsomeness, but he had the face of a warrior, a man who was willing to fight for what he wanted, a man who laughed at danger. The hard recklessness of him was more apparent now, as if he'd torn aside a veil that had hidden him from view. She'd thought that his beard had made him look like more of a desperado than he really was; now she realized that the reverse had been true. The beard had disguised the ruthlessness of his face.

He was looking down at her with mockery in his eyes, as if he had known that the beard had been a camouflage. The years and the mileage were etched on that hard, slightly battered countenance, but she wasn't repelled by it; she was drawn, like an animal from the depths of a cold night to crouch by the warmth of a fire. In a fleeting moment of despair, knowing herself lost, she realized that the more attractive the lure, the higher the risk, and she would be risking her entire way of life if she allied herself with him. She was by nature cautious and reserved, yet as she stood looking at him in silence, she accepted that risk; for her heart, she would disregard the past and the future, and count the reward well worth the danger. With an inarticulate murmur, she lifted her arms to him.

An odd look of strain tightened his feature; then with a harsh, wordless sound, he picked her up and carried her into the bedroom, lying down on the bed with her still in his arms, twisting until he was half on top of her. His left hand buried itself in her hair, holding her head still, and his mouth came down to imprint his possession on hers. She parted her lips willingly to the demanding thrust of his tongue, giving a tiny sigh of bliss as she curled herself against him, twining her arms around his neck and shoulders, pressing her breasts into the hard, warm plane of his chest. She kissed him with fire and delicacy, offering herself to him with gentle simplicity. He lifted his mouth a fraction of an inch from hers, his breath coming in fast, irregular gulps. "I think... I think I'm going to lose my head over you," he muttered. "Why couldn't you be what I'd expected?"

Before Susan could ask what he meant, before it even occurred to her to wonder at it, his mouth was on hers again, and his arms were tightening about her with a force that would have bruised her if she hadn't been boneless with need. Everything combined to overwhelm her senses. She was aware, with every pore of her body, of the warm fragrance of the new day, the slight breeze drifting in the open window, the sweet trilling of the birds as they darted about among the huge trees; then there was nothing, nothing but the touch of his hands and mouth.

He unzipped her dress, pulling it down to bare her

breasts to him, and he took them hungrily, first with his knowing hands, then with the furnace of his mouth. She cried out as the strong suckling sent shock waves of primitive pleasure crashing along her nerves, and she arched into his hard frame.

The phone beside the bed began ringing, and he lifted his head, muttering a violent curse under his breath, then settled himself more fully on her, his muscular legs parting hers and making a cradle for him. Her nipples were buried in the curly hair of his chest, her hands clutching urgently at him; she wanted all the layers of clothing between them gone, but she hated to release him long enough to remove them. She twisted against him, wanting more, more...

"Susan! Telephone!"

Emily's voice wafted up the stairs, startling them as much as if a bucket of cold water had been dashed over them. Susan drew a sobbing breath, unable to answer. No, no! Why now?

"Susan?" Emily called, raising her voice in question.

She bit her lip, then managed to call out, "Yes, I'll get it. Thanks, Emily." Her voice didn't even sound like her own, but Emily must have been satisfied.

Cord rolled off of her with a sigh. "Go ahead, answer it," he said gruffly. "She'll be up here checking on you if you don't." He lifted the receiver and handed it to her, stretching the cord across his chest, then relaxing against the pillows.

Susan wet her lips, and took a deep breath to steady herself. "Hello."

"Hello, dear," came Imogene's brisk voice. "I wanted to congratulate you on your quick thinking last night. I knew you wouldn't let us down."

Susan frowned in puzzlement, her thoughts still too fogged by desire for her to understand what Imogene was saying. How could she think when she was lying half on Cord's chest, his heady scent rising to her nostrils like an aphrodisiac. "I'm sorry, I don't understand. What do you mean?"

"Why, playing up to Cord," Imogene replied impatiently. "Remember, you have just as much to lose in this as we do. String him along and find out all you can. Last night was a brilliant move—"

Susan darted a quick, agonized look at Cord, and her blood congealed in her veins when she saw the iciness of his eyes and realized that he'd heard every word; how could he not, when she was practically on top of him? A cold, cruel smile curved his mouth as he gently took the telephone receiver from her nerveless fingers and cradled it on his shoulder. "You jumped the gun on the congratulations, Aunt Imogene," he purred with silken menace. "That was a tactical error; you should've let Susan call you when the coast was clear."

With a deliberate movement he dropped the receiver back onto the hook, then turned back to her. The smile on his face was deadly, and she could do nothing but wait, her breath halted, her heart stopped.

"My God, you're lovely," he murmured, still smiling, his eyes dropping to her bare, creamy breasts. "And so willing to give me anything I want, aren't you? No wonder you let me talk so much last night; did you think I'd spill my guts to you, tell you everything I'd planned?"

A fine trembling invaded her limbs. "No," she whispered. "You needed to talk; I was available."

She was so close to him that she could see his pupils dilate, the inner blackness expanding until only a thin circle of blue remained. "Are you available?" he drawled, deliberately covering her breast with his hand. "Are you as available for me as you are for Preston?"

She felt as if he'd kicked her, and she tried to jerk away, but he locked his other arm around her and held her to him. His fingers kneaded her soft flesh with a slow precision that frightened her, and tears stung her eyes. "I'm not available for Preston! Except as a…a friend. I'm not a sexual release valve for anyone!" She could feel her cheeks burning with mortification, and she tried to pull away again, an attempt that was useless against his effortless strength.

"Sure you're not," he crooned. "That's why you're on this bed with me. You offered yourself to me, darling, for a little fun and games. But dear Aunt Imogene, bless her nosy soul, couldn't stay off the phone, and she blew it for you. Now what are you going to do?"

"It's not like that!" she cried desperately, pleading with him to understand. "Imogene wanted me to sleep with you so I could try to find out what you're planning to do, but I refused—"

He laughed, a low, harsh sound of disbelief. "It really looks like you refused," he taunted, stroking her breast. He adjusted her squirming body to his in a way that branded her with his male heat. "For once, she had an idea that I like. We shouldn't let a little phone call interrupt us—"

"No!" She wedged her arms between them and braced her hands on his chest, pushing against him in a useless effort to create more of a space between them. It took a tremendous effort to prevent herself from bursting into tears, but she refused to give in to that weakness and blinked her eyes fiercely.

"Why not? You'd enjoy being—"

"Used?" she broke in bitterly.

"Now, darling, I wasn't going to be crude. I was going to say that you'd enjoy being with a man again, because I don't count Preston as a man. What do you say? I promise that when I...*use*...you, I won't leave you unsatisfied."

"Stop it!" she almost shouted, horrified at what had happened, at how swiftly something that had been so *right* had deteriorated into something so ugly. "I've never had sex with Preston. Let go of me!"

He laughed and recaptured her as she almost wriggled free, his hand going to her buttocks and cupping them, pressing her into him. "Settle down," he advised, still laughing, though how he could laugh when she felt as if someone had torn her heart out was more than she could understand. "I'm not going to attack you. Though, my God, woman, if you don't stop squirming against me like that, I may change my mind!"

She stilled. After a long moment she said rawly, "Please, let me get up."

With a mocking lift of his eyebrows, he opened his arms and released her. She sat up away from him, fumbling with her dress, trying to straighten the fabric over her breasts. He got up from the bed and sauntered into the bathroom, returning with his shirt. He pulled it on and buttoned it, then unzipped his pants to tuck the shirttail in, standing nonchalantly before her. Susan sat in frozen horror, too miserable to do anything but stare numbly at him.

"Don't look so unhappy, darling," he advised in a mockery of tenderness. "I probably wouldn't have told you anything, anyway." He strolled over to where she sat on the bed and leaned down over her, his weight braced on his arms. Briefly, firmly, he kissed her, a little rough in his anger. When he straightened, a tiny fire was burning in his eyes. "Pity she couldn't have waited another half hour before she called," he said, touching her cheek with his finger. "See you around." With that nonchalant goodbye he was gone, and she sat in paralyzed agony, listening to his sure steps going down the stairs. Then there was the sound of the door, and a moment later the throaty roar of a powerful, well-tuned engine.

After a long time she managed to slide stiffly off the bed, but that was all she could force her body to do. She leaned against the wall, her eyes closed, while she tried to come to terms with what had happened. She almost hated Imogene for coming between her and Cord, even though it had been unintentional. No, if Imogene had known that Cord had been there, she wouldn't have done anything to rock the boat! She simply couldn't believe that Susan would balk at prostituting herself for the good of the Blackstones, namely Imogene herself and Preston. To her mind, if Susan had anything to do with Cord, it was based on ulterior motives.

It was particularly painful because, for a little while, he had seemed to be lowering his formidable barriers just a bit. Their kisses had been building a frail bridge of understanding between them, until Imogene's heavy touch had shattered it. For a few hours Susan had been on the verge of an ecstasy so deep and powerful, so wide in scope, that she had difficulty in believing the richness that had hovered just beyond her fingertips.

Black despair engulfed her, a depression so deep that only Vance's death compared to it. After Vance's burial, when she had been forced to admit to herself that there was no miracle that would restore him to her, for a time it had seemed that there was nothing worthwhile left in her life. If it had been possible, she would have died quietly in her sleep during that time, so bitter and helpless had she felt at the irrevocable chasm of death. Time had healed her, time and the gentle steel of her own nature, but she hadn't regained the utter delight in being alive, capable of experiencing pleasure again, until Cord had walked into her life and touched her with his hard fingers, bringing fires that had been banked for five years back into full blaze.

It was an hour before spirit began to return to her numbed brain. She had learned at Vance's death that even the most precious life could be extinguished, and she had also learned that death was final. But she was very much alive, and so was Cord. She couldn't let him just walk away from her like that! If you truly loved someone, then you had to be willing to fight for them, and she was willing to fight the entire world if need be. Thankfully, it wasn't necessary that she take on the world, but the one stubborn, dangerous man she had to face was bad enough. If it hadn't been so necessary to her life that she make him listen, she would never have been able to summon the courage. She could face down almost anyone, but Cord could intimidate the devil himself.

Without giving herself time to think, because if she paused, she'd stop altogether, she told Emily that she'd be gone for the rest of the day, then grabbed her purse and ran to the car. She broke the speed limit getting to the cabin, not daring to rehearse what she would say to him, but knowing that she had to make him listen.

She thundered across the old bridge over Jubilee Creek, and the car fishtailed when she slung it around the long, sweeping curve of the incline going up to the gentle rise where the cabin sat. A bright red Blazer with enormous tires was parked at the front steps, and she pulled up behind it, scattering rocks and dust. Before the wheels had stopped rolling, she had the door open and was out of the car, bounding up the steps in a very unladylike manner. She had pounded on the door twice with her fist when a piercing whistle reached her ears, and she spun around. Cord was standing down at the creek, about a hundred yards away. He lifted his arm, beckoning her to come to him, and she was in too much of a hurry to use the steps; she jumped off the end of the porch and headed down the slope at a fast walk.

He went back to work, his powerful arms swinging a slingblade with easy rhythm, sending showers of rioting greenery flying into the air as he sliced through a section of heavy overgrowth. Her pace slowed as she approached, and when she reached him she stood to one side, well out of the way of the slicing blade. He stopped after a moment, leaning on the handle and giving her an unreadable glance, a little smile pulling at his lips. "The honeysuckle is out of hand," he drawled, wiping his forearm across his sweaty face. "If we ever decide to conquer the world, all we have to do is ship out some cuttings of honeysuckle and kudzu, then wait a year. Everyone else would be so worn-out from fighting the vines that we could just waltz in."

She smiled at the whimsy, but to Southern farmers, it wasn't that much of an exaggeration. Now that she was standing before him, she couldn't think of anything to say; for the moment, it was enough to simply be there, staring at him, drinking in the sight of his magnificent masculinity. He was glistening with sweat, his dark hair wet and stuck to his skull, and he'd twisted a white handkerchief into a band that he'd tied around his forehead to keep the sweat out of his eyes. His shirt had been discarded and was lying on the ground; his jeans were dirty. None of that mattered. He could have been wearing a tuxedo, and he wouldn't have looked any better to her.

When she didn't say anything, he tilted his head in question, a devilish gleam entering his eyes. "Did you come here for a reason?"

She swallowed, trying to conquer her voice. "Yes. I came to make you listen to me."

"I'm listening, honey, but you're not saying much."

She searched for the perfect words to use, the ones that would make him believe her, but with a sinking heart she knew that there weren't any. He was still watching her in amusement, letting her squirm, and suddenly it was unbearable. She blurted out, "When Imogene asked me to spy on you, I refused, and she's not used to anyone telling her no. Someone must have told her what happened last night, and she assumed that I'd changed my mind. I haven't."

He laughed aloud and shook his head in amazement. "So what were you doing on that bed with me? My ego isn't so big that I'll fall for the line that you just have the hots for me. I know your reputation, lady, and it's the straight and narrow all the way, as far as anyone knows. I have my doubts about Preston—"

"Shut up!" she cried, knotting her hands into fists. "I've told you and told you—"

"I know," he interrupted wearily. "You haven't slept with Preston."

"It's the truth!"

"He's in love with you."

Startled by his perception, she admitted, "Yes. But I didn't know until a few days ago. That doesn't change anything. I'm very fond of Preston, but I'm not in love with him; there's never been anything sexual between us."

"Okay, say there's nothing between you," he attacked sharply, changing positions. "That means there's been no one in your life, romantically speaking, since Vance died, which makes it just that much more unlikely for you to suddenly take up with me. There has to be a reason."

Susan turned pale. "There is. When I met you, I realized that I'm not dead. I've mourned Vance for five years, but he's never coming back, and I'm very much alive. You make me *feel* things again. I'm not like you; I've never been brave or adventurous, or taken a gamble on anything, but when I'm with you I feel just a little braver, a little more free. I want to be with you for *me,* not for Imogene or Preston or any amount of money."

His eyes had darkened as he listened to her, and now he stared at her for a long, taut moment, taking in the tension of her slim figure, the almost desperate earnestness in her eyes, eyes of such a dark blue that they looked like the deep Pacific. Finally he untied the handkerchief from his forehead and began using the square of cloth to wipe the rivulets of sweat from his face and arms, then rubbing it across his chest. He was silent for so long that Susan could bear it no longer, and she grabbed his arm. "It's very simple," she said desperately. "All you have to do is not tell me *anything!* Since you're forewarned, how can I possibly find out anything? How can I possibly be using you?"

He sighed, shaking his head. "Susan," he finally said, his voice so gentle that she shivered at the sound of it, "you said it yourself: We're nothing alike. I've lived a hard life, and it hasn't always been on the right side of the law. You look as if you've been carried around all of your life on a satin pillow. If you think you want pretty words and pretty flowers and hand-holding in the moonlight, you'd better find some other man. I'm not satisfied with hand-holding."

She shivered again, and her lashes drooped to veil her eyes in a sultry, passion-laden manner. "I know," she whispered.

"Do you?" He moved closer to her, so close that the heady scent of his hot, sweaty body enveloped her, tantalizing her senses. "Do you really know what you're asking for?" His hands closed on her waist, his fingers biting into her soft flesh. "I'm not much on genteel gropings in the dark, on schedule every Saturday night. I'm a lot rawer than that, and a lot hungrier. I want to take your clothes off and taste you all over," he rasped, hauling her close to him so that their bodies touched. A fire alarm of pleasure began clanging inside her, and she let herself flow up against him like a tide rushing to shore. "I want to take your nipples in my mouth and suck them until they're hard and aching for more. I want to feel your legs wrapped around my back, and I want to go so deeply into you that I can't tell where I stop and you begin. That's what I want right now, and what I've wanted every time I've seen you. And if that's not what you want, too, you'd better run, because you're about to get it."

Susan sighed in delirium. Her body was alive, aching, throbbing, wanting to do those things he'd described, and more. She wanted to give her heart to him, and with it, the soft, burning ardor of her body. She couldn't give him the words; she sensed that he didn't want love, that he'd feel burdened if she admitted that she loved him, so she would bite the words back and instead content herself with the offering of her body.

"I'm not running," she said into the damp refuge of his neck.

"Maybe you should," he said roughly, releasing her. "But it's too late for that. You had your chance, honey. My sense of honor doesn't go that deep!" He leaned down and lifted her into his arms, his brawny back and shoulders taking her slight weight easily. He began walking up the slope with a determined stride, and when Susan dared to slant a quick look up at his face, she quivered at the fierceness of his expression. The thought of the risk she was about to take in giving herself to him made her feel faint with apprehension, and she turned her face into his warm shoulder. Only one man had made love to her in her life, and that with love, with deep tenderness. Cord didn't trust her; he would take her in lust but not in love, and she didn't know if she was strong enough to handle that. On the other hand, she knew beyond doubt that she had to try to reach him, that she had to try to show him with the gentle offering of herself that she wasn't a treacherous or mercenary person. She had to show him what love was, because he'd never known it.

Her sheltered life had not prepared her for this, but

neither had it prepared her for the reality of her husband dying in her arms, with his blood soaking through her clothing. Since Vance's death, she had held a small part of herself sealed off from the world, protected against hurt, allowing even those closest to her only the shallowest portion of her love. The seal had remained intact until she'd met Cord. He had awakened her to a deeper knowledge of herself, an awareness that she wasn't such a creature of convention as she'd always thought. She wasn't as wild as Cord, as free, nor had she ever been a gambler, but she was willing to take a chance that she could make him care for her. She *had* to take that chance. There were many things she didn't know about him, but that made no difference to the essence of her, the combined power of heart and soul and body, which had recognized him on sight as the mate of her lifetime, the one man who could mean more to her than anyone else could even begin to imagine. She had loved Vance, loved him deeply, and yet that emotion now seemed as mild when compared to the way she felt about Cord as a light spring shower compared to the thunder and fury of a towering electrical storm. She would gladly follow this man anywhere on earth that he wanted to go, because there was no physical discomfort that could rival the hell she would endure if deprived of his presence.

His long legs ate up the distance as he moved up the slope, showing no sign that her weight in his arms was hampering him in the slightest. He leaped up the steps and shouldered the cabin door open, then turned sideways to enter with her. His boot heel collided with the door and sent it slamming back to the frame. He carried her straight through to the bedroom and set her on her feet, his narrowed eyes on her pale, strained face.

A cool, cynical smile touched his face as he dropped to the bed and sprawled on its surface, dragging a pillow over to crumple it into a ball which he placed behind his dark head. He crossed his booted feet and let his gaze rake over her. "All right," he drawled. "Strip."

Susan put out a hand to steady herself as she swayed. The room was dipping crazily, and a sudden roaring in her ears made her think that she might not have heard him correctly. "What?" she asked soundlessly, then swallowed and tried it again. The second time, her voice was a weak croak.

In an insultingly casual manner, he eyed her breasts. "Strip. Take your clothes off. Since you're so all-fired anxious to try me out in the sack, I'm giving you the chance. You may have been planning on a quick flip of your skirt, but what I have in mind will take longer than that."

He didn't think she'd do it. She suddenly realized that as she stood there trying to regulate her breathing. He hadn't believed anything she'd said. He probably thought that all he had to do was push her a little and she'd run crying back to Preston. What had made him so wary that he couldn't trust anyone?

Slowly, with trembling fingers, she reached behind herself and tried to grasp the zipper of her dress. She found the tiny tab, but couldn't manage to hold it. After it slipped out of her jerky fingers for the third time, she took a deep breath and let her arms drop, turning her back to him and sitting down on the edge of the bed beside him. "I can't manage my zipper," she said thinly. "Would you do it for me, please?" For a long, silent moment, he didn't move, and she felt his eyes boring into her back. Then the mattress shifted, and he touched the zipper. Slowly, like thickened molasses, the zipper moved down, and her dress loosened. When he released the tab, she stood up before she lost her nerve and turned to face him again.

His face was expressionless, his black lashes dropping to shield anything his eyes might have told her. An insidious quiver began in her legs and spread upward, turning her insides to jelly. She stepped out of her sandals and caught the straps of her sundress, dropping them off her shoulders and pulling her arms out of them. The cloth dropped to her waist, baring her breasts. She hadn't worn a bra with her little-nothing dress, and a fragrant spring breeze wafted in the open window, touching the pale brown of her small nipples and puckering them into soft, succulent buds. Though Cord hadn't moved, she sensed the tension that pervaded every muscle of his body. Still his eyes were veiled, but she felt them on her, visually touching the creamy slopes that she offered to him. Her breasts were high and firm, deliciously rounded, and she was suddenly, fiercely glad that her woman's body could entice him.

Deep inside her, welling up from the bottomless reservoir of her love, was the inborn need to belong to him. She was woman, and he was man. She was *his* woman, in any way he wanted her, if only he'd take her. There was nothing else as important to her as the time she had with him; that time might be fleeting, and she would have to carefully garner every precious second of it. Circumstances might separate them, or he might leave without notice, his restless spirit leading him on. He'd spent too many years wandering the dark corners of the earth to ever completely settle in one place. For whatever time she had with him, she would take each day as it came, enjoy it totally, as if that were all there was, all there would ever be. She couldn't set a limit on how much of herself she would give to him. She had to give him everything, every ounce of her love.

With precise, graceful movements she pushed the dress down over her hips and dropped it into a billowy puddle around her feet. She stepped out of it, her body completely bare to him now except for her lacy panties, letting him see her sleek, shapely legs, her flat tummy and rounded hips, the graceful curve of her waist. She stood motionless before him, letting him look all he wanted, sensing the coiling need that was beginning to throb through his body.

If time still existed, she wasn't aware of it. It could have been seconds or minutes that she stood there, waiting, hearing nothing but the cheerful songs of the birds in the trees outside the window, the drone of insects. When he didn't move, she slid her fingers inside the waistband of her panties and began sliding them down over her hips, baring the final mystery of her womanhood. Her heart was slamming so wildly in her chest that her ribs hurt. What if he didn't do anything? What if he just lay there and looked, then got up and walked out? She thought she'd die on the spot if that happened. Taking a deep, wavering breath, she pushed the panties down her thighs and dropped them to the floor.

Perhaps he hadn't meant for her to realize his reaction, but she heard the audible intake of his breath, and that gave her the courage to continue standing there before him, vulnerable in a way only another woman could understand. By offering herself this way she was exhibiting a deep, enormous trust in him as a human being, taking it on faith that even though he possessed the strength to hurt her badly, if he were cruel or careless, he would instead treat her tender flesh and heart with the care they deserved. She stood motionless in the bright morning sun, yet she was a statue with warm, supple skin, and the coursing warmth of her life's blood gave her a faint, rosy glow. Her eyes were deep pools of midnight-blue, beckoning him, enticing him to enter the world of sensuality and love that was waiting for him.

He was still stretched out on the bed, but every muscle in his body was taut, the tight fabric of his jeans doing more to outline his arousal than conceal it. Burning color had flared on his high, chiseled cheekbones, and his tongue edged along his lower lip in an unconscious move, as if he were already tasting her sweetness. Finally he began to move, sitting up in slow motion, his eyes never leaving her body, glittering hotly as he explored every inch of her with visual hunger. He reached down to take off his boots and socks, tossing them to the side, where the boots landed with muffled thuds. Then he stood, unfolding his tall frame to tower over her. All moisture left her mouth. Without her shoes, she was suddenly aware of the differences in their sizes, their strength, the very shape and texture of their bodies. He was male, powerful and aggressive. She was completely feminine, soft and satiny, yet capable of taking all of his aggression and power and turning it into an expression of love. She hoped, oh, how she hoped!

His lean hands were pulling at his belt buckle, releasing it and stripping the belt free of his pants with one firm tug. When he moved to unsnap his jeans, Susan came to life and reached out to cover his hands with hers. "Let me," she whispered. His arms fell to his sides, and he sucked in another deep, shuddering breath.

Slowly, drawing the time and the moment out, she released the snap and slid down the zipper, her tender hands moving inside the opened garment to trace his hip bones, explore the tight little cavity of his navel, then move around to palm the hard, taut roundness of his buttocks. Gently she ran her hands down his thighs, taking the jeans with her, delighted as she realized that he wore no underwear. When the jeans were below his knees, he moved suddenly, as if his patience had abruptly worn out. He stepped out of the entangling denim and kicked it away, seizing her simultaneously and falling back on the bed with her in his arms, cradling her against his chest.

Like a willing sacrifice on his sensual altar, she entwined her arms around his muscled neck and lifted her lips to his, her body writhing against him in a slow, delicate dance. His mouth closed over hers with hard, fierce possession, and he pulled her more fully onto him, mingling his legs with hers as he mingled his breath with hers, his tongue with hers, his taste with hers. The tartness of desire lay like a heady wine on his lips, and she sipped it eagerly. She was alive, soaring, her entire existence focused on him and exulting in the intensity of her being. She trembled in his arms, her entire body quaking.

He released her mouth to slide his lips like a burning brand along the curve of her jaw, then down the soft column of her neck. As if he'd discovered a rare treasure, he pressed his face into the tender hollow of her shoulder. His tongue darted out and tasted her, and

Susan shivered in blind delight, her fingers lacing into his hair and pressing him to her.

"My God," he muttered thickly, nipping at her flesh with his sharp white teeth, leaving little stinging points of sensation that stopped short of pain and instead raised her internal temperature by several degrees. "You make me crazy. Sometimes I think I'd kill to get to you, even knowing that Preston has had you."

For a moment pain so intense that it blinded her tore at her insides, and she inhaled sharply. Then she managed to push it away, accepting that she would have to prove to him that he could trust her, in all things. She moved against him in a way that wrenched a groan from his lips. With a lithe, powerful twist of his body, he rolled and placed himself above her, his muscled legs controlling hers.

With one shaking finger, he outlined the small circles of her nipples, watching as the velvet flesh puckered into succulent buds. "Sweet Susan," he breathed, and lowered his head to offer homage with his mouth. Like fire, his lips burned over the soft mounds of her breasts, and he teased the quivering slopes with his devilish tongue. Susan moaned, a sound unnoticed except perhaps by the deeper, primal instincts of the man who bent over her. Her insides were molten, her body liquid with the flow of desires that urged her relentlessly onward. He suckled strongly at her breasts, and the moans became whimpers, little sounds of pleading.

But he lingered over her, as if determined to enjoy everything about her. With hands and mouth he explored her, discovering the different textures and tastes of her body, searching out her most sensitive places with probing fingers and a curious tongue. She writhed under his touch, her hips undulating as she arched higher and higher toward the sun, her skin breathing the perfume of passion. She cried out in hoarse, mindless reaction when his hand moved with sure, heart-stopping intimacy to discover the degree of her readiness, and he sucked in a deep breath. "Now," he said with fierce intent, his hand moving her thighs apart, opening her legs to him. Susan obeyed the demanding touch instantly, unable even to think of not doing so, opening herself to him like a vulnerable flower, chaining him with her trust more surely than he could chain her with his strength.

He moved over her, his eyes feverish with desire, his strong body shaking as he covered her softness with the hard power of his own frame. He slid his hands under her, cradling the satin curves of her buttocks in his palms and lifting her up to his thrust. Susan whimpered softly, wanting him so much that she was aching with it, and she arched invitingly. He took her with a powerful surge that drove him deeply into her, sheathing himself completely in the searing velvet of her flesh. The whimpers in Susan's throat caught as a shock wave thundered through her body, her chaste body that hadn't known a man's passion since Vance's death. A reflexive cry of pain slipped from her lips, and her fingers dug into his biceps, feeling them bulge with the strain as he reached desperately for control.

He hung over her, staring down at her with astonishment freezing his expression. "My God," he muttered hoarsely.

Her lips were parted, her breath moving swiftly in and out between them, as her body struggled to accept him, adjust to him. "Cord?" she gasped, asking for reassurance, a little frightened with an instinctive, feminine fear.

He held himself very still. "Do you want me to stop?" he asked. "I don't want to hurt you."

"No, no! Don't stop! Please, don't stop." The words turned into a moan as they trailed out of her mouth. She felt as if she would die if he left her now, as if a vital part of her would be torn away. But he didn't pull away; he lay motionless atop her until the tension had eased out of her body and he felt the inner relaxation, until she began to move under him with little instinctive undulations of her hips. She clung to him, her arms around his neck, her legs locked around his waist when at last he began to answer her movements with his own. He was slow and gentle, taking incredible care of her, making certain that she was with him every step of the way as he pushed his body toward satisfaction. His hands and mouth buried her conscious thought under a flurry of hot caresses that intensified the fire in her loins, pushing her out of control, past any semblance of serenity or decorum. In his arms she wasn't the quiet, demure Susan Blackstone; she was a wild thing, hot and demanding, concerned only with the riptides of pleasure that were sucking her out to sea. She clutched at him with damp, desperate hands, and her heels dug into his back, his buttocks, the backs of his thighs. He was no longer gentle, but driven by the same demons that drove her, pounding into her with a wild power that had only one goal.

"I can't get enough of you," he gritted, his teeth clenched. It was a cry that erupted without conscious thought, and he heard it but scarcely realized that he'd said it. But it was true; he couldn't get enough of her. He couldn't get deeply enough into her to satisfy the burning need that was torturing him; he wanted to blend his flesh with hers until the lines of separateness faded and he absorbed her into himself. He wanted to bury himself so deeply within her that she could never get him out, that her body, the very cells of her flesh, would always have the imprint of his possession.

While he was branding her with his touch, Susan branded him with hers. She'd never realized how incomplete she felt until this moment when she knew the shattering satisfaction of being whole. She tried with her hands, her mouth, the undulant caress of her body, to show him how much she loved him, giving him everything she had to give, declaring her love with every movement, mingling herself with him in an act of love that transcended the physical.

There, on a sun-washed bed, she gave her heart to an outlaw and found a heaven that she hadn't known existed.

In the silent aftermath of passion they lay together with their bodies slowly cooling, their pulses gradually resuming a normal rate. Time drifted past, and still they lay together, reluctant to move and break the spell, reluctant to face the moment when their flesh would no longer be joined. Her fingers threaded through the tousled softness of his dark hair, stroking gently, and he settled his full weight on her with an almost soundless sigh of contentment. Susan stared at the ceiling, so happy that she felt she might fly into a million little pieces of ecstasy. Her lips trembled abruptly, and the image of the rough, timbered ceiling blurred. She bit her lip to stifle the sob that rose in her throat and demanded voicing, but she couldn't prevent the identical tracks of moisture that ran out of the corners of her eyes and disappeared into the hair at her temples. He was relaxing into sleep and she tried to keep from disturbing him; it was silly to cry because the most wonderful thing in her life had just happened to her!

But he was a man who had stayed alive by paying attention to his senses and gut instincts, and perhaps he felt the fine degree of tension in her body. His head lifted abruptly, and he surveyed her brimming eyes with sharp attention. He levered himself up on one elbow and lifted his hand to wipe at the tears with his thumb, the callused pad rasping slightly across the sensitive skin of her temples. He was frowning, the dark, level brows lowered over narrowed eyes that searched her delicate features so intently that she felt he could see inside her mind.

"Is it because I hurt you?" he rumbled.

Quickly she shook her head and tried to give him a smile, but the stretching of her lips wobbled out of control and vanished. "No. You didn't really hurt me. It was only at first... I wasn't expecting..." She couldn't get the words out, and she swallowed, forcing her will on her voice. "It was just so...so special." Another tear escaped her eye.

He caught that one with his lips, pressing an open-mouthed kiss to her temple and darting his tongue out to cleanse the salty liquid from her skin. "Susan," he breathed almost inaudibly, saying her name as if he could taste it, as if he savored the sound of it. "I want you again."

Golden sunlight washed the room with brightness, allowing no shadows to hide their passion, and no shadows at all on her heart. Her lips trembled again, and she reached for him, drawing him into the tenderness of her embrace. "Yes," she said simply, because she couldn't deny her heart.

CHAPTER SEVEN

THERE WERE ISOLATED MOMENTS, during the hours that followed, when she was able to think, but for the most part she was overtaken by the unstoppable tidal wave of desire. He knew just how to touch her, how long to linger, how to bring her time and again to the heart-stopping peak of pleasure. His hard hands learned every inch of her as he taught her to accommodate his desires, and she gave herself to him without reserve. She was incapable of holding any part of her heart back, all thoughts of protection left behind in the dust of the past. She had to love him with all the strength and devotion she could, because she could give no less. He'd known too much coldness, too much pain, and she sought to heal him with the soft, searing worship of her body. He was wild, hungry, sometimes almost violent, but with her love she absorbed the bitterness from him, soothing away the loneliness of his isolation. A combination of many things had made him a loner, a man without hearth or home, who lived on the razor's edge of danger and stayed alive by his wits and his finely honed body. Without words she accepted his passion and gentled it with her unquestionable trust. She tried to show him that he was safe with her, that he had no need for the wall that he'd built to keep himself apart from the rest of the world.

The sun was past its zenith and sliding down to the horizon when he relaxed abruptly and fell asleep, as if a light had been clicked off. Susan lay beside him and almost cried again, this time in thankfulness. He *did* trust her, at least a little, or he wouldn't have been able to sleep in her presence. She somehow had a mental image of him taking his pleasure with innumerable women, faceless and nameless; then, when they slept sated in his arms, he would slip away from them to find his solitary bed. She watched him as he slept, his powerful body sprawled across the bed, his mouth softened under the black silk of his moustache. He had long, curling lashes, like a child's, and she smiled as she tried to imagine him as a toddler, with his cheeks still showing the chubby innocence of a baby.

But the innocent child had grown into a hard, wary man whose body was laced with scars, evidence of the battles he'd fought just to stay alive. He'd told her about Judith, but other than that he'd kept his past locked away in the depths of his mind. Other men would have had tales to relate of their adventures, or at least mentioned the different cultures and lands they'd seen, but not Cord. He was a silent warrior, not given to rehashing past battles, and when he was wounded, he crawled away to lick his wounds alone.

The thought of him being hurt made her heart clench painfully. She couldn't bear it if he were ever hurt again; just knowing that he had already borne wounds was almost beyond bearing. She leaned forward in blind desperation and touched her mouth lightly, tremblingly, to the round, silvered scar on his right shoulder. His skin twitched under her touch, but he didn't awaken, and she drifted to the long, thin line that ran down under his left arm, trailing her lips along the length of the scar, with aching tenderness trying to draw from him even the memory of those wounds. She found every scar on his body, licking and kissing them as she crouched protectively over him, guarding him with her slender, delicate woman's body, healing him. She felt him quiver under her mouth and knew that he was awake, but still she roamed over his body, her gentle hands caressing him. He began to shake, his body taut and ready.

"You'd better stop," he warned hoarsely. She didn't stop, instead turning her loving attention to a scar that furrowed down the inside of his thigh, then moving on to a newer, still-angry scar that snaked down his abdomen. He groaned aloud, his hands clenching on the sheet. She lingered, more intent now on the tension that she could feel building in him, intensifying to a crescendo, wanting to make him writhe with need as he had done to her.

He endured her loving torment until he was a taut arch on the bed, then his control broke and he reached for her, a primal growl rumbling in his throat as he swept her over him, thrusting up to bury himself in the sweet comfort of her body. His movements were swift and impatient, his hands grasping her hips so tightly that tiny smudged spots would mark the placement of his fingertips for a week. He held her still for his sensual assault, rotating his hips in a manner that drove her to a fast, hard culmination, then followed her while she was still submerged in the powerful waves of satisfaction.

Afterward he cuddled her against his side, and she curled into his hard, strong body with a sigh that reflected her bone-deep exhaustion. His hand stroked over her hair, smoothing it away from her damp face.

"I'm sorry I hurt you, that first time," he murmured, his thoughts turning lazily to the morning, remembering the shock he'd had at how *virginal* she'd felt. "But I'm glad as hell that Preston hasn't had you."

So he'd realized what her difficulty in accepting him had signified. She wished that he had trusted her enough to take her word in the matter, but he'd learned the hard way not to trust anyone, and it would take time for her to teach him that he didn't always have to guard his back. She ran her hand through the dark curls on his chest in an absent manner. "Since Vance—" She stopped, then continued so softly that he had to strain to hear her. "You're the only one."

She didn't look up, so she missed the expression of almost savage satisfaction that crossed his hard face. She knew only the momentary tightening of his arms before his embrace relaxed and he shifted his weight, coming up on one elbow to lean over her. His hand settled proprietarily on her soft stomach, a little gesture that said a lot. "I don't want you going anywhere else with him," he informed her in a voice so darkly menacing that she looked up at him in quick surprise.

She hesitated, wondering if she dared presume that this day of naked passion had established any sort of stable relationship between them. Very steadily she asked, "Are you offering your services as an escort if I need one?"

A guarded look came over his face, and he stroked his jaw in a restless manner, as if missing his beard. "If I'm available," he hedged.

Susan slowly extricated herself from his arms and sat up, feeling a little chilled by his answer. "And when will you be unavailable?" she queried. "When you're with Cheryl?"

Surprise pulled his brows together, but she couldn't tell if it was the thought itself that surprised him, or that she'd thought she had a right to ask the question at all. Then his face cleared, and amusement began to sparkle in his pale eyes. Very deliberately he let his gaze wander over her, noting the tumbled dark hair, the soft flush that his lovemaking had left on her creamy skin. Her lips were swollen and passionate-looking, and he remembered the way they'd drifted over his body. Her breasts, high and round, fuller than he'd expected, also bore a rosy glow from his caresses and ardent suckling, and as he stared at them he noticed that her pert little nipples were hardening, reaching out as if for another kiss. Swiftly he glanced at her face, and his amusement deepened when he saw the way she was blushing. How could she still blush? For hours she'd lain naked in his arms, totally unselfconscious, allowing him the complete freedom of her body, yet now it took only a slow, enjoyable visual tour of her nakedness to have her blushing like a virgin.

Then he had still another surprise as he felt the lower hardening of his body in response to her. How could he even think about sex again right now? Five minutes before, he'd thought that the day had been fantastic, the most sexually satisfying day of his life, but that he probably wouldn't be able to respond again for a week. Now his body was proving him a liar. He wanted her, again and again. The sensual pleasure he felt with her was staggering, but no sooner had his pulse calmed than he began to feel the nagging need to possess more of her. From the moment he'd seen her, he'd wanted to lie on her tight and deep, immerse himself in her tenderness. He'd never been jealous of a woman in his life, until he'd met Susan. It knocked him off balance, the fury that filled him whenever he thought of her dancing with Preston, kissing Preston, letting him put his arms around her. He'd wanted to hurt her because it drove him crazy to think of Preston making love to her. Now he knew that she'd been chaste, yet still there was the possibility that her loyalty was to Preston. Women were hard to read, and a treacherous one was deadly. If he were smarter, he'd keep this one at a distance, at least until everything was settled and he wouldn't have to watch every word he said to her, but he couldn't force himself to say the words that would send her away, just as he hadn't been able to resist her rather innocent striptease that morning.

Susan watched him, waiting for his answer, but his eyes had gone opaque and his face was a blank wall, his thoughts hiding behind it. She was aware that he was becoming aroused by looking at her body, so why should he suddenly lock himself away? Was it because he didn't think she had any right to question him about his relationships with other women? Well, if he thought she'd sit quietly home while he danced the night away with Cheryl Warren, he'd just have to think again! She balled her fist and thumped him on the chest.

"Answer me," she demanded, her blue eyes darkening with fire. "Will you be out with Cheryl? Or any other woman, for that matter?"

He jackknifed to a sitting position and swung his long legs off the bed. "No," he said shortly, getting to his feet and leaning down to scoop his jeans from the floor. "I won't be with any other woman."

Did he resent having to give her that reassurance? Suddenly she felt embarrassed at her nakedness, and she snatched up a corner of the tumbled sheet to hold it over her breasts. Until then she had felt protected by the closeness she'd shared with him, but now he was suddenly a stranger again, and her bareness seemed much more vulnerable.

He gave the sheet a derisive glance. "It's a little late to try to protect your modesty."

Susan bit her lip, wondering if it would be better simply to get up, get dressed, and leave, or if she should try to talk him out of his sudden ill-temper. Had she gotten too close to him today? Was he reacting by trying to push her away with hostility? Looking at him worriedly, she thought that he looked uncomfortable, the way a man looks when a woman is making a nuisance of herself and he doesn't know how to get rid of her. She paled at the idea.

"I'm sorry," she heard herself say in swift apology, and she scrambled off the bed, abandoning the flimsy barrier of the sheet in favor of dressing as quickly as she could. Without looking at him, she grabbed up her panties and stepped into them. "I didn't mean to push you. I realize that having sex doesn't mean anything—"

"Whoa, lady!" Scowling, he dropped his jeans to the floor and grabbed her arm, pulling her upright as she bent to retrieve her dress, then drawing her into the circle of his arms. Her soft breasts flattened against his chest, and she quivered with enjoyment, her thoughts instantly distracted. How could she want him again? Her legs were distinctly wobbly after the day's activities anyway, and she was already feeling achy in various places, but she knew that if he wanted to tumble her back on the bed again, she would tumble gladly and worry about her aches tomorrow.

He frowned down at her. "Don't try feeding me that free-and-easy hogwash, because that isn't you, and I know it. I'm just feeling uneasy. Things are getting complicated all of a sudden." He stopped without explaining any further and cupped her face in his warm fingers. "Are you sorry it happened?"

She put her hand over his, rubbing her cheek against his palm. "No, I'm not sorry. How could I be? I... I wanted it, too." She'd started to say, "I love you," but at the last moment she'd choked the words back and substituted others that were true, but lacked the depth of what she felt. He didn't want the words, didn't want to be burdened with her emotions, and she knew it. As long as she didn't say the words aloud, he'd be able to ignore the true depth of her feeling, even though he had to know how she felt after these past hours spent in his arms, when she had given herself to him completely in a way that only a woman in love could give. He had to know, yet until the words were spoken, the knowledge didn't exist.

"I don't want you to get hurt," he muttered.

She leaned against him, wrapping her arms around him. He was warning her, letting her know that she shouldn't expect anything permanent from him. Pierced by a stiletto pain at the thought of one day watching his back as he walked away, she was also grateful for his honesty. He wasn't going to hit her with a blow from behind. And maybe, just maybe, she could change his mind. He wasn't used to being loved, and it was obvious that, even unwillingly, he felt more for her than he was comfortable with. She had a chance, and she would risk everything on that.

"Everyone gets hurt," she murmured against his warm skin. "I'm not going to worry about what might or might not happen someday in the future. I'll worry about someday when it gets here."

Someday she might have to do without him, a little bit of her dying every day of emotional starvation. But that was someday, and she had today. Today she was in his arms, and that was enough.

LATER THAT NIGHT, facing Imogene across the width of the kitchen, she tried desperately to hold on to the memory of what she'd shared with him. Imogene's first words to her had been of concern, but that had quickly faded when Susan told her flatly that she wasn't going to play spy. "I told him what your plan was," she confessed remotely. "Then I told him to make certain he didn't tell me anything, so he couldn't think I was with him just to whore for information."

Imogene whitened with fury. She drew herself up to her full height, her anger making her seem six feet tall, Imogene in a rage was a formidable sight, but Susan stood her ground, her soft mouth set in a grim line, giving back stare for stare.

"Susan, my God, are you a fool?" Imogene shouted. "Haven't you realized yet that we stand to lose everything?"

"No, I haven't realized it! Cord hasn't made any move at all, other than threatening to press charges if the ridges aren't leased to him. I've agreed to that, and he's waiting for the geological surveys. Stop painting him as the devil, Imogene!"

"You don't know him like I do!" Suddenly Imogene realized that she was yelling, and she drew a deep breath, visibly forcing herself back under control. "You're making a big mistake if you take him at face value. He's planning something; I *know* it. If I just had some inkling, so I'd know what to protect! You could have found out," she said bitterly. "But instead you've let him turn your head and make you forget about where your loyalty lies."

"I love him," Susan said quietly.

Imogene gaped at her, her eyes going wide. "You... what? But what about Preston? I thought—"

"I *do* love Preston, as a friend, as Vance's brother." Susan groped for the words that could explain. "But Cord...makes me feel alive again. He gives me something to live *for*."

"I hope you're not banking too much on that! Susan, where's your common sense? He'll willingly take you to bed, but if you expect more from him than that, you're a fool. When he gets tired of you, he'll drop you without thinking twice about it, and you'll be left to face everyone you know. You'll always be Cord's leftovers."

"If I'd gone along with your plan, I would have been, anyway," Susan pointed out. "I won't stab him in the back, even if it means I lose everything I own, but I don't think he means to do anything else at all. I think all he wanted was the oil leases."

"You're not the only one who's involved here! You're not the only one who's at risk. Preston and I also stand to lose everything. Doesn't that mean anything to you?"

"It means a great deal to me. I simply don't think he's a threat to you."

Imogene shook her head, closing her eyes as if in

disbelief at Susan's blindness. "I can't believe you're so blind where he's concerned. You love him? Well, that's just fine! Love him if you have to, but don't be fool enough to trust him!"

Susan went white. "I have to trust him. I love him too much not to. I'd trust him with my life."

"That's your decision, I suppose," Imogene snapped sarcastically. "But you're also trusting him with ours, and I don't like that at all. He must really be something in bed, to make you so willing to turn your back on the people who love you, knowing that all he'll every offer you is sex."

Susan felt as if she were staring at Imogene from a great distance, and a faint buzzing sound in her head warned her that she might faint. Dizzily, she groped for one of the kitchen chairs and almost fell into it. They were tearing her apart! The awful thing was that she could see Imogene's side of it. Imogene fully expected Cord to take some sort of revenge against her, and she was frightened, as well she should be. Imogene was lashing out, reacting to a driving need to protect her own, and in her desperation she was willing to hurt people if they got in her way.

Imogene hesitated for a moment, staring at Susan's pale, damp face as she slumped in the chair; then her face twisted, and for a moment tears brimmed in her pale gray eyes. She blinked them back fiercely, because Imogene Blackstone never wept, and moved swiftly to the sink, dampening several paper towels and taking them to Susan. She slid her arm around the young woman and gently blotted her face with the cool, wet towels. "Susan, I'm sorry," she said, her voice steady at first, then wobbling dangerously. Imogene never apologized. "My God, he's got us fighting among ourselves."

The damp coolness of the paper towels banished Susan's momentary dizziness, but it couldn't banish the ache in her heart. She wanted to run to Cord, to throw herself into his arms and let his kisses make her forget that there was an outside world. But despite the hours she'd spent in his bed, she wasn't entitled to dump all her worries on his shoulders, even though all her worries centered around him.

She clasped her hands on the table, entwining her fingers so tightly that they turned white. "I haven't turned my back on you or Preston," she said with hard-won steadiness. "I simply can't do something that's so completely against the things I believe in. Please don't try to make me take sides, because I can't. I love all of you; I can't stab any of you in the back."

Imogene touched Susan's bent head briefly, then let her hand drop. "I only hope Cord has the same reluctance to hurt you, but I can't believe it. I don't want you to be caught in the middle, but it seems that you'll have to be, if you won't take sides. He'll smash anything that gets in his way."

"That's a chance I'll have to take," Susan whispered. She'd already accepted the risk she had to face in loving Cord; what else could she do?

The next morning she went to church as usual, but she couldn't keep her mind on the sermon. Imogene, sitting beside her, was quiet and withdrawn, not entering into conversation before the services began, her gaze fixed on the minister, but Susan felt that Imogene wasn't really concentrating on the sermon either. Preston had shadows under his eyes, and to Susan's concerned eye he seemed to have lost a little weight, though she'd seen him only two days before. The strain was telling on him, but he managed to smile and greet everyone as normal. Susan wondered if Imogene had told him anything that had been said the night before, then decided that it wasn't likely. Imogene was too reserved to cry on anyone's shoulder, even her own son's.

Susan declined Imogene's invitation to Sunday dinner and went home to prepare a light meal of a crisp salad and potato soup. The spring day was too beautiful to sit inside, so she took her needlepoint out on the patio and worked on it for a couple of hours. She was outwardly serene, but she was aware of the coiling tension inside her as she sat and listened for the sound of a car coming up her long driveway. Would Cord drive over today? The thought made her breath catch. He would take her upstairs to her bedroom, to the bed where no man had ever slept, and on the cool, pristine sheets he would blend his body with hers.

She closed her eyes as desire built in her, making her lower body feel heavy and tight, and painfully empty. Surely he would come; surely he could hear her silent call for him.

Stately, towering thunderheads began to march in from the west, and the wind developed a brisk chill, but still she sat there until the first fat raindrops began to splatter on the patio tiles. Gathering her needlework, she ran for the sliding doors and slipped inside just as the weather broke and the rain became a downpour, filling her ears with a dull roar. A sharp crack of thunder made her jump, and she hastily pulled the curtains over the glass doors, then moved around and turned on lights to dispel the fast, early dusk.

It was after eight o'clock that night before she admitted that he wasn't going to come, so she locked up the house and readied herself for bed. The storm had passed, but the rain continued to fall, and she lay awake for hours listening to the hypnotic patter, wishing that he was in bed beside her, warm and virile. The big house was silent and empty around her, emptier even than it had been after Vance's death, and that was strange, because Vance had lived here, and she had memories of him in every room. But Vance was gone, and Cord's personality was too strong to fight.

Because the day was so muted and gray when she woke up in the morning, and because she felt so depressed at not having seen Cord, Susan made a determined effort to cheer herself up. She chose a dark red silk sheath for work, and belted it with a snazzy wide black belt that she'd never worn before. A short black jacket pulled the outfit together, and Susan arched an inquiring eyebrow at her own reflection in the mirror as she leaned forward to put on her earrings. The sharply stylish woman in the mirror didn't quite look like Susan Blackstone, who usually preferred more conservative garments. But then, the Susan Blackstone who had looked in that mirror the Friday before had never spent the day making love with Cord Blackstone. She was gambling for the first time in her life, and the stakes were higher than she could afford. A woman who would risk her heart, knowing from the outset that the odds in her favor weren't too good, couldn't be as staid and conventional as Susan had always thought herself to be.

She kept her cheerful demeanor in place all day long, but after she got home and had eaten the dinner Emily prepared, after Emily had gone to her own house, she waited hopefully until long after dark, but still she didn't hear anything from Cord. A chill began to tighten her muscles. If the day they had spent together had meant anything to him at all, why hadn't he made any effort to see her again? Had it just been a…a convenience for him? A casual sexual encounter that he wouldn't think of again?

She thought of driving out to Jubilee Creek, but the lateness of the hour and the steady rain dissuaded her. Surely tomorrow she'd hear from him.

But she didn't, and the hours dragged past. She called Information to see if he'd had a phone installed, but they had no listing in his name. She could no longer even keep up the pretense of being cheerful, and her face was tight with strain, an expression that was duplicated on Preston's face. Susan knew that he had extended himself to the limit, liquidating assets to replace the money in Cord's account, and she wanted to ask him if he needed help, but an intimate knowledge of Blackstone pride kept her from making the offer. He'd refuse, and even if he later changed his mind, if things became desperate enough that he would want to accept her help, he wouldn't mention it to her.

Thursday afternoon she drove out to Jubilee Creek, but there was no sign of Cord. She looked in the windows and could see no lights, no dirty dishes, no clothing strewn about. She tried both the front and back doors, and found them securely locked. The thought that he might have gone permanently made her sag against the door, and bitter tears of regret seared her lids before she forced them back; not regret for what had happened, but regret that she'd had only that one day in his arms. She should have had more! It wasn't fair to give someone a brief glimpse of heaven, then draw heavy curtains over the scene! Where Cord was concerned, she wanted it all: all of his smiles, his kisses, his company every day. She wanted to be the one to calm his anger or incite his passion. She wanted to wake up beside him every morning and look at his sleepy, beard-stubbled face, and at night she wanted to lie close against his tall, hard body.

Of course, she could just be borrowing heartache; the cabin hadn't been emptied, so she had to assume that he would be returning. It was just… Why couldn't he have let her know that he was leaving, or when he would be back? Would a phone call have been so difficult for him to make?

But those were the conditions she'd set: He wasn't to tell her anything. Her eyes widened in realization. What if his absence had something to do with Imogene and Preston? They were convinced that he was scheming against them, and though she had defended him, suddenly she was unsure. What did she know about him, other than that he was so exciting and dangerous that he made her heartbeat lurch out of rhythm every time she saw him? He was a hungry, demanding lover, but considerate in controlling his strength and handling her carefully. He danced with wild grace, and his body was laced with the scars that a warrior collected over the years. She loved him, but she was painfully aware that he kept most of himself hidden away. If he had lived by the law of fang and claw, could she expect him to do anything other than strike back at people who had wronged him? Was she a fool to trust him? She'd always thought that a trainer who walked unarmed into a cage with a snarling tiger was extremely foolish, but she had been just as foolish. Suddenly she knew that Cord was more than capable of taking revenge; he could raise it to the level of fine art.

The next day Preston came into her office and dropped tiredly into the comfortable chair next to her desk. "Well, I've done it," he said in a voice hollow with exhaustion. "I've stretched myself to the limit, but Cord has been repaid in full."

She was overcome with sympathy for him, looking at the dark shadows under his blue eyes. "I wish you would let me help—"

"No, thanks, sugar." He managed a slow smile for her. "It wasn't your doing, so you shouldn't have to pay. Now that the debt is covered, if you don't want to lease the ridges to him, you don't have to. I've pretty well blocked any move he can make to cause trouble about the money; I've even paid him interest."

"I wish you could talk with him and settle your differences," she said wistfully. "It's not right for a family to tear itself apart like this. All of that happened so long ago; why can't you put it in the past?"

"There's too much resentment, on both sides," Preston replied. He stretched his long legs out in front of him and crossed them elegantly at the ankle. "We never got along, for one reason or another. That thing with Judith Keller just topped it off, as far as he was concerned. And as far as I'm concerned…" He gave her a direct look. "As long as you're interested in him, I have to hate his guts."

Susan blushed, distressed at causing him any pain. "Don't feel like that, please. Don't add to the trouble. I can't stand the thought of being a bone of contention between the two of you."

"But such a sweet, lovely bone," he teased, his blue eyes lightening momentarily. He really was an extraordinarily good-looking man, she realized with some surprise, slim and elegant, with a smooth style that sometimes made him seem misplaced in this century. But Preston wasn't out of place; he was supremely suited for his occupation. He was cool, levelheaded, and fair in his practices. He was also completely out of his league in fighting Cord, because he lacked the ruthlessness that had kept Cord alive in a lot of dim back alleys.

The light had already faded out of Preston's eyes. "Do you see him often?" he finally asked, his tone gruff as he struggled to hide his emotions.

It was only the painful truth when Susan replied, "No, not often at all." In moments of mental detachment she was astonished at the way she had given herself to a man whom she didn't know that well, hadn't seen that often, and who was a direct threat to her way of life. Then the memory of the heat of his kisses would banish her detachment, and she would no longer wonder at the way she had lost herself in his arms. He wasn't a man who inspired a sedate love; he evoked the deepest, wildest passions a woman's heart was capable of feeling.

Preston sat there, a frown puckering his brow as he thought. After a moment he said, "I'd like for him to know that the money has been repaid. Will you tell him for me?"

"If I see him again," Susan agreed steadily. "I don't know where he is." The bald confession stabbed her as she realized anew how empty she felt at the thought that she might not see him again.

Preston sat upright. "Has he left town?"

"I don't know. But I haven't seen him for a week, and he's not at the cabin."

"He's either gone again, or he's making some sort of move against me," Preston muttered absently, tapping his fingertips on the top of Susan's desk. "Let me know if you hear from him." He got up and left her office, still preoccupied with the news that Cord had dropped out of sight.

After a moment Beryl appeared with an armload of correspondence to be signed, pulling Susan away from the chasm of loneliness, but inside herself she was aware that she had only stepped back, not walked away from it entirely. It was still there, cold and black in its yawning emptiness, a bleak, bottomless pit where she would fall forever, locked away from the fire of the man she loved.

CHAPTER EIGHT

JUST AS SHE turned into her driveway a swiftly moving
thunderstorm swept in from the Gulf, and it threatened
to drown her as she dashed the short distance from her
car to the covered side patio. Emily met her at the door
with an enormous towel, having seen her drive up. Just
as Susan stepped out of her soaking shoes and wound
the towel around her hair, the rain stopped as swiftly as
it had come, leaving only the cheerful dripping of water
from the trees and the eaves of the roof. A split second
later the thundercloud was gone and the sun was shining merrily on the wet landscape, making the raindrops
sparkle like diamonds. Susan gave Emily a rueful look.
"If I'd waited in the car for a minute, it would've been
over with and I wouldn't have gotten soaked."

Emily couldn't suppress a chuckle. "If you wanted
predictable weather, you'd live in Arizona. Go on upstairs and get dried off, while I finish your dinner."

Fifteen minutes later Susan was downstairs again,
helping Emily put the finishing touches on the small
but tasty meal she'd prepared. Emily watched her set
a single place on the table, and the older woman's protective instincts were aroused. Putting her big spoon
down with a thunk, she braced her hands on her hips.
"I'd like to know why you've been eating alone every
night, instead of letting Cord Blackstone take you out."

Susan flushed, not certain how to respond. Because it was what she feared most, she finally said, "Just because he passed out on the couch and spent the night here doesn't mean he's interested—"

"Baloney," Emily interrupted in exasperation. "I've got eyes, and I saw the way he was looking at you the next morning. You were looking back at him the same way, and don't try to deny it. Then he went upstairs with you, and it was quite a while before he came down."

"I don't know where he is," Susan admitted helplessly, staring down at the table. "He's not at the cabin. He hasn't called; he didn't even tell me he was leaving, or where he was going. For all I know, he won't be back."

"He'll be back, mark my words." Emily sniffed. "He's not used to accounting for himself to anyone, but if he had it in mind to leave for good, he'd have let you know."

"You knew him when he was a boy," Susan said, looking up at Emily with the hunger to know more about him plain in her eyes. "What was he like?"

Emily's careworn features softened as she looked at the pleading face turned up to her. "Sit down," she urged. "I'll tell you while you're eating."

Susan obeyed, automatically eating the tiny lamb chops and steamed carrots that were one of her favorite meals. Emily sat down at the table across from her. "I loved him as a boy," she said, turning her mind back over twenty years. "He was always ready to laugh, always up to some prank, and it seemed like he was more relaxed at my house. He never fit in with the people his parents expected to be his friends, never really fit in here at all, and that just made him wilder than he naturally was anyway, which was wild enough. He was always ahead of everyone else, stronger than anyone else his age, faster, with better grades, more girlfriends. Even the older girls in high school were after him. Everything came so easy to him, or maybe he made everything come to him; I've never seen anyone more stubborn or determined to have his way. Thinking back on it, I know that he had to be bored. Nothing challenged him. He pulled off every wild stunt he could think of, but he had a golden touch, and everything always worked smooth as silk for him. I've never seen anything like his luck."

Susan's breath caught at the image Emily had given her, of a boy growing up too fast, without any limits to guide him. He wouldn't accept any limits, she realized. He'd been propelled by the extraordinary combination of genes and circumstance that should have made him the prototypical Golden Boy, with all the comforts and privileges of wealth and class: handsome, unusually intelligent, athletic, gifted by nature with charm and grace. But his restless, seeking mind had soared beyond that, driven him to test the limits of chance. He had pushed and pushed, seeking a boundary he couldn't push beyond, until he'd gone too far and been driven away from his home.

There had been dark years in Cord's life, times when he'd been close to death, when he'd been cold and hungry, but she couldn't imagine him ever being frightened. No, he'd face everything that came his way, the mocking twist of his lips daring everyone and everything to do their worst. The remaining vestiges of the Golden Boy had been obliterated by the harshness of the life he'd led. Perhaps he had money now, perhaps he lived comfortably, but it hadn't always been so, and his senses were still razor-sharp. She thought of the scars on his body and her heart twisted.

"Everyone acts as if he's a wild animal," she said painfully. "Why are they so afraid of him?"

"Because they don't understand him. Because he's not like they are. Some folks are afraid of lightning; some think it's beautiful. But everyone's cautious around it."

Yes, he was as wild and beautiful as a bolt of lightning, and as dangerous. She stared at Emily, her eyes glistening with tears. "I love him."

Emily nodded sadly. "I know, honey. I know. What are you going to do?"

"There's nothing I can do, is there? Just…love him, and hope everything works out."

A foolish hope, doomed from the start. How could it work out? It was impossible to hold a bolt of lightning.

He was gone, and every minute seemed to drag by, rasping on her nerves. An hour was a lifetime; a day, eternity. No book, no gardening, no sewing, could ease her bone-deep sense of yearning. All she could think of was Cord, overwhelming her with his reckless charm and the impact of his forceful sensuality.

If only he was with her! In his presence she wouldn't care about Preston, or Imogene, or whatever was going on. In Cord's arms, she wouldn't care about anything. She could lose herself in him, and count the loss well worth the cost in pain. She loved him simply, completely, and she had to follow only the dictates of her emotions.

She slept restlessly that night, and was jerked out of sleep a little after midnight by a boom of thunder that rattled the windows. Susan lay snugly in her warm bed, listening to the lightning crackle; then a hard, driving rain began to pound against her windows and the wind picked up. Deciding she'd better turn on the radio and get a weather report, she sat up and turned on her bedside lamp. When she did, another pounding reached her ears and she paused, a small frown touching her brow. Then it was repeated, and she jumped out of bed. Someone was trying to beat her door down.

She grabbed her robe and raced down the stairs, turning on lights as she went. "Who is it? What's wrong?" she called as she neared the door.

A deep laugh answered her. "The only thing that's wrong is that you're on that side of the door and I'm on this one."

"Cord!" Her heart jumped into her throat and she fumbled hastily with the lock, throwing the door open. He sauntered in, as wild as the night, and as dangerous. The wind had tumbled his dark hair into reckless waves, and his pale eyes were glittering. He brought the fresh scent of rain in with him, because the wind had blown a fine mist of moisture over him. He was dressed in a conservatively cut, dark business suit, but the coat was hanging open, his tie was draped around his neck, and his shirt was open to the waist. The suit couldn't disguise the desperado that he was, and her mouth went dry with longing.

Unthinkingly, she clutched at his sleeve. "Where have you been? Why haven't you called? I've been so worried—" She stopped, suddenly realizing what she was saying, and stared up at him with eyes full of vulnerability.

"Uh-uh," he crooned softly. "No questions, remember? I'm not telling you anything, not where I was, or when I'll be going again." A savage enjoyment lit his face as another crash of thunder reverberated through the house, and his teeth flashed in a grin. "I like storms," he murmured, taking a step toward her and lacing his arm around her waist in an iron embrace. "I like making love while it rains."

Something was wrong; she couldn't quite catch her breath. She stared up at him dazedly, and she clutched his lapels for support. "I was just going to turn on the radio to get the weather report," she stammered.

He grinned again. "Thunderstorm warning, with possible high winds," he said, pulling her closer until she was pressed full against him. "Who cares?"

The gleam in his eyes was still interfering with her breathing. "When...when did you get back?" she asked, hanging suspended over his arm, her feet having somehow lost touch with the floor. "Or is that another off-limits question?"

"Tonight," he answered. "I was driving home, thinking about how dead tired I was, and how good it would feel to fall into bed. Then I thought how much better it would feel to fall into bed with you, so here I am."

"You don't look tired," she observed cautiously. He didn't. He looked as if he could rival the storm for energy. He was almost burning her with his touch.

"Second wind," he said, and kissed her. His approach was direct and without hesitation, and he kissed her for a long time. She clung to him, first to his lapels; then her clutching fingers somehow found their way to his shoulders, and finally her arms were locked around his neck. He lifted her and started up the stairs, leaving all the lights on behind him, because that was the last thing on his mind.

He set her on her feet in her bedroom and watched her with lazily hooded eyes as he stripped his tie from around his neck and tossed it carelessly over a chair. The tie was followed by his coat; then his shirt was pulled free of his pants and discarded. When he kicked off his shoes and leaned down to pull his socks off, Susan swallowed at the sight of his half-naked body, so sleek and powerful, and she untied the sash of her robe and removed the garment, folding it over the chair. She could feel his eyes on her, on the ice-pink nightgown that half revealed her body.

He dropped his pants and left them lying on the floor. His only remaining garment was a pair of jogging-style shorts, dark blue silk with white edging, which did nothing to hide his arousal. A thunderbolt of excitement raced through her as he nonchalantly stepped out of his underwear and came toward her, as naked and powerfully beautiful as an ancient god.

Quickly she raised the hem of the nightgown over her head and drew it off, the silk whispering over her bare skin. His look of hunger became almost fierce as he reached for her. When he placed her on the bed, Susan reached out for the lamp and he halted her, his hard fingers closing around her wrist.

"Leave it on," he instructed in a voice gone gravelly rough. "I thought of this all the time I was gone. I'm not going to miss seeing one minute of it."

She couldn't help the blush that tinted her breasts and spread upward to her cheeks, and he found it fascinating. Without a word he took her in his arms.

Their loveplay extended as he explored her body as

thoroughly as if he'd never made love to her before, had never spent a lovely sun-drenched day sprawled across a bed with her. When she was writhing against him in frantic need, he paused for a moment to reach for his pants, and Susan realized what he was doing. Without a word, he assumed responsibility for their lovemaking. Then he turned to her and swiftly moved between her legs, sliding into her so powerfully that moans of pleasure were wrenched from both of them. His patience was at an end, and he thrust strongly, his rhythm hungry and fast. Susan wound her legs around him and absorbed the power of his thrusts with her eagerly welcoming body, so dizzy with pleasure at being in his arms again, kissing him, giving herself to him in the most intimate act between man and woman, that he couldn't leave her behind in his relentless quest for pleasure. The powerful coil that had been tightening within her was released suddenly, and her entire body throbbed with the pulsating waves that raced down her legs to curl her toes and spread upward through her torso in a splash of heat. She heard the wild cries that were ground out through his clenched teeth, felt him arch into her helplessly; then it was suddenly quiet again as the storm passed and he let himself down to lie on her in contented exhaustion.

After a moment he sighed and carefully eased himself from her, rolling over on his side. Susan touched him, her fingers gentle. "This might not have been necessary," she murmured. "I... I'm not sure I can get pregnant. Vance and I never used any protection, but I never got pregnant. I'm very...erratic."

He closed his eyes and a tiny grin touched his mouth. Relaxing, he threw one arm behind his head. "Somehow, that's not very reassuring. I get the feeling that if there's any man walking this earth who could get you pregnant, I'm him. We took a big chance last week, but we'll be more careful from now on." He opened one eye a slit and pinned her with the narrow ribbon of his gaze. "Let me know if it's too late to be careful, or if we hit it lucky. As soon as you know."

"Yes," she agreed, sinking down onto the pillow and closing her eyes as contentment claimed her. It felt so natural to be in bed with him, talking about very intimate things, feeling the heat of his body so close to her. She nestled closer to him and rubbed her face against the hair of his chest, feeling the soft curls catch at her eyelashes.

He drifted into sleep with her lying against his side, but woke when the storm, forgotten in their own storm of loving, renewed itself with a snap of lightning so close that the thunder was simultaneous, and Susan sat upright in bed at the unmistakable sound of a limb splitting away from a tree and crashing to the ground. Before she had time to voice her alarm, he seized her from behind and tumbled her back to the mattress.

"Just where do you think you're going?" he growled with mock roughness.

"The trees—" she began, and just then the lights flickered and went out.

"Oh, hell," he said into the sudden darkness. Another bolt of lightning flashed to earth and the eerie blue-white light illuminated the room. He was sitting up, too. "Where's a flashlight and the radio?"

"There's a flashlight in the top drawer of the nightstand," she said, pulling the sheet up around her as the damp chill of the air reached her. "The radio is downstairs in the den."

"Battery?"

"Yes." She listened as he fumbled around in the nightstand, finally locating the flashlight and clicking it on, the beam of light dispelling the darkness. He swung his long legs out of the bed.

"I'll bring the radio up here. Sit tight."

What else could she do? She pulled her knees up and rested her chin on them, her eyes on the storm erupting right outside her windows. It was loud and magnificent, full of fury, but she mourned the damage to the enormous old trees that surrounded the house. If one of the trees came down, it could take the roof of the house off and crush the walls.

Cord came back into the room, the battery-powered radio in his hand. He had it turned to a local Biloxi station. Placing the radio on the nightstand, he clicked off the flashlight and got into bed with her, pulling her down to nestle in his arms.

In only a few moments the amused drawl of the radio announcer was filling the room. "The thunderstorm warning for the Biloxi area has been canceled. I guess those folks at the weather bureau haven't looked out their windows lately. Now, this is what I call *rain*. There aren't any reports of any serious damage, though several power outages have been reported, and there are some signs blown down. Nothing major, folks. We're in touch with the weather bureau, and if it turns serious—"

Cord stretched out a long arm and turned the radio off, silencing the announcer in midsentence. "It's already passing," he murmured, and she noticed that the lightning was indeed less intense, the thunder growing more distant. The lights suddenly blinked back on, blinding both of them with their unexpected brilliance.

He laughed and sat up. "I was going to stay with you as long as the power was off," he said, getting out of bed and reaching for his underwear.

Bewildered, Susan sat up too, staring at him. He pulled on his underwear, then his pants, before she spoke. "Aren't you staying?"

"No." He slanted her a look that was suddenly cool and remote.

"But—it's so late, anyway. Why drive to Jubilee Creek—"

"Three reasons," he interrupted, a harsh note entering his deep voice. "One, I like to sleep alone. Two, I really need the sleep, which I wouldn't get if I stayed here with you. Three, Emily didn't turn a hair at finding me asleep on your couch, but finding me in your bed is something else entirely."

A hard, cold pain struck her in her chest, but she looked at him and saw the way he'd closed himself off, and she summoned all of her strength to give him a smile that wavered only a little. "Are you worried about your reputation?" she managed to tease. "I promise I'll take the blame for seducing you."

Her attempt at lightness worked; he smiled, and sat down on the side of the bed to cup her soft cheek in his palm. "Don't argue," he murmured. But when he was that close he could see her pain, though she was doing everything she could to hide it, and his level brows pulled together. He wasn't used to explaining himself, or talking about his past at all, but he found himself trying to explain his actions for the first time in years. The urge to take the uncomprehending pain out of those soft blue eyes was almost overwhelming. "Susan, I don't feel comfortable sleeping with another person, not anymore. I've spent too many years guarding my back. I may doze off after making love, but I don't fall into a deep sleep. Some part of me is always alert, ready to move. I can't rest that way and I'm really tired tonight; I need some sleep. We'll go out for dinner tomorrow night…make that tonight, since it's almost morning. Seven-thirty?"

"Yes. I'll be ready."

He winked at her. "I won't mind if you aren't dressed."

As he finished dressing, Susan watched him and hugged the sheet up over her nudity. She bit her lip, trying to force her own feelings away so she could consider his. She'd sensed that he was uneasy about allowing himself to relax when anyone else was with him, and she knew that her vision of him leaving his women alone in their beds had been an accurate one. *His women.* She had joined them, that long line of women who had held him in their arms for a taste of heaven, then lain weeping in their cold beds after he had gone. Yet she wouldn't have turned him away, wouldn't have missed her own chance at heaven. If she could turn time back, she would go with him that first night she'd met him, and not waste one moment of the time she had with him.

He completed dressing and reached for his coat, then leaned down to give her a swift kiss. Susan dropped the sheet and rose up on her knees, entwining her arms around his strong neck as she lifted her mouth. He paused, looking down at her gentle mouth, already pouty from his kisses; her eyes were serene pools, with thick black lashes drooping in a drowsy, unconsciously sexy manner. She was a naked Venus in his arms, soft and warm and feminine, and his hands automatically sought her curves as he kissed her long and hard, his tongue deep within her mouth. Despite his weariness, desire hardened his body, and it was all he could do to pull away from her.

"You're going to be the death of me," he muttered, giving her a look that she couldn't read before he left the room. Susan remained on her knees until she heard the sound of the front door closing; then she sagged down on the bed, fighting the hot tears that wanted to fall. For a moment she'd sensed that he'd been tempted to stay, but only to slake the urges of his amazingly virile body, not because he trusted her, not because he felt he could sleep in her arms. She knew that she could have touched him, wriggled herself against him, and he would have tumbled her back down to the mattress, but that wasn't what she wanted. That hot, glorious madness that seized her at his lightest touch was wonderful, but she wanted more. She wanted his love, his trust.

The tiger is a majestic beast, savagely beautiful and awesome in its power, but it's locked alone in its majesty. The beautiful tiger is solitary, hunting alone, sleeping alone. A tiger mates, and for a time is less alone, but the moments of physical joining are soon gone, and the tiger once again roams in solitude. Cord was a tiger in nature, and after mating he had gone to seek his bed apart from every other creature on earth, because he trusted no other creature.

She pounded her fist on the mattress in mute frustration. Why couldn't she have fallen in love with a man who *liked* cuddling up and falling asleep, a man who hadn't spent years of his life kicking around the globe in a lot of godforsaken places, who did all the normal things like going to work during the week and cutting the grass on weekends? Because, she interrupted her own thoughts fiercely, a man like that wouldn't be Cord. He was wild and beautiful, and dangerous. If she had wanted a man who wasn't all of those things, she'd have fallen in love with Preston long ago.

She lay awake, her eyes on the ceiling as the hours slid past and dawn came and went. Part of her was hurt and humiliated that he had come to her for sex, then left as soon as he was satisfied, but another part of her was glad that he had come to her at all, for any reason. Certainly, if he made love to any woman, she wanted it to be herself. She wanted to believe that he felt something for her besides physical desire, but if he didn't, she would try to use that desire as a base to build on. As long as he came around at all, she still had hope.

SHE WAS TAKEN by surprise the next afternoon when sudden cramps signaled that their reckless day of love-making hadn't borne fruit; she'd been feeling listless all day, but credited that to her lack of sleep the night before. She was further surprised when she burst into tears, and it wasn't until that moment that she realized she'd been unconsciously hoping that Cord's seed had found fertile ground. She almost hated her body for being so unpredictable, so inhospitable; she wanted his child, a part of him that would be hers forever. She wouldn't use a pregnancy to chain him to her, ever, if he wanted to go, but how she would love a baby of his making! Her arms ached at the thought of holding an infant with soft dark hair and pale blue eyes, and their emptiness haunted her.

She was pale and shadows lay heavily under her eyes when Cord arrived to take her to dinner; she told him immediately that he had no need to worry about a pregnancy, and almost winced at the relief he didn't bother to hide. Despite that, they had a pleasant dinner, and after eating they danced for a while to some slow, dreamy forties-style music. He'd taken her to a restaurant in New Orleans where she'd never been before, and she liked the place-out-of-time atmosphere. He knew that her energy level was low, and she thoroughly enjoyed the way he coddled her that evening. She drank a little more wine than she was accustomed to, and was floating slightly above the earth as he drove her home in the sleek white Jaguar that he had arrived in, though she had expected the red Blazer. The man has style, she thought dreamily, stroking her fingers over the leather of the seats. In the light of the dash his face was hard and exciting, the virile brush of his moustache outlining the precision of his upper lip. She reached out and let her fingers lightly trace his mouth, causing his brows to arch in question.

"You're so beautiful," she murmured huskily.

"Feel free to admire me anytime you like, madam," he invited formally, but the wicked, sensual glint in his eyes was anything but formal as he glanced at her. She was a little high, her eyes filled with dreams, and he knew that she would come willingly into his arms if he stopped the car and reached for her right then. He shifted uncomfortably in his seat as his body reacted to his thoughts. He wanted her, but he knew that she didn't feel well, and he wanted her to enjoy their lovemaking as deeply as he did, not just allow her body to be used for his pleasure. He thought of how she looked in the throes of passion, and desire slammed into his gut so hard that he jerked in his seat. When this was over, when he had accomplished all that he wanted, he promised himself that he'd take her on a long vacation, maybe a cruise, and he'd make love to her as much as he liked. He'd satisfy his craving for her once and for all, sate himself on her slim, velvet body that was so surprisingly sensual. Her sensuality was so unconscious, so natural, that he sensed she wasn't even aware of it. A perfect lady, he thought, until he took her in his arms; then she turned into a hot, sweet wanton who took his breath away.

He didn't plan any further into the future than that; Cord had learned not to make long-range plans, because they inhibited his ability to react to circumstances. When some people formed plans in their minds, they locked their thoughts on course and couldn't deviate from them, couldn't allow for unforeseen interruptions or detours. When Cord plotted his course of action, he didn't tie himself down; he always allowed for the possibility that he might have to jump to the left instead of to the right, or even retrace his steps entirely. That flexibility had kept him alive, kept him in tune with his senses. In that way, he was a creature of the moment, yet he always kept his goal in mind, and changing circumstances only meant that he would have to reach that goal by a different route. He was usually prepared for anything and everything, but when he'd returned to Biloxi he hadn't been prepared for the primitive desire he would feel for a woman who had one foot in the enemy camp and seemed determined to keep it there. To the victor belonged the spoils, and he looked at Susan with hard determination; when he had won, she would be his, and he would force all thoughts of her in-laws out of her head. He wouldn't allow her any time to think of anyone but him. The savagely possessive need he felt for her had forced him to adjust his actions, but in the end... in the end, everything would be just like he'd planned it, and Susan would be his, on his terms.

Susan sensed the control he exercised when he kissed her lightly and left her at her door; she was too tired, too sleepy from too much wine, to try to understand why he left so abruptly. She only knew that she was disappointed; she could have made a pot of coffee and they could have sat close together and watched the late news, just as she and Vance had often done....

But Cord wasn't Vance.

Susan stood in the darkened foyer and looked around at the beautiful, gracious home Vance had built for her. The light she had left on at the head of the stairs illuminated the pale walls and the elegant floor-to-ceiling windows, the imported tiles of the foyer. Her home was warm and welcoming, because it was a home that had known love, but now she stood in the darkness, surrounded by the things that Vance had given her, and all she could think of was another man. Cord filled her days, her nights, her thoughts, her dreams. His pale lodestone eyes compelled her, like the moon silently controlling the tides. She tried to visualize Vance's face, but the features refused to form themselves in her mind. He had taught her about love; his tender care had helped shape her into a warm and loving woman, but he was gone, and he had no more substance for her than that of the drifting mist. *Vance, I really did love you,* she called out to him silently, but there was nothing there. Vance was dead, and Cord was so vitally alive.

Instead of going up to bed she went into the den and turned on the lights, then walked unerringly to the precise spot in the bookshelves that held a small album, though it had been at least four years since she'd looked at it. She took down the leather-bound volume and opened it, staring at the pictures of Vance.

How young he looked! How fresh and gallant! She saw the familiar mischievous sparkle in his blue eyes, the rather crooked smile, the strong Blackstone features. She traced the lines of his face with one gentle finger, seeing the resemblance he bore to Cord. He looked much the way she imagined Cord would have before experience had worn away his youthful wonder at the world, before all his ideals had been blasted out of existence. "I loved you," she murmured to Vance's smiling face. "If you could have stayed, I'd have loved you forever."

But he hadn't, and now Cord had stolen her love like the renegade he was.

Gently she replaced the album and left the room, walking slowly up the stairs to her empty bed, her mind and her senses filled with the memory of the night before when Cord had swept in with the rain, wild and damp, the air about him almost crackling with the heat of his passion. She hadn't even thought of denying him, even though he'd disappeared for a week without a word of warning. She'd simply undressed, so eager for his touch that she wouldn't have protested if he'd taken her there in the foyer.

She creamed the makeup off her face, closing her eyes slightly to combat the faint giddiness caused by the wine. How passionate he'd been the night before, and how considerate he'd been this evening. She tried to convince herself that he cared for her, but the thought kept coming back that he hadn't wasted any time getting away from her after driving her home. And the night before, he'd left after making love to her. He only wants me for sex, she silently told her reflection, and shut her eyes tightly against the words. It had to be more than that, because she wasn't sure she could keep from falling apart if it wasn't.

CHAPTER NINE

BY THE TIME another week had come and gone, Susan was convinced that she knew nothing about Cord. He was the most enigmatic man she'd ever met; just when she'd decided that he was only using her as a convenient sexual outlet, he confounded her by taking her out every evening, wooing her with wine and good food, and dancing with her into the wee hours of the morning. Dancing with him was special. He was the most graceful man she'd ever known, and he enjoyed dancing. Between them, rituals of dancing were both flirtation and foreplay. She could feel his powerful body moving against her, sending her senses tumbling head over heels, and the unabashed response of his body told her that he was reacting the same way. Held in his arms, she felt secure, protected, locked away in their private world. She could have dreamed her life away in his arms.

He was a gentleman in every sense of the word, tenderly solicitous of her, courting her in a manner so old-fashioned that it stunned her even though she deeply enjoyed every moment of it. He gave her the grace of a few days' privacy, then brought his abstinence to an end with hungry impatience; instead of kissing her gently good-night, as he had been doing, he picked her up and carried her to her bed. When he left several hours later she lay sprawled nude on the tangled sheets, too exhausted to get up to find a nightgown or even pull the sheet over herself. She slept with a heavenly smile on her passion-swollen mouth.

The nights that followed were just as passionate, and she should have been wilting from lack of sleep, but instead she was radiant, full of energy. She sailed through the hours at work, too immersed in her own happiness to really pay attention to Preston's growing depression, knowing that when the night came she would be in Cord's arms again.

Her happiness made the blow, when it came, just that much more cruel. She was going over a productivity report from the small electronics plant they owned when Preston appeared at her office door. Susan looked up with a ready smile, but the smile died when she saw the taut expression that had made his face a gray mask. Concern snapped her to her feet, and she went across the room to him, taking his arm. "What is it?"

He stared at her for a minute, and she silently reproached herself for not having paid more attention to him this past week. She'd known that something was bothering him, but she hadn't wanted anything to dim her happiness. Her selfishness made her writhe inside.

Wordlessly, he extended the papers in his hand. Susan took them, her brow wrinkling as she stared at them.

"What is this?"

"Read it." He moved over to a chair and lowered himself into it, his movements slow and jerky, strangely uncoordinated.

She flipped through the papers, reading slowly. Her eyes widened, and she read them over again, hoping that she hadn't understood correctly, but there was no way to misunderstand. The meaning of every word was perfectly clear. Cord had bought up an outstanding loan against the Blackstone Corporation and was calling it in. They had thirty days to pay.

Almost suffocated by the thick sense of betrayal that rose in her throat, she dropped the papers to the top of her desk and lifted her stunned gaze to Preston. She couldn't speak, though she wet her lips and tried to force her throat to form the words. How could he have done that?

"Well, now you know where he went on that mystery trip," Preston said bitterly, nodding toward the papers. "Dallas."

She braced one hand flat on the desk, trying to support herself as acid nausea rose in her throat. She conquered the moment, but she couldn't conquer the pain that threatened to bend her double. Why had he done it? Didn't he realize that this hurt her as much as it did Preston? This wasn't just Preston he was striking at; he was threatening the entire corporation, her livelihood as well as the livelihoods of thousands of workers who depended on their jobs to put food on the table. He had to know, so the only supposition she could reach was that he simply didn't care. After the week she had spent with him, the passion she'd shared with him, the brutal realization that it all meant nothing to him was like a slap in the face, and she reeled from the impact of it.

"I thought we were protected against this sort of thing." Lifelessly, Preston stared at the floor. "But he found a way, and he's bought up the loan. He's called it in. God knows where he got the money to buy it up, or even how he knew where to go—" He broke off suddenly, his blue eyes narrowing as he stared at Susan with bitter accusation.

For a moment she didn't read the expression on his face; then her eyes flared with understanding. She went even whiter than she had been. How could he so readily believe that she would betray them to Cord, after all she had done to try to convince Cord not to seek vengeance? But why not? Why should Preston trust her? Cord didn't trust her, despite the passionate devotion she revealed every time she gave herself to him.

"How can you believe that?" she choked. "I haven't told him anything."

"Then how did he know?"

"I don't know!" she shouted, then stopped, pressing her hands against her mouth, aghast at her loss of control. "I'm sorry. I didn't tell him; I swear I didn't."

His blue eyes were suddenly sick, and he drew a deep, shaking breath. "My God, he's got us fighting each other," he said miserably, getting to his feet and coming around to her. He took her in his arms and held her tightly to him, rocking back and forth in a comforting motion. "I know you didn't tell him; you don't have a deceptive bone in your body. I'm sorry for being so stupid. I'm rattled. Susan, he's trying to bankrupt us."

The evidence lay on her desk, so she couldn't even try to deny it. She pressed her face into Preston's shoulder, vaguely aware that she was shaking. The awful thing was that, even with her knowing that Cord was capable of being so ruthless and devious, the aching, burning love she felt for him didn't diminish at all. She had known the chance she was taking in mating with that human tiger.

How long they clung together like frightened children trying to comfort each other, she didn't know. But gradually she calmed, and their embrace loosened.

There were things to do, strategies to plan. "How badly will we be weakened?" she asked in a voice that was flatly calm.

Preston's arms dropped away completely, and he turned to drag a chair around so he could sit beside her at her desk. "Dangerously. He couldn't have timed it better. At the moment, our cash flow is restricted because we've invested so heavily in projects that won't begin paying for at least another year, possibly two years. You handled the paperwork on the laser project in Palo Alto, so you know how much we've sunk in that one project alone."

She did. "Then what about our personal assets? If we liquidate, we can raise enough money to cover the loan—"

He was shaking his head to stop her, and he smiled wryly at her. "How do you think I raised the money to repay him for the money we used?"

She sat back, stunned. How neatly Cord had boxed them into a corner! He must have been planning this all along. First he had threatened to bring charges against Preston for stealing, then he had sat back and done nothing, giving Preston time to replace the amount taken, knowing that Preston would have to stretch himself thin to cover that much at one time. He had maneuvered them like pieces on a chessboard.

Still, she cast around for a solution. "Imogene and I can cover it. We have stocks we can sell, and property in prime locations—"

"Susan, stop it," he said gently. "Mother and I were both involved in using Cord's money, and we both had to sacrifice to replace it. She's stretched as thinly as I am, and you can't handle this all on your own. You wouldn't have anything left if you did."

Susan shrugged. The thought of being penniless didn't bother her. "If we can hold on for a year, two years at the most, then the corporation would be safe. That's what matters."

"Do you really think I'd let you sell off everything Vance gave you? From the moment he married you, he worked to make certain you'd always be comfortable, no matter what happened. He cherished you, and I won't let you undo all of the things he did for you."

"If we can stay out of bankruptcy, everything can be replaced."

"Covering this loan won't guarantee that. What if he buys up another one? He's obviously got money behind him, enough money to destroy us if he wants to keep pushing. If he buys up another loan, we end up in the bankruptcy courts, even if you do sell everything you own to cover this one."

Preston's logic was irrefutable, and she went cold to the bone. "Then there's nothing we can do?"

"I don't know. We're going to have to consider everything. The damnable part of it is, he has a stake in this corporation himself, and that isn't stopping him. He'll take that loss in order to get back at me. I can't believe he went this far. I know he hates me, but this is...this is crazy!"

It was unnerving to think of someone so determined, so ruthless, that he would go against his own best interests in his quest for revenge. He was tightening the screws, pushing, enjoying tormenting Preston. He'd said that he wanted to make the other man squirm.

He might have reason enough for the way he felt; she could only guess at the hellholes he'd been in since he'd been turned away by his family, though she had seen the marks they had left on his body. But no matter what the past had been, it was time the senseless hurting was ended. It had gone on long enough, tearing families apart, creating bitter enemies of the same blood. She wanted to take Cord by the neck and shake him until he'd regained his senses, and for a moment she could almost smile at the image of herself shaking someone who was almost a foot taller than she was, and who outweighed her by about a hundred pounds.

She was exhausted when she went home that day. They had spent the hours poring over financial statements, marshalling their forces to meet this challenge. Preston was a superb corporate tactician, but she'd never before realized the extent of his subtlety and expertise. He knew exactly how much they could sacrifice without dealing themselves a mortal blow, and he'd set the wheels in motion to liquidate the assets he thought the corporation could spare.

She was late getting home, but Emily was waiting for her with a hot meal, which the older woman made certain she consumed. Somehow, Emily always knew when Susan was tired or depressed, and she would dispense an extra measure of coddling, but not all her tender concern could erase the tension from Susan's face that night. Thinking that all of her nights out with Cord might be tiring Susan out, Emily asked, "Are you going out with Cord again tonight?"

Susan started at hearing the name that had been reverberating in her thoughts. "Oh... I don't know. He said he might be over later tonight. He had to drive to

New Orleans to take care of some business." She felt sick at the thought. What sort of business? Finding another nail to drive into the coffin of Blackstone Corporation?

"Well, I think you need to get more sleep then you've had this past week," Emily scolded. "You look like a dishrag. Send him home early if he does come over."

Somehow, Susan managed a smile for the woman, grateful for her concern. "Yes, I will." She loved him, but right now she couldn't be with him. She had the feeling that if she looked over her shoulder, she'd be able to see the handle of the knife that was sticking in her back.

Perhaps he wouldn't come. She hoped he wouldn't. She was too tired, too hurt, too raw from the knowledge of his betrayal. But why kid herself? He wouldn't see it as a betrayal, because he'd never promised her anything. All he had given her was the coin of physical passion, not a hint of commitment beyond the moment.

She hoped he wouldn't come, yet she wasn't surprised later that night to hear the rumble of the red Blazer that he used for his casual driving. She'd begun to think that she was safe for the night; it was after nine o'clock, and she'd been thinking about taking her bath and going to bed. But now he was here, and she stood in the den, her heart beginning to pound in apprehension. She felt sick; her hands were cold and clammy, and she pressed them against her skirt. How could she face him? Why couldn't he have waited until tomorrow, when she might be calmer?

The doorbell rang, but still she stood rigidly in the middle of the floor, unable to force her legs to move. Cold dread rippled down her spine. Seconds ticked past, and the doorbell began an insistent peal as he jammed his finger onto it and held it there. It wasn't until he began to pound on the door with enough force to rattle it on its hinges that she managed to move, her legs shaking. She crept into the foyer and released the bolt on the door.

The door crashed open under the impact of his fist, narrowly missing knocking her down. Cord loomed over her, his face dark and savage. He seized her by the arms, his fingers biting into her soft flesh. "Are you all right?" he bit out. "The lights were on, but when you didn't answer the door I thought something must be wrong. I was going to go around and break out the glass in the sliding doors—" He never finished the sentence, instead pulling her to him with one iron arm locked around her waist, his other hand cupping her chin and turning her face up to him. He bent his head and his mouth closed over hers, hard, hungrily, and for a moment she forgot everything. She was swamped by the exciting maleness of his scent, the coffee taste of his mouth. She clung to him, her fingers digging into the heavy muscles of his back as she rose on tiptoe to fit herself to him.

His desire rose swiftly, launched from the perfect condition of his superb body. Before she could think, he had lifted her off her feet and started up the stairs, after kicking the door shut. Feeling the last vestiges of control slipping away from her, Susan freed her mouth from his and gasped, "Wait! I don't—"

He caught her mouth again, his tongue plunging deep inside, stifling her desperate words as he placed her on the bed. If he had released her then, stepping back to remove his clothes, she might have had a chance, but he stayed with her. He covered her, his mouth taking hers with hard, deep kisses, while his hands delved under her skirt and peeled away her underwear. Stunned by his urgency, after a moment she forgot about the rift between them and held tightly to his neck, her slender body arching to him as he parted her thighs and fit himself between them. He paused a moment to adjust his clothing and insure her protection, then thrust deeply into her, the impact of his body making her jerk.

She wasn't the only one taken by surprise by his urgency. Cord had been unpleasantly surprised by the desperation that had knotted his stomach when she hadn't answered the door, and he'd had a vision of her sprawled lifeless at the foot of the stairs. Or someone could have broken in on her, and raped her before killing her. That last thought had made the hair on the back of his neck lift up, and he had been snarling silently as he pounded on the door. Then it had opened and she'd stood there, pale and silent, but obviously healthy, and his desire had bloomed with his relief. He had to have her right then, bury himself in her and satisfy his body as well as his mind that she was still there, still healthy, and still his. The taste of her, the silken feel of her under his hands, the intimate clasp of her body, were all that could drive the fear from his mind. He luxuriated in his possession of her, feeling her response building and the tension in her growing tighter, and the knowledge that she wanted him, that he could satisfy her, was a pleasure as great as that he was taking from her soft flesh.

Susan heard the soft little whimpers in the back of her throat, but she was powerless to stop them, powerless to control her body. She reached blindly for satisfaction, her fingers clenched in his hair, her body arching up to meet his. He was crushing her, yet she didn't feel his weight; his heavy shoulders and chest were holding her down, yet she was soaring high and free, everything forgotten except for this moment in time. She was completely physical, yielding to his rampant masculinity and demanding that he give her all of himself.

He caught her legs, pulling them high to coil them around his back, and the whimpers turned into sharp, breathless cries. Deliberately he paced his movements, keeping her on the edge but not allowing her to go over it, not wanting the act to end. His strong hands on her hips controlled her, guided her, held her when she would have taken over the rhythm he'd set. She clenched her teeth on the agony of pleasure that boiled in her; then suddenly it was too much to be held in, and she heard the words of love that she gasped, the words that she'd always longed to say but had held inside.

A rumble in his chest and the tightening of his hands on her flesh signaled the end of his control, and he began to thrust hungrily into her. Instantly an incredible heat exploded inside her, washing through her with ever-widening waves, making her shudder beneath him. She sank her teeth into his shoulder in an effort to control the sounds she was making, and the primitive, sensual act pushed him over the edge. Short, harsh cries tore from his throat as his satisfaction thundered through him, and he clasped her to him with a wild strength that made her gasp for breath, as if he could meld her flesh with his for all time. When he'd finished, he slowly relaxed until he lay limply on her, his body still quivering with small aftershocks. She smoothed his sweat-damp hair, her fingers gentle on his moist temple. His hot breath seared her throat, and she felt the flutter of his eyelashes against her skin as he began to doze.

But he lay there for only a moment before rousing himself and gently moving from her. He rolled heavily onto his back and lay there, one brawny forearm thrown over his eyes.

Susan lay beside him, tension and dread growing in her again now that the appetites of her body had been satisfied. She should never have let that happen, not tonight, not when she had so much on her mind. And she had told him that she loved him. He couldn't have misunderstood her; it seemed to her that the words still lingered in the air, echoing with ghostly insistence. Would he say anything, or would he just ignore what she'd said? He hadn't asked for any commitment from her any more than he'd offered one. He probably wasn't even surprised; it couldn't be the first time that a woman in his arms had cried out that she loved him.

Caught in her misery, she was only half-aware when he left the bed. The sound of running water caught her attention, and she opened her eyes to look at him through the open door of the bathroom as he stood drinking deeply from a glass of water. His strong brown throat worked as he appeased his thirst. He'd already straightened his clothing, she saw, and her hands clenched into fists. He'd be leaving now that his sexual appetite had been satisfied.

He came back and stood over her, his level dark brows lowered over eyes so pale and fierce that she almost flinched from them. "You scared the hell out of me," he said flatly. "Why didn't you answer the door?"

Restlessly, she sat up, and flushed wildly when she saw that her skirt was still tangled above her waist. Quickly she fumbled with the cloth, straightening it and pushing it down to cover her nakedness, an act that sparked a flash of fury in his eyes. But when she darted a glance up at him, she saw only the same iron implacability that had been there before as he waited for an answer. Pushing her tumbled hair back from her face, she said in a dull tone, "You bought up a loan against us and called it in."

Silence lay thickly between them for a long moment; then he sliced it by saying harshly, "You're not involved in that."

A laugh broke from her throat, a laugh that was almost a sob, and she got quickly to her feet, leaving the bed where she had given herself to him so thoroughly. For a moment she feared her legs wouldn't hold her, but after an initial wobble she regained control of them and moved a few paces away from him. "I have to be. You know that everything is tied together. If you attack them financially, you're attacking me financially. If you bankrupt them, you bankrupt me."

"You don't have anything to worry about. I'll take care of you."

The cool arrogance of his words almost made her choke, and she whirled on him in disbelief. "Is that supposed to make it all right? You'll reduce me to a...a kept woman, and I'm supposed to be grateful?"

One dark eyebrow quirked. "I don't see your problem," he said, and added with casual cruelty, "after all, you said that you love me."

She winced, unable to believe he'd attacked her so soon, even though she'd put the weapon in his hand. Suddenly she was too close to him, and she put the width of the room between them, withdrawing from him as far as she could. She bent her head, unable to look at him and face the contemptuous knowledge that she knew must be in his eyes. "Would you…would you actually push us all into bankruptcy just to get back at Preston? Even knowing that a lot of other people are involved, that they'd lose their jobs?"

"Yes." His voice was hard, as hard as he was, and the last vestige of hope died in her. Until then there had been one small shred of faith left; she had been able to hope that he was only punishing Preston and would stop before things went too far.

"You'd be hurting yourself!" she cried. "How can you do this?"

He gave a negligent shrug. "I've got other things to fall back on."

She'd begged before, with no result, but now she was reduced to doing it again. "Cord, stop this! Please! Don't push it until it's gone too far. When will you be satisfied? After you've ruined us all, then what? Will it have brought Judith back for you?"

His face turned into stone, and his eyes narrowed. Wildly, goaded by her own pain, she lashed out at him, sensing that she'd found a way to wound him. "You're just trying to ease your own guilt about Judith, because of your part in what happened to her—"

With a growl he strode across the room, seizing her before she could dart to the side and avoid him. His hands bit into her shoulders and he shook her lightly. "Shut up about Judith! I made a mistake in telling you about her, but you'll be making an even bigger one if you ever mention her to me again. For the last time, stay out of this."

"I can't. I'm already in it." She stared up at him with eyes so huge that they eclipsed her entire face, eyes so filled with pain that any other woman would have been weeping uncontrollably. They were going to destroy each other, Cord and Preston, and she was helpless to stop it. There could be no winners in this family war, because when the bond of common blood goes bad, it causes a rift that can never be healed. She saw the chasm that was already widening between herself and Cord, and she wanted to scream out in desperate protest, but there was nothing she could do. She held herself rigidly in his painful grip, trying to control the shrieking agony that was tearing her heart apart.

His grasp on her eased, and he stroked his thumbs over the fragile ridges of her collarbones. "You're too soft for this," he murmured to himself; then he eased her back into his embrace, shifting his arms to hold her against him. She was silent, letting herself rest against him because she hadn't the strength to deny herself what she feared might be the last time he'd hold her like this. He bent his head to press his warm lips into the sensitive curve where her neck met her shoulder, and a delicious shiver ran over her body. Just like that, with only a casual caress, he was able to make her want him again. She loved him too much, too dangerously, because she could hold nothing of herself back. There was no way she could protect herself.

"Don't go back to work," he instructed softly, brushing his lips against her hair. "Stay at home, and stay out of this. Vance left you secure, and whatever happens to Preston won't affect you at all." His big hands stroked slowly over her back and shoulders, their effect on her hypnotic. "You said that you love me; if you do, you won't take his side against me."

For a moment, for a weak, delicious moment, she wanted nothing more than to do just as he said, to let his hard embrace protect her and make her forget all other considerations. Then she stiffened and slowly pushed herself away from him, her face taut and pale.

"Yes, I love you," she said quietly, because there was no use in trying to hide it from him any longer. How could she deny it, when her body told him the truth every time he touched her? "But I have to do whatever I can to stop you from bankrupting the family."

His eyes narrowed. "You're choosing him over me?"

"No. But I think you're wrong in what you're trying to do, and if you won't stop, then I have to help him fight you."

Black fury gathered in him, sparking out of his pale eyes, but he held it in. "Is it asking too much for you to trust me in this?" he rasped, watching her carefully.

"The same way you trust me?" she shot back. "You told me yourself, just a moment ago, that you're trying to bankrupt us! Is that supposed to reassure me?"

He gave a derisive snort, the fire in his eyes turning to ice. "I should've known! You spouted that garbage about loving me, *then* you asked me so sweetly to ease up on Preston. You're good in the sack, baby, the best I've had, but you don't have that kind of a hold on me."

"I know," she whispered blankly. "I've always known that. But I wasn't trying for any emotional blackmail. I think... I think you'd better go."

"I think you're right."

As he moved past her, she blinked at him with eyes suddenly blurred by a film of tears. He was going, and she knew he wouldn't be back. "Goodbye," she choked, feeling herself shatter inside.

He gave her a grim look. "It's not goodbye, not yet. You'll be seeing me around, though you'll wish you weren't." Then he was gone, lightly taking the stairs with graceful bounds. Slowly she followed him, and she reached the door in time to watch the red flare of the Blazer's taillights disappear as he rounded a curve. She shut the door and locked it, then methodically moved about and made certain the house was secure for the night. She even sat down and watched the late movie until it went off, then realized that she hadn't absorbed any of it. She didn't even know the name of it, or the names of the actors. She hadn't been thinking of anything, just sitting there, her mind numb. She wanted it to stay numb, because she knew that when the numbness wore off, she was going to hurt more than she could bear.

She went through the motions of going to bed; she showered and put on her nightgown, moisturized her face, neatened up her bedroom and put her discarded clothing in the laundry basket. Then she lay in bed until dawn, her eyes open and staring at the ceiling. He was gone.

He was gone! It was a litany of pain that echoed through her endlessly, an inner accompaniment to the gray, dreary days that followed. The sun could have been shining; she simply didn't know. But she couldn't see any sunshine, and she functioned only through instinct and sheer grim determination. She'd kept going after Vance's death, and now the same steely determination kept her upright even when she wanted nothing more than to collapse in a corner of her bedroom and not ever come out again.

She'd had to accept the bleak truth of Vance's death because she had seen his lifeless body, had buried him. It was worse with Cord. He was gone from her, yet he seemed to be everywhere. They met at several functions, and she had to act as if it didn't almost double her over with pain to see him. He was usually with Cheryl, of course, though she heard that he wasn't limiting himself to the other woman. She had to see him, had to listen to him say all the polite things while his icy eyes cut her, had to watch him slide his arm about Cheryl's waist, had to imagine him kissing the other woman, touching her with his hot, magic fingers, drawing her beneath him in his big bed at the cabin.

To stay sane she drove herself at work every day, working longer and longer hours, working frantically with Preston in an effort to raise enough cash to pay off the loan without seriously weakening the corporation. It was an impossible task; they both knew that if Cord chose to attack them again, they wouldn't be able to meet his demands.

Quietly, without letting Preston know, Susan sold some prime property in New Orleans that Vance had left her and added the proceeds to their cash fund. Preston would have died rather than let her sell off any of her personal property, though she knew he'd been heavily liquidating his. Sometimes, when she thought about the fact that Cord was deliberately forcing them to sell off land that had been in the family for generations, she hated him, but always that hate was mingled with love. If she hadn't loved him so much, she wouldn't have felt so betrayed by his actions, wouldn't have been so deeply angry when she saw Preston, without complaint, destitute himself personally in order to keep the corporation out of bankruptcy.

This had shaken Imogene, too, to the very basis of her foundations. Since the night she and Susan had argued so violently, she had been a little quieter, as if some of the spirit had gone out of her. Perhaps she had sensed then that she couldn't fight Cord, that by the very act of returning he had won. Always before, Imogene had been actively involved in any corporate decisions, but now she let Preston and Susan carry the weight. For the first time she was showing her age.

At last it was done. They had enough to cover the loan, and though Susan and Preston shared a moment of relief, it wasn't without worry. They had used every ounce of spare reserve they had, and another blow would be too much. Still, the relief was strong enough that they celebrated in the French Quarter that night, in a far noisier restaurant than the one Cord had taken her to. But she was glad of the noise and distraction, and for once she ate a good meal. In the time since Cord had sauntered out of her house she'd lost several pounds that she hadn't been able to spare. It was as much over-work as depression, or so she told herself every morning when she frowningly examined herself in the mirror, noting that her clothing was too loose to fall correctly on her increasingly slender body.

On the drive home Preston startled her by apologizing. "You've broken up with Cord because of this, haven't you?"

There was no denying it, no use in concocting a lame excuse that they simply hadn't gotten along, so she simply murmured, "Yes," and let it go at that.

"I'm sorry." He cast her a frustrated glance. "I should be glad, because I didn't like you being with him, but I'm sorry that you've been hurt. I didn't want you in the middle like this."

"I made my decision. He insisted that I choose sides,

and I simply couldn't watch him cost a lot of people their jobs without trying to do something about it."

"I hope he knows what he's lost," Preston said violently, and returned his attention to his driving.

Even if he knew, he wouldn't care, Susan thought dully. He certainly wasn't pining away for her; he looked better every time she saw him, his hard, dark face becoming darker as the late-spring sun continued to bronze him. Had he finished clearing off the land down by the creek? Was he doing any more work on the cabin?

When he had pushed her out of his life, he had left her lost and desolate, without any emotional focus. She wondered if the rest of her life would be like this, a dull misery to be endured as she went through the motions of living.

CHAPTER TEN

IF SHE HAD known what awaited her when she walked into the office three days later, she would never have gone. Beryl was already there and had a fragrant pot of coffee brewing. "Good morning, Beryl. Is Mr. Blackstone in yet?"

"No, not yet. Do you want a cup of coffee now?"

Susan smiled at the young woman. "I'll get it. You look like you have enough to handle right now," she teased, nodding at the stacks of paperwork that littered Beryl's desk.

Beryl nodded ruefully. "Don't I, though? Mr. Blackstone must have worked until midnight last night. He left all of this, and enough tapes on the Dictaphone to keep me typing through the weekend."

"Really? I didn't know he'd planned to come back to the office last night. He left when I did, and I can't think of anything that would have been so urgent."

She poured herself some coffee and carefully balanced the cup as she went into her office, keeping a cautious eye on the sloshing liquid. She placed the cup on her desk and walked around to pull the curtains open, letting the brilliant morning sunlight pour into the room. The day was hot already, with a sultry feel to it that had dampened the back of her neck with perspiration even before she'd left the house that morning.

She was beginning to think of taking a vacation, finding a beach somewhere and doing nothing more strenuous than lying in the sun. Somehow, sweating on the beach didn't sound nearly as hot as sweating at work.

After fingering the blossoms of her favorite geranium, she went to her desk and sat down. It wasn't until then that she saw the thick manila envelope lying there with her name printed on it in big block letters. Frowning, she opened the sealed envelope and pulled out a sheaf of papers. On top was some sort of legal document, and she turned it around to read it.

Immediately she went deathly white, not having to read further than the front page to know it for what it was. Cord had bought up another loan and called it in.

My God, he was going to do it. They couldn't weather this. They couldn't pay, and the shock waves he was going to make would reverberate throughout the corporation and the banks they were involved with. Their credit would be ruined. They simply couldn't pay this and keep operating.

Where was Preston? She wanted to run to him, wanted to hear him say that he would be able to work another little piece of magic and somehow come up with the money they needed. It was selfish of her, and she controlled the urge. He would have to know, yes, but let him have a few more hours of peace, of not knowing.

How had the envelope gotten on her desk? The office was always locked when they left, and Preston had worked late the night before....

Then she knew, and she felt sick. Preston already knew about the loan, and he'd left the envelope on her desk.

She flipped through the legal document, and behind

it she found a letter to her, in Preston's handwriting. His usually elegant style was a scrawl as if the letter had been written in agitation, but the writing was unmistakably his. She read the letter through carefully, and when she was finished she let it fall to the floor, tears searing her eyes.

If Cord had wanted only to defeat Preston, he'd won. Preston had gone. His letter was both defeated and desperate. He'd done all he could, but he couldn't fight Cord any longer. Perhaps, if he left, Cord would let up. By taking himself out of the picture, Preston hoped that Cord would cease his vengeance.

Cord had had the legal paperwork delivered to Preston at home, by special messenger, an act that chilled Susan with its calculated cruelty. Preston had then returned to the office, methodically finished all the work currently on his desk, left the letter for Susan, and disappeared.

She couldn't blame Preston for leaving; she knew that it was his last-ditch effort to save the corporation, to keep Cord from putting it under. He hoped that when Cord found that Susan was running the corporation he wouldn't call in the loan, knowing that his prime target had fled and that now he was attacking only a woman he'd previously been very interested in.

As if that would stop him! Susan thought despairingly. Then her spine stiffened. As if she would run crying to him now, asking him to have mercy on her!

She'd begged him before, for Preston's sake, for everyone's sake, and he'd turned a cold shoulder to her. She wouldn't beg him for herself now.

Susan didn't recognize the fierce anger that seized her, but she wasn't going to just give up. If she had to fight him until she didn't have a penny left, then that's what she would do.

She picked up the telephone and quickly punched out a number. She wasn't surprised when Imogene answered herself.

"Imogene, do you know where Preston is?" she asked directly, not wasting time with polite greetings.

"No. He only told me that he was going." Imogene's voice sounded tired and a little thick, as if she'd been crying.

"Do you know why he left?"

"Yes. I tried to talk him out of it, but he wouldn't listen. He just wouldn't listen," she sighed. "He thinks that this is the only way he can get Cord to stop. What... what are you going to do? Are you going to see Cord?"

"No!" Susan said violently. She inhaled swiftly, searching for control and finding it. "I'm not going to tell him anything. I'm going to fight him with everything I have, and I need your help."

"Help?" Imogene echoed blankly. "What can I do?"

"You've been involved with this corporation for years. You have a lot of contacts, and you know everything that's going on even if you don't come to the office. There's too much to do on an everyday basis for me to handle it by myself and fight Cord, too. Will you come? Do you want to fight him?"

There was a long silence on the other end of the phone, and Susan waited tensely, her eyes closed. She really needed Imogene's help. She didn't fool herself that she'd be able to carry on for long by herself. The burden would break her. But Imogene hadn't been herself, and she wasn't sure what her mother-in-law would do.

"I don't want to fight him," Imogene finally said

softly. "This insanity has gone on long enough. If I thought it would stop him, I'd sign everything I own over to him this minute just to bring peace to our family. I have to share in the responsibility for this mess, and I'm not proud of it. I shouldn't have turned on him; he's family and I forgot that. I regret it so much now, but regrets don't do any good."

Susan's heart sank. "You won't help?"

"I didn't say that. I'll be there as soon as I can get myself ready and make the drive. But it's not to fight him, dear. It's to help you, and to do what I can to keep the corporation out of bankruptcy. That's the only important thing now, and when it's over, I'll crawl on my hands and knees to Cord if that will satisfy him and stop this war."

The thought of proud Imogene being willing to humble herself in such a way left Susan fighting tears again. "I'll be waiting," she whispered, and hung up the phone before she embarrassed herself by sobbing into it.

If she had worked before, it was nothing compared to the way she drove herself now. She arrived in the office shortly after dawn and often remained until nine or ten in the evening. On the surface, it didn't seem possible that she would be able to meet Cord's demands, but she didn't give up. Imogene was on the phone constantly, calling in favors, trying to arrange a loan that would keep them going. But even old friends were suddenly wary of the Blackstone Corporation, for the business grapevine was remarkably sensitive, and word had filtered through that they were on shaky financial ground. Their common stock was trading hands rapidly, and in desperation Susan put some of her own stock up for sale. Preston and Imogene had already sold some of their stock in order to replace the money they'd embezzled from Cord, hoping to buy more when their cash flow had improved. But Cord had kept them on the ropes and hadn't let the pressure ease at all. At least the price of the stock was holding up, due to the brisk trading, but Susan knew that she had to take even more desperate measures.

She had stock in other companies, blue-chip investments, and ruthlessly she turned them into cash. She kept it secret from Imogene, knowing that Imogene would be as horrified at the idea, as Preston had been. Imogene was holding up wonderfully, attacking the work with increased vigor, and as she settled into it she began to display a wonderful panache for the job. Susan didn't want to do anything to throw the older woman back into the mild depression that had held her in its grip lately. She knew that Imogene worried about Preston and fretted over the absence of her only living son; that burden was enough.

Every morning when Susan looked in the mirror she realized anew that she was living on her nerves, and sometimes she wondered how much longer she could keep going. The shadows under her eyes seemed to have become permanent fixtures that she carefully disguised with makeup. She always left the house now before Emily arrived, and she was too tense to prepare breakfast herself and eat it. There was always a meal left for her when she got home at night, needing only to be warmed, but more often than not Susan was too exhausted to eat it. She was existing on pots of coffee and hasty bites taken out of sandwiches, sandwiches that were seldom finished and instead left to grow stale while she worked.

The steamy weather further sapped her strength, the heat and humidity weighing her down like a smothering blanket. She couldn't sleep at night, even with the air-conditioning on, and she would lie watching the flash of heat lightning, hoping that the bursts of light meant thunderstorms and rain, but the clouds never came and each day dawned hotter than the one before.

Lying on her bed in the thick, humid nights, the light cover kicked down to the foot of the bed because even a sheet was too oppressive, she thought of Cord. During the day she could resent him, hate him, fight him, but when the nights came she could no longer hold the memories at bay, and she would hug her pillow to herself, keening her pain almost soundlessly into the pillow. He had been on that bed with her, his dark head on the other pillow; he had wrapped her graceful legs around him, linking her to him with a chain of flesh while he drove deeply into her body and her heart. She wanted him so much that her entire body ached, her breasts throbbing, her thighs and loins heavy with need. She wanted just to see him, to watch his beautifully shaped mouth quirk into one of those devastatingly wicked smiles. Whenever she dozed she dreamed of him, and she would jerk herself awake with a start as she reached out for him. Sometimes the impulse to go to him was almost too strong to ignore, and in the hot, heavy nights she suffered alone.

She heard, through the grapevine of gossip that always yielded an astonishing amount of information, that Cord was gone again, and this time she didn't wonder if he'd ever come back; now she wondered what new weapon he was readying to use against her. No, not against *her* personally, but against them all in general. Though she wasn't able to pinpoint the exact date when he'd left, she knew that it was about the same time Preston had gone; it was possible that he didn't know Preston had bowed out and left the corporation in her lap. As far as all their acquaintances were concerned, Preston was on a business trip. That was the tale she and Imogene had decided to put out, rather than trigger a flood of gossip that would grow larger and wilder with every turn.

Despite everything, when the grapevine informed her that Cord had returned, she didn't feel the dread that should have overwhelmed her. For a sweet moment of insanity she was simply glad that he'd returned, that he was once more close by geographically, if not emotionally. Somehow she felt that if he was at least in Mississippi, then it wasn't all over. When it was finished for good, he'd leave for good.

If she hadn't been so tired, so desperate, pushed beyond common sense, she'd never have considered the idea. But late one afternoon she thought again of the ridges. She hadn't slept at all the night before, with her thoughts whirling around in her mind like a rabid squirrel in a cage, until she felt as if her very skull were sore from being banged from within. The air conditioner couldn't handle the heat and humidity, and her lightweight tan suit clung to her sticky skin. She'd already shed the jacket, since it was late and everyone else had already gone home, but even the thin cotton camisole top she'd worn with the suit seemed to be restricting her. A distant rumble of thunder held out the hope of rain to a parched region, but Susan had ceased believing in the thunder's promise. It had proved to be deceptive too often lately.

She had done everything she could think of, and still she hadn't managed to scrape together enough cash to pay off the loan. She'd liquidated a large portion of her stock in Blackstone Corporation, all her stock in everything else, and had disposed of all of the property Vance had accumulated for her...all of it except for the land the house stood on, and the ridges.

The ridges. The thought of them was like a jolt of electricity, straightening her in her chair. *The ridges!* With their promise of oil or natural gas, they were a gold mine, and she'd had it under her nose all the time. The money she could get from leasing them would be enough to finish covering the loan, and in her exhaustion she thought that it would be only fitting that the money from the ridges be used to defeat Cord; after all, it had been the ridges that had brought him back to Mississippi in the first place.

In the back of her mind she knew it was odd that Cord hadn't pressed her about signing the lease, but she simply couldn't follow his reasoning. She loved him, but even after weeks of agonized wondering, she couldn't understand him.

The thought of the ridges gave her a spurt of strength, rather like a marathon runner's last desperate burst of speed. She would drive out to the cabin and offer the lease to Cord, and he could take it right now or leave it. If he didn't take it, then she'd lease the land to the first oil company she could interest in it, but she was going to give him the first chance at it. She knew that her excuse was flimsy, but suddenly she had to see him. Even if he were an enemy now, she had to see him.

Without giving herself time to reconsider, she locked the office and left the building. If she thought about it, she'd begin to worry, and she'd let the doubts change her mind. Her hands were trembling as she guided the Audi out of Biloxi. A distracted glance at the fuel gauge warned her to stop for gas, but even that small interruption in her progress was too much to tolerate. She thought she'd have enough gas to get home, and that was all she cared about at the moment. She'd worry about getting to work later.

The radio volume was low, but even the background noise was rasping on her nerves, and she snapped the radio off with a quick, irritable movement. It was so hot, and she felt so weak! A moment of dizziness alarmed her, and she turned the air-conditioning vents so the cold air was blowing right on her face. After a moment she felt better, and she urged the Audi to greater speeds.

The Blazer was parked under one of the giant oak trees that kept the fierce sun away from the front of the cabin, and the front door stood open. Susan guided the Audi to a hard stop in front of the porch, and as she opened the door to get out, Cord strolled lazily out of the cabin to lean against one of the posts that supported the porch roof. He had on boots, and jeans so old that one of the pockets was missing, and that was all. She looked up at him and her heart stopped for a moment. He'd begun to let his beard grow again, and the several days' growth of whiskers on his jaw made him look like an outlaw out of a Western. His hard, muscled torso was darkly tanned, his hair longer, and if anything, his pale eyes were even more compelling than she'd remembered. Her mouth went dry, and her legs wobbled as she went up the steps, clinging with all her strength to the rough railing.

She'd tried to imagine what his first words would

be, and her imagination had supplied any number of brutal things that would wound her. She braced herself for them as his narrowed gaze went over her from head to foot.

"Come on in and have a glass of iced tea," he invited, his rough, callused hand closing on her elbow and urging her inside the cabin. "You look like you're about to melt."

Was that it? She had to swallow an almost hysterical giggle. After all her panic, he calmly invited her in for iced tea!

Somehow she found herself sitting at his table while he moved around the kitchen. "I was just about to eat," he said easily. "Nothing hot in this weather, just a ham sandwich and a tossed salad, but there's plenty for two."

She started. He wanted her to eat? "Oh, no, thank you—"

He interrupted her refusal by sliding a plate in front of her. She stared down at the ham sandwich, wondering if she could possibly swallow a bite of it, and his hand entered her field of vision again, this time placing a chilled bowl of salad beside the plate. A napkin and cutlery were placed by her hand, and a big glass of beautiful, amber tea over ice finished her instant meal. When she lifted her stunned gaze, she saw that he'd set the same for himself, and he draped his tall frame into the chair across from her.

"Eat," he said gently. "You'll feel better after you do."

When had she last had a meal, a real meal? The days had merged into one long, steamy nightmare, and she couldn't recall her last meal. Half-eaten sandwiches, coffee, and an occasional candy bar had constituted her diet since Preston had left. She began to eat slowly, and the crisp, fresh flavor of the salad, only lightly coated with tart dressing, was suddenly the best thing she could imagine eating. She savored every bite of it, and the cold tea seemed to cool her from the inside out. Because she'd been eating so little she was unable to eat all of the sandwich, but Cord made no comment on the half left on her plate. Instead he swiftly cleared the table, placing the dishes in the sink before coming back to the table and refilling her glass with tea.

"Now," he said, dropping into his chair again, "you don't look like you're going to pass out at my feet, so I'll listen to whatever you came to say."

Susan held the frosty glass between both hands, feeling the refreshing chill on her hot palms. "I want to talk to you about the ridges," she said, but her mind wasn't on her words. She was staring at him, her eyes tracing the lines of his features as if etching them permanently on her memory.

"So talk. What about them?" He folded his arms across his chest and leaned back, bringing his booted feet up and propping them on the chair beside him.

"Do you still want to lease them?"

His lids dropped down to hood his eyes. "Get to the point, Susan."

Nervously, she took a sip of tea, then fidgeted for a moment with the glass, returning it to precisely the same spot where it had been before, making certain that it matched the ring of water that marked its position. "If you want them, then lease them now. I've decided not to wait for the report from the survey. If you don't want the lease any longer, I'm going to lease them to some other company."

"Oh, I still want them," he said softly, "but I'm not

going to give you any money on them right now. You'd run all the way to Biloxi to give the money to Preston, and I'll be damned if I'll give you a penny until this is all over. The money from the ridges is for you, to keep you in your accustomed style after Preston doesn't have a penny left." He gave her a cynical grin, one full of wry amusement at himself. "I'll keep you in silk underwear, honey."

Susan choked and jumped to her feet, her cheeks scarlet. "Then I'll lease them to someone else!"

"I don't think so," he drawled, swinging his long legs to the floor and getting to his feet, moving gracefully to put himself between her and the door. "If you think I've used every club I have against Preston already, then you're mistaken. If you lease that land to anyone else, I'll crush him, and you can bet your sweet little life on that."

Susan drew back from him, stumbling a little as she tried to circle the table without turning her back on him. She was slowed by her exhaustion, and totally unable to react when he moved suddenly, cutting her off. His hands closed on her fragile waist, and he felt the slenderness of her under his fingers. His black brows snapped together in a forbidding frown. "How much weight have you lost?" he demanded curtly, glaring down at her.

Despite the tremors that quaked through her insides, Susan held herself stiffly. "That's none of your business." Her fingers dug into his biceps as she tried to push him away, but he was as immovable as a boulder.

He held her with one arm and swept his other hand over her body, exploring her newly frail contours. He slid his hand over her hips and buttocks, her slender thighs, then up to rub gently over her breasts, making her cry out and writhe in a desperate attempt to escape him. He held her easily, his eyes blue with fury. "What in the hell has he done to you?"

Shards of pain pierced her, and she twisted suddenly, a gasping cry breaking from her lips. She managed to break his grip, and she shoved herself away from him, her face pale, her hair straggling out of its once-tidy knot. She hurt so much, and she was so desperate, that she screamed at him, "He hasn't done anything to me! You've done it; you've done it all! You're not crushing him, you're crushing *me!* He left—" Horrified at what she was saying, she stuffed her hand into her mouth to stop the mad tumble of words, her eyes huge and so dark they were almost black as she stared at him.

If he had been angry before, he exploded now. Hammering his fist on the table with a force that upset her glass of tea, he roared, "What do you mean, 'He *left?*' That damned weasel!"

"He's not a weasel!" She'd been pushed too far to be wary of his temper, to even consider the questionable wisdom of defending Preston to Cord. "He left because he hoped you'd stop when you saw that you weren't hurting him any longer! He's trying to save the corporation, save thousands of jobs—"

"You mean he thought you'd come running to me with the information that you were trying to do it all on your own, and I'd back off. Damn you, Susan, why didn't you do just that? Why have you driven yourself into the ground like this?"

"Because I think you're wrong! Preston isn't using me as a sacrificial lamb; if you'd stop hating him long enough, you might see that he's not the same person he was years ago. You can try to ease your own guilt by making him pay, but you're wrong to do it!"

"Is that why you've run yourself half to death, to show me how wrong I am?"

He was never going to listen to reason. The realization slapped her in the face, and she reeled from the force of it. "No," she whispered. "I've run myself half to death trying to keep a corporation alive. I don't sleep because I lie awake trying to think of a way to raise money, and I don't eat because I don't have the time to spare." She'd gone completely white now, her eyes blazing at him. "I've sold everything I own, except my house and the ridges, trying to stay afloat. Do you want them, too? Or maybe the keys to my car? Or how about my record collection? I've got some real golden oldies—"

"Shut up!" he thundered, reaching out a hand to catch her.

She twisted away, unable to bear his touch. "Leave me alone," she said rawly, then almost ran out of the cabin and tumbled into the Audi. Slamming the door, she savagely turned the key in the ignition and the engine caught immediately, but when she put the car in gear it gave a shuddering jerk and died. "Don't do this to me," she said through gritted teeth, turning the key again. The motor turned over but didn't catch, and in horror her eyes flew to the fuel gauge, where the needle bumped against the E. "Damn you!" she shrieked at the car. "Don't do this to me!" She began to pound on the steering wheel with both fists, screaming, "Damn! Damn! Damn!" with every impact, and tears burst from her eyes.

"Susan!" The door was wrenched open, and Cord

caught her wrists, hauling her out of the car. "Susan, stop it! Settle down, honey, just settle down. Don't fly apart like this. Let me see if I can get the car started."

"You can't," she blurted, pulling her hands free to bury her face in them and weep uncontrollably. It was just too much. She, who always controlled her tears no matter how much she hurt, had dissolved into sobs because she had run out of gas. "The gas tank is empty."

He slid into the driver's seat, keeping one long leg on the outside of the car, as he turned on the ignition and checked it for himself. Sighing, he got out of the car and closed the door. "I'll drive you home."

"I don't want you to drive me home!" She turned to walk down the slope and he made a grab for her, hauling her back just as an enormous clap of thunder shook the earth. She jumped, startled, looking up at the horrendous black cloud that had suddenly taken over the sky. A brisk wind had begun blowing, but she hadn't noticed it until then. As they both looked up, the first enormous raindrops splattered them in the face with stinging force, and Cord put his arm around her, hustling her up on the porch just before the heavens split open and dropped a deluge so thunderous that they had to shout to make themselves heard.

"You can't walk home in this," he yelled, bending down to put his mouth close to her ear. "We'll wait until it lets up; then I'll take you home."

Despairingly, Susan looked at the gray curtain of rain. Already it had turned the area around the cabin into a shallow river as the water ran down the slope, rushing downward to the creek. She knew that it would splash up to her ankles, and gave in to his opinion that she couldn't walk home. But neither could she stay here, so close to him, in the cabin where they'd made love the first time. Her nerves were at the breaking point. "I want to go home!" she half screamed at him. "I'm not going to stay here! I simply won't!"

A look of savage impatience twisted his face; then he brought himself under control by sheer effort of will. He caught her arm and dragged her into the cabin, slamming the door shut in an effort to close out the roar of the rain.

"All right, all right!" he snapped. "We're going to get soaked just getting into the Blazer, you know."

"I don't care." Obdurately she stared at him, and he stared back at her in frustrated fury, but evidently he saw something in her face that made him hesitate. She had no idea how frail she looked, or how deeply the shadows of exhaustion lay under her eyes. He shoved his hand through his too-long hair, making the silky strands tumble down over his forehead.

"I'll pull the Blazer up as close to the porch as I can," he muttered. "There's a newspaper on the table in front of the fireplace; put it over your head and make a run for it. But I warn you, it's not going to do much good against this downpour." He stalked to the cabinet and pulled out a plastic trash bag, then disappeared into the bedroom. Susan remained where she stood, feeling icy chills race over her body, too dispirited to wonder what he was doing. He came out a moment later wearing one of those disreputable T-shirts that hugged his magnificent body so faithfully. He had the trash bag folded and tucked under his arm, and a battered khaki-colored baseball-style cap was jammed on his head. He looked as stormy and furious as the cloud outside.

Without speaking to her, he went out on the porch,

and she followed him. He didn't bother with the steps; he walked to the end of the porch nearest to the Blazer and paused a moment to stare in disgust at the pounding rain. Then he leaped off the end of the porch, and was in a dead run by the time his feet hit the ground. As depressed as she was, Susan watched him in admiration, admiring the speed and grace of his powerful strides. He looked like a linebacker closing in on a pass receiver, every movement purposeful and deadly.

A bolt of lightning, blindingly white, snapped to the ground close to the creek, and the earsplitting crack made Susan shriek and jump back as the entire earth shook. The tiny hairs on the back of her neck lifted at the electricity that hummed through the air, and suddenly she realized how powerful this storm was, how dangerous it was to be out in it. The limbs of the giant oaks were waving back and forth as the trees bent before the onslaught. She wanted to call Cord back, but he was already in the Blazer; she heard the engine roar into life, and the headlights came on. She stumbled back into the cabin to get the newspaper he'd indicated, only to find that the storm had blotted out the lingering twilight and it was so dark inside the cabin that she had to switch on a lamp to find the newspaper.

Her fingers trembled as she turned the light off again. As Cord maneuvered the Blazer up close to the porch, inching it between her car and the steps, the headlights threw twin beams of light through the open door, illuminating the wet floor where the gusting wind had blown the rain across the porch and into the house. She touched her hair and found it was damp, and her clothes were equally damp; she hadn't even noticed that she'd been getting wet.

He blew the horn, and she started. Why was she standing there in the dark? Quickly she crossed the room and struggled out onto the porch, the wind making a strong effort to push her back inside. It took all her strength to tug the door closed, and the newspaper she held over her head was blown uselessly to one side. She grabbed it with both hands and held it; without giving herself time to think, she dashed down the steps, splashing in icy water that was over her ankles. She was soaked through to her skin immediately, and she gasped at the iciness of the rain. Cord had leaned over to open the door of the Blazer for her, but when she let go of the newspaper with one hand to reach for the hand that he extended to her, the paper was promptly whisked away and the deluge struck her unprotected head. The Blazer sat so high on its huge wheels that she couldn't jump up in it, so she caught the edge of the seat in an effort to haul herself up. Cord cursed, the word drowned out by the pounding rain, and leaned over to catch her under the arms. He lifted her bodily inside, then leaned in front of her to slam the door shut.

"There're a couple of towels in the trash bag," he informed her curtly, sliding back under the steering wheel and putting the vehicle in gear.

She pulled one of the towels out and patted it over her bare arms and shoulders, then blotted her dripping hair. That was the best she could do, and she stared in dismay at the soaked seats and floorboards of the Blazer. "I'm sorry," she choked, realizing now that they should have remained at the cabin until the storm had passed.

Rain still glistened on the rock-hard planes of his face, and drops were caught like liquid diamonds in the black silk of his beard. He pulled the soggy cap from his head and dropped it on the seat between them. In silence she offered him the towel, and in silence he took it, rubbing it over his face and head with one hand as he eased down the driveway.

The headlights caught the swirling, muddy waters of Jubilee Creek as they crossed the small bridge, and she was frightened at how high the water had risen in the short time it had been raining. Cord gave the water a grim look. "I hope I can get back."

He had to keep both hands on the wheel to hold the Blazer steady against the gusts of wind that pushed at it; one particularly strong gust pushed them so far to the side that the two left tires left the road and dug into the soft earth on the side. Cord wrestled them back onto the roughly paved secondary road, but they could proceed at nothing more than a crawl. The headlights did no good against a blinding curtain of rain, and the windshield wipers, though going full speed, couldn't keep the windshield clear.

Making a sudden decision, he glanced at her and pulled the Blazer over onto the side of the road, then cut the ignition. As the engine died, the roar of the rain hitting the metal top sounded even louder. He'd turned off the headlights but left the dashlights on, and in the dim glow she turned frightened eyes on him.

"I can't see to drive," he explained. "We're going to have to wait until this blows over."

She nodded and clasped her hands tightly in her lap, staring out through the windshield. She couldn't see anything; the darkness was absolute, the rain cutting them off from everything else, isolating them in the small sanctuary of the Blazer.

Seconds ticked past and became minutes; if anything, the rain fell harder. Cord turned on the radio, but the static was so bad that they couldn't make out what the announcer was saying, and he snapped it off again. Out of the corner of his eye, he caught her shivering, and he reached out to touch her chilled arm.

"You should have said something," he scolded, and started the motor, then flipped the heater switch to high.

The blast of warm air felt good on her feet and legs, and she slipped her icy feet out of her soggy shoes to stick her toes up close to the vent.

Silence thickened and grated on her nerves. "It's been a long time since I've seen it rain like this," she ventured, if only to break the quiet.

He drummed his fingers on the steering wheel.

She controlled a shiver. "Why did you start letting your beard grow again?"

"Because I don't like to shave."

The curt sentence slapped at her, and she winced. So much for conversation. She hugged her arms around herself, for the first time thinking of the suit jacket she'd left in her car, as well as her purse. She'd been acting like a wild woman, so desperate to get away that she hadn't given a thought to anything else.

A metallic sound began to reach her ears, just barely detectable above the pounding of the rain. She sat up straighter and cast a puzzled glance in Cord's direction, to find that he was listening, too. "What is it?"

"Sleet."

No sooner were the words out of his mouth than the sound of the sleet began to intensify. He turned off the motor, his eyes alert and wary.

"The thunder and lightning are farther away," Susan

said hopefully, not admitting until that moment that she was a little frightened.

"Shhhh," he cautioned, his head turned slightly in a listening position. He reached out and caught her hand, his hard fingers wrapping securely around hers. Susan caught her breath and listened, too, becoming more uneasy as she realized what they were listening for. The sleet stopped, then abruptly the rain stopped, leaving behind a silence that was broken only by the dripping of water from the battered leaves of the trees.

It was the silence, the utter stillness, that was so unnerving. There was a tense, heavy waiting quality to the air, making it difficult to breathe, or perhaps she was simply too frightened to draw in a deep breath. She was clinging so hard to his hand that her nails were sinking into his flesh. "You can see to drive now," she said nervously.

He slid across the seat until he was pressed warmly against her, his body heat making a mockery of the soggy condition of his clothes. He put his arm around her shoulders in a comforting gesture and briefly pressed his lips to her temple. "We'll wait awhile," he told her mildly. "We won't be able to hear it coming if the motor is running."

Susan shivered and closed her eyes. "I know." Her every muscle was tight, her heart pumping faster. The quiet before the storm wasn't just a cliché, it was a reality. As a native of the warm Southern climes where the heated Gulf bathed the region in warm moisture, triggering wild and magnificent storms whenever a cooler system from the west swept in to collide with that warm, damp blanket of air, Susan knew all too well the lethal power of the twisting tornadoes that were spawned out of the towering thunderheads. She knew all the signs, the warnings, and as a child had been drilled in school in the best way to survive a tornado. The Number One Rule: Don't get caught by one.

"If we think we hear something, get out of the truck as fast as you can," Cord instructed quietly. "There's a small ditch on the left of the road; it's probably full of water, but that's where we'll go anyway."

"Okay." Her voice was strained but calm, and she rolled down her window a little, making it easier to hear. Only the dripping of the water, splattering down on the undergrowth, reached her ears.

The first hailstone hit the windshield of the Blazer with such force that they both jumped, and Susan bit back a shriek. Cord uttered a short, sharp expletive, then anything else he might have said was drowned out as golf ball-size hail began to pound the Blazer, ripping the leaves of the trees to shreds, taking small saplings completely down. The din was incredible. Susan felt that they were on the inside of a giant drum, with some maniac beating wildly on it. She tore her hand from Cord's grip and pressed her palms over her ears.

Then it was gone, racing away, leaving the ground covered with shimmering balls of ice, a deep rumble following after it.

With a quick, hard motion Cord reached over her and shoved the door open, then used his body to force her outside. He grabbed her around the waist, keeping her from falling as her feet hit the ice and skidded out from under her. She was barefoot except for her stockings, and the ice was unbearably cold, bruising her soft feet, but she knew that she had better traction without her shoes anyway. High heels would have been more

than useless, they would have been dangerous, unsafe
for picking her way across a road covered with ice balls.
Heedless of the pain, she ran, hearing the rumble come
closer, feeling the earth begin to tremble beneath them.

They splashed into the ditch, the freezing water taking her breath. There was an eerie yellowish cast to the
sky, an absurd lightening of the night sky, and she was
able to see the taut lines of Cord's face. With one hand
on her shoulder he forced her to lie down in the ditch,
and the rushing stream of water splashed up in her face,
filling her mouth with the taste of mud. She spat it out
and looked up at him, her eyes burning. If she had to
die, then thank God it was with him. Then he was covering her, pressing her down deeper into the foul water,
putting his body between her and the fury of the storm
that was thundering toward them.

Somehow, it didn't seem quite real. Inside she was
terrified, but on the outside she was not only calm but
oddly detached. She felt the wind buffeting their bodies,
so fierce and strong that the tumbling water was blown
out of the ditch to splash across the field in tandem with
the gargantuan rain that had begun slashing down out
of the abruptly inky sky. It had been raining hard before, but that was nothing to the way it rained then. The
water that had been blown out of the ditch was instantly
replaced by the downpour. Her skin was bruised and
stinging in a thousand places as small stones and debris
were hurled through the air, and she could hear nothing but the roar of the enormous, thundering monster
as it tore across the earth. She clung to Cord, her slender arms wrapped about his head in an effort to give
him as much protection as she could, and her desper-

ate strength was so great that he couldn't dislodge her arms to tuck her more securely under him.

A deep, bull-throated bellow of destruction assaulted her, and she screamed, a sound that went unheard in the greater scream of the storm. Cord's grip on her increased until she thought her ribs would snap under the force of it, and he pressed her harder, deeper into the ditch. She fought for breath, but couldn't drag any oxygen into her lungs, as the monster's suction pulled all the air away into its rotating, twisting maw. Her only thought was, I'm glad I'm with him.

She must have fainted, though she could never be sure. Certainly she was dazed by the storm, her senses scattered. One moment she was suffocating, feeling as if any moment the tornado would come down on them, and the next the world was strangely normal, even serene. It was still raining, but it was a normal rain, as if the violence of a moment before had belonged to another world. There was no lightning, no thunder, no hail…and no wind. Cord was still lying heavily on her, his chest heaving as he too sucked in much-needed oxygen, his arms outspread and his fingers sunk into the mud as if he would physically anchor them to the earth with his own body. They remained like that for several minutes, lying in the ditch with the rain slanting down on them, as they tried to assimilate the fact that they were not only alive, but relatively unscathed.

Susan moved beneath him, turning her face into the hollow of his throat, and her fingers moved through his hair.

He rolled off her and sat up, his arm behind her as he eased her into a sitting position. "Are you all right?" he demanded hoarsely.

"Yes," she said, and was surprised to find that her throat was sore, her voice so husky that she could barely form the word.

They stumbled to their feet, clinging together, and Susan heard Cord swear quietly as he peered through the darkness and the rain, searching for the Blazer. "I'll be damned," he muttered. "It's turned completely around, and pushed off the road on the other side."

Susan put her hand over her eyes to keep the rain out and was finally able to make out the black bulk of the Blazer, farther away now than it had been when they'd jumped out of it so long ago…or had it been only a few minutes ago? Cord must have eyes like an eagle, she realized, because she could tell only where the Blazer was, not what direction it was facing.

"It missed us," he said suddenly, with hoarse jubilation. "Look where it came across the road."

Following his pointing hand, she could make out a twisted, broken mass that was evidently an enormous tree, lying across the road. There was an odd, flashing illumination, so bright and blue-white that it almost hurt the eyes to look at it. The falling trees had taken down the power lines with them, and now a live wire was lashing back and forth just above the ground, throwing sparks like a Fourth of July celebration. The tornado had dipped down to earth and exploded everything in its path, bypassing them by no more than fifty yards.

Seeing her pick her way, limping, across the hailstones, Cord turned to her and swung her up against his chest. Susan felt as if she'd used her last reserves of strength, and she was just as glad to let him carry her; wearily, she let her head fall against his shoulder, and his arms tightened momentarily about her. He carried her to the Blazer, placing her inside it before walking around and vaulting into the seat behind the steering wheel. He turned the key in the ignition, and to her amazement the engine started immediately. He flashed her a quick grin. After the last hour it was a pleasure to have something going right. He changed gears, easing the Blazer along, the big tires churning in the mud until they gained the hail-slick surface of the road.

"We're going back to the cabin," he said, letting the truck move slowly to keep it from skidding on the ice. "I can't get you home until morning, when I can see how to pick my way around those trees and power lines that are down."

Susan didn't say anything, merely clung to the edge of the seat. She was certain the power would be off at the cabin, but he could build a fire, and the thought of being warm and dry again seemed like heaven. Her muscles were still tense, and she found she couldn't relax, her gaze fixed on the stabbing beams of the headlights as they probed through the gray curtain of rain.

They reached the crest of the gentle incline that led down to the creek, and Cord brought the Blazer to a halt. "I'm going down to check the bridge," he said, and left the truck before she could cry out that she wanted to go with him. Somehow, she didn't want him out of her sight for even a moment.

He came back in only a few minutes, his face harsh in the blinding glare of the headlights. He got back into the Blazer. "The water's over the bridge; we can't chance crossing it. We have to spend the night in the truck."

CHAPTER ELEVEN

SUSAN BIT HER LIP, thinking of the fire that had been warming her in her imagination. She was silent as he shifted into Reverse and turned the Blazer around, then drove a little farther back the way they'd come. Finally he pulled to the side of the road and parked.

She had been so frantic to get away from him, she thought dimly, but now she was glad that he was here, that he was all right. They had come so close to death... but what if only she had been spared? The thought of him lying dead from the brute force of the storm was unbearable.

Her shaking hand went to her dripping hair, and her fingers combed through it. The driving rain had evidently washed the mud out, but she found a few twigs that she pulled out and dropped to the floorboards. But what did it matter, anyway, if her hair was a mess? She began to laugh.

Cord's head jerked around at the sound, and he reached out to touch her shoulder. Susan covered her mouth with her hand, trying to stifle the unwilling mirth, but she couldn't. "Baby, it's all right," he murmured, sliding out from under the steering wheel and taking her in his arms. "It's over; you're all right."

The hard strength of him surrounded her, and Susan burrowed into it, her arms lacing around his waist. The strained laughter turned into choking, dry sobs, then slowly diminished as he continued to hold her, talking to her in a quiet, gentle voice, his hand stroking her head.

But her shaking didn't diminish, and finally his hand moved down over her bare shoulder and arms. "My God, you're freezing," he muttered, taking his arms from around her. He found the two towels that he'd brought when they'd dashed through the rain from the cabin to the Blazer, and wrapped one around her hair. "Get out of those wet clothes," he ordered, but in a voice so calm and matter-of-fact that she didn't balk. "There's a blanket in the back; I'll wrap you up in it." He turned the heater on high.

Susan looked at him, her eyes enormous. "You need to get out of your clothes, too; you're not impervious to cold, either."

The normal tone of her voice reassured him, and he flashed her a grin that shone against the darkness of his growing beard. "I'm warmer than you are, but I'll admit that wet jeans are damned uncomfortable." He peeled his T-shirt off over his head and wrung the excess water out, then draped it over the steering wheel.

The sight of his bare, powerful torso agitated her, and she jerked her gaze away, beginning to unbutton the flimsy camisole top while he struggled to take off his boots in the limited space they had. Her cold fingers wouldn't cooperate, and she had managed to get out of only the camisole and the strapless bra she'd worn under it by the time Cord had completely stripped and was wiping himself down with the other towel.

When he'd finished, he came to her assistance, pushing her shaking hands aside. He dealt with her skirt, panty hose and panties in short order; then he dried her vigorously, the rough fabric of the towel speeding her circulation and driving some of the chill away.

He reached in the back for the blanket, unfolding it and draping it across the seat. He sat in the middle of it, then scooped her up and placed her on his lap, and wrapped the rest of the blanket around both of them like a cocoon.

Blessed warmth enveloped her, and Susan gave a blissful sigh, cuddling against his amazing body heat. She felt suddenly peaceful; they were completely alone and isolated from the world, at least until morning. They were naked together, rather like Adam and Eve, and for the moment she wanted nothing except that they be warm and dry. Everything else could wait until morning. For now she was in his arms, and the feel of him was heaven. The scent of his skin, of his warm masculinity, both soothed and aroused her, and she turned to press more fully into the hair-softened contours of his hard chest.

Cord held her, his hands on her satin curves, his face troubled. "I've never in my life been as scared as I was tonight," he admitted in a rumble, his words startling Susan.

She lifted her head from his shoulder, her eyes wide with astonishment. "You?" she demanded, her voice rising in disbelief. "*You* were afraid?" That didn't seem possible. He had nerves of ice, an imperviousness to danger that both alarmed and reassured her.

"I kept thinking: What if I couldn't hold on to you? What if something hit you? If anything had happened to you—" He bit his words off, his face growing darker.

Susan was stunned. "But you were in danger, too."

He shrugged, utterly indifferent to his own fate.

Perhaps that was how he faced all dangers, with complete unconcern, and perhaps that was why death hadn't found him yet. He didn't fear it, and therefore it didn't seek him. But he had been afraid for her... Her mind stopped, almost afraid to take the thought any further. She simply pressed close to him once again, her hands clinging to his neck.

He rubbed his bristly cheek against her forehead, his hands tightening on her. "Susan."

She loved the sound of her name on his lips. With unconscious sensuality, she moved her breasts against him, the hair on his chest feeling like rough silk against her sensitive nipples. "Ummmm?" she murmured bemusedly.

"I want to make love to you. Will you let me?"

The thought, the rough thread of need in his voice, made her shiver in delight. She lifted her mouth to him, simply and without reserve, and he took it with a tender fervor. He kissed her for a long time, their tongues meeting in mutual need, while his hard fingers found her breasts and stroked them until they hardened and thrust out for his touch.

He lifted his head and gave a low, shaky laugh. "Is that a yes?"

"That's a yes." Despite the weeks they'd been apart, the anger between them, she wasn't shy with him. She was his, in the purest sense, and always in his touch she had perceived his genuine pleasure, the care and concern he gave her. His passion might border on roughness in his urgency, but he never hurt her, and she knew that he never would. Her trust in his physical care of her was so great that despite the rift between them, she knew that she had nothing to fear from him. And for this moment, there was no rift, no pain or disagreement; all of that had retreated, and would arrive with the sunrise, but for now there was only the sweet fever between them.

She could have fought him, could have insisted that he preserve the distance between them, but in the aftermath of the storm, none of their reasons for argument seemed very important. She loved him; she didn't want to fight him. After what they'd just been through, she wanted only to hold him and feel his hard, warm flesh against her, reassure herself that he was unharmed. He was so infinitely precious to her that she didn't want to waste a moment of this time they had together by holding him off. She'd worried herself sick about their situation anyway, and it hadn't changed anything. Let the sunrise bring its troubles; she had the nighttime, and for now that was enough.

He was slow, and exquisitely gentle, using his kisses and the boldness of his stroking fingers to bring her to fever pitch before he stretched her out on the seat, his hard hands controlling her even when she reached for him, trying to pull him down to her. Susan writhed in blind delight, small cries escaping from her throat, her eyes tightly closed as her head rolled slowly back and forth. He was suckling leisurely at her breasts, his tongue curling around each of her aching nipples in turn, a caress that sent bolts of ecstasy shooting through her body. She was no longer cold, but burning with a radiant glow, her body arching up to his.

Deftly he moved her, rearranging her legs, and his mouth left her breasts to trail down her stomach, his beard softly rasping her satin flesh and making her gasp at the rough pleasure. His tongue found her navel and he kissed her, paying homage to her for a long, sweet moment before moving on to a richer treasure.

A startled cry tore from her when he claimed her with his mouth, kissing her deeply, making lightning forays with his tongue that pushed her toward the edge so swiftly she couldn't breathe. Then she forgot about breathing as her fingers tangled in his damp hair; he was killing her with pleasure, stabbing her to death with his devilish tongue, and she rushed to meet her small death. He held her securely until she was calm again, lying peacefully in his arms; it was several moments before she realized he was doing nothing but holding her.

"Cord?" His name was an expression of bewilderment. "What about you?"

"I'm all right." Very gently, he tilted her face up and kissed her. "It's just that I'm unprepared; I don't have any way to protect you."

His unselfish consideration jolted her, but the ecstasy he'd just given her wasn't enough. She didn't want just simple release; she wanted him, with all his delicious masculinity, his driving power, the very essence of the man. She reached out for him, her soft hands touching his face. "I want *you*," she said in a low voice. "Would you mind, very much, if we took the chance?"

A shudder rippled through him, and he moved swiftly to lie over her, parting her thighs and taking her, a groan of pleasure breaking from his lips. He held nothing back from her, his urgency communicating itself to her. He was shaking in a way she'd never seen before, and she tried to soothe him with her yielding softness. All too soon he was hoarsely crying out his satisfaction; then he sagged against her to rest.

After only a moment they were both shifting uncomfortably. During the heat of their lovemaking, neither had noticed their awkward positions or cramped limbs, but now they seemed to be fighting a tangle of gearshift, steering wheel, and door handles, all of which were in uncomfortable places. Cord chuckled as he tried to untangle himself from her and still manage not to maim himself.

"I think we'll be more comfortable in back; God only knows why we didn't get in back anyway."

With the backseat folded down they had considerable space, though still not enough for Cord to stretch out his long legs. He'd cut the motor, so they had to depend on the one blanket and each other for warmth, but now that Susan was dry she didn't feel the chill so much. They lay on half of the blanket, and he pulled the other half around them. Susan nestled in his arms, quietly happy. "I'm so tired," she murmured, then smothered a yawn. She didn't want to sleep, didn't want to waste any of the time they had together, but her body was demanding rest. The stress of the past weeks, the emotional tension and fear she'd experienced today, had all taken their toll. Her limbs felt as heavy as lead, and her eyelids simply would not stay open.

She yawned again, her eyes slowly closing. She put her hand on his chest, where she could feel the strong, steady beating of his heart. He was so big and tough; she felt infinitely safe and protected when she was with him. "I do love you," she told him quietly, not needing anything now beyond the telling of it. She'd just wanted to say the words aloud this once, when there was peace between them. It was a gift, a simple gesture from her heart.

"I know," he whispered against her temple, and held her while she slept.

He hadn't expected to sleep at all; his senses were too raw. He had been sure that he would feel the restlessness that always seized him if there were anyone else about while he slept. But the rain kept drumming on the roof of the Blazer, and the darkness enclosed them like a cave; he was warm and dry, and his body pleasantly satisfied. She was soft in his arms, small and delicate, so completely feminine that from the moment he'd met her he'd found himself tempering his strength lest he accidentally hurt her. This afternoon, when she'd been crying and beating on her steering wheel, he'd felt as if he'd taken a punch in the chest; she simply wasn't the weepy type, yet he'd hurt her enough to make her cry, and he hadn't meant to. He'd been infuriated to hear that Preston had run off and left her to shoulder everything, that instead of Preston knuckling under and sacrificing, it had been Susan. He had to end this, as soon as he could, for Susan's sake. She was at the end of her rope, physically and emotionally.

She loved him. Once a woman's offering of love would have made him impatient, restless to be gone. He couldn't offer anything in return, and he hadn't wanted the complications of clinging hands, teary scenes, or the incredible plots of revenge some women could concoct when they felt they'd been wronged. Judith's death had scarred him deeply, left him so wary of being wounded like that again that he'd instinctively protected himself...until Susan. She'd gotten in under his guard, and because she didn't demand anything of him, he found himself giving more.

Still, he hadn't realized, until she'd practically ordered him out of her house and out of her life, just how close she'd gotten to him. He'd felt lonely, and he was a man who treasured his solitude. His healthy body had burned for sexual release, but other women seemed unattractive in subtle ways he'd never noticed before. He didn't want other women; he wanted Susan, with her serenity like a halo around her. Susan, who became a sweet, loving wanton for him, only for him.

Now she was in his arms again, pressed against his heart, just where she belonged. He moved drowsily, seeking a more comfortable position, and she moved with him, her soft hands holding him even in her sleep. It was the most uniquely satisfying experience of his life, and a slight smile touched his hard mouth as he went to sleep.

As often happens after a storm, the next day dawned sunny and warm, but without the suffocating humidity that had been weighing down on everyone. It was as if nature were pleased by the destruction it had wrought. Cord's eyes blinked open, and for a moment he stared at the expanse of innocent, deep blue sky. The interior of the Blazer had already heated under the morning sun, and a trickle of sweat ran down his side, tickling him. He twitched, and Susan stirred, stretching. He rolled to his side and watched as she slowly came awake, her eyelashes fluttering. The blanket fell away, revealing her slender bare body, her full, pretty breasts and succulent nipples. His loins tightened, and he put his hand on her hip. "Honey, we have to leave soon," he said huskily. "Before we go…?"

Susan heard the question, the intent in his voice, and she turned to him. "Yes," she said drowsily, reaching out for him.

He took her gently, slowly, holding the world at bay while they loved each other. When it was done he leaned over her, his weight supported on one elbow, his eyes very clear and demanding. "Stay with me. Don't go back to the office. I'll take care of you, in every way."

Tears blurred her eyes, but still Susan managed a smile for him. As the salty liquid seeped from the corners of her eyes, she said shakily, "I have to go back; I can't just turn my back and walk away from everyone who's depending on me."

"What about me? How can you turn your back on me?" His words hit her hard, and she flinched.

"I love you, but you don't *need* me. You want me, but that's entirely different. Besides, I don't think I have what it takes to be a mistress." She reached up and stroked his bearded cheek, her mouth trembling. "Please, take me home now."

Silently they dressed in their damp, incredibly wrinkled clothing, and Cord began the torturous drive, detouring time and again as their way was blocked by fallen trees or downed power lines. They passed utility crews who were hard at work, trying to get new lines up, and in some cases new poles. The sounds of chain saws split the peaceful morning air as men began cleaning up the debris. What was normally a fifteen-minute drive took well over an hour, but finally Susan was tumbling out the Blazer's door into Emily's arms. The older woman's worn face was tight with concern.

"My lands, just look at the two of you," she breathed, and tears sparkled in her eyes.

Cord managed his devilishly casual smile. "I think we look pretty good for two people who've been lying in a ditch." Actually, every muscle in his body was protesting, not only from sleeping on a hard, cramped surface, but from the beating he'd taken from the hailstones. For the first time he saw a bruise high on Susan's cheekbone, and he reached out to touch it with his thumb. She stood very still under his touch, her eyes filled with pain and longing.

Emily wiped her tears away, and hustled them both inside, bullying them shamelessly now that she knew they were safe.

"Both of you get upstairs right now and take a hot shower, and toss those filthy clothes out so I can wash them—"

"I'll be leaving in a minute," Cord interrupted her. "I've got to see if I can get to the cabin and check for damage. But if you have any coffee brewed, I'd appreciate some."

She brought him a cup and he sipped it gratefully, the hot liquid sending new life into his body. Susan stood watching him, her arms limp at her sides, wanting to do as he said and go with him, forget about everything. Without knowing that she had moved, she found herself in front of him, and without a word he set the cup aside and folded her tightly in his arms. He kissed her roughly, almost desperately, as if he would imprint his possession on her mouth, and as Susan clung to him she felt the acid tears burning down her cheeks.

"Shhhh, shhhh," he soothed, lifting his lips at the salty taste. With his fingertips, he wiped her cheeks dry; then he framed her face between his big hands and held it turned up so he could see into her drowning eyes. "Everything will be all right. I promise."

She couldn't say anything, so he kissed her again,

then released her. He gave Emily a swift hug and left, not once looking back.

Susan jammed her fist against her mouth, trying to hold back the sobs that shook her, but they burst out anyway. Emily led her upstairs and helped her undress, then took away her soiled clothing and laid out fresh garments while Susan stood under the shower and cried.

She knew there were a thousand things that needed doing, but she couldn't summon any interest in any of them. She wanted only to curl up on her bed and cry until she couldn't cry any more. It was all just too much; she couldn't fight any longer. It was a measure of her willpower that she had controlled her tears by the time she left the bathroom; she sat down and dried her hair, then applied a careful blend of makeup to hide the traces of her tears. After dressing in the casual slacks and shirt that Emily had put out for her, she went downstairs for the meal that she knew Emily would have ready. She wasn't hungry, but eating was a necessity that she'd been neglecting lately, all to no good. She wouldn't be able to keep the corporation from bankruptcy, even if she divested herself of everything she owned except her clothing, then held a yard sale to get rid of even that.

She sat on the patio all day, soaking up the sun, dozing, thinking, but her thoughts only went in circles and produced nothing. She called Imogene and explained why she wouldn't be at the office that day; she had no idea when Cord would be able to get the Audi back to her, but she found that it was the one bright spot she could see right now: She would be able to see him again when he did bring it to her.

She was probably a fool not to have taken him up on his proposition, she thought tiredly. She should just forget about tomorrow, about all the duties and obligations that she'd always served; she should go with Cord and take what love she could get from him. He cared; she knew he did. Perhaps he didn't love her, but she knew that he'd offered her more than he'd ever offered any other woman, except Judith. Poor, hurt, confused Judith, who was now the point of all this enmity years after her death. Because everyone had failed her, because she'd died, Cord was trying to make it up to her now, to get revenge for her, and for himself, perhaps, so he could be at peace.

She'd told him that she didn't have what it took to be a mistress, but what did it take, really, except a woman in love? She thought longingly of spending every night with him, of traveling around the world beside him. She'd always been a woman who was happy with her hearth and home, but for Cord she would learn to wander, and lay her head on a different pillow every night if that was what he wanted.

It was only a matter of time, anyway, before the life she knew was all over. She had failed; she couldn't pay the loan.

When Cord still hadn't brought her car back by the next morning, Susan called and asked Imogene to pick her up; there was nothing more she could do, but she would continue to handle the office and make the myriad decisions that still had to be made every day. The ship might sink, but she wouldn't make a confused mess of it. Dignity and grace in defeat, that was the ticket.

Giving herself pep talks didn't help much. She was agonizingly aware that she'd lost on both sides. She'd tried to heal the rift in the family, but instead it had grown deeper. Cord might want her, care for her, but

how could he ever trust her? He'd asked her to stay
with him, but instead she'd given her aid to Preston.
Knowing that Cord was wrong didn't ease the hollow
ache inside her.

She had to face everyone at the office, where they
had all somehow heard that she'd almost been caught in
a tornado. Several tornadoes had ripped through Mississippi that night, and one close to Jackson had hit a
residential area, leaving two people dead, but her acquaintances and employees were only interested in the
local one, which had missed all the populated areas and
destroyed only trees and newly planted crops. She managed to be very casual about it, and her lack of detail
soon killed their interest.

When she went home that night she found the Audi
there, and disappointment speared her. Why couldn't
he have brought it when he knew she would be home?
But perhaps he was avoiding her. She stared at the car
for a long moment before thanking Imogene for the ride.

Imogene reached over and patted her hand. "Is there
anything I can do?" she asked. "Anything I can say to
Cord? I know you're not happy, and I feel like it's all
my fault."

"No, it's not your fault," Susan denied, managing a
smile. "I made my own decisions, so I imagine I'll have
to live with them."

Emily was still waiting, and she made a pretense
of cleaning up the kitchen while Susan ate, but Susan
had a feeling that she had caught on to Susan's habit of
disposing of the food instead of eating it. As she dutifully ate the last bite, Emily nodded in satisfaction.
"Cord told me to make certain you were eating. You're

too thin. This business is tearing you apart, and I'm ready for it to end."

"It won't be long," Susan sighed. She hated herself for asking, but she had to know. "Did he say anything else?"

"He said he lost one of his trees, but it fell away from the cabin, and there's hail damage to the roof, but other than that everything came through the storm okay."

"That's good." It wasn't personal news, but it was better than nothing. She refrained from asking if he'd looked tired.

Emily had just left when Imogene phoned. "Susan, can you come over?" she asked, urgency filling her voice. "Preston's back, and he's found out something about Cord!"

"I'll be right there." Susan dropped the phone and ran to get her purse. Something about Cord? Her heart clenched. Had he done something illegal? Whatever it was, if there were any way, she'd protect him. No, it couldn't be anything illegal; he was far too visible, and he made no attempt to disguise his identity. It was far more likely that he'd crossed some powerful people. Preston might plan on using his knowledge against Cord, but she'd make certain that Cord knew all about his plans.

As she drove over to Blackstone House she was hardly aware of the turns she took, or the speed at which she traveled. Her heart was slamming wildly in her chest, hurting her ribs. She'd been longing for Preston to come back, but now that he had she could only fear that he'd try to hurt Cord in some way.

Preston looked surprisingly normal when he opened the door to her as she ran up the steps. He was casually attired; his tan was deeper, and he looked relaxed. He was startled when he saw her. "Good Lord, Susan, you've lost a good ten pounds. What've you been doing?"

She brushed his comment aside. "It doesn't matter. What have you found out about Cord?"

He ushered her into the den, where Imogene was waiting, and waited until she was seated before speaking. "I've been doing some detective work while I was gone," he explained. "I wanted Cord to think that I'd chickened out so he wouldn't make any attempt to cover his tracks. It worked, thank God. He must've thought he'd won without a real battle."

"I doubt that," Susan interrupted. "He didn't know until the day before yesterday that you'd gone."

He frowned. "But why? Didn't you tell him?"

Susan's eyes widened, and she sat up straight. "That's what you wanted me to do, wasn't it? You dumped all of that on me, thinking I'd run straight to him and beg for mercy. He said that was what you were doing, but I didn't believe him." She stared at him, her eyes clear and accusing, and he shifted uncomfortably.

"What else could I think?" he tried to explain gently. "Are you saying that I completely misread the situation?"

"I don't know; I haven't any idea how you read it."

He turned away from her distinctly chilly gaze. "Anyway, I went to New York. I'd noticed that the prices of our stock had remained high despite the rumors that had to be going around, so it followed that someone was buying. I suspected then, but I wanted to be certain. Cord has been buying up all the stock that came on the market. He's not pushing the company into bankruptcy;

he's been pushing us into selling stock, which he's been buying. He's mounting a takeover!"

A takeover! For a moment Susan was dazed; then a spurt of admiration for Cord's nerve made her laugh. "A takeover!" she giggled, clapping her hands. "All of this for a takeover!"

"I don't see that it's so funny."

"Of course you don't! After all, *I'm* the one who's been selling stock in an effort to raise money to pay off that loan!"

Imogene went white. "Susan! Your own assets!"

Preston stared at her; then he swore quietly, and rubbed his eyes in a disbelieving manner. "Susan, we talked about that. I told you not to liquidate anything of yours."

"You also walked off and left me in a sink-or-swim situation," she pointed out. "I thought I had a company going under; I didn't know it was just corporate games! The stock isn't all that I've liquidated!"

He looked ill. "My God, you've done all that…and he had no intention of calling in that loan. He just wanted us to panic and sell enough to give him a majority. Susan, how much did you sell?"

"Nine percent."

"That still leaves you six percent. I have eleven percent, and Mother has eleven. Twenty-eight percent total. Cord has, I think, twenty-six percent. We still have a majority."

"If his takeover doesn't succeed, he may still collect on that loan," Imogene pointed out, but Preston shook his head decisively.

"No, that would be killing his own source of income. It didn't make sense from the beginning that he'd hurt himself financially just to get back at me, but I thought that maybe he did hate me that much. Then when the stock sold immediately whenever any shares went on the market, I began to think that it was something else entirely he was after."

"Why didn't you tell me?" Susan inquired. "Never mind; I know the answer to that. You didn't trust me because I was seeing Cord, and Cord didn't trust me because I was helping you."

"I'm sorry," he said softly. "I had no idea it would be this hard on you. I swear, I'll replace everything you sold."

She dismissed that with a wave of her hand. "It doesn't matter." She just wanted it over with.

Preston decided not to pursue the issue, because she was looking tired and dazed. "I drove out to see Cord as soon as I got in this afternoon," he continued. "I called a board meeting for ten in the morning, and this will be put to a vote. He'll have to take his chances on snapping up any more stock before we get to it, so he knows his game is up."

It had all been just a game. That was all she could think of that night. Just a game.

She didn't know how all of the shares had been originally divided; when she'd married Vance, she'd known only that the family had owned fifty-one percent of the stock, and the rest of it was in others' hands. Others owned chunks of shares, but with the majority in family hands it hadn't mattered. Imogene had owned fifteen percent, Preston fifteen percent, and Vance fifteen percent. Susan had inherited Vance's shares. That had left six percent of the family majority, which she had always assumed was scattered around to distant cousins. She hadn't known of Cord's existence until the day he'd come back; he'd been gone for so long that no one talked about him. But now it was evident that he'd owned the remaining shares.

Preston and Imogene had both sold four percent of their stock in order to cover what they'd used of Cord's money; that gave Cord fourteen percent, assuming that he'd bought it, which he must have done. She'd sold nine percent, giving him twenty-three percent. If he had twenty-six percent, he'd bought some common stock as well, and possibly had acquired voting proxies from other stockholders. Preston also had voting proxies. It was all just a game of numbers, nothing else. If anything, the corporation was stronger, since Cord had essentially paid off an outstanding debt. The family now owned fifty-four percent of the stock. Everything was just fine.

Now Cord's reassurances made sense. He'd known that the company was in no danger of bankruptcy, but he hadn't trusted her enough to tell her what was going on, just as Preston hadn't trusted her enough to tell her his suspicions. She'd tried to be a mediator, and instead had become the sacrificial goat.

She was glad that the morning would bring the end of it. She was tired of games. They seemed to be fine for everyone except the goat.

CHAPTER TWELVE

OF THE FIVE people in the boardroom the next morning, Cord looked the most relaxed. He was dressed impeccably in a summer-weight pin-striped suit, the cut of which had a definite European flair. His growing beard gave him a raffish look that kept the suit from being *too* impeccable, but then his rampant masculinity allowed him to wear anything with elan...or wear nothing at all, her imagination whispered, conjuring up a vision of how magnificent he was in the nude.

Imogene was calm, almost remote. Preston was all business. Beryl looked as calm as ever. On the other hand, Susan felt disoriented and none of the familiar boardroom rituals or words made any sense. She darted another glance at Cord, only to find him watching her, and he gave her a slow wink. Was he that unconcerned about the outcome? Was that elaborate scheme nothing more to him than another way of irritating Preston? If so, his practical joke had been enormously successful.

She was so detached that she missed what they were saying. It wasn't until she caught a surge of anger that she was able to gather her senses and pay attention.

"This is my birthright," Cord was saying, his tone hard and his eyes cold. "It took me years to realize that, but I'm not giving it up. I decided to fight for it, and there won't be any compromising."

"That's your loss," Preston said crisply. "Shall we put it to the vote?"

"By all means."

Cord sat there, so confident, but then it wasn't in him to be any other way. He had to know that he hadn't enough to best their combined shares, but that knowledge couldn't be read in his face.

He'd been shoved out of the family circle. What was in his mind now, when victory danced before him? Thoughts of revenge? Or just a determination to be in that family once again, wanted or not? To assume responsibility for what was his, to finally settle in his home?

"I vote yes," Cord drawled easily, and Susan jerked her thoughts back.

Imogene sat quietly, not looking at either Preston or Cord, but how else could she vote? She wouldn't vote against her own son. "I vote nay," she finally said.

"I vote nay," Preston followed promptly. "Susan?"

He was sure of her, Susan realized. She looked at him, and found him watching her impatiently, the gleam of victory already in his eyes. What a shark he was! He was a perfect chairman, conscientious and bold, and able to use guerrilla tactics when they were called for.

There was nothing for her to read in Cord's eyes. He simply waited. He hadn't contacted her, hadn't tried to persuade her to vote in his favor. Why should he? She'd come down solidly on Preston's side in every skirmish. No wonder he didn't trust her! He would be a good chairman, too; he'd shown his expertise in gathering enough money to mount this campaign.

"Susan!" Preston prodded impatiently.

Trust has to start somewhere, she thought painfully.

Cord was so used to guarding his back that it was second nature to him now. "I vote yes," she said in a low tone, and total silence descended on the room, except for the quick rasp of Beryl's pencil across the pad as she recorded everything.

Preston looked to be in shock; he was pale, his mouth compressed to a thin line that was bracketed on each side by grooves of tension. The meeting was quickly adjourned, but only Beryl left the room. Everyone else remained in their seats; perhaps even Cord was stunned by the turn of events. Susan's motives were too murky for her to explain them even to herself, but she was aware, deep inside, of a feeling that she simply couldn't fail him now. If he had lost, he wouldn't have returned to being an absentee board member, his shares automatically voted by Preston; Cord entered a fight to win. He would have gone on and on, and the conflict would have continued to tear the family apart and drain the company. Let it end, even if she made herself an outcast with Preston and Imogene. Why not? She was tired, too tired to really care, and she was doubly bitter at being played with so callously by both Cord and Preston. She'd just been a pawn in their games, moved around according to their whims, and kept in the dark by both of them.

Imogene leaned forward, clasping her hands on the table. "Let it end," she said quietly, looking from her son to Cord and back. "We were a family once; I'd like us to be one again. I was wrong for my part in it, and if you can possibly forgive me, Cord, I'll be very grateful." The steel that was an inherent part of her personality shone clearly out of her gray eyes, and in that moment Susan knew that she'd never liked or respected her mother-in-law more.

Without waiting for an answer from Cord, Imogene turned her determined regard to Preston. "I know this will be difficult for you; you've been an outstanding chairman, and it won't be easy for you to turn over the reins. But I'm asking you to do it without bitterness, and to do whatever you can to ease the transition. Cord is family; he's as much a Blackstone as you are. I hope you're big enough to let this end now, before it totally destroys us. People have already been hurt, and others will be if this continues. Susan was the only one of us with enough sense to realize that from the beginning. If you won't stop it for yourself, then stop it for me…and for her. God knows she's paid enough for your enmity."

Susan flinched, hating to have her feelings dragged out in the open like this. She sat very still and pale, her eyes focused on her hands. Now it was up to them to either settle their differences or draw new battle lines. Either way, she'd withdrawn from combat, retreated to lick her wounds. She was simply too tired to care any longer.

Preston sat with an abstracted frown on his brow, his gaze turned inward to long ago, when he'd first become enemies with his cousin. "I always envied you," he said absently, reviewing his memories. "Everything always came so easily to you. Vance was a hard act to follow, but with you… My God, when you were around, I became invisible. Everyone watched you."

Cord stared across the length of the table at his cousin, his dark face hard and expressionless. What he thought of Preston's admission was impossible to guess.

Giving an unbelieving little shake of his head, as if he couldn't quite take in how far their enmity had taken them, Preston straightened his shoulders and looked

at Cord directly. "When I was sixteen I started dating
Kelly Hartland, and I fell hard for her. You were just
starting your sophomore year in college, and I suppose
to a high school girl that was irresistible. You came
home for a weekend, met Kelly at a party, and just like
that she dropped me flat."

A startled look flared in Cord's eyes. "Kelly Hartland? A little strawberry-blond cheerleader type? I can
barely remember her. I dated her a couple of times, but
it was nothing heavy."

"It was for me. I hated you for taking her away from
me when you obviously didn't care about her. At sixteen I thought she was the love of my life. When your
affair with Judith blew up in your face, I saw a way to
get back at you, and I took it. I'm not proud of it, but
there's no way to undo it."

Cord inhaled deeply, and even without looking at
him Susan knew that the mention of Judith was lashing
at him, uncovering the deep pain and guilt he felt at the
way she'd been treated. Yet the bonds of common blood,
weakened by years of bitterness and hatred, were reaching out again, and the two men looked at each other,
seeing their common heritage in each other's face. The
serrated edge of pain rasped in Cord's voice when he
spoke. "Judith was my wife. We were married after we
left here; she died the next year. I could've killed you
for what you did to her." A crystalline sheen was suddenly in his eyes. "I'm guiltier than anyone else for what
happened to her." Even now, he was bitterly angry at
the way she'd died, her spirit gone, her laughter stilled.

Silence fell, and suddenly Susan couldn't bear any
more. Without looking at anyone, she pushed her chair
back and got to her feet, walking out swiftly before

she could be called back. Her chest was aching, yet she didn't think she could cry. The time for that was past.

Her senses were dulled as she went to her office, walking past Beryl who looked up eagerly, full of questions, but Susan didn't see her. She felt chilled to the bone, so cold that she could never be warm again.

All of this had been because of women who had long ago faded into the mists of the past. There was a certain irony in her own situation; did either of them want her for herself, or merely because each thought the other wanted her?

She had barely moved away from the door after closing it when it was thrust open again, and Cord loomed behind her, so close that she felt oppressed by his size, and she moved instinctively away from him. At her action, his eyes narrowed, and he closed the door behind him.

"Why did you leave the meeting?" he asked evenly.

"I'm going home." Her legs felt wooden as she walked to her desk and retrieved her purse, tucking it under her arm. She avoided his gaze and moved to the side to step around him.

He took one stride and stood in front of her, blocking the door. "I need you here, Susan. You know it won't be easy, making the transition. Up until now only the family has been involved, but now everyone else will have to be informed and dealt with. I need your help. You can do more with a look than most people can manage with a baseball bat."

"If I hadn't thought you could handle it, I wouldn't have voted for you," she said tiredly. "Please, let me by."

"Why did you vote for me? Everyone else was as surprised as I was." He put his hand on her bare arm, the warmth of his fingers searing her, seeking a response, some sign of the quiet radiance he associated with her.

Susan couldn't give him one. She simply stared woodenly at the light gray fabric of his suit. "I'm tired; I want to go home," she repeated.

He looked at her pale, tense face, seeing the shadows around her eyes, and though all of his instincts screamed against letting her slip away now, it was obvious that she was almost at the breaking point. "I'll drive you home."

"No." Her reply was immediate, and firm.

He bit back a curse. "All right, if you don't want me to drive you home, I'm sure Imogene will—"

"I drove myself here; I can drive myself home. I'm not going to tangle with any power poles."

Forcing himself to compliance, he said, "All right. I'll come by tonight—"

"No," she interrupted, looking at him now, pain and betrayal plain for him to read in her eyes. "Not tonight."

It was a hard battle that he fought with himself, evident in the grim set of his jaw, the drumming of the pulse in his temple. "We have to talk."

"I know. Maybe later; I don't think I can handle it right now."

"When?"

She managed a shrug, but her lips were trembling. "I don't know. Maybe six or seven years."

"Hell!" he roared, his control shattered.

"I'm sorry, but that's the way I feel! Please, just leave me alone! I don't have anything else you want, anyway; you've already got my stock and my vote." She pushed past him, ducking her head to keep from looking at him. She just watched her feet, mentally commanding them to function. She left the building, and the hot Mississippi sun burned down on her, blinding her momentarily with its brilliance. She blinked and fumbled in her purse for her sunglasses, finally extracting them and sliding them on her nose. The sun felt good on her chilled skin, she noticed dimly. She would go home and sit on the patio in the sun, and sleep if she could. That was the most ambitious plan she could make at the moment, with her mind so dulled by pain.

She drove home slowly, carefully. Emily, bless her, didn't ask any unnecessary questions. Moving like an automaton, Susan shed her dress and slip, and peeled the hot panty hose away from her legs. The freedom afforded her by an old pair of shorts that she usually wore only while gardening, and a plain white sleeveless blouse with the tails tied in a knot at her midriff, made her breathe easier for the first time in days. It was over. She had lost more than anyone else, but she could rest now.

She pulled a chaise longue out into the full strength of the sun and lay down, letting the heat begin the healing process in her exhausted body. Her eyelids each weighed a thousand pounds; she was unable to keep them up, and after a moment she stopped trying. She dozed in the sun, her mind blank.

Emily woke her once with an offering of iced tea, which Susan accepted gratefully. The chill was gone now, and she felt pleasantly hot, her skin damp with perspiration. She drank the tea, then turned over on her stomach and slept again. During the worst of the heat Emily came out and pulled the big patio umbrella into position to shield Susan, then went back in to finish the chores Cord had set for her.

Susan awoke late in the afternoon and wandered in to eat the light salad and stuffed tomato that Emily had prepared. Her eyes were still heavy, and she yawned in spite of everything she could do to prevent it.

"I'm sorry," she murmured. "I'm still so tired."

Emily patted her arm. "Why don't you go watch the evening news? Just put your feet up and relax."

"That's exactly what I've been doing for *hours*," Susan sighed, but it was still an outstanding idea.

It was inevitable that she'd go to sleep in front of the television. Her last memory was of a stalled low-pressure system on the weather map.

She was stiff when she woke, and she stretched leisurely, trying to ease the kinks out of her back and legs. Her lashes fluttered open, and she stared straight into Cord's eyes.

With renewed energy she sat up abruptly. "What are you doing here?" she demanded, her eyes wide, the haunted look creeping back into them.

"Waiting for you to wake up," he returned calmly. "I didn't want to startle you. Now I'm going to do exactly what I wanted to do the first time I saw you."

She pressed herself back into the corner of the couch, watching him warily as he approached and leaned over her. "What was that?"

"Throw you over my shoulder and carry you off." He gripped one of her wrists, gave a gentle tug, and to her astonishment she found herself being hoisted over his shoulder. He settled her comfortably, one arm locked around her legs to hold her steady, while he patted her bottom with the other hand.

Dizzily she grabbed at his belt loops to anchor herself. "Put me down!" she gasped; then, as he moved deliberately around the room, switching off the television, turning off the lights, she said, "What are you doing?"

"You'll see."

It wasn't until he carried her outside into the warm, fragrant night air that she began to struggle, kicking futilely against the band of his arm. "Let me down! Where are you taking me?"

"Away," he answered simply, his boots crunching on the gravel of the drive. In an effort to see Susan braced her arms on his back and raised herself, looking over her shoulder. His Blazer was sitting there, and he opened the door, then very gently lifted her off his shoulder and placed her on the seat.

"Emily packed your clothes," he informed her, leaning in to kiss her sweetly astonished mouth. "I've already put them in the Blazer. Everything's taken care of, and all you have to do is ride. I still have that blanket in the back, if you'd rather sleep," he finished huskily, his tone telling her how clearly he remembered the last time he had used it.

Susan sat in dazed astonishment as he shut the door and walked around to the driver's side. He was really kidnapping her, with Emily's cheerful aid! She supposed she should feel more indignant, but she still felt slow and drowsy, and it just didn't seem worth the effort to protest.

When he slid under the steering wheel, she asked quietly, "How did you know I wouldn't try to run while you went around to get in?"

"Two reasons." He started the motor and shifted into Reverse, turning to look over his shoulder as they backed up. "One, you're too smart to waste what little energy you have in a useless effort." He braked, then changed to first gear and smoothly let out the clutch, his powerful legs working. "Two, you love me."

His logic was ironclad. She did love him, even though she was still trying to deal with the hurt he'd inflicted. She supposed that she could best describe her feelings as those of being ill-used, shuffled about with little regard in the high-stakes game he and Preston had been playing.

Cord slanted her a searching look. "No fervent denials?"

"No. I'm not a liar."

The simple dignity of her statement, coupled with her listlessness, shook him to the core. She loved, but without hope. He felt as if a flame that had been given into his care was flickering on the brink of extinction, and it would take tender nurturing to bring it back to full strength. His first thought, when she'd left the office earlier in the day, had been to give her time, let her rest and recover her strength, but as the day wore on he'd been seized by an urgent need to do *something,* to bring her back into the circle of his arms where she belonged. His arrangements had been hurriedly made, as he swept all obstacles and protests out of his path.

He'd thought she would sleep, but she sat very still and erect in the seat, her eyes on the highway. When he'd gone past every destination that she'd guessed, she finally asked, "Where are you taking me?"

"To the beach," he answered promptly. "You're going to do nothing but eat, sleep, and lie in the sun until you gain back the weight you've lost and lose those smudges under your eyes."

Susan pondered his answer for a moment, since they

were evidently not going to the stretches of beach that she was familiar with. She sighed. "What beach?"

He laughed aloud, a rare sound. "I'll narrow it down to Florida for you. Does that help?"

She did sleep, finally, before they reached their destination. In the early hours of the morning Cord pulled the Blazer up to a darkened beach house and put his hand on her shoulder to gently shake her awake.

The house was right on the beach, and the luminescent Gulf stretched out before her as far as she could see. The white sand of the Florida panhandle looked like snow in the faint starlight. When she climbed from the Blazer, the constant wind off the Gulf lifted her hair, bringing with it the scent of the ocean mingled with the fresher scent of rain.

It was a basic Florida beach house, built of white-washed cement blocks, with large windows and low ceilings. Following Cord as he moved through the house turning on the lights, she saw a small, cheerful kitchen in yellow and white, a glass table in an alcove, with a ceiling fan above it, and a living room with white wicker furniture; then Cord led her to a small white-painted bedroom. He brought in the single suitcase Emily had packed for her and placed it at the foot of the bed.

"Your bathroom is through there," he said, indicating a door opening off the bedroom. "I'll be in the room straight across the hall, if you need me for anything."

Of all the things she had considered since he'd put her in the Blazer, that she would be going to bed alone wasn't one of them, yet that was exactly what happened. He kissed her on the forehead and walked out, closing the door behind him, and she stood in the middle of the room, blinking her eyes in astonishment.

But the bed beckoned her, and she took a swift shower, then crawled naked between the sheets, too tired to see if Emily had packed a nightgown for her.

Over breakfast the next morning, a meal that he cooked before awakening her, she commented, "You know, this isn't very wise behavior for a man who's just taken control of a firm. You should be in the office."

He shrugged and liberally spread his toast with jelly. "There's wise, and then there's wise. I think I have my priorities in the right order."

Pursing her lips, Susan carefully cut her toast into thin strips. She wasn't quite certain why he'd brought her to the beach, but her questions could wait. She'd slept until she was almost dopey, and consequently she was rested for the first time in weeks. She didn't think she could handle any personal questions right then, but there were a lot of things she wanted to know.

"You had it all planned out before you came back, didn't you?"

He glanced up, his blue eyes glittering as the morning sun fell on his face. "It all depended on the first step. When I put pressure on him, he had to sell off stock and weaken himself financially in order to replace the money that he'd taken in order for any of it to work. He literally financed my takeover; the money that he replaced was used to buy up the first loan. Then, when that loan was paid, I used the money again to buy up the second loan."

His nerve and gall were truly astonishing, leaving her shaking her head in awe. "You didn't have any other money to back you?"

"Of course, I have money," he snorted. "I'm a hell of a good gambler, regardless if it's cards, dice, horses...or oil. I've lost my shirt a few times, but more often than not I come out on top."

"Oil?" she asked blankly. "You wanted to lease the ridges yourself? You weren't acting for any company?"

He shrugged, his powerful shoulders rippling under the light blue polo shirt he wore. "The ridges were a smoke screen," he admitted. "They were a way to put pressure on Preston; I wanted him to refuse to lease them to me, giving me an excuse to use my lever against him."

Susan remembered feeling, at the time, that he'd deliberately pushed Preston into refusing; he'd manipulated them all like a master puppeteer, and they'd danced whenever he pulled the strings. "So there's no oil in the ridges? No wonder you weren't in any hurry to sign the leases!"

"I didn't say that." He reached out and put his hand on hers. "Stop butchering that slice of toast and eat it," he commanded. "Haven't you received the geological survey you ordered?"

"No, not yet."

"Well, the part about the oil is true, or at least there's a good chance of either oil or natural gas."

She ate a piece of toast, and fiddled with another one until she looked up and saw him glaring at her. She hastily took a bite, then put the remainder on her plate. "I'm really not very hungry. I'm sorry."

"That's all right. You'll get your appetite back soon." He rose and began to clear the table; when Susan moved to help him, he stopped her with a lifted hand. "Whoa, lady. Put that plate down. You're not to do any work."

"I'm fairly certain I'm still strong enough to carry a plate," she informed him mildly.

"Sit down. I think I'm going to have to explain the rules to you."

At the mock sternness in his voice, she sat down like a naughty schoolgirl, her hands clasped on her knees. He sat down in the chair opposite her and explained the situation to her slowly and carefully. "You're here to rest. I'm here to take care of you. I'll do the cooking, the cleaning up, everything."

"How long will heaven last?" she asked, and for the first time a tiny smile lit her face, catching his eye like a ray of sunshine after a storm.

"As long as it takes," he replied quietly.

He was serious. The next few days passed leisurely, even monotonously, but after the stress of the last weeks, that was exactly what Susan needed. Time was measured only by the rising and setting of the sun. At first she slept a lot, as much from mental fatigue as any physical tiredness. She didn't occupy her thoughts with tormenting questions of "What if?"; her mind was curiously blank, as if it were just too much trouble to think about anything. She rested, she ate, she slept, all under the mostly silent guardianship that Cord offered.

She not only slept alone, she was completely undisturbed, and as she regained her strength she began to wonder about that. It was a sign of her returning vitality that she wondered about anything, but she was young and healthy, and the coddling she'd been receiving was rapidly restoring her strength. Her depression and fatigue had been feeding on each other, and with the weariness banished, the uncharacteristic depression began to lift. It was almost like rebirth, and she quietly enjoyed it. But she knew that it was also obvious to Cord that she was feeling much better, and every night she expected him to come to her bed. When he didn't, she had the panicked thought that perhaps he didn't want her any longer; then she realized that he was waiting for her to make the first move, to indicate that she was ready to resume their relationship.

Uncertainty kept her silent. She wasn't certain that it was what she wanted; she still loved him, but there was still that lingering sense of betrayal that she couldn't shake, and she knew that as long as she had doubts about him she had to hold herself aloof. Nor did she want simply to resume an affair; she wanted far more from him than that. She wanted his love, his legal commitment, and, if possible, his children.

The fifth night they were at the beach house a thunderstorm blew in from the Gulf and dumped its fury on them, rattling the windows with its booming claps of thunder. Susan awoke with a start, a cry on her lips, as for a confused moment she thought a tornado was bearing down on her. Then she realized where she was and curled up under the sheet, listening to the drumming rain against the window. She'd never been frightened of storms in the past; in fact, she rather enjoyed the display of power and grandeur, as long as it didn't escalate into a tornado. She would forever have a healthy respect for those snaking, dancing storms.

Her door opened abruptly, and Cord stepped into the room, his nakedness revealed in the flashes of lightning.

Susan stared at him, feeling the tart taste of desire on her tongue, the slow, heated coiling in her abdomen and thighs.

"Are you all right?" he asked softly. "I thought you might be nervous, after the tornado."

She sat up, pushing her tousled hair away from her

face. "I'm fine. I was a little startled when it first woke me, but I'm not frightened."

"Good," he said, and started to leave the room.

"Cord, wait!" she called, not planning to say the words, but they burst out of her anyway. He hesitated and turned back to her, standing silently, waiting. "I think it's time to talk," she ventured.

"All right." He moved his shoulders in a strange manner, as if bracing himself. "I'll go put on some pants and be back."

"No." Again she stopped him, holding her hand out to him. "There's no need, is there?"

"I didn't think so," he returned. "But I wasn't sure how you felt."

"I feel the same... Please, sit on the bed." She moved to one side and pulled the covers about her waist, sitting up in the circle of them.

He dropped down to her bed, confiscated one of her pillows and stuffed it behind his back, stretched his long legs out on the mattress and turned on the lamp. "If we're going to talk, I'm going to be comfortable, and I want to be able to see you."

She tucked her legs under her, trying not to stare at the wonderfully masculine form sprawled in front of her. She couldn't imagine a man made any more beautifully. Every time she saw him, she only admired him the more; he seemed to improve with age. But his body was distracting her, and she forced herself to look at his face. The small, knowing, infinitely pleased smile that lurked on his lips made her flush; then she laughed a little at herself.

"I'm sorry. You have a knack for making me blush."

"*I* should be blushing, if I'm reading your mind correctly."

He was, and they both knew it. She quickly sought control, and found it. This was far too important for her to let herself be sidetracked. "Before I say anything else, we might as well get one thing out of the way. I love you. If you can't deal with that, if it makes you uncomfortable, then we have nothing to talk about. You might as well go back to your own room."

He didn't move an inch from his comfortable position. "I've known for some time," he said, his eyes darker than she'd ever seen them before. "I knew the first time I made love with you. If you hadn't loved me, you never would have stripped for me like that, or put yourself in my hands so completely."

"But you couldn't trust me? You left me in the dark, knowing how much I was worrying, how it tore me apart to have to fight you?" A jagged edge of pain tore into her again just at the memory, and she drew a quick breath, fighting to keep from falling apart, but still the hurt was evident in her voice.

"In my defense, let me say that I hadn't expected you. You blindsided me, sweetheart, and I've been floundering ever since. Except for my parents, I can't say that I've ever known anyone I could trust until I met you, and so many years had passed since I'd been able to turn my back to anyone that I couldn't let myself believe it. You defended Preston so stubbornly, even though you said you loved me; how could I be sure you wouldn't run and tell him immediately if I let it slip that I wasn't trying to bankrupt the company, only to pressure him into selling enough stock for me to have the majority?"

"Don't you see?" she cried. "I defended Preston *pre-*

cisely because I thought you were trying to bankrupt him to get revenge for Judith!"

"No, I wasn't after revenge, though I wanted him to think so. I'm far too guilty myself to have any right to take revenge. But the way things were when I left… honey, you have no idea how bitter and violent it had become. I wanted to come back home, and I knew the only way I could do it was from a position of power. I didn't want to simply live in the area again; I wanted to be accepted, to be a part of what I'd had before, when I was too young and too hotheaded to appreciate it."

"And if you'd told me all of that, you thought I'd still ruin it for you?" she asked, blinking back tears.

He cupped her cheek in his palm, his fingers caressing her jaw. "Don't cry," he murmured. "I told you, I'm out of the habit of trusting people. I've spent a lot of time in dives and jungles and back alleys that—well, never mind. But, damn it, you know I never planned for you to be the one to sell! I never thought he'd dump it all on your shoulders, but he's a smart bastard, I'll say that for him. His idea almost worked. If I'd known that *you* were the one being beaten down, I'd have stopped on the spot. It was your own stubbornness in not telling me that kept things going for so long, that gave me enough time to buy the stock I needed."

"Along with my vote," she reminded him thinly.

"Yes, along with your vote." He watched her intently, reading the myriad expressions as they flitted across her lovely face. She looked incredibly sexy, he noticed, with her hair all tousled and her eyes still heavy-lidded, her skin softly flushed from sleep. The dark shadows were gone from beneath her eyes, and the soft curves of her breasts shone beneath the thin silk of her nightgown, with her small nipples pushing against the fabric in an enticing manner that made him want to lean forward and take them into his mouth, silk and all. He felt it again, that punch in his chest, and he realized anew that she lit his life like an eternal candle, pure and white. If that serene flame ever went out he'd be doomed to darkness for the rest of his life.

"I was wrong not to trust you," he said softly. His voice went even quieter, so deep that it rumbled in his chest. "I knew that you loved me, and it was almost too much for me to believe. I was afraid to believe. My God, Susan, don't you know? Don't you have any idea what you do to people? Everywhere I turned, there were people falling all over themselves to please you, to get you to smile at them, to have your attention for just a little while. Even Imogene would fight her weight in wildcats for you! If I'd let myself believe that sweetness was all mine, then found out that it wasn't, I couldn't have handled it. I had to protect myself by not letting you get too close."

Susan stared at him, bewildered by his words. "People fall all over themselves for me? What do you mean?"

She truly didn't know, he realized, had never noticed the effect her radiant smile had on people, or the almost inevitable softening that crossed their faces whenever they talked to her. My God, he had a treasure that men would fight for, possibly kill for, and she didn't even know her own power, which he supposed was part of her elusive, but hauntingly sweet charm.

"Never mind," he told her gently. She wouldn't believe him even if he told her. "The important thing is, do you love me enough to forgive me?"

"I have to," she replied obliquely, but the truth was

plain in her eyes. She had to forgive him, because when she searched down to the deepest recesses of her heart, she loved him too much not to forgive him anything.

Very tenderly, he reached out and caught her waist, drawing her out of her tangle of covers and pulling her atop him, resting her weight on his chest. "I'm glad," he said gravely, his diamond-eyes so close that she could see her own reflection in the dilated blackness of his pupils. "Because I love you so much that I think I'd go crazy if you sent me away."

Susan's eyes widened, and her heart gave a great bound, then resumed beating with thuds that hammered against the delicate cage of her ribs. "I...what?"

"I said, I love you," he repeated, sliding his hands up her back in a slow, heated caress. She quivered, tried to speak, but her trembling lips couldn't form the words, and instead she gave up and dropped her head to his shoulder, her hands holding tightly to him. He folded her to him, pressing her soft, deliciously feminine body against his. Sudden tears, hot and acid, burned his eyes. He'd almost lost her, almost let her love slip away from him, and the thought tormented him.

"I love you," he said again, this time whispering the words into the dark cloud of her hair. The searing tears slid down his hard, sun-browned cheeks, but he wasn't aware of them. His world had narrowed to the wonder he held in his arms, the slim, delicate body that held such sweetness and gallantry, such an endless capacity for love, that he was staggered by it.

Susan drew a little away from him, her heart stopping when she saw the wet tracks on his face, and in that moment she knew beyond doubt that he loved her. He was looking at her with a deep, consuming love that he made no effort to hide. The last of his bitterness was drained away in the salt of his tears, the last grief and guilt he felt for Judith. She put her cheek against his, rubbing the wetness away.

Knowing that she would never refuse him, that what they felt burning between them needed to be consummated, had to be sanctified by their union, he rolled and deftly placed her beneath him, his legs parting her thighs. He rose to his knees and lifted her nightgown, then drew it over her head. After tossing it away, he regarded her slim beauty for a moment, then let his weight down on her. He kissed her fiercely, then drew back with masculine satisfaction stamped on his bearded features. "I'm going to marry you."

Again shock reverberated through Susan, but now it was a joyous shock, as at last she began to believe what was happening to her. She looked up at him, and suddenly a smile curved her lips. Just like that; it wasn't a proposal, a question, but a statement. He was going to marry her, and she'd better not try to argue with him about it!

"Yes," she said, then caught her breath as he entered her. Her moistly yielding body accepted him without difficulty, the sweet honey of her flesh welcoming him. He moved against her, probing slowly, and he groaned aloud in pleasure.

Then he raised himself on his elbow to look down at her, his gaze burning with desire. "It might be a good idea if we get married as soon as possible," he murmured. "After the night in the Blazer, you could well be pregnant."

"I know." She slid her hands over his shoulders to his neck, and smiled up at him. "I hope so."

An answering smile touched his lips. "Just to be on the safe side, let's do it again." He kissed her again; then their bodies began to move in unison, with a passion that was wild and tender and sanity-destroying, their love binding them together with an electrically charged force field of devotion. What had begun with a dance on a crowded ballroom floor had become a sensual dance of love, sanctified by the tears of a hard man who'd had to learn how to cry.

EPILOGUE

CORD LAY HEAVILY on her, sweetly limp after the whirlwind of their lovemaking. Susan nibbled on his shoulder, and he put his hand in her hair to pull her head up. He began kissing her again, slow, drugging kisses that lit the fires between them again, fires that burned higher and hotter than ever after a year of marriage. Just as he began moving within her, a faint, fretful cry caught their attention, a cry that quickly escalated into an all-out bellow.

He cursed luridly as he slid off of her. "She's got the most incredible timing!" he grumbled as he stalked naked from the room, outrage evident in every line of his powerful body.

Susan pulled the sheet up over her nude body; she was cool without the heat of him next to her. A slow, gentle smile touched her lips as she envisioned the scene in the next room. Cord might grumble and grouse, but he'd melt as soon as he set eyes on his tiny daughter, who had just learned how to blow bubbles. As soon as she saw her father, she'd stop her bellowing, and her arms and legs would go into overtime as her entire body wriggled in delight. She'd treat him to her entire repertoire of accomplishments, from kicking to blowing bubbles, and he'd be lost in adoring admiration. Alison

Marie was a four-month-old tyrant, and she had Cord wrapped completely around her dainty finger.

It was a good thing they'd gotten married so swiftly, because within a month it had become evident that Susan was indeed pregnant. Cord had teased her before Alison had been born, insisting that if the baby were a girl, he was going to name her Storm, and if it were a boy, it had to be called Blazer. She'd been a little worried at how he would accept fatherhood, but she'd worried over nothing. No man could have been more delighted over his child.

She prepared herself to nurse the baby, and in a moment Cord came back into the bedroom, cradling Alison in the curve of his strong arm and crooning to her as her plump little hands waved in the air, trying to catch his beard. "We're going to have to trade her in for a model that doesn't leak," he said, getting back in bed, still holding Alison, while Susan stuffed a pillow behind her back.

When she took the baby, he moved to put his arm around her, holding her so most of her weight rested on his chest. "Look at that little pig," he drawled, as the baby latched onto the milk-swollen nipple with starving ferocity. He was fascinated by everything about her, and had been from the moment he'd known of Susan's pregnancy.

Despite it being her first child, she'd breezed through the months with almost boring ease. She'd had little morning sickness, no cravings, and had carried the baby easily. Her biggest problem had been Cord, who had hounded her if she even tried to change a lightbulb. She had Alison with a minimum of fuss, and Cord had been there to hold his daughter, who weighed in at a tiny five pounds and two ounces.

Now his big hand touched the small, round head, smoothing the black curls that covered it. She opened her eyes briefly, revealing pale blue irises surrounded by a ring of darker blue. She was his image, and he adored her. But the delights of her mother's breast occupied her at the moment, and she closed her eyes again, suckling vigorously.

Soon she slept again, and Susan's nipple slipped from the relaxed rosebud mouth. "I'm going to have to wean her soon," she sighed.

"Why?"

"She's starting to teethe."

He laughed softly, sprawling naked on the bed. "Dangerous, huh?"

"Extremely." She carried Alison back to the nursery, and stood for a moment holding the infinitely precious little bundle in her arms. The baby grunted as she was placed on her stomach, but a tightly curled fist brushed her mouth and she latched onto it in her sleep, sucking noisily on her knuckles.

He was waiting for her when she came back into their bedroom, and he drew her back down into his embrace. Susan curled against him, placing her head on the broad, hairy chest. Being married to him was better than she'd dreamed, because she'd never thought that her restless renegade would have been so content.

He and Preston had reached a truce, a working relationship that allowed peace between them. Preston remained as president of the company, because his experience and ability were too good to waste. Cord's own daring and verve had blended with Preston's attention to detail, and together they were creating a company that was innovative but not reckless, sure-footed but not too cautious. The challenge kept Cord fascinated, and at night he came back to her arms, which was all she'd ever asked of heaven.

He reached out and clicked off the lamp, yawning in the sudden darkness. He settled her in his arms, in their sleeping position, and she nuzzled her mouth against his flesh. Just as she'd dreamed months ago, sleeping with him every night was deeply satisfying. They talked in the darkness, sharing the things that had happened to them during the day, planning what they wanted to do together. His hand moved lazily over her soft body, then found her breasts and became more obvious in his attentions.

"Susan? Do you think she'll wake up this time?"

Susan laughed, winding her arms around his neck. Her beloved desperado, her darling renegade, still swept her away into his dark, magic world of love.

* * * * *

 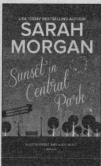 

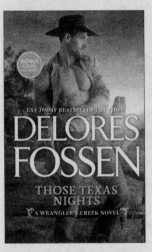

**Trouble comes to town for the
Cahill Siblings of Gilt Edge, Montana,
in this captivating new series from
New York Times bestselling author**

B.J. DANIELS

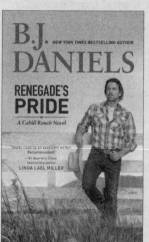

In the nine years since Trask Beaumont left Gilt Edge, Lillian Cahill has convinced herself she is over him. But when the rugged cowboy suddenly walks into her bar, there's a pang in her heart that argues the attraction never faded. And that's dangerous, because Trask has returned on a mission to clear his name—and win Lillie back.

When a body is recovered from a burning house, everyone suspects Trask…especially Lillie's brother Hawk, the town marshal. Will Lillie give Trask a second chance, even if it leaves her torn between her family and the man she never stopped loving?

Available February 28!

HQN™

REQUEST YOUR FREE BOOKS!

2 FREE NOVELS
FROM THE ROMANCE COLLECTION,
PLUS 2 FREE GIFTS!

YES! Please send me 2 FREE novels from the Romance Collection and my 2 FREE gifts (gifts are worth about $10). After receiving them, if I don't wish to receive any more books, I can return the shipping statement marked "cancel." If I don't cancel, I will receive 4 brand-new novels every month and be billed just $6.49 per book in the U.S. or $6.99 per book in Canada. That's a savings of at least 18% off the cover price. It's quite a bargain! Shipping and handling is just 50¢ per book in the U.S. and 75¢ per book in Canada.* I understand that accepting the 2 free books and gifts places me under no obligation to buy anything. I can always return a shipment and cancel at any time. Even if I never buy another book, the two free books and gifts are mine to keep forever.

194/394 MDN GH4D

Name	(PLEASE PRINT)
Address	Apt. #
City	State/Prov. Zip/Postal Code

Signature (if under 18, a parent or guardian must sign)

Mail to the **Reader Service:**
IN U.S.A.: P.O. Box 1867, Buffalo, NY 14240-1867
IN CANADA: P.O. Box 609, Fort Erie, Ontario L2A 5X3

Want to try 2 free books from another line?
Call 1-800-873-8635 or visit www.ReaderService.com.

*Terms and prices subject to change without notice. Prices do not include applicable taxes. Sales tax applicable in N.Y. Canadian residents will be charged applicable taxes. Offer not valid in Quebec. This offer is limited to one order per household. Not valid for current subscribers to the Romance Collection or the Romance/Suspense Collection. All orders subject to credit approval. Credit or debit balances in a customer's account(s) may be offset by any other outstanding balance owed by or to the customer. Please allow 4 to 6 weeks for delivery. Offer available while quantities last.

Your Privacy—The Reader Service is committed to protecting your privacy. Our Privacy Policy is available online at www.ReaderService.com or upon request from the Reader Service.

We make a portion of our mailing list available to reputable third parties that offer products we believe may interest you. If you prefer that we not exchange your name with third parties, or if you wish to clarify or modify your communication preferences, please visit us at www.ReaderService.com/consumerschoice or write to us at Reader Service Preference Service, P.O. Box 9062, Buffalo, NY 14240-9062. Include your complete name and address.

ROM15R